PENGUIN BOOKS

LACE 2

Shirley Conran went to St Paul's Girls' School, London, followed by a finishing school in Switzerland. She then trained as a painter and sculptor at Southern College of Art, Portsmouth. She was the first women's editor of the *Observer* colour magazine and women's editor of the *Daily Mail*, where she launched 'Femail'. She also has great experience as a textile designer and as a colour consultant and she has designed her own paint range. She handled the publicity for the Women in Media campaign for legislation against sex discrimination and was one of the selection committee for the Council of Industrial Design for eight years. She was formerly married to design tycoon Sir Terence Conran and they have two sons, Sebastian and Jasper, both of whom are designers.

Shirley Conran has also published *Superwoman* (1975); *The Superwoman Yearbook* (1976); *Superwoman in Action* (published in hardback as *Superwoman 2*, 1977); *Futurewoman*, with Elizabeth Sidney (published in hardback as *Futures*, 1979); and *The Magic Garden* (1983). *Lace 2* is the sequel to her bestselling novel, *Lace*, which was published by Penguin in 1983.

Lace received sensational publicity:

'Superwoman author, Shirley Conran, has really hit the literary jackpot . . . you can spend a few enjoyable hours finding out if it's more than sex and scandal that's the secret of its success' – *Sunday* magazine in the *News of the World*

'One of the most richly entertaining reads of the year' – *Options* magazine

'*Lace* is like a large bag of potato crisps (garlic and gorgonzola flavoured), rather delicious and absolutely unputdownable' – *Image* magazine

'Riches, bitches, sex and jetsetters' locations – they're all there' – *Sunday Express*

LACE 2

SHIRLEY CONRAN

PENGUIN BOOKS

Penguin Books Ltd, Harmondsworth, Middlesex, England
Viking Penguin Inc., 40 West 23rd Street, New York, New York 10010, U.S.A.
Penguin Books Australia Ltd, Ringwood, Victoria, Australia
Penguin Books Canada Ltd, 2801 John Street, Markham, Ontario, Canada L3R 1B4
Penguin Books (N.Z.) Ltd, 182–190 Wairau Road, Auckland 10, New Zealand

First published 1985
This edition first published 1985
Reprinted 1985

The lines quoted on page 229 from
'You Must Have Been A Beautiful Baby', words by John Mercer,
are copyright © 1938 Remick Music Corporation
and are reproduced by permission of
B. Feldman & Co. Ltd, London.
© (renewed) Warner Bros. Inc.
All rights reserved used by permission.

Printed and bound in Great Britain by
Cox & Wyman Ltd, Reading
Filmset in 10/13pt Linotron Plantin by
Rowland Phototypesetting Ltd
Bury St Edmunds, Suffolk

For Peter
With Love

PROLOGUE

31 August 1979

They are the most expensive breasts in the world, thought Lili as she soaped them. Lace rivulets of foam slipped over her rounded flesh and, as she touched one cinnamon-tinted nipple, Lili shivered with sensuous pleasure. She stretched one rose-tipped toe to push the old-fashioned, ivory-handled dial which released hot water; then she stroked her other nipple with the sea sponge, and again her body quivered in response. It was as if the tips of her breasts were part of an electrical circuit of sensation which connected directly with the sensual core of her body, Lili thought as she watched the two cinnamon buds grow hard, then break through the carnation-scented foam.

Everything was in perfect working order; Lili's body was fully practical, as technicians said when they checked props on the set. But the satin slopes that started to swell immediately below her collarbone were considerably more than practical; Lili's breasts had been her passport, her work permit, her meal ticket, and now they were her fortune. Currently, those two impertinently rounded breasts were insured for a seven-figure sum by Omnium Pictures, which had just negotiated a record fee for Lili to play Helen of Troy.

Nowadays my breasts are worth far more to other people than they are to me, Lili reflected wistfully; but for almost fifteen years, whatever power she had possessed over her destiny had been derived from these two pounds of flesh which, to Lili, were as familiar as her knees and hardly any more remarkable.

Lili sighed, threw the sponge aside, slowly rose from the over-full bath and carelessly splashed a lake of water over the pink marble floor. She wrapped herself in a buttercup-yellow towel and wandered into the sitting room. A bowl of figs stood on her breakfast tray, each fruit cut in quarters to expose the red flesh; Lili nibbled at a segment as she glanced at the newspaper: 1979 was not proving a good year for President Carter, she thought as she read about the siege of the American Embassy and the hostages held in Iran. Lili knew what it felt like to be suddenly confronted by violence.

Born in Switzerland, Lili had never known her mysterious mother, but when she was six years old she had been on holiday with her foster family in Hungary. They had been trapped by the 1956 Hungarian uprising against the Communists, and Lili had seen her beloved foster parents shot by border guards before she had managed to escape. From an Austrian refugee camp she had been sent to

Paris where she had been adopted by an ageing, childless couple. By the age of seven she had virtually become the unpaid servant of Monsieur et Madame Sardeau, a skivvy who longed for the love, peace and happiness that she had once known and still hoped for.

It had been easy for the rich American playboy to seduce Lili, and easier still for him to abandon her when she found herself pregnant. Thrown out by the Sardeaus, Lili had paid for her abortion by posing naked for a truck drivers' calendar. Overnight she became famous as a lewd, baby pin-up. Terrified, helpless and dependent on her exploitative manager, Lili had eventually been rescued by Jo Stiarkoz, a Greek shipowner who had encouraged Lili's natural acting and painting talents, and who gradually changed her from a suspicious, wary child of the gutter, unable to equate sex with love, into a cultured, discerning beauty.

When Jo was killed in a car accident Lili sought oblivion in her film career, and then had flung herself into a notorious year-long affair with Abdullah, King of Sydon, a tiny oil-rich state on the Persian Gulf. But eventually Lili could no longer tolerate her position, described by some as an unofficial concubine and others as the Western Whore. Lili then returned to her home in Paris to search once more for dignity, love and peace. And so far she had not found them.

Sighing, Lili threw aside the *Herald Tribune* and slowly walked through the carved cedarwood shutters on to her balcony, which hung over the grape-green water of the

•

•

Bosporus. Around the balcony the domes and sharp minarets of Istanbul sparkled in the hazy morning sunlight
of August. The sounds of the city, muted and distorted,
travelled over the waters of the Bosporus as shouting
voices, bicycle bells and the occasional goat bleat blended
with the roar of the traffic. Lili hugged the golden bath
sheet around her as she absorbed the sights and sounds
of Turkey. There were worse places to want love, peace
and happiness.

Across the Straits, on the Asian side of the water, the
sun also warmed the stubby grey barrel of a Smith &
Wesson Magnum .357, UZI 9mm, a Kalashnikov and
two hand grenades. They lay on a rickety table in a small
room that smelt of stale marijuana smoke.

He hadn't been able to risk bringing the hardware
through customs, but when he'd arrived in Istanbul he'd
obeyed instructions and everything had gone smoothly.
He'd ordered two cups of coffee, simultaneously, in the
small Bazaar café, then he'd sent them both back, complaining that the coffee wasn't strong enough. After a few
minutes a dark-suited, dark-featured man had appeared
before his table, and he had followed the dark stranger
as they walked through a maze of narrow streets, then up
a dirty staircase to a small dark room, where he had shown
his passport. From the poor selection of guns that he had
been offered he'd picked three, realizing that he had very
little choice in the matter.

He'd hoped for a .44 Magnum because that stopped

•

anyone close up; even a big man would be thrown, dead, on his back. The UZI sub-machine-gun was easy to get anywhere in the Near East because it was used by Israeli infantry. It weighed seven and a half pounds and was the shortest sub-machine-gun (twenty inches folded), which made it not impossible for you to strap it inside your trouser leg. It could fire 600 rounds a minute as well as single shots, and used 9mm ammunition, which was easy to get hold of because it was a common size for pistols as well as SMGs. He'd also chosen the Kalashnikov because it was handy and reliable. It was slower than the UZI but the longer barrel made it more accurate. God knows how it had ended up in Istanbul, because it was a Chinese '56 model with a wooden stock and a permanently attached folding bayonet, which might well be useful.

Beside the hardware lay an untidy heap of bullets, two ammunition clips, a coil of nylon rope, 500 millilitres of clear solution in a glass bottle, a roll of three-inch-wide white surgical tape, two maps of the city, a water pipe with a few crumbs of half-burned resin in the bowl and a copy of *People* magazine.

The man moved to the rusting, metal-framed window and swept the opposite shore with high-powered, army field glasses. He saw low hills wooded with cypresses and pines; too high, he thought, and corrected. He saw a blurry mass of buildings pierced by the decorated spires of minarets; he was still too high. Then he was focused at the correct level, but the jumbled, dirty-brown houses were confusingly similar and only the larger shapes of a mosque, shrine or palace offered directions to the watcher. Impatiently the man picked up his tourist's map and peered at a photograph. Again he raked the distant shore with the field glasses, this time slowly tracking along the water's edge.

At the point at which Galata bridge spanned the Golden Horn the man fiddled with the focus until the image was so sharp that he could see the faces of the passengers on the ferry, which was pulling away from the landing. Carefully he watched the laden boat begin its journey towards him, then he swept the binoculars further to the right and saw the gleaming façade of a palace, a small park shaded by Judas trees, and the ruined shell of a fortified tower. Finally, with a grunt of satisfaction, he was focused on a large terracotta-coloured building directly on the edge of the water. Systematically he checked each window, beginning with the square casements of the top floor and working down to the tall French doors on the first floor, some of which opened on to small domed balconies, suspended over the water like white birdcages. While the man watched, a pair of shutters was pushed open and Lili, wearing her golden towel, walked out on the balcony.

The man dropped the field glasses and grabbed the copy of *People* magazine. Those tawny, almond-shaped eyes, the mass of black curls, the provocatively out-thrust breasts were unmistakable. He had found more than he had expected.

★

•

Lili wandered back into the sitting room of her suite, squashed another fig segment into her mouth and moved into the dressing room, where she stepped into a loose white linen shift, the only thing which offered her any hope of navigating the Grand Bazaar without being pinched black and blue by lecherous fingers. Yesterday she had spun round after a particularly insulting nip to find that the fingers had belonged to a ten-year-old boy. Lili slipped her feet into snakeskin sandals, pinned up her mass of dark hair with antique tortoiseshell combs and applied as little make-up as possible because, thank heaven, she wasn't the photographic target for today. Leaving clothes and cosmetics scattered all over her suite, she left it, then knocked on the next door.

'That you, Lili? Come on in, honey, I'm waiting for this to dry.' The preoccupied voice held a hint of Louisiana. Sandy Bayriver (born Flanagan) was finishing a delicate job of restoration. The area on which she was working had been cleaned and rubbed down, and she was draping a minute web of strengthening gauze over the fingernail crack. In Sandy's business, a girl could not afford to be seen without a perfect set of ten matched talons.

Lili wandered around the opulent, brocade-furnished drawing room, picked up a tawdry diamanté crown slung rakishly over the marble ear of a bust of Alexander the Great and held it on her head. 'How d'you keep this thing on, Sandy?'

'Bobby pins, honey. Once, when I was Lake Pontchartrain Oyster Queen, I clean forgot to pin it on and the damn thing fell off halfway across Churchill Plaza.' She looked up. 'It really suits you, Lili – maybe you should take over as Miss International Beauty and I'll just go shopping today.'

'You won it, you wear it,' Lili threw the coronet back on the statue's head. Sandy never missed an opportunity to say something sweet, the way some people never missed an opportunity to say something nasty. It was easy to forget that she was in the piranha pool of competition for these gaudy crowns, Lili thought, as Sandy wriggled her toes into scarlet sandals.

'Four-inch heels would cripple me,' said Lili.

'Hell, honey, I'm used to them.' Sandy tripped into the bathroom where she carefully removed the heated rollers from her wild tawny hair which curled naturally, but Sandy preferred a disciplined cascade of shiny ringlets. 'Let's go find your mamma.' Sandy giggled, ever conscious of the two notorious women with whom she was travelling.

At the top of the immense double staircase, which swept down to the foyer of the Harun-al-Rashid Hotel, Sandy hung on to Lili's arm as, carefully, she moved sideways down the slippery marble steps. Waiting at the bottom of the ornate staircase was a small, delicately boned woman in a red silk dress.

Judy Jordan, founder of *Verve!* magazine for working women, was not sure that she was enjoying her role as travelling companion to two of the most beautiful women

•

in the world – one of whom happened to be her long-lost daughter.

The guide in baggy black trousers led them to the water gate of their elegant, rose-washed hotel, which had once been the summer palace of a queen, built at the water's edge for coolness.

'Where are we going today?' asked Lili as the three women settled into the canopied private launch.

Judy pointed. 'Over there. The Topkapi Palace, where the Ottoman kings lived. That enormous pile of buildings on the hill; you're both being photographed in the Palace Harem.'

'Surely not me, too?' exclaimed Lili. 'I'm not made-up.'

Judy looked at her, thinking now that patience was the outstanding quality required by any mother as she said, 'Lili, last night I told you that we needed shots of you, as well as Sandy. Anyway, you look fine.'

Of course Lili looked fine; Lili always looked fine, thought Judy wistfully. I always looked fine when I was her age. Now if I watch my diet and work out every day and only drink wine at Christmas, I can still look good, but not as good as I did when I was Lili's age. Judy knew that in her red Chloë dress, with its rippling bias-cut skirt, her figure was still girlishly slim; she still had the waif-like appeal of an exhausted Little Orphan Annie, in spite of her present problems. Judy thought, I wouldn't have to be involved in anything as tacky as a beauty queen competition if I wasn't so broke, and Lili hadn't been so indiscreet, and Tom hadn't taken one business risk too many.

•

And there was one other problem. After almost a year as Lili's mother, and a week travelling with eighteen-year-old Sandy, Judy was forced to acknowledge that she was of a different generation, and that made her feel uneasy. Not jealous, of course, just uneasy. If Judy felt uneasy, by now she knew that millions of her women readers felt the same way about the same things. Putting her life into her magazine, and knowing when to trust her gut instincts, had made Judy her first million dollars.

She found Lili the more disturbing of her two travelling companions because elegance, to Judy, meant neat hair and formal clothes, not expensive garments that were *intended* to look crumpled and hair that had been carefully dressed to look untidy. Nevertheless, since gaining a daughter Judy had stopped arguing with her fashion editor when spreads were proposed on street-chic or models swathed in knotted muslin.

Sitting with her back to the Bosporus, Lili dearly wished she had not forgotten about today's photographic session. Eventually she leaned towards her mother and said, 'I'm sorry I forgot. I'm so glad you persuaded me to come on this trip, Judy.'

Judy smiled politely, recognizing the peace offering. It was the politeness that came between them, thought Judy, but she didn't know how not to be polite. A real mother isn't polite; she yells at her kids, hollers when her daughter pinches her pantyhose, then goes without a new winter coat so that her daughter can have a really pretty first formal. A mother washes your clothes, and her time

•

and her love are the ingredients that go into every stack
of lunchtime sandwiches she cuts. A mother's always at
you about your galoshes (putting them on, taking them
off, putting them away) and you ignore her or groan
theatrically, but her scolding is comforting because you
know it means that she cares. Every day, between a
daughter and the mother she's grown up with, there are
a thousand unspoken reference points which add up
to the feeling of comfortable, affectionate intimacy, the
feeling that a puppy has for the blanket in its basket.
Without discussion, a mother knows that you like goat's
milk cheese and don't like Aunt Bertha. A mother knows
your temper tantrums, and where they come from, and
how to stop them before they start. Between Lili and
Judy there was liking, respect and even the start of a
touching friendship, but both of them were silently aware
that there should have been love, and there was no love
– yet. They both pinned their hopes on that 'yet'.

From the other side of the boat Lili watched her
mother's short blonde hair ruffle in the breeze. Lili had
always expected her unknown, mysterious mother to be
a quiet, kindly madonna, an apron-covered, ample figure,
always stirring something delicious on an old-fashioned
kitchen range. But when, almost a year ago, Lili had
finally tracked down her mother, she had found this
glamorous, lonely public figure instead of the comforting
creature of her daydreams.

Both Lili and Judy were alone in life and they both
longed not to be; so they tried to behave as they imagined

•

a mother and her daughter should behave. They made odd little stabs at what they thought was the appropriate way to act. But although she had made such a great effort to discover her real mother, Lili was suspicious of her own feelings. Lili was an instinctive actress; her fame was the result of having the raw talent, then slowly acquiring the craft, then polishing the talent. She had always had to play her life by ear, so her impulses were important, but she was suspicious of her facility to take on a mood when she wanted to act it. Lili did not want to act love. She wanted the real thing. She wanted what she had always felt she had been deprived of – mother love. Lili knew she was not getting the real thing, she felt it deep in her heart and her bones and her being, but she did not want to face it; so she continued hopefully to grope for it.

Lili also feared that something else might sabotage the relationship with her mother that she was trying so hard to establish. Lili knew from her acting work, and from watching other people's stage work, that when a coach or a director asks an actor to play affection, what sometimes unconsciously comes up is bitter rage, always followed by sudden tears and breakdown. This was another reason why Lili feared that she might unconsciously be acting the love for her mother that she so longed to establish with Judy. Lili did not want suddenly to cause an unforgivable but unforgettable resentment of her mother's abandonment.

The pink fringe of the canopy swayed in the breeze as

their little launch darted over the grey-green water. Lili leaned over to Judy. 'After the photo session, can I go shopping? I want to buy a carpet in the Grand Bazaar.'

'I'll come with you, it's better to bargain with two people, you'll get a lower price if I stand behind you looking grim. Offer one third of what they ask and settle for half.'

'That's not really the way I hoped to do it. I want to buy you a present, Judy. I want to buy you the most beautiful carpet in the Bazaar.'

'That's sweet of you, Lili, but you know it's not necessary.'

Without realizing it, Lili had expected her real mother to be a duplicate of her beloved Swiss-peasant foster mother, Angelina, and Lili had expected her mother to be poor, like Angelina. Lili had expected to be able to show her love by helping her mother financially. She had had a little fantasy of taking her mother to the best store in town and buying her mother her first fur coat. But then her mother had turned out to be a millionaire. So Lili kept trying to buy Judy expensive presents, which embarrassed Judy. Any show of affection embarrassed Judy, especially touch. Her strict, Southern Baptist parents had never touched each other; they had not kissed or cuddled their children or each other and, consequently, there was a distance in all Judy's relationships, because, to her, touch was related to sex, not affection.

Lili sensed the loneliness that Judy would have fiercely denied. Judy had achieved everything that spells success

•

– she was a Liz Smith regular, a Page Six standby, she had expensive designer clothes, maids, secretaries, an East Side apartment, a place on Long Island, plenty of men friends and three very special women friends. But nobody . . . close. Perhaps that stemmed from her feelings of guilt.

Judy had spent many years feeling guilty about abandoning her child, feeling responsible for her child's death, feeling guilty that her life hadn't turned out as planned, and all because she hadn't been an instant success in the Big Apple.

However much she justified her actions, however tenderly her friends reassured her, there was no getting away from the fact that she had – as Lili felt it – abandoned her own daughter when she was three months old. There had been plenty of justification. Judy had been a sixteen-year-old waitress, working her way through the Language Laboratory in Gstaad, Switzerland, when she had been raped. Judy's three rich girlfriends at the nearby finishing school had all helped to pay for Lili's birth and then for her keep. But no matter how hard Judy had tried, business success always, at first, seemed just beyond her reach, and whatever way Judy turned, she came up against an impersonal blank wall at the end of a cul-de-sac. And all the time she knew that she had to succeed as fast as possible, because – her own ambition apart – she couldn't support her baby daughter until she was successful and made money. Judy's lack of early success had made her feel helpless and unloved, as well as a failure.

•

•

With the cheery arrogance of youth, Judy had expected quick success to be the result of brains and hard work. She didn't realize that you can put all your heart and energy into your work but the opportunities you deserve just aren't offered to people who are only moderately attractive; it can make you bitter when the other, less gifted people get the opportunities that should be yours.

Sure, Lili had suffered, but nevertheless Lili had all the things that Judy had never had at her age: beauty, sexuality, money and time. Time to play, time to go out in the evening without feeling exhausted, time for men. Judy remembered once wondering whether she would be successful while she was still attractive or whether she would ever be able to afford to wear a wonderful dress, to go to a wonderful place and perhaps meet a wonderful man there?

Perhaps it would all have been much easier if only she had been a little bit more beautiful. Judy was ashamed of the fact that she was jealous of Lili's beauty.

On the opposite side of the water, in the Asian part of the city, the man with binoculars still slung around his neck pushed his way through the boys selling chewing gum and evil-eye beads until he reached the Galata ferry. A few minutes later the wide wake of the flat-bottomed ferry crossed the wash of the pretty little launch that carried the three famous women as they sped towards the shore, where richly decorated palaces and mosques crowded together at the water's edge; the entire view

•

•

rippled in the heat, so the buildings seemed to be part of the water itself.

'Problems, Judy, problems,' warned the photographer at Topkapi Palace. 'They say we can't shoot in the Harem. It's impossible.'

People with longer experience of Judy Jordan never used the word 'impossible'. If you told Judy that something was impossible she merely lifted her little nose an inch or so and said, 'Only impossible people use the word "impossible",' or simply, 'It *must* be done.' Now Judy said, 'We *must* shoot in the Harem; the copy has already been written, all the headlines are set and your film is going straight back to New York tonight to be developed and printed in time for Friday's deadline.' She turned to the guide from the Turkish Tourist Board, 'What's the problem?'

'The Harem quarters are enormous, Mrs Jordan . . .'

'Can't we use part of it for us to get a few shots? Everything was cleared with your office.'

'There must have been a misunderstanding. Photography is forbidden because of the restorations.'

'But isn't there even one room . . .'

'Please understand, Madame. The Topkapi Palace is a magnificent national treasure and the government would be most unhappy if it were not seen at its best. All the most beautiful rooms are in the part of the palace which is open to tourists. Let me show these to you.'

'OK, do that,' agreed Judy. She looked at her watch

•

and thought, an hour to set up, another hour to get the shots. Yes, there would be time for a quick tour.

'Do you suppose they'll let us come back and have a proper look?' Sandy asked Lili as they hurried through a library lined with carved wooden bookshelves, inlaid with mother-of-pearl and tortoiseshell.

'No.' Lili was listening to the guide's heavily accented voice as he told a story about some favourite concubine.

'Is it always like this? Being on tour?' asked Sandy, still reluctant to learn that the glamorous life looked better than it lived.

'Yes,' said Lili. 'You never have enough time, except in airports; it doesn't matter where you are, all you really see is the inside of dressing rooms and studios; you can't go to the discotheques because you'll have bags under your eyes tomorrow; you can't sunbathe because you'll look browner in some pictures than others; you can't eat most of the food so you won't either get fat or sick; and everyone is always late and frantic. Isn't success wonderful?'

'Time to get ready, girls,' said Judy. 'We're going to shoot in the king's dining room.' She led them to a tiny chamber with walls and ceilings covered in gold-embellished paintings of lilies and roses, pomegranates and peaches. The photographer looked doubtfully at his light meter. 'All this interflora stuff might look like psychedelic oatmeal by the time the pictures are printed.'

'Then let's do a few more shots outside, by the Harem gate, where you'll get better light,' Judy suggested.

•

After the photo session was finished and the film had been dispatched to the airport, Sandy and the photographer stayed behind for a more leisurely look at the palace. 'After all, honey,' said Sandy, as they headed for the treasure chamber, 'how often does a girl get a look at rubies the size of pigeon's eggs?'

Judy and Lili climbed into their limousine, kicked off their shoes and asked the driver to take them to the Grand Bazaar.

As she got out of the car Lili's tiny snakeskin bag slipped off her shoulder and fell on to the cobbles, spilling coins, lip-gloss and letters. Quickly Lili snatched them up, but Judy had spotted the airmail letter.

'Not fast enough, Lili.' Judy couldn't stop herself saying it. 'He's still writing to you, isn't he?'

Lili opened her mouth and then shut it again; after all, whatever she said would be wrong.

Still Judy couldn't stop herself. 'Do you think I don't know my lover's handwriting after all these months?'

'Judy, *I* can't stop Mark writing to me. *I* don't want anything to do with him, I never did . . .'

'But he wants *you*, Lili, doesn't he? And he certainly doesn't want me any more.' Judy knew she was being destructive and knew that she should stop, but now that she had begun she could not stop; she had been suppressing this for weeks. 'Lili, don't tell me you didn't know that Mark was falling in love with you in New York, right under my nose. You can't pretend that you don't know what effect you have on men – Lili, the world's most famous sex symbol.' Judy knew Lili's most sensitive point.

'You're not being fair, Judy. What kind of a woman do you think I am?'

Suddenly Judy's self-control snapped as jealousy, unhappiness and fear controlled her. 'The kind of woman who might seduce her mother's lover. The kind of woman who could ruin her mother's business – that's the kind of woman you are!'

Lili burst into tears of rage. 'You're impossible! I wish I'd never found you. I wish I'd never met you. I never want to see you again.' Impulsively she turned, plunged into the jostling crowd, and vanished. Grimly Judy watched her go. Their raised voices, the faces twisted with anger and misery, had gone unremarked in the noisy crowd. But both women knew that their play-acting was over. Within two minutes the fragile relationship that both had tried so hard to establish had been wrecked.

The man with the binoculars watched them argue, then saw Lili burst into tears and disappear under the great stone gateway of the Bazaar. Quickly he followed her, elbowing his way through the heaving mass of people, determined to keep Lili in sight.

'Where the hell can Lili be? She should never have gone off alone like that.'

'Going off alone is her idea of luxury,' Sandy reminded Judy as she tipped back her chair, crossed her feet on

·

•

the balcony rail and watched heavy black clouds gather behind the minarets. 'You know that Lili doesn't like the usual star entourage. The rest of them may not move an inch without PR people, bodyguards, a couple of studio executives, two gofers and a hairdresser, but that's exactly the part that Lili hates. Nobody can make an entrance better than Lili but, although she's not exactly Garbo, Lili doesn't care for all the fuss and glitter that I long for.'

'But she knows we're supposed to meet the agency people in ten minutes.'

'Maybe she doesn't want to meet the agency people. Why don't we just go ahead and eat?' Sandy stood up and pulled down the zipper of her gold lamé jumpsuit. 'Lili can follow us when she turns up.'

But when Judy tried to leave a message for Lili the clerk pointed out that Lili's key was still in its pigeonhole. 'Miss Lili went out many hours ago. No, not alone. With a man.'

'What sort of man?'

'Not a guest. Maybe Turkish. I don't remember his clothes. A dark suit, maybe.' In luxury hotels in Turkey the clerks speak impeccable English.

'That's odd; we don't know anyone Turkish, except the agency people,' Sandy said as they turned towards the dining room. Judy said nothing.

As the agency people made over-polite conversation, Judy picked her way through a series of dishes with suggestive names: Holy Man Fainted (stuffed eggplant

•

with tomatoes, onions and garlic), King's Delight
(sautéed lamb with onions and tomatoes), Ladies' Navels
(fried pastries with pistachio nuts and whipped cream).
Then the lights dimmed and six plump girls in neon-pink
gauze undulated across the dance floor. After the belly
dancers came the fire-eaters, then the snake-charmer. Not
until two o'clock in the morning, when the last cobra had
been re-coiled in its basket, could Judy stand up and
leave.

Back at the hotel reception desk her anxiety increased
as she stared at Lili's key, still in its pigeonhole. 'This is
not the kind of town for a girl to be out with a strange
man,' Judy said to Sandy. 'However angry Lili was, she
would have sent us a message. After all, she wouldn't
want the police looking for her if she was just romancing.'

Feeling increasing guilt, Judy turned to Sandy. 'We'd
better not call the police. We don't want to upset the local
people and we don't want to look foolish if Lili, if she
only . . .' she paused.

'Exactly,' agreed Sandy.

As soon as Judy woke she telephoned Lili's suite. No
answer. In her red silk dressing gown, Judy hurried down
to the reception desk. The clerk, a nervous new boy on
the daytime shift, refused to give her the key to Lili's
rooms. Judy demanded to see the hotel manager and,
together, they hurried up the marble staircase. An anxious
Sandy waited outside the double doors of Lili's suite.

They rushed across the empty drawing room and threw

•

open the bedroom door. The billowing pink silk canopy of the elaborate antique bed was caught back with golden rope, but the plump velvet pillows in their lace coverings were undented and the ivory chiffon sheets were still as smooth as when the maid had turned them down the night before.

Sandy ran into the dressing room and opened the closets. 'Her clothes are still here.' She pulled open the bathroom door. The make-up was scattered on the marble counter as Lili had left it.

Sandy dashed back to the sitting room to see Judy on her knees, tearing at a cylindrical brown-paper parcel on the floor. She pulled out an exquisite silk rug. 'Lili must have bought that after she left me in the Bazaar.'

'Maybe the man she went out with was a rug merchant?' suggested Sandy.

'Maybe she met someone in the Grand Bazaar?' Judy worried aloud.

Sandy always told people what they wanted to hear. 'Lili might have taken up with some good-looking guy and decided to have a little fun,' she soothed.

The discreet tap at the door made both women jump, then hurry towards it. Judy was the first to reach the handle. 'Lili, thank God you're . . . oh!' Outside stood a hotel page boy, carrying a gigantic bouquet of red roses.

'Who would send us flowers when we're leaving to-morrow?' Sandy wondered as she unpinned the tiny envelope and handed it to Judy. She pulled out the card and read it, then gasped, 'Oh, no!' and dropped the card.

·

•

Sandy snatched up the card and read it aloud. 'Wait in your hotel suite to hear from Lili's father. He must pay the ransom.' Slowly she turned to Judy. 'So now we know. Lili's been kidnapped.'

ONE

15 October 1978

Standing, dazed, in her hotel room, gazing at the beautiful bunch of red roses which had accompanied the kidnap letter, Judy said nothing. But she thought, this is my fault. Once again I have been responsible for a disaster in my daughter's life. Why, oh why, doesn't God stick up red flags when you accidentally do some little thing that's going to lead to calamity? *I* persuaded Lili to come with me on this tacky trip because I never had enough *time* for her back home in New York; there I told myself that it wasn't my responsibility, I hadn't been expecting a long-lost daughter to drop in on me. I had a magazine to run and a business to run and my charity commitments, and my lover to look after. But that article on Lili in *Verve!* was my idea. I should have known that article was asking for trouble – and that we'd all get it in shovelfuls. I wish I could turn the clock back to a year ago, to that first meeting at the Pierre Hotel.

★
●

It had been a warm October evening; nevertheless, a log fire had burned softly in the quiet, cream hotel suite, with the spectacular view across the purple dusk of Central Park. Firelight had flickered across the faces of the two women as they moved towards each other. Judy had felt the strange animal magnetism that emanated from Lili. Looking at Lili's black, soft curls, falling to the folds of her white Grecian tunic, Judy felt a new appreciation of that world-famous oval face with the high cheekbones that looked both innocent and predatory, the thickly lashed chestnut eyes that always glistened as if tears were about to fall. Judy found it hard to accept that her daughter, believed dead, was alive – let alone that she was Lili, the most famous professional waif since Marilyn Monroe. It was impossible to match this sensuous creature with the image that Judy had treasured of a well-behaved, six-year-old girl with braided hair.

Judy had always imagined that her long-lost daughter would look exactly like herself, but their only resemblance lay in the slim-boned frames of their bodies. The three other women in the room sat motionless – hypnotized by the drama of the moment – as Lili took a hesitant step towards Judy. Pagan, elegant in pink wool, suddenly noticed that Judy and Lili had the same doll-like hands. She leaned across to the green-eyed woman in the mulberry suit. 'Do you think we should leave?' she whispered to Kate, who was sitting next to her on the apricot silk sofa.

Kate Ryan shrugged her shoulders, unable to take her

•

eyes off Lili. She found herself mentally taking notes, as if writing one of her articles, as Lili moved towards Judy, but Judy stood motionless and silent. Kate opened her mouth to say something but the third onlooker, an elegant blonde in blue silk, lifted her fingers to her lips as all three women watched the mother and daughter hold each other in a nervous embrace. Sharing a natural impulse to dissolve the pain and embarrassment of the moment by reaching towards physical contact, they were hugging each other, but not kissing each other, Kate noticed.

As she held her daughter Judy realized that this was the first time she had touched Lili since the sad moment when she had handed her three-month-old baby to her foster mother that morning years ago in the Swiss hospital where Judy's illegitimate child had been born. As she held Lili close to her heart Judy realized that, since that day, they had shared a physical need for each other that was close to hunger; their embrace was an expression of that need, rather than of warmth, of affection, even of liking; but both women realized that this was an expression of goodwill.

This is my daughter, thought Judy, as she felt the trembling warmth of Lili's body; this voluptuous woman once came out of my body; those wild brown eyes and slanting cheekbones – once they were a part of me, I made them. She looked down at Lili's gold-skinned forearms and thought, that is flesh of my flesh.

She does not *feel* like my mother, thought Lili, hugging the slender Judy in her brown velvet suit. A mixture of

•

resentment and relief swirled in Lili's mind; she had built up her unknown mother's identity into a romantic mystery because the alternative was to face her mother's brusque rejection of her as a baby. When she finally met her mother Lili had expected to feel as protected as a child, but when she looked into Judy's eyes and saw pain, fear and guilt, Lili felt unexpectedly protective towards her mother.

Oblivious of the three seated women who watched, Lili was also near to tears as she remembered her deep-rooted restlessness, the profound anxiety and uncertainty that had shadowed her adult life. Now she instinctively recognized it as a sense of loss – sad and constant – even though it was for a woman that Lili had never known, her *vraie maman*, as Lili used to think of her mother, in the little Swiss village where she had been raised by the local seamstress. 'Mother?' Lili said the word softly, as if forming it for the first time, and then tried it again. 'Mother.'

The two women drew back, gave tearful laughs and simultaneously said, 'You're not what I expected!' Then Judy added, 'How did you find us?'

'It wasn't difficult,' said Lili. 'I hired a detective. He discovered that my mother had been one of four teenage girlfriends who had been students in Switzerland, and then he followed the trails until he identified you.' She turned to the green-eyed woman in the mulberry suit. 'You were the most difficult to track down, Kate, because the world is full of Katherine Ryans. But, once he did find you, my detective couldn't discover *which* of you four was that teenage mother, which is why I arranged this confrontation.' She hesitated, and nervously bit her lower lip. 'I hope you'll forgive me; I do so hope you'll understand why I had to know who my parents are, why I had to know *who I am*.'

The last thing Kate had expected to feel for this sex goddess was a sudden rush of affection and pity. Gently she said, 'We do so hope, Lili, that you will understand why Judy couldn't keep her baby. In 1949 a sixteen-year-old girl from a poor family, who had to earn her own living, couldn't also look after a baby.'

Anxiously Judy said, 'Did you . . . were you . . . did your foster mother look after you?' She added in a rush, 'I can never forgive her for taking you to Hungary after the Russians occupied it.'

Lili said, 'I shall always love Angelina. She loved me and she never lied to me; she always told me that one day my *vraie maman* would come for me.'

'She did come for you.' The elegant blonde in the blue silk dress spoke, for the first time, with an unmistakable French accent. 'We knew you were on holiday in Hungary and, when we heard there'd been a revolution, Judy flew over to Europe and we went straight to the Hungarian border. The situation was chaotic: a hundred and fifty thousand Hungarian refugees were pouring over the Austrian border into camps for displaced persons. We visited every one of them. But nobody could trace you.'

Maxine remembered Judy's frenzy and self-accusation as

they stood in the snow outside hut after hut, waiting to see yet another refugee committee official.

As Judy remembered her constant self-reproach for having abandoned Lili, for not having done enough to find her, she sat down heavily on the apricot silk sofa and buried her face in her hands; her little gulps, splutters and sniffs were the only sounds to break the silence.

Kate picked up the ivory telephone and said, 'Champagne is what you celebrate a new baby with, isn't it? D'you think they have any Krug '49?'

'I would prefer you to order our champagne,' said Maxine firmly. 'Ask for a magnum of Chazalle '74.'

After a great deal of emotion and champagne Pagan suddenly said, 'How is the press going to react to this news? Do you think we should keep it secret?'

'It's bound to get out somehow,' said Maxine. 'We're all public personalities as we all live our lives in the spotlight. Why, within a week, someone would have overheard a telephone conversation, stolen a letter and sold the story to the *National Enquirer* for a meagre fifty dollars.' She turned to Kate. 'You're a journalist, right?'

Judy remembered the cruel descriptions that she had quite enjoyed reading about Lili, as maliciously enjoyable as any tidbit about Elizabeth Taylor, Farrah Fawcett or Joan Collins. 'We'll be able to set the record straight, Lili. We'll print your *true* life story, as told by you.'

'No!' Lili looked frightened and anxious. 'You know

•

the lies, the filth that's published about me. They'll all just dredge it up from their files again.'

'Don't worry, Lili,' said Kate. 'I'm the editor of *Verve!* magazine, so you can control the story. We'll print whatever you want.' She turned to Judy for confirmation. 'If we get in first with an exclusive story and splash it big enough, we'll have scooped the rest of the world; nobody will want to run it after that.'

Lili said, 'It's quite a story.'

As Maxine poured champagne all four women listened to the quiet voice of Lili reciting the tale of her life since 1956, the success story of the Paris porn model who became an international movie star, the sad story of an exploited, lonely girl as incapable of controlling her own destiny as the autumn leaves that fluttered from the trees below them in darkened Central Park.

It was two o'clock in the morning before Kate let herself into her apartment. She stood in the doorway of her huge living room, rubbing her tired eyes as she looked across at the man who lay asleep on the thirty-foot-long, beige suede sofa that ran along one wall. Above the sofa hung a collection of antique paintings and engravings of tigers. On the floor below the man lay a pair of loafers, a pair of socks, a crumpled copy of the *Wall Street Journal*, and a silver salver upon which was a slice of cold, leftover pizza and a half-empty glass of beer. Tom would never be a gourmet, no matter how many elegant meals she served him, thought Kate as she tiptoed over to her husband and gently shook him awake. 'Bedtime, darling,' she whispered, as he leaned against her, blinking, then suddenly hugged her in a hard grip. 'How'd it go, darling? Did you reach an agreement with Tiger-Lili?'

'Tell you in the morning. Everything's fine, but right now I'm exhausted and I just want to be in bed. How I wish that someone would invent a machine with a button that you press and suddenly you find yourself undressed, showered and in bed with your teeth cleaned.'

'With me.'

'You'd be an optional accessory. Very expensive.'

In her softly lit bathroom at the Plaza Hotel Maxine carefully broke open three glass ampoules, mixed the clear liquids together, then patted the solution carefully around the delicate skin of her eye socket. She used a pink cream to remove her make-up, a clear solution to exfoliate her skin and a white preparation to stimulate cell renewal while she slept. Along the fine lines of her forehead, no more definite than the veins on a leaf since her face-lift, she traced a tiny paintbrush dipped in a solution of synthetic collagen. Finally, her generously rounded right buttock, smooth as a peach thanks to regular treatments to dispel *la cellulite*, received a slimming injection. Carefully she hung up her blue silk dress, then wrapped herself in an oyster silk peignoir edged with point-de-Chazalle lace. She brushed her hair with a hundred strokes, then climbed into bed, opened her maroon leather travelling office and dictated half a dozen

•

memos to be telexed to her secretary on the following day. Then, in her large, loopy handwriting, she thanked Judy for making her so welcome in New York and wrote an encouraging note to Lili. She always wrote her thank-you notes at night, when she was still feeling grateful, no matter how late the hour. Maxine never considered it an excuse to neglect her body, her business, or her gift for expedient politeness.

Pagan sprawled across her old-fashioned brass bed in her room at the Algonquin and again tried to direct-dial her husband.

It was two in the morning in New York, which meant seven in the morning in London, so with luck she'd catch Christopher just before breakfast, she thought as she looked around the small pretty room. Her Jean Muir pink coat was thrown carelessly over the rose velvet armchair and her discarded underwear was scattered over the malachite-green carpet.

'Darling, that you? How are the dogs? Is Sophia doing her homework *directly* when she comes home from school? Are you helping her with geometry? . . . Sorry, it doesn't seem like twenty-four hours, it seems weeks since I saw you last, darling . . . Yes, I've met Lili, but I don't want to talk about it on the telephone . . . No, we didn't discuss the possibility of a donation to your laboratory, darling, you're even more tactless than I am . . . No, there simply wasn't a chance to discuss the importance of cancer research.' She pushed her heavy, wavy mahogany

•

hair away from her face and wriggled her long-legged, lean, naked body into a more comfortable position on the lace blanket cover. '. . . Yes, I know I forgot to pack my nightclothes, but nobody's noticed, darling, I'll hide in the loo when they bring breakfast up . . . Oh, damn, did I really forget the grocer order again? Thank heaven for Harrods and Globe Car Service . . .' Eventually, in a carefully casual voice, Pagan said, 'How are you feeling, darling?' After his heart attack, she always worried when she was away from Christopher.

'. . . No, I hardly slept at all last night, you know I mustn't take sleeping pills or anything addictive. But tonight I'm prepared to enjoy a sleepless night. I've bought this absolutely gripping book called *Scruples* . . .'

Judy had also spent a sleepless night. Huddled under the red-fox spread of her big, luxurious, peaceful bedroom, she restlessly gazed at the peach-coloured walls and matching wild-silk curtains, at the pretty Victorian oil paintings of peaches and grapes, apples and apricots that hung from the walls. She was almost glad that Griffin wasn't here; he'd had to fly to the West Coast for a couple of days to launch a new decorating magazine, the first of his many publishing ventures to be based in San Francisco. Only the previous evening Griffin had asked Judy the question that she'd been waiting to hear from him for ten years. Although Griffin was a major shareholder of *Verve!*, and although they'd been lovers for over ten years, there had always been a subject that she was forbidden

•

to discuss. That subject was Griffin's home life. Everyone in the media world knew that it had been clearly established years ago, before he'd met Judy, when that tough, clever bastard, Griffin Lowe, was still being seen around town with the best-looking models and young actresses in New York, that none of them stood a chance: Griffin would never leave his wife and three children because he'd fought too hard to climb his way up the ladder of success and he wanted all of it, the successful, respectable life that he'd established as well as his notorious, amorous adventures.

And then, a few days ago, Griffin's wife had left him for another man; they were going to Israel together, to start a new life on a kibbutz. The long-suffering Mrs Lowe had walked out on her handsome, rich, debonair, double-crossing husband.

What was equally surprising was that Griffin had immediately asked Judy to marry him. What was even more surprising was that, after hearing the words for which she'd waited ten years, Judy found that she didn't want to marry Griffin. Griffin had developed a habit of cheating on his wife and therefore she wasn't too sure that she wanted to become his wife. Old habits die hard.

Silhouetted against the russet shade of the bedside light, the slim, naked figure looked like an alabaster Praxiteles; slowly his fox-shaped face broke into an intimate smile. 'No, darling, it's absolutely safe; Lili's out there playing the biggest role of her life.' Softly he laughed into the ivory

•

telephone. 'I'll be back in Paris on Saturday . . . promise, darling . . . you can save it for another couple of days . . . you'd better . . .' The man's head jerked up as the door was flung open and Lili stood there smiling. Hastily the man said to the telephone, 'Sorry, this is suite 1719. I think you've got the wrong number.' He replaced the telephone and held out both his arms to Lili, who hurled herself into them. 'You were right, Simon! It worked just as you said it would!' She threw her arms round his neck and kissed him full on the lips. 'At last I know who I really am, at last I know who my mother is!'

Simon Pont was an actor. A good stage actor who needed an audience to produce his best work, who hated movies and only occasionally made one, strictly for the money. He and Lili had lived together for two years and it was Simon who had originally persuaded Lili to search for her mother. A quiet, intelligent thirty-five-year-old, he seemed secure enough to handle Lili with firm indulgence, seemed to understand that she needed more protection and attention than most men are prepared to give a woman. It was Simon who had given Lili the reassurance she had needed, and it was he who had realized that Lili needed to trace her mother in order to firmly establish her own identity. Simon had pointed out that if Lili found her real parents, then she might stop looking for substitute parents to love in almost everyone with whom she became involved – which is why she was so vulnerable to the exploiters, the con men and the con women that the rich and the famous invariably attracted.

•

Now Simon held Lili to his handsome, naked body and licked her ear with his long, curly tongue. 'Tell me who your mother is, darling. Lady Swann?'

'No, not Pagan Swann; it's Judy Jordan. She admitted it almost at once, but I remembered what you'd said – that they'd be bound to pin it on the only woman who wasn't married and didn't have to explain me to a husband!'

He pushed the white silk from her shoulder, and nipped the golden flesh with his little wide-spaced teeth. Lili wriggled. 'So I suddenly asked Judy who my father was and – just as you said – the other three all snapped round to look at Judy, so I knew that she was telling the truth, that she really *is* my mother.'

Simon pushed Lili's dress from both shoulders, and gently flicked one sandalwood nipple with his finger and thumb. Lili wriggled again. 'Listen, Simon, she wasn't some rich bitch who'd just dumped me because she couldn't get an abortion.' Simon tugged at Lili's white belt as she continued. 'Judy was poor, from one of those grim Baptist families in West Virginia, a scholarship student in Switzerland, working her way through college by waiting on tables. And she was only fifteen when it happened.'

'And who helped it to happen?' Simon's voice was gentle. 'What about your father? Who's he?' He tugged again at Lili's belt, and the white Grecian tunic slithered to the floor. Simon pressed her naked body against his and stroked Lili's hair.

•

'That part's sad,' said Lili, sorrowfully. 'He's dead. He was an English student that she met in Switzerland, but he was drafted into the British army and died fighting the Communists in Malaya. He never even knew she was pregnant.'

'Do you believe that?' Simon put his arms round Lili and grasped her buttocks.

Lili thought for a moment. 'There was something odd about the way she told me. Pagan Swann started to say something, then thought better of it.'

'What about the rest of his family?'

'I haven't asked Judy yet. There was so much to talk about. It's a really strange story. Apparently all four girls paid Angelina for my keep. Judy didn't dare to tell her parents, you see. Judy intended to come to Switzerland for me as soon as she was able to support me by herself. But she was only a twenty-two-year-old secretary when I disappeared.'

'I'm glad she didn't get an abortion.' He rubbed himself against Lili's big, soft breasts.

'She couldn't have done that in Switzerland in 1949. It was illegal and dangerous.'

He trickled his finger up her spine. 'So now, can we start a family of our own?'

'What, right now?'

'Right now.' Gently he pushed her backwards on to the grey silk bedcover. She always felt safe with Simon, Lili thought as he began to kiss her. She trusted him. There was no need for him to dominate her, envy her or exploit her, because he was a successful actor in his own right. And she knew that he had her interests at heart. Why else should he have encouraged her search for her mother?

After her sleepless night Judy didn't feel tired. She felt contented and apprehensive. A fizz of anticipation coloured all the chores of planning future issues of her magazine, because the future was now the future for both Judy and her daughter. She picked up the telephone. 'Dick?' she said, unable to keep the excitement out of her voice as she spoke to New York's most famous portrait photographer, 'I want you to take a very special picture for me . . .'

Next she called her florist. 'Do you have tiger lilies?' she asked, her voice quivering. 'Then please send every single one to Mademoiselle Lili at the Pierre, and put a card with it saying . . . "With all my love, Mother".' As she hung up she savoured that word. All her life she had thought of a mother as someone like her own mother – disappointed and inwardly desperate. The picture of that ineffectual woman setting out for chapel every Sunday flashed into Judy's mind. Sin and its avoidance were the only things in which her mother had seemed interested, and when Judy's father had plodded home from the grocery store to break the news that he had lost everything, all her mother had done was to kneel and pray; she had merely accepted the disaster, and hadn't tried to fight it. Motherhood, to Judy, meant drudgery, dependence and the sublimation of all the joy of living into faith

•

in an unforgiving God. But now that Judy herself was a mother – truly a mother – with a living daughter to prove it, the notion of motherhood began to become exciting. Her morning rushed by in a froth of delight.

'D'you suppose there's a new man in Mrs Jordan's life?' wondered the junior secretary as, one after another, the magazine's senior staff came out of the pastel-painted office looking startled, but pleased, because for once their proposals had been received with uncritical enthusiasm. 'Did you know that Griffin Lowe's wife walked out on him last week?' the senior assistant whispered as she stood up to take in Judy's morning mail. 'I think that's why she's lit up. When your lover's wife finally concedes after ten years it must feel pretty good.'

Every Friday Kate the editor and Judy the publisher of *Verve!* had an editorial conference for all staff. It always took place over lunch in Judy's office. The ten men and women who created the magazine pulled up lucite chairs and hurled ideas at each other for an hour and a half over the long table, cold meats, cheese and sodas. Judy found the Friday conference an excellent way to channel the thoughts of her staff for the weekend, and Monday always produced a satisfying stack of memos which crystallized the ideas that had been thrown about during the Friday brainstorming session.

Today Kate's green eyes flicked over her agenda as she tried to work up the necessary enthusiasm to motivate her staff. Thank heaven, next week she'd be away from

●

the highly polished, shallow world, where, at the end of the day, nothing could happen without the lipstick advertisements. It had been eleven years since her last bestseller, eleven years since she'd done something worthwhile on her own, and now she was itching for the end of the month, when she was to start her first sabbatical – a year on her own.

Suddenly Kate was startled to hear Judy ask, 'What do we think about working mothers?' She picked up a stick of celery and nipped off the end. 'I'm concerned that our feature coverage is getting too heavy on emotional and sexual issues; we didn't get two million readers by treating them as if they had nothing more important to think about than multiple orgasms. I want some solid feature ideas about the basics of our readers' lives.'

The team couldn't believe it. Family life was a no-no on the magazine. Few principles were written on tablets of stone in that office, but one of the unbreakable commandments was that children should never be mentioned between those assertive, glossy covers. Both Judy and Kate were childless.

The youngest assistant editor tentatively said, 'The last readership survey showed that the majority of *Verve!* readers planned on working again after they had started their families.' She picked up a celery stick with the same gesture as Judy; she was editing an article on body-language-in-the-workplace, which advised that mirroring a superior's movements was a good way to establish subliminal empathy.

●

'Let's have a breakdown of those figures.' Judy snapped the celery stick. 'I want to know everything we can find out about our readers' attitudes towards children, childcare, step-parents – that whole important area.'

There was an astounded silence as Judy continued, 'And I'd like to see us become a little less parochial, a little more international. How about a regular feature on successful European women? Starting, of course, with internationally known actresses.'

'Our readers don't relate to these European stars.' Judy's business partner, Tom Schwartz, raised his eyes from the hot dog he'd had sent up. He winked across the table at his wife, Kate, and Kate knew that the idea was about to get firmly kicked at as Tom continued, 'My instinct is that our readers are interested in the new identity that women are creating for themselves and these sexy actresses from over the ocean merely represent everything they want to reject. They aren't relevant to a girl who's focused on getting her qualifications and her business skills in shape.'

Judy was about to protest when she realized she was overreacting. Twenty-four hours ago she, too, had considered Lili a glamorous, irrelevant, continental pain in the ass.

Kate wished that Tom hadn't taken a stand on European stars, since she was about to do as Judy asked and propose the feature on Lili without telling the magazine staff the full significance of the story. Now she was forced to override her husband's opinion in public and, despite

Tom's unsinkable self-esteem, she felt ungracious as she announced, 'There's always an element of risk when we're trying a new idea. But I've decided that we're going to run a major interview with Lili in the December issue.'

The production editor looked as if she'd swallowed a toad instead of a caviare canapé. 'It's already too late. Unless we put it in the Hither and Yon section, it'll cost us a fortune. The printers will probably need to replate.'

'It'll be the cover story, so whatever it costs we're going to do it,' said Kate. 'I want it run over two spreads and we're getting a special cover picture from Avedon. Tomorrow.' Kate raised her eyebrows at Judy, who nodded behind her tortoiseshell spectacles. The rest of the staff, who respected Kate's sure judgement and professionalism, were irritated, but not surprised. Kate's background in newspapers had given her what the staff called a 'hold-the-front-page, I'm changing-the-comic-strip' mentality. Correctly, they felt that she rather enjoyed wrecking editorial plans at the last moment, for the sake of squeezing in the most up-to-the-minute material.

'We're going to tell Lili's story right from the beginning,' Kate went on. 'She's agreed to tell us everything about her early days, even that blue-movie stuff when she was thirteen. Things she's never talked about before.'

'Small wonder,' somebody muttered (but very quietly).

'Can we dig up one of those classic tyre-calendar shots of her?' the art director wondered from the far end of the table. 'Maybe that one with a sunflower in the navel?'

Judy shook her head. 'No early shots. Only the Avedon

•

portrait.' Kate threw a warning glance at Judy, catching the protective, emotional tone of her voice.

'What about the men in Lili's life?' Tom reached for another prawn, wondering what his wife was up to. This morning over breakfast Kate had been oddly reticent about her meeting with Lili.

'All of them,' Kate explained. 'The photographer who put her in dirty movies and ripped her off until . . .'

'Until she had a nervous breakdown on the promotional tour I managed for her first straight film. I'll never forget that.' Judy found that the memory of that television tour – previously nominated as the worst fuck-up of Judy's career – now seemed less painful; but she tried to sound correctly resentful in front of the staff.

'We all know about her relationships. What we're dying to know is *more* about some of them. That Greek shipping millionaire, Jo Stiarkoz and then, after he died, King Abdullah. And what's it like with Simon Pont? And are they going to marry?'

Kate gave her tight smile. 'If they are, she'll tell us. Lili's promised to tell us the whole truth and I think you'll find it's quite a story.'

After lunch, as they all left Judy's pretty cream-and-green office; Kate felt a hand on her shoulder. 'Wait a minute, Kate,' said Judy, 'I want a word with you . . .'

Kate threw herself on to the cream art deco sofa. 'It's no use. You can't stop me. I'm off,' she said, her British accent still distinct in the clipped short 'o' sound. 'It's been terrific, Judy, but I feel smothered under equal opportunities programmes and contraceptive sponges. I want to get back to hard news.'

'Kate, for heaven's sake – the goddamn magazine was your idea in the first place.'

'You can run it with Pat Rogers for a year – she should have been promoted long ago. I'm going to Chittagong.'

'But Kate, who *needs* a book about settlement wars in the hill tracts of Chittagong. It won't sell two thousand copies.'

'That's not the point. And anyway, I've a feeling that the situation's going to escalate.'

'Where the hell is Chittagong anyway?' Judy's new maternal euphoria started to disperse. Sure, Judy and Kate's deputy could run the magazine while she took a sabbatical, but Judy's plans for 1979 had included launching a new magazine, aimed at the generation of readers who had grown up with *Verve!* and now had mature lifestyles, families and spending power to match. Unless she made a last-ditch attempt to stop Kate leaving, she'd have to postpone the new magazine.

'Bangladesh, east of the Ganges delta. It hasn't changed location since I told you about it last month, Judy. The Bengalis have been fighting the hill tribes there ever since the state of Bangladesh was created seven years ago, and it virtually amounts to jungle genocide. Thousands of people have died, but because the war area is so remote nobody knows what's going on.' Kate was becoming irritated. 'It's a terrific assignment, Judy. You bullied me

•

into becoming a writer. I wouldn't have written my first book if you hadn't pushed me into it. Now be a pal and let me bug out.'

After leaving Judy's office Kate poked her head back around the door. 'There's an enormous Tarzan figure out here waiting to see you. Who's he?'

'Our new exercise instructor,' said Judy. 'I've decided we can all work out for an hour.'

Kate laughed. 'It's the mean Irish in you. You don't want the staff to even leave for lunch.'

Under their continental quilt Tom's elbow gently prodded Kate. 'Sure you want to go?'

'Sure. Judy won't really miss me, once I'm gone; she's more identified than I am with the magazine. That's one of the reasons I want to get out and do something on my own.' Kate turned on her back and watched a little wink of light from a passing 747 travel from one corner of the window to the other. 'I'll be on that shooting star next week.'

'How do you know I'll be here when you come back?'

Kate gently prodded Tom. 'You'd better be.' The reason she hadn't gone off earlier was that she couldn't bear to leave this wonderful man, who loved her without wanting to own her, encouraged her without patronizing her, and admired her talent without exploiting it. 'I'll miss you, too. Be careful.'

'Come over here, woman.'

•

'What's on your side of the bed that isn't on my side?'
'Me.'

Judy handed Griffin his vodka martini with olive on
the rocks and sat down in her living room, which had
just been restyled by David Laurance in soft turquoise,
an excellent background colour for blondes. Judy drove
her decorator crazy by decorating one room at a time
instead of having the whole apartment done over.

Griffin said, 'So when are we doing it?'

'I'm not sure, Griffin.'

'Not sure about what?' He ate his olive. 'Tell me
about it while you get dressed. We're due at the Sherry
Netherland in twenty-five minutes.'

Judy hurried to her dressing room, not because she
was late but because she wanted to put off the discussion.
But, as she started to select her clothes, Griffin followed
her and, leaning against the door, he repeated, 'Have you
decided when you want to get married?'

'Not yet.' She turned away from him and selected a
black sequinned jacket, then thought, better get it over
with, and gently said, 'Maybe not ever, Griffin. I don't
really want to share the whole of my life with you or
anyone.' She carefully avoided looking at him. 'I think
we should face the fact that we're both independent
people – and that's why I suited you as a lover. I didn't
pester you to get divorced and marry me . . .'

'But we've waited so long! I always thought . . .'

'*I've* waited so long, is what you mean, Griffin. I've

•

53

waited too long. It's become a way of life with me. I've had to make too many excuses for you; I've had to spend too many Thanksgivings without you, too many Christmases, too many holidays and too many Sundays – *they're* the loneliest days of the week, Griffin.'

She looked at Griffin and a hundred tall, dark, astounded Griffins looked back. The entire dressing room, including the ceiling, was covered in mirror glass. Judy could stand in the middle of the room and see herself from every angle without craning her neck. She could also, in a playful mood, give a high kick and see herself reflected to infinity, like a one-woman Busby Berkeley chorus.

'Do you really mean you *don't* want to marry me?' Didn't all women want to get married? Was she really turning down one of the most successful publishers in the country, whose empire included some of the best magazines in America? Was she turning down the maroon Rolls-Royce, the money, the servants, the old-English manor house in Scarsdale, the social position, the sensational times in bed? Griffin's forehead wrinkled in perplexity. 'What's got into you tonight? Is it the wrong time of the month?'

'Griffin, it isn't premenstrual tension, it's common sense.' Judy thought she'd better be firm or she'd duck out. 'After all, what do I really know about you except that you're in the habit of cheating on your wife? How do I know that when I'm your wife you won't want the same surreptitious excitement?'

•

Carefully Griffin put his drink on one of the glass shelves that lined a complete mirror wall but did not interrupt the reflected perspective into infinity. 'That's a cheap shot after all these years. You didn't complain when you were getting your share.'

Judy looked at him. He thinks he's a great lover and he's right, she thought. But, for him, the satisfaction is being seen to be a great lover, not simply enjoying himself with me. His constant craving for admiration will always make him flirt with other women, because his ego is insatiable.

Griffin rubbed the scar on his left hand, a sure sign of irritation. 'So where do we go from here?'

'How about the Sherry Netherland? What's wrong with business as usual, Griffin? Can't we continue as we are? You keep that mansion in Scarsdale, I'll stay here, and we'll be together three or four times a week. And maybe Sunday.'

What Judy really meant to say was, 'This relationship will stand or fall on how we feel for each other, moment by moment. I do not want you to take me for granted, Griffin. I do not want cosy warmth and domestic security. Or even domestic insecurity, which would be more likely.'

Griffin wasn't used to earning a woman's affection. He wanted his mate dependent, tied, safe and always there – waiting. Workaholic Griffin needed a steady partner because his kind of insecurity meant that he needed to know that there was always someone waiting at home for him, no matter what he did or where he went.

•

Suddenly Judy realized that she didn't like having a man watch her while she got dressed. She opened the walk-in shoe closet, newly covered in jet-black moire to match the carpet. 'Griffin, I've got something really important to tell you.' She picked a pair of silver sandals. 'Yesterday my past caught up with me.'

'What happened?' Was that why she was acting so strangely tonight?

'You know I was a scholarship student in Switzerland. I got pregnant while I was there. The baby was adopted.'

'Well, that was a long time ago.' Now that Griffin understood, he knew when to be magnanimous. 'That shouldn't come between us. Don't let it upset you.'

Suddenly the love affair, which had seemed overwhelmingly important to Judy for ten years, looked very insignificant beside the new fact that she had a daughter. 'Griffin, will you listen? My child is alive and she's tracked me down.'

'Huh?' He was suddenly all attention. 'I'll get the lawyers on to it first thing tomorrow. Boy, has she picked the wrong lady to touch for a few bucks!'

'Griffin, she isn't short of a few bucks. She's Lili – the actress, *the Lili*.'

'Tiger-Lili?' That was what she was called by the press. 'Yes.'

Griffin thought for a moment. 'There must be a reason for it. She's after the publicity.'

'Griffin, she can get all the publicity she needs by simply appearing in public.'

•

•

'Don't worry, I'll fix it. She's bound to be after something.'

Judy gave up.

Maxine leaned forward and sighed with pleasure as the navy-blue Peugeot crested the gentle hill and she saw her vineyards spread below her. She always enjoyed flying Concorde on a Sunday, when it was never crowded. The car cruised quietly out of the snow-speckled forest and began the gentle descent towards the Château de Chazalle. Maxine's mind was already running down the list of arrangements she needed to make for the forthcoming week, when she and Charles were to meet a rider from the French Olympic equestrian team, and Maxine's first boyfriend, Pierre Boursal, now the trainer of an exciting young skier who had already won the European women's slalom. Since Maxine had decided that Chazalle was going into sponsorship they had entertained more suitors than a fairy-tale princess, she reflected with satisfaction.

The car scattered a flock of white doves on the crescent-shaped gravel drive and the cooing birds bustled out of Maxine's way as she walked happily up the wide stone steps to the imposing doorway, where the butler waited with a footman behind him.

Eagerly Maxine ran upstairs to her bedroom. 'Honorine, have all my bags put in the dressing room,' she called over her shoulder to her maid as she pulled off grey kid gloves. 'Send the jewel box to the strongroom and please run me a bath . . .'

•

She was fully inside the bedroom before she realized that the room was not as it should have been. Instead of being smooth and perfectly in place on the enormous boat-shaped Empire bed, the pale-blue silk bedcover was crumpled on the floor. On tousled sheets her husband Charles lay naked on his back, and astride him sat a big, dark woman wearing the shreds of a green silk camisole. Charles clutched her breasts so tightly that flesh bulged between his fingers as, with one arm, the woman held up her mass of dark hair; her other hand was busy between her legs, helping herself to climax.

Like a stunned animal in an abattoir, Maxine buckled at the knees. Her first instinct was to step back and swing the doors shut, to blot out the sight of her bed, her husband and his mistress. She leaned against the wall of the wide corridor, shaking with shock, but then her tactician's mind told her what to do.

Maxine pulled on her gloves, then she flung open the double doors of her bedroom and strode furiously up to the disordered bed. She grabbed the writhing woman by the hair and pulled her away from her husband's body. 'Charles, how dare you?' Maxine demanded in fury. 'In *our* bed! Why couldn't you keep this whore in Paris, with all your other *divertissements*?'

TWO

17 October 1978

Unhappily for Maxine, the dark woman was no cheap *jupon*; after the hallucinatory flash of the first few seconds Maxine realized that the girl making love to her husband was Simone, his impressively qualified personal assistant.

'We thought you were coming back tomorrow.' His explanation was hardly an excuse, thought Charles, and his habitual expression of mild astonishment changed to frantic alarm. The girl in the shredded green slip shook herself free of Maxine, then calmly sat on the side of the bed, grabbed Charles's limp hand, and twitched the sheet over his long, thin, naked body with a gesture of possession.

'Charles has something to tell you, Madame la Comtesse.' Charles's assistant looked Maxine straight in the eyes. 'Go ahead, Charles, don't let your wife push you around.'

For an instant husband and wife looked silently at each other, then Charles cleared his throat and said, 'Maxine, I want a divorce.'

Maxine could not believe her ears. 'Never,' she said softly, sounding far more resolute than she felt. Then her voice rose. 'Get her out of this bed! Get her out of this room! Immediately!' Maxine's legs shook and she felt as if she were running in slow motion across the treacherous surface of the moon as she ran into her bathroom and slammed the door against those two naked bodies on the wrecked bed.

By the following morning Charles's assistant had disappeared and a frosty silence had settled on the Château de Chazalle. Maxine was still in a shocked trance, but she plunged into a frenzy of work to distract her mind from her grief and pain; she attacked her accumulated mail, demanded to check the china and linen lists, and sent servants scurrying on different errands all over the château. Maxine's secretary left her office with enough work for a month; without being told, Mademoiselle Janine, who had been with Maxine for twenty-two years, knew the reason for Maxine's frantic activity, and silently sympathized with her mistress for being faced, yet again, with one of the count's regrettable indiscretions.

By midday Maxine's competent mind had worked out that her charming, correct husband would never have acknowledged the existence of his mistress to her – let alone have asked for a divorce – had Maxine not surprised them together, had that bitch not forced Charles to speak. Too late Maxine realized that the cleverest action would

•

•

have been quickly to close the bedroom door and walk away, then later to have tackled Charles on his own, when, Maxine knew, he would have agreed to whatever she demanded. But now it was too late.

It was not the first time Maxine had felt her marriage to be in danger. Traditionally, aristocratic French couples often lived discreetly separate sex lives, but they never allowed anything to threaten the sanctity of their family, their home and – most important – their inheritance. But Charles was too easily seduced, and Maxine too romantic, to follow this civilized way of life, and their friends considered the mixture of Charles's *déclassé* mistresses and Maxine's perfect fidelity to be an immature invitation to trouble.

After Charles's first serious affair, what had brought them together again had been Judy's intervention. A little of her Yankee common sense had made Charles realize what he stood to lose. So if she couldn't handle this situation by herself, Maxine thought, she'd send an SOS to Judy in New York.

Lili yawned as she answered the telephone. 'Who? Paul Kroll? For Simon?' Damned directors thought they could phone an actor at any time of the day or night. 'Paul, can't it wait until tomorrow? It's eleven o'clock in New York and Simon's in the shower.'

'Simon never minds what time I call him.'

'Well, I mind. Are you in London or Paris? I'll get him to call you tomorrow when we wake up.'

•

'Why not wake up now, Lili?' Paul's voice was slurred and backed by party noise.

'What do you mean? I am awake.'

'No, dear, you're in Dreamland.' The silky, bitter note in his voice reminded her that Kroll was gay.

'What the hell do you mean?'

'What I mean, lil ole Lili, is that you won't face what we all know.' Now his words were running into each other, but there was a triumphant note in Kroll's voice.

'What *do* you mean?'

'I mean that no matter how hard Simon tries to pretend he's straight . . . he's only pretending. We've been at it together for years, darling. We all know that any actor will do anything for a good part, but Simon does it because he likes it. He *loves* it, darling. He hates to admit it, but that long tongue gets in the strangest places, don't you find? When you were shooting *Chérie*, Simon and I were in Marrakesh. When you were making *The Sun King*, Simon and I were in Tangiers. When you . . .'

Unable to speak, and unable to put down the telephone, hypnotized by Paul's disgusting, detailed story of lust and treachery, Lili listened with tears falling down her face until Simon's wet forearm reached over her shoulder and snatched the telephone from her. Without saying a word he, too, listened. Then he shouted, 'Shut up, Paul, you're drunk . . . because I can tell . . . you've wrecked everything, you stupid idiot.' Simon slammed the phone down and stared defiantly at Lili. 'Paul doesn't mean anything to me.'

•

•

Lili knew that Simon was lying.

The massed narcissi and pink rosebuds of La Grenouille
defied the November mist outside; the cheery buzz of the
lunchers – mostly elegant women – was a counterpoint to
the white, strained face of Lili as she leaned across the
restaurant table to Pagan and said, 'I never meant to tell
you about Simon, but I'm so miserable that I haven't
been able to think about anything else for the last few
days. I didn't want to tell Judy because . . . it would just
make our situation more complicated, when I want it to
be simplified.'

'Lili, your reactions are understandable,' Pagan
soothed her. 'That would have been a devastating experience for anyone. It was a rotten way to learn the
news, and Simon did a rotten thing in walking out on
you.'

'I suppose he was forced to choose. I suppose he was
being honest with himself at last. We didn't have a row,
you know. We both just sat on the bed crying. But after
the things that Kroll had told me, I couldn't bear for
Simon to touch me. And, as well as his homosexuality,
there's his deception; the thought that I would have been
used as camouflage; that we would have had children –
just to make Simon look normal . . .'

'Be fair, Lili, he may really want children.'

'I can't be fair. I feel so . . . humiliated.'

There was a pause, then Pagan leaned across and
pressed Lili's hand. 'There *is* life after humiliation, Lili,

•

●

I promise you. As you get older, you'll find out. You have to learn to overcome humiliation, to live through it. And although you never want anyone to know about it, it's always much easier for you if you tell somebody, because *everybody* has known the bitterness of humiliation at some time; everyone's experienced it, and that's why any sensitive person sympathizes with someone who's been humiliated.'

'I certainly know about humiliation, but I don't believe that any of you four rich, successful women really know the meaning of the word.'

After another pause, Pagan said, 'Yes, I do.' Even after all these years Pagan still felt a twinge of jealousy as she remembered the nineteen-year-old Prince Abdullah and the happy intimacy they had shared until he had contracted a political marriage at the command of his grandfather, then assumed the role of Sydon's ruler and embarked on his philandering career as the Playboy Prince of the Western World.

When his father died Abdullah's time was fully taken up with the political problems of his country and the gynaecological problems of his wife, who had a series of miscarriages, a stillborn child and a son who died two weeks after birth. King Abdullah, as a Muslim, could have four wives. Four childless years later he was on the point of taking a second wife to provide him with heirs when his son Mustapha was born, and from the moment his father held the tiny body in his arms, Mustapha was the only person in the world that he loved.

In 1972 Abdullah, piloting his own helicopter, was

●

flying his wife and ten-year-old Mustapha to their hunting lodge in the eastern mountains of Sydon. Because of faulty servicing, the engine failed, the helicopter had crashed, and the 150-pound propeller blade roughly slashed the Queen's head from her body; then the helicopter had exploded, throwing Abdullah through the air and across the desert sand, where, severely injured but not unconscious, he watched the helicopter turn into a roaring ball of fire that reduced his son, Mustapha, to a twisted black crisp.

During the following three years Abdullah, racked by grief and guilt, had rarely appeared in public until he met Lili. For the next year, Pagan remembered, Lili and Abdullah had been inseparable, until Lili had suddenly returned to Paris and her career.

Pagan looked across the narcissi and rosebuds on the restaurant table to Lili, the only white woman that Abdullah had ever openly taken to Sydon. Suddenly Pagan remembered Abdullah's arrogance and the commanding voice which masked his apprehension and, sometimes, fear. Lili had had what Pagan had never been allowed – and Lili had turned it down; she had walked out on Abdullah.

Pagan couldn't resist mentioning it. She said, 'If we're talking of humiliation, we must remember that you humiliated King Abdullah.'

'No, I didn't,' said Lili. 'He didn't feel humiliated when his Western Whore went back to the West.'

Again Pagan couldn't resist asking, 'Why did you leave him?'

•

'I was kept in a gilded cage, his courtiers spied on me, they didn't trust me. I was an infidel and there was no possibility of his marrying me, because Abdullah needs a wife – preferably a Muslim wife – to provide him with heirs, and my . . . shall we say my "exotic" past rendered me unsuitable wife material. In a word, Pagan, I was not respectable enough for the job.'

'But immediately after you left he adopted his only blood kin, his nephew Hassan, as his heir, so it doesn't look as if he intends to marry again. Haven't seen a word about him in the gossip columns lately.'

'He's too busy with his civil war.'

'No, Lili, it isn't a civil war. Abdullah's army is fighting the Communist-backed guerrillas in the eastern hills of Sydon.'

Lili gave Pagan a sharp look. 'I know that, but most people don't realize how complicated the political situation is in Sydon at the moment. You seem to know a lot about Abdullah.'

'We were all at school in the same little town in Switzerland. Abdullah and I used to be pretty good chums.' Pagan thought she needn't tell Lili more than that.

Lili threw a quick look of reassessment at Pagan; she noticed the Englishwoman's long legs, tucked awkwardly around the table legs, the mahogany-coloured hair that fell carelessly around her pale-blue eyes, and the beautifully cut tweed jacket with a man's cream silk handkerchief flopping out of the breast pocket. Lili asked, 'What happened to you after Switzerland, Pagan?'

•

•

'Something nasty happened to me. I married Mr Wrong and then found out that he didn't really love me, he was just after me for my money. Funny thing was, I didn't have any money. I'd inherited my grandfather's estate in Cornwall, but it was mortgaged to the hilt. Robert never forgave me for not being rich. I cheered myself up with vodka, which blotted out the reality of Robert, and eventually ended up a drunk most of the time.' She raised her glass of Perrier. 'You see before you a card-carrying member of Alcoholics Anonymous. I can assure you that I know about humiliation, because I was responsible for my own humiliation.' She took a sip of water. 'Kate saved me. Kate's always been my best friend since we were at school together. She took me over and wouldn't let me give up. I'll never forget what she did for me.'

Lili, who hadn't touched her avocado and salmon salad, said wistfully, 'There's something about the four of you that I can't put my finger on, something warm and protective. I could almost feel it when we were in the room together.'

Pagan finished her last forkful of mushrooms. 'That's friendship. Since we were in Switzerland together we've helped each other through thick and thin – or sick and sin as Maxine calls it. Like most French people, she pronounces "th" as "s".'

'Don't tell me that Maxine knows about sin!'

'Maxine may be a bit of a prig, but she certainly knows about sin – and humiliation. Her husband, Charles, finds other women . . . difficult to resist. Maxine felt

•

humiliated for years until one day she couldn't take it any longer. Crunch point. Separation. Judy flew over to France and had a colossal stand-up fight with Charles, pointing out what he was going to lose if he was idiot enough to let Maxine walk out on him. Since then he seems to have toed the line. Judy can be a fierce little thing when she believes she's fighting for the right.'

'What was my mother like when she was young?'

'Brave, like a little drummer boy marching into war. Her father had gone bust in the depression and that made her determined to be successful. She always worked very hard. Unlike the rest of us, she had an iron discipline. The poor girl never even had time to learn to ski.'

'And my father? What was he like?' Lili's innocent question was the reason that she had invited Pagan to lunch. 'What did he look like?'

Damn, Pagan thought, I'm hopeless at fibbing, but I must make this sound good for Judy's sake. She said, 'He was – um – was very good-looking. He had black hair and aquamarine eyes and beautiful manners. He was terribly shy, like most English boys.

'Judy met him first because he was a waiter learning hotel management at the Imperial, where Judy worked. He was like a brother to us and we all adored him – but he had eyes for nobody but Judy.' Pagan didn't add that, although Judy liked him, she simply didn't feel sexually attracted to Nick. And if a girl doesn't, she doesn't. No matter how handsome, rich and eligible a boy was, if the chemistry wasn't present, there was no use trying to force it. Poor darling Nick had been potty about Judy – when he left he'd given her those two carved rosebud rings from Cartier, but, although Judy liked him, she had drawn away from a physical relationship.

'Judy said he was an orphan.'

I'll bet she did, thought Pagan. That meant that Judy would have no further questions from Lili to answer. 'He charmed us all,' Pagan said. 'Then he went to do his National Service as a soldier in Malaya, and the next thing we heard was that he'd been killed. We were heart-broken.'

Lili did not miss the hesitancy in Pagan's description, or the overcarefulness of her speech, so unlike Pagan's normal easy frankness. So there is something more to find out, Lili thought, mechanically brushing toast crumbs off her white leather trousers. 'Was Judy . . . er . . . popular with boys when she was a student?'

'Judy? She worked so hard that she hardly had time for dates. Why do you ask, Lili?' Attack is the best method of defence, Pagan thought, returning Lili's velvet-brown gaze.

She's challenged me, Lili thought, sensing the bond between the four women, so strong it was almost tangible, an invisible wall between her and the last shreds of the mystery of her identity.

'I suppose there was no doubt that Nick was my father?' There, I've said it, Lili congratulated herself.

'I should think not,' Pagan's tone was firm with a scandalized edge. Lili realized that she would get no

•

further, as Pagan continued, 'What happened to Judy could have happened to any one of us. We were all experimenting with life, we all had our first love affairs in Switzerland and we shared everything, so it seemed natural to us to share the responsibility for you until Judy could afford to give you a home. But she was only earning a secretary's salary when you disappeared.'

'How did she start her business?'

'She worked in public relations, and then Maxine pushed her into starting her own business. In fact, Chazalle was Judy's first client. It was rough for Judy with no experience, no reputation and no money. She keeps quiet about it now, but she was twice evicted because she couldn't pay the rent. She was almost as broke as the Research Institute is today.' Pagan thought she might as well do what she'd come to New York to do. 'My husband was so excited when I told him you were considering a donation to the Anglo-American Cancer Research Institute. He desperately needs a new electron microscope.'

Lili wriggled, feeling guilty. She had certainly lured Pagan to that meeting at the Pierre with the promise of money for cancer research. 'I could ask my agent if we could open my new film with a benefit première in New York. Or a gala in London.'

'Or both?' Pagan had come a long way since, quivering with fear and shame, she had first asked for a charity donation.

'I'll do my best,' Lili said, then added, 'I wish that

•

Maxine hadn't had to return to France. I wanted so much to get to know you all properly.'

'You will, in time. We don't see that much of each other these days, not that it matters.'

'Why doesn't it matter?' asked Lili as the waiter served their lobsters.

'A real friend is someone you don't have to be with. These days a friendship between two women can last longer than their marriages.' Pagan picked up her lobster crackers. 'If both women accept that there will be tough times as well as good ones' – she sucked the juicy flesh from the claw – 'and that sometimes you'll want to strangle your friend and sometimes she'll want to strangle you. A true friendship isn't static, it comes and goes.'

'Then what pulls friends back together?' Lili wondered.

'You just feel more comfortable, more at home, with certain people than with anyone else.'

'But why?' Lili persisted.

'Oh – shared experience, understanding, tolerance and trust, that sort of thing.' Pagan gestured with a red lobster claw. 'A good friendship is like a marriage is supposed to be, but very rarely is. Today the men seem to come and go in a woman's life, but our female friendships are often more enduring. In fact, as marriages crash and the generation gap widens, female friendship seems to be the only growth area in relationships.'

'What do you mean?' Lili was fascinated.

'Lots of relationships are now being questioned and

•

rethought, because it's clear that the old relationships aren't working as we had been led to expect when we were young.'

'So what were you led to expect?' Lili licked a scrap of pink carcass.

'We were all taught that our purpose in life was to get a man,' said Pagan. 'So we all hung around, waiting for Prince Charming to turn up.' She separated shreds of flesh from shell. 'After I married I thought that I'd live in pink bliss for ever; I never imagined that my Prince Charming husband would be unkind or unfaithful. We've turned out to be pioneers, just as much as those women in covered wagons.' Pagan wiped her fingers on her pink napkin. 'But we are pioneers of the emotions, and one of our problems is that we don't realize this.' Lili had hardly touched her lobster, Pagan noticed as she continued. 'Those pioneers knew when they were travelling through hostile territory; they could hear the war whoops, see the Indians and feel the arrows. Today some of us are under fire, some of us are walking wounded and some of us on crutches; but our scars are invisible, and often you don't even realize that you've been in battle.' Pagan paused as they ordered coffee, then continued, 'The pioneers end up scalped, of course; it's the next generation that reaps the benefit and enjoys the promised land.'

'Where the hell is the promised land?' Lili demanded.

'A place where men and women can be honest with each other, and share their responsibilities, and base all relationships on truth, not inadequacies and fear.'

•

'What do you mean by fear?'

'Most relationships are based on fear to varying degrees; fear that your mother will be cross, fear that your teacher will be angry, fear that your boyfriend will leave you, fear that your boss will fire you, or fear that the Russians will kill you.'

'What do you mean by inadequacy?'

'An example of a relationship based on inadequacy is a marriage that a woman enters into because she's frightened that she's unattractive, or she's frightened that she'll never get married, or she's frightened that she can't support herself.'

Slowly Lili said, 'Then we are pioneers and explorers, and what we are discovering is a better way to live.'

'Hopefully, yes.'

Sand and rock spurted into the shell hole where the American war photographer and three Sydonite soldiers pressed themselves into the shuddering earth. Another shell burst at the far lip of the crater, half burying their legs. The next one will get us, thought Mark, his lean body cringing against the hot earth. I must not panic, I must not panic, I must not panic, he chanted silently to himself like a mantra; if the next one does not get you, you will have to run, and if you panic, your legs will turn to water, and you'll move so slowly, you'll get hit immediately. I must not panic, I must not panic. He brushed his dirty-brown hair off his forehead and knuckled the dust from heat-sore grey eyes.

•

At his side two soldiers leapt up as another shell whistled overhead; they struggled up the sliding sides of the crater, trying to run forward as the ground crumbled under their legs, and the shell ploughed into the sand behind the crater.

A burst of gunfire caught the men squarely in the neck and chest, and flung them back into the shell hole. Their blood splashed over the two remaining men crouched in the crater and Mark wiped some of the spattered drops off his camera. Mark's wide mouth was bleeding, his big lips were sun-cracked and his thin face was covered with sun blisters; his small, pugnacious nose was pink and raw because he always forgot his sunblock.

Another shell howled overhead, and bullets smacked into the sand around the crater. 'No way I'm going to get killed while being unprofessional,' Mark muttered as he reloaded his camera. 'When they roll my carcass over, the last shot will be fit to print.'

In the few seconds the distant mortar took to reload, two Sydonite soldiers and an officer hurled themselves forwards into the shell hole, falling over their dead comrades. They scrambled to their feet, pushed the bleeding bodies to one side and started to position a missile-launcher.

Mark noticed that the young officer was using an infra-red tracking device to aim the missiles. For once, thought Mark, King Abdullah's petrodollars have been well spent. The officer was calm and businesslike – they would have been proud of him back at Sandhurst. Did this quietly

•

competent youth know that he was in charge of a suicide mission? Mark wondered. Major Khalid had tried to stop the photographer from coming out with this patrol. With hindsight, Mark realized that the major was *too* insistent that this was merely to be a routine reconnaissance mission, of no interest to the Western press. But because so much desert warfare was carried on at night, when it was impossible to take photographs, Mark had argued with the major. What the callous bastard had not chosen to spell out to Mark was that the platoon had been sent out as cannon-fodder, to draw the guerrillas' fire, and the major didn't want any half-baked heroics from an American journalist.

Again Mark wiped the lens of his Nikon, composed the shot in his mind's eye and carefully photographed the dead men, who were huddled together in the dirt like sleeping children; both were drenched in blood and the smaller soldier had a boot print clearly stencilled in carmine across his face. Concentration steadied Mark's hands and wiped the panic from his body as he cleared his mind to get the high definition which made his pictures look so vivid. A Mark Scott picture could be sent by wire around the world and not be reduced to a blur when it was printed.

Mark's panic surged back as soon as the shutter clicked, and he watched the other three men in the shell hole work to wipe out the enemy position, grimly aware that this was their only chance of getting out alive. One soldier loaded the first slim missile down the launcher's muzzle,

•

and the officer watched his tracking device as it hurtled forward in a high arc.

From the hillside ahead another shell roared over the shell hole as the angle of the missile-launcher was lowered and again fired at the mortar emplacement ahead, which was tucked under a rocky overhang behind a wall of sandbags.

Mark focused carefully on the intent faces around the launcher. These men would have no chance of leaving this crater alive unless they could get a rocket into the eighteen-inch gap between the rocky overhang and the sandbags to blow out the gun and the men manning it.

Another adjustment to the weapon, another rocket down the spout, another retort as it was fired. This time no answering shell screamed back from the hillside ahead.

The Sydonite officer ordered another round and again there was no response.

The air was harsh with heat, smoke and the sweetly pungent stink of war. Now Mark fought relief with the same intensity that he had earlier fought panic. Cool it, cool it, for Chrissake stay cool, stay down, stay alive. Mark had often seen men jump up in elation, believing they had been snatched from the jaws of death, only to be mown down by an enemy who understood that his last chance would be the other side's carelessness.

The young officer ordered his two remaining men to crawl forward, one by one, taking advantage of every rock and every rise in the cracked earth as they snaked forward until they were below the rocky hill.

They started to scramble upwards. When they were closer to the enemy mortar emplacement a grenade was thrown into the gap from which the gun barrel still projected. Caution saved them. With a howl of pain, a man's body was catapulted out by the blast. Behind the billowing pall of dust and smoke Mark saw the machine-gun whipping to and fro on its tripod.

'Better use the back door,' said the officer. 'Grenades may have weakened the roof of that cave.'

They crawled out of the heat into another opening in the rock, part of an interconnected labyrinth across a limestone cavern, packed with stores which looked like the usual guerrillas' jumble of substandard or obsolete arms and explosives. Over a hundred crates, containing 1000-gram sticks of TNT were stacked by polythene bags, each containing twenty-four sticks of gelignite. Beyond was a box of safety fuses and a crate of No. 27 instantaneous aluminium detonators, half-hidden by a tangle of Cordtex detonating cords. Further back in the cave were a few primer sticks of TNT and two boxes of TNT flakes. The hot desiccated air of Sydon had preserved the arms from rust, but nitroglycerine had soaked through the wax coating of some of the cartridges, so the pile was liable to explode at the slightest impact.

'Why did we bother?' The young officer was cheerful as he spoke to Mark in his correct, but guttural English. 'One cigarette would have done our job for us.' It was a weak joke, but to the four survivors of the fourteen-man platoon which had set out that morning it was hilarious.

•

Bright sunlight slid through slits in the rock and illuminated the interconnected caves as Mark wandered below the stack of old equipment. Seeing that some of the crates were marked in Cyrillic script as well as English, Mark used his Swiss army knife, the only weapon he ever carried, to lever out the nails. The crate was full of Russian MUV igniters for use in priming booby traps.

Further back in the cave Mark found crates of Kalashnikov rifles, Chinese grenades, 122mm BM 21 Katyusha rockets with twenty-kilo warheads and a Goryunova SG-43 machine-gun. The inner cavern was a treasure trove of Soviet arms and, unlike the elderly Western supplies near the entrance, they were clean and new.

Mark quickly moved to the devastated front of the cave, where the mortar still stood among the debris of fallen rock and torn flesh. The six bodies wore ragged US army surplus battle fatigues. One man was still alive, although his chest was a gaping hole filled with blood; his lips stretched wide in agony as he tried to speak. Realizing that the man might live long enough to give them useful information, the Sydonite officer reached for his water bottle and dribbled some liquid into the cracked mouth. As the dying man mumbled a few words, Mark realized that they were not Arabic. The man was dark haired and olive skinned but, as Mark looked at the dirt-caked face, he realized that those features were unmistakably Latin.

'Cubanos?' Mark asked.

The man hissed his last words. '*Si. Viva . . . re . . . revolución.*'

•

Four of the dead men were Cubans. One of the corpses wore a neck medallion with Castro's head on it. The other two enemy corpses were unmistakably Arabs; one had a prayer written in Arabic script on a scrap of cloth tied around his right wrist. 'He asked the Prophet to guide his hand,' explained the officer, tossing away the rag.

'Mercenaries?' asked Mark.

'Sure,' the young officer answered. 'Intelligence warned us that the Fundamentalist guerrillas had Soviet equipment. It's not surprising that they also brought the men to use them.'

He ordered a soldier to carry the damaged explosives down the hillside; they then threw a grenade into the lethal pile and destroyed it.

The four survivors waited until starlight before approaching the nearest village. They entered the settlement with caution and were similarly greeted, then escorted to the headman's house. A young boy in white came forward and offered a brass bowl of dates. Wearily Mark pushed the food away.

'You will eat!' the young officer angrily told him. 'While you are with my men you are my responsibility, so you will eat and drink when I tell you.'

Mark apologized. He never remembered his physical needs while he was working; his goal was first to get his pictures, then to get back alive.

'And now we sleep,' the officer told him. Obediently, Mark stretched out with the three soldiers on the mud floor of the hut.

•

At dawn Major Khalid drove into the village and Mark shipped out on a truck that was crammed with wounded men. This was going to be a stinking, uncomfortable ride, Mark thought. Then, to his surprise, two black-veiled peasant women also climbed on to the truck. Between them they carried a seven-year-old girl, her abdomen greatly swollen above filthy swaddling bandages which bound her legs together like a mummy. The child was running a high fever, her eyes rolling upwards and her cheeks dry and flaking as she lay across the legs of the two peasant women.

When the truck reached the hospital Mark helped to carry the wounded into the building. Then he heaved his kit bag on to his back and set off for the gate. He was almost out of the hospital grounds when a male nurse ran up to him. 'Come,' said the nurse, 'come – take picture.' Mark followed him along the hospital corridor. Outside the casualty room stood a grey-haired, tired, skinny woman, with her hands thrust into the pockets of her white coat. 'You are a journalist?' she asked Mark.

'Sure.'

'To whom do you sell your photographs?'

'*Time*, *Newsweek*, all the European magazines; my agency sells worldwide.'

'Then I want you to photograph that girl. It must be done without her mother's knowledge or she will prevent it.'

Mark followed the white-coated woman to a small beige room where the girl lay on a stretcher, her stomach bloated as if she were pregnant. A female nurse was gently unwinding the bandages that held the child's legs together. Mark had asked no questions because the urgency in the doctor's voice had told him that whatever he was going to see might be important. In silence he prepared his cameras, while the nurse rigged a drip into the girl's thin arm; as she increased the volume of the liquid flowing into her vein, the girl slipped into unconsciousness. The smell of septicaemia pervaded the small room.

As the bandages were removed Mark saw a mass of pus and blood oozing between the little legs; her delicate young genitals were caked in a brown paste of what looked like chewed grass. As one nurse gently sponged water over the stinking mass, another held the small dusty feet together, then eased the girl's thighs apart, allowing the coltish knees slowly to fall outwards.

The lips of the girl's vulva were speared by a row of long acacia thorns lashed across with black twine. As the caked paste and scabs of blood were washed away from the cat's cradle of thorns and string, Mark saw cloudy green pus trickling from a tiny opening at the bottom of the closed slit. Quickly, he photographed as the nurse snipped the threads, picked each piece off with tweezers, then carefully, so as not to break them, pulled the thorns out, one by one. The last thing Mark saw was the child's mutilated genitals gaping bloody and rotten as the last thorn came out. Then he fainted.

Mark opened his eyes in an emergency room, reached

•

for a kidney bowl and vomited the remains of the previous night's milk and dates into it. The woman doctor heard his retching and came over to him. Mark said, 'What had they done to that girl? That's the most horrible thing I've ever seen.'

'They made her into good marriage material.' The doctor was unable to keep the fury out of her voice. 'A virgin bride and a docile wife. They do that in most of Africa and also some of the most primitive communities in the Arab states. They circumcised her, they deliberately mutilated her genitals. First, they cut out her clitoris and all of her labia minora; a wife that cannot fully enjoy sex is less likely to stray.'

'But who did it?'

'Probably the village midwife used the razor, while the girl's mother and her sisters held her down. Of course they have no anaesthetics. Then, earth or ashes would have been rubbed on the wound to stop the bleeding. Then they sewed her up, as you saw, with thorns and twine. They leave a minuscule opening for urine and menstrual blood. Then they bind her legs together to immobilize them.'

'Why is her stomach so swollen?'

'It is swollen with blackish, foul-smelling blood.'

'But what happens after she's married?'

'What do you think? Her husband cuts her open with a dagger, then runs around the village, waving the blood-stained blade so they can all see that the bride has just been deflowered. It goes without saying that mutilated

women feel severe pain during intercourse, and sometimes the husband doesn't cut enough, so when the girl
has her first child, she splits open like a melon.'

'Are they all . . . operated on at such a young age?'

'The earlier a child is mutilated, the greater is the
damage, since infantile and adolescent masturbation
teaches the orgasm.'

Mark heaved a further mouthful of bile into the bowl.
'What do you want me to do with the pictures?'

'Photographs may alert the Western World to what is
happening here.' The doctor pulled off her heavy-framed
spectacles and rubbed her tired eyes. 'I was one of the
doctors who gave evidence to the United Nations Com-
mission that investigated female circumcision in the Gulf
States, but their report was ignored. However, as you
know, a picture is worth a thousand words. I see cases like
that girl every month; some are even worse.' She sighed.
'But the government of Sydon, which pretends that this
practice no longer exists, would be unable to ignore a photograph in an American magazine. Western pressure would
force the Sydonite government to take action.'

'Do you mean King Abdullah?' asked Mark.

'No, not the King. The Department of Health sup-
presses all information. I think they keep the facts from
the King because many of his Western reforms are unpopular.'

Mark felt a quick sympathy for this doctor. Pity for
the wretched peoples of the earth was the driving force in
his life; however many corpses he photographed, however

•

•

many of his friends disappeared in combat zones, Mark's compassion was as profound as it had been ten years earlier when, an idealistic teenager, he had run away to his first war. He said, 'Before I leave Sydon, I am to photograph King Abdullah. I will try to show him the pictures.' Behind the doctor's spectacles Mark saw gratitude and hope.

From his army helicopter Mark saw Semira on the skyline. The political capital of Sydon rose in tiers of white fortified walls from the green plain that lay below it, on the bank of the country's only river. As the helicopter flew over the white-domed rooftops Mark could see the royal standard flying from the castellated towers of the palace that crowned the ancient town. Even though he was stuck in the desert, Major Khalid had been able to pull the necessary strings to arrange Mark's audience with King Abdullah because the major wanted full credit for the discovery of the enemy arms dump, the existence of which had been proved by Mark's photographs.

Mark was conducted by two ADCs into the King's presence. The King rose from behind his elaborate antique French desk.

'*Salaam Alaikum.*'

'*Alaikum a Salaam.*' King Abdullah preferred the simple traditional greeting of peace to the elaborate extended courtesies which were his birthright, as the fourteenth hereditary ruler of his country. 'Intelligence tells me you have been in the eastern hills with Major Khalid,

•

and that you are one of the survivors of the major's assault
on the guerrillas in Wadi al Hasa. Let's look at your
pictures.'

Mark knew better than to point out that Major Khalid
had nothing to do with the success of the operation,
as he opened his folder of photographs and spread the
still-damp prints on a mahogany table at the side of
the room. Mark handed him a magnifying glass and,
carefully, the King bent over the shots. 'These are really
magnificent pictures of desert warfare.' He peered closer
at the prints. 'You are obviously a brave man, Mr Scott.'
He looked again at the shots of the Soviet arms cache.
'As every discontented man calls himself a Communist,
we could not be sure of Soviet infiltration; we suspected
it, but we had no proof. You have done my country a
great service. Thank you.'

Mark saw his moment. 'Your Majesty, I have some
other pictures I would like you to see.'

'By all means.' Swiftly Mark gathered up the pictures
that proved Russian intervention in Sydon and replaced
them with pictures of the circumcised child being tended
by the nurses.

Abdullah looked in silence at the helpless, feverish face
and mutilated young body, then softly he demanded,
'Who committed this atrocity? What kind of soldiers are
guilty of this perversion?' Mark could see from the faces
of the two ADCs that they knew what they were seeing,
but that Abdullah's mistake was genuine.

'Your Majesty, this is not an atrocity committed by

•

the guerrillas,' Mark explained, 'this is the result of an infibulation operation on a young girl. I was asked to take these pictures by a doctor at the Dinada hospital.'

Abdullah's calm was chilling as he walked slowly back to his polished leather wing chair and asked Mark to sit down and tell him about this barbaric practice. He scribbled the doctor's name on his note pad and ordered one of the ADCs to summon the Minister of Health immediately. The King then fixed the other young ADC with his black glare. 'Did you know of this custom?'

'Yes, Your Majesty.' The ADC stood stiffly at attention. 'But it is only practised by the most primitive peasant women . . .'

'Ninety-five per cent of our people are primitive peasants.' King Abdullah's voice was still quiet but his eyes were angry. 'Why was I never told of this? Is there any reason for it?'

'Nothing beyond superstition, Your Majesty,' the ADC answered, 'but the Muslim Fundamentalists approve it. There is no reference in the Holy Koran to such a practice, but some of the great learned men of the past regarded the tradition as commendable.'

'May Allah preserve us from the evil that is done in his name.' Abdullah turned back to Mark. 'What will you do with these pictures?'

'Offer them to *Time*,' said Mark at once. 'They'll certainly take the shots of the Russian armaments.'

'But what about these?' Abdullah asked, indicating the pictures of the suffering child.

•

'I'll also offer them to *Time*, but they may not take them; they're too shocking.'

Abdullah nodded, sharing Mark's opinion. 'Do you appreciate my difficulty? I can give the order for this practice to cease immediately, and the women will obey me. Thirty years ago no house in Sydon could be repaired, no man could even leave his village, without permission of the King, and the simple people will still obey royal commands without question. The simple people are not the problem. The problem is that if I make a dictatorial gesture, the fanatics will use it to foment revolt. If I am to succeed in stopping this disgusting custom, it must seem as if I am bowing to the will of the people, not trying to impose my will upon them.'

'So you need the Western press to shift the climate of popular opinion?'

'As well as Western politicians, scientists and diplomats . . . Have you ever exhibited your photographs in a gallery, Mr Scott?'

'Yes, I'm with Anstruthers, in New York.'

'Then please arrange a gallery exhibition of these photographs. We will pay for it, of course. Our ambassador will see you when you get back to America.'

Quietly, a side door opened six inches. King Abdullah's head jerked round. Two nervous brown eyes looked round the door, then a twelve-year-old boy entered. He was wearing an elaborate miniature white military uniform. King Abdullah thought his heir should enter the room like a prince, not peer round the door like a servant.

•

•

'I'm sorry to bother you, Uncle. I thought you'd finished.' Prince Hassan had been waiting outside the door for two hours, torn between love and dread of his uncle, his guardian, and the King whose throne he would inherit.

THREE

November 1978

'Do you mind answering the door, Zimmer? That'll be the hotel maid with my dress.' Lili was, as usual, in the tub.

Zimmer stuck his head round the bathroom door. He had directed Lili in most of her best movies, including the scandalous *Q*, which had made her an international star. 'When you're ready, darling, a small jungle has just been delivered.'

'Check there isn't a small journalist swinging from the trees.' Since the news of her break-up with Simon Pont had flashed around the world, Lili had once again been besieged by photographers. Zimmer thought, thank heaven for Lili's sake that nobody had discovered the real reason for the break-up; but then, they never did.

Lili wandered out into the luxurious sitting room wearing a white bathrobe with her wet hair wrapped in a peach towel. With care, she approached the luxuriant orchid plant. From an arching spray of unnaturally perfect, succulent, pale-yellow flowers dangled a small emerald velvet pouch tied with silk cord. Lili opened the little bag and tipped out a small scarlet jeweller's box. Inside, a pair of dazzling blue-white diamond earrings sparkled in the weak November sunshine.

On the apricot couch by the fireside Zimmer clicked his tongue approvingly. 'That's the third packet this week – now you've got the complete set: Madame Pompadour's thirtieth birthday present, auctioned in Monte Carlo last month. No one can say Spyros doesn't try.'

'Shut up, darling.' Lili threw a kiss to the small, slender man on the couch and put the little scarlet box on the coffee table. 'You know Spyros Stiarkoz is only after me because I was his brother's girlfriend; I'm just another part of the old Stiarkoz empire to be annexed.' Lili tugged the white sash even more tightly round her slim waist. 'And, Zimmer, I'm not letting you bully me into a high-profile, low-satisfaction relationship just to make your next movie a little bit more bankable.'

'Not many women would turn down someone as rich and powerful as Spyros Stiarkoz.'

'I don't care about his riches and his power. After Simon I want a bit of peace and quiet. I want to be left alone. Don't you understand?' Lili sat on the other end of the apricot sofa and started to towel her hair. 'Stiarkoz is *just another man* to me, another man chasing me because of something in his own imagination. Being pestered by Stiarkoz is just the same as being chased by photographers, or any of those sickies who write filthy letters to me.

•

To them, I'm hardly human; I'm some sort of fabulous sex goddess. All that's important to them is how *they* feel! They never think of *my* feelings, of what *I* want.'

'Spyros knew as soon as Simon left for Paris. He's just trying his luck as fast as possible, before anyone else gets on the field.'

'Exactly, Zimmer.' Lili leaned forward and ruffled his greying blond curly hair. 'I am the hare, I am the quarry. This is the nightmare of my life, the obverse of the cost of success.'

'But basically it's flattering, Lili.' Zimmer waved his small, neat hands in the air, begging her to be reasonable. 'You're love-hungry, Lili, that's your problem and always has been. But you can't stand men being "in love" with you because you're more intelligent than the *average* sex goddess; you don't want to mesmerize them, you want communication, not lust. You want loving warmth instead of the heat of passion.'

'Exactly.' Lili stopped towelling and flung her still-wet hair backwards. 'I have had it up to *here* with sex.' She touched her nose. 'My allure, sex appeal, whatever the hell it is, brings me nothing but trouble, Zimmer.'

'At least you don't have to worry about that with me, darling.'

'No, but I come up against your naked-eyed, beer-swilling MCPs every time I set foot outside the door. *You* can't imagine how it depresses me. *You* think it's a joke. But I sometimes wonder if anyone will ever love me just for myself, as Angelina did, instead of being mesmerized

•

•

by the superstar, or loving because they really want
something from you. There are so many star-fuckers,
Zimmer, who just want to bed me and run out and tell
all their friends, so many people who want me to endorse
some body stocking or bicycle, so many people who want
me to invest my money in their sure-thing project.' She
turned to Zimmer and gently touched his hand, saying,
'That's why it's so important for me to establish a loving
relationship with my mother.'

As he looked into the glowing dark eyes, although he
wasn't the worrying sort, Zimmer thought, she can't
really blame men for the effect she has on them.

'And that's why we can't persuade you to do this film?
That's why you're wasting your career time hanging
around New York, turning down all the parts that Swifty
and I suggest?'

'That's why.'

'I don't want to press you, Lili, but please think again.
Mistinguett is such a wonderful part; she was the Marilyn
Monroe of the twenties, all Paris was in love with her,
she was the girl who put the Ooh-la-la into the *Folies
Bergère*, and her legs were the toast of Europe.'

And you, Lili, have the most wonderful legs, Zimmer
thought but knew better than to mention it. '*The Best
Legs in the Business* is going to be *the* biggest musical of
the year. Glitter! Glamour! Fishnets! Showgirls! Sequins!
Feathers! And we're after Richard Gere to play the young
Maurice Chevalier.'

'Sounds over budget before you start shooting.'

•

Briskly, Lili tossed the diamond earrings back into the scarlet box and threw it to Zimmer, who caught it with one hand. 'In the hotel safe?'

'If we've now got the complete set I'll return them to Spyros tonight.'

'God, how I hate women who are too pure to accept jewellery. Why are you going out with him tonight if you want nothing to do with him?'

'I'm going to say no politely.'

Lili and Stiarkoz sat stiffly in their private box, hardly speaking to each other as, on the distant stage, Prince Albrecht danced with the vengeful spirits of maidens deserted at the altar.

'Why do you have to tell me here?' Stiarkoz hissed.

'Because,' Lili said steadily, 'I don't want to tell you in public but in private.' In fact, she wanted to be in a protective atmosphere. She didn't want to be taken out to sea, abducted by white Rolls to Greenwich, Connecticut, or flown to Spyros's private island in the Grenadines while he 'reasoned' with her for five days nonstop. 'Spyros, I'm flattered by your attention, but the answer is no. I'm sorry.' Lili's voice sounded suitably contrite. On stage the white net corps de ballet moved relentlessly towards Prince Albrecht, their pink slippers dancing lightly over the hallowed areas of the misty graveyard. 'You've been very generous to me, Spyros, but I cannot accept this beautiful jewellery from you.'

'Don't thank me, Lili. I want to give you everything
•

you want.' He touched her soft hand with his wrinkled one, and Lili could not imagine anyone enjoying the touch of that claw.

Below them, fickle two-timer Prince Albrecht collapsed before the onslaught of ghostly brides. In the box an inch of cigar ash fell on the crimson carpet. 'I am a careful man, as you know, Lili, and I consider all my decisions. Is there nothing I can give you to persuade you?'

Prince Albrecht staggered on, but as far as Lili was concerned, the scene was over, and she hoped to escape. Lili whispered fiercely, 'How many times do I have to tell you, Spyros? All I want you to do is to leave me alone. So long as I'm dependent on a man, I'm frightened that I won't be able to cope on my own. That's why I want to start out again – by myself.'

'What rubbish! All women like to play hard to get. If you don't want to see me, then already there must be another man.'

Lili shook her head in frustration, and her pearl earrings shone as they caught the light. 'You men can't believe that when a woman says no, she means no.' She leaned forward. 'There isn't anyone else. The only other person in my life is *me*. Can't you understand that at the moment I don't know who I am or what I want, or what I can do? I have found my mother, I have the beginning of my new identity, and I want to be left in peace to discover the rest – that's all. That's why I want to be left alone.'

'Left alone? For twenty-four hours, perhaps.' Angrily,

•

he ground out his cigar in the bank of white chrysanthemums that fronted the private box.

In the Stiarkoz white Rolls-Royce Lili thought, Spyros is a greedy old reptile. How surprising that two brothers could be so similar and yet so different. Spyros had Jo's twinkling black olive eyes and the rough, tough business acumen, but he lacked his dead brother's vitality and charm. Then, suddenly, in the hushed, padded interior of the car, Lili realized that Spyros was about to pounce, and that she was in a luxurious, pale pigskin prison. Lili panicked as she remembered being told that when a Greek shipowner meets a woman and likes her, he wants sex with her straight away.

Spyros was tough, coarse and muscular. He went straight for Lili's breasts, ripping the embroidered white chiffon gown. Seed pearls bounced over the carpet as his stubby hands reached for her. Lili cast a frantic look at the back view of the chauffeur. No hope there. She managed to shove Spyros away from her.

Spyros muttered, 'I don't need to rape you, you'll find you will belong to me. I will look after you better than Jo did. When he died my brother left you penniless, didn't he? But I will give you everything you want, Lili. Your place is on my yacht, *Persephone*, without a care in the world, except to go shopping.' Again he fumbled at her breasts and, this time, Lili let him. She realized that if she continued to resist, he might rape her. No, her only thought was how to get out of the Rolls.

·

'Spyros, you can either force me, or you can give me time. It's not . . . the right day of the month.'

His unblinking, tortoise-like stare searched her eyes. Lili held up her flower-like face to his lips and suffered his embrace until they arrived at the Pierre.

She was sweating with relief as she hurried down the long, cream corridor, pulling her chinchilla wrap around her wrecked chiffon dress. At the elevator she paused, then turned on her heel and approached the reception desk. She handed the night manager the scarlet jewel boxes. 'Would you please have security deliver these to Lady Swann at the Algonquin.'

Nothing would irritate Spyros more than giving his diamond bribes to charity.

Angrily Lili stood naked in the mirrored bathroom and looked at her breasts, where bruises were already starting to form. She remembered how her body had ripened early, at twelve; how embarrassed she had felt as her breasts had swelled. Young girls always worried about their growing breasts; they were either too big or too small or too low; but whatever they were like, they attracted attention. Lili remembered how she had hated the new interest of the unknown men who lounged on the street corners of the shabby Paris suburb where she had grown up; even her adoptive father, Monsieur Sardeau, from behind his prim, civil servant's pince-nez, had furtively swivelled his eyes over her body as Lili worked her way through the household chores each day after school.

•

From the age of six Lili's existence had been a vortex of catastrophe, a downward spiral of misery over which she had had no control. Lili had been one of life's victims – until she had learned how to use the power of her body, the power of those two upthrusting breasts.

Lili had once asked Jo Stiarkoz why men had this automatic, knee-jerk response. Why – even when they were talking to her – men would gaze helplessly at Lili's breasts, and not at her face; what was so compelling about those two pounds of flesh?

Jo had laughed and said, 'I've never thought about it.' Then he added thoughtfully, 'What's so good about breasts is that they *wobble*; when they bounce and they jiggle, a man just wants to grab them. I can't say why; it's an instinctive reaction, it's gut lust.'

'But *why*? When a woman sees a group of workmen in the distance, she knows that when she draws close, there'll be this glazed-eyed, following-the-tennis-ball-at-Wimbledon reaction as she passes them. *Why?*'

Jo had said, 'I really can't tell you. A man has no control over these feelings. But if a woman isn't wearing a bra, so that you can see her nipples and watch them bounce, or if she's wearing tight clothes that make her breasts look as if they are bursting to escape, then a man feels that there's a special conspiracy between himself and that woman because he's wanting to touch them and knows that he can't, and he knows that this unknown female knows just how the man feels.'

'What an impertinent assumption. So they wobble;

•

so does Jello and men don't go glassy-eyed about that.'

'To a man, a woman's breasts are something hidden, mysterious, forbidden. And that soft lilting movement is both a hint and a promise of that woman's sexuality: those breasts convey a secret, sensual message from the female to the male.'

'Rubbish,' said Lili. 'That's the cause of all the trouble. No message is sent. When a woman's not making love, then her breasts just get in the way if she's doing anything athletic, or trying to look elegant, because clothes hang better on a flat body. *That's* what a woman thinks about her breasts; they're just *there*, like her knees. I'm not promising every man *anything*, simply by having breasts.'

'You may not be, but that's how it appears to the man.'

'That's just a man's excuse for bad behaviour,' Lili had sniffed. '*She was asking for it*, is what men say, conveniently shifting the responsibility for *their* attraction on to the woman. A woman likes to be admired by, and attracted to, men – but only the men of her choice.'

It was a typical New York small gallery opening. Clutching glasses of white wine, intellectual men wore jeans, and intellectual women wore Martha Graham robes or black dresses: standing with their backs to the dramatic photographs of Sydon battlefields, they bitched about the gallery owner, the other critics, and Beverly Sills. Mark Scott said even less than usual as Anstruther led him from the *Village Voice* critic to the *New York Times* critic, then turned to a small blonde woman who was actually inspecting the pictures through huge, tortoiseshell spectacles.

'These pictures of the little girl are shocking,' Judy said. 'I'd like to discuss what we could do about it in *Verve!* magazine. And I like your other work. We can't use war photography, but I'd like to see your portfolio. I'd like our art editor to see your work.'

Suddenly another man was at her elbow, a tall, muscular, swarthy man with coarse features and an expression that veered from anxious to menacing. 'Everything all right, Judy?'

'Yes, Tony, everything's fine. Would you mind getting my coat, please?'

Judy turned back to Mark. 'Tony is just being protective, he's a little overzealous sometimes. He thinks I work too hard and I do too much and that people take advantage of me. I'm afraid he's especially protective when he sees me talking to a handsome young man.'

'Then let's talk where Tony can't see us. How about dinner?'

Tony's daily aerobics class at *Verve!* had been an instant success, and Judy fell into the habit of inviting her friends in to work out, instead of taking them out to lunch.

As Judy told Pagan about her new friend, the war photographer, Lili pulled on several pairs of dirty leg warmers, all full of holes. 'Zimmer calls these my refugee rags,' she laughed as she arranged the knitted layers over

•

•

her black sweat trousers, then flopped over to tie her shoes with the well-trained suppleness of a Degas figure.

Pagan could admire with detachment the beauty of the slim young woman; Pagan had always been blithely unconcerned about her appearance until she met Christopher.

After forty minutes in the exercise class Pagan's face was flushed with effort and she was gasping for air. On either side of her, Judy and Lili seemed to be barely sweating. 'Thank God I'm going home at the end of the month – much more of this would kill me,' Pagan panted.

Tony's glistening muscles were set off by white satin shorts and a white T-shirt with rolled sleeves. His muscles bulged, knotted, quivered and twitched as he demonstrated the next exercise in front of a panel of mirrors that now lined one wall of the *Verve!* boardroom.

'This exercise increases flexibility.' He demonstrated. 'Feet apart, pointing forward. Now bend your knees, shoulders down and relaxed – don't stick your ribcage out, Pagan. Now move your hips forward right, back, left, swing your hips in a circle. Don't move any other part of your body.' Blank-faced with concentration, he rotated his pelvis.

Somebody snickered. 'Go to it, Tony.'

Tony stopped moving. 'This isn't funny. It's a basic jazz isolation exercise, also found in many other schools of dance.' He scowled. 'Even classic Eastern belly dancers perform this movement . . .'

Without thinking, Pagan interrupted him. 'No, they

•

don't, Tony. Belly dancers don't bump and grind, that's far too crude a movement. They sort of . . . shimmy all over.'

Tony didn't like being contradicted. 'No girl gets to be the king's favourite unless she can shake her ass, and if she won't practise her exercises, she's whipped by the chief mistress of the harem.'

Stubbornly Pagan said, 'I don't know where you studied your Eastern philosophy, but you've got it wrong. There's no such person as a chief mistress; a proper harem is run by the king's mother and the chief eunuch and no wives would ever be beaten because royal blood must never be spilled. They used to strangle naughty wives with silken bowstrings.'

Judy didn't want Pagan to tease the not-overbright exercise instructor. 'OK, everybody, that's enough,' she ordered. 'Let's switch to inner thigh exercises and stop this nonsense.'

The girls groaned and started spreading out on the floor. As they stretched out on foam mats Judy muttered to Pagan, 'If they're not gay, they're health food nuts, or Harvard Business School robots, or Eastern philosophy freaks. I sometimes think that Mark Scott is the only normal, good-looking guy in New York. And that's not saying much!'

Later, in the changing room, Judy reprimanded Pagan. 'Listen, Tony hasn't had the benefit of your background and education, so it's unkind to tease him. He may be

•

only an exercise instructor, but he's a damn good one and I don't want to lose him.'

'He *used* to be only an exercise instructor.' Pagan wriggled out of the black leotard which made her legs look four inches longer and her hips two inches smaller. 'Do you realize, Judy, that Tony's turning into your shadow?'

'Maybe he's a little over-devoted, but it's because he's been a garbage collector, a guard in a detention centre, a subway cleaner. He's merely grateful that he's now working in an attractive, clean office among a lot of attractive, clean women who all appreciate him.' Judy carefully smoothed on her coffee-coloured silk lace teddy. 'And Tony's very useful, very strong, very willing to do odd jobs for me that don't exactly fit into anyone else's job specifications. And he's touchingly devoted to me, simply because I gave him this chance. In fact, he's almost become . . .'

'. . . Your damned personal bodyguard,' snorted Pagan.

'Is that such a bad thing, considering the state of Manhattan today?' Judy checked herself in the mirror. 'As a matter of fact, if he's becoming anything, he's becoming my driver. I never realized how useful a driver could be until Tony came along.'

'They're useful, but drivers can also be a royal pain in the ass,' said Pagan, wriggling into her sheer black tights. 'They're never there when you really want them, which is late evenings and the weekends; you always have to see they're fed, and they're often sulky. The only way to have really efficient transport is to have three drivers, each working an eight-hour shift. I must say, that would be heaven.'

Pagan paused as she remembered what her grandfather had once told her, after reluctantly dismissing his driver for theft. Her grandfather had said that passengers often forget to close the sliding glass panel between the front seat and the back and, consequently, a driver gets to know everything about his employer's life, because the people riding in the back seat forget that the driver is a person, not an anonymous, automatic robot, not a piece of impersonal mechanism like a faucet. Pagan remembered her grandfather saying that a driver carried two dangerous weapons: his ears.

'Be careful,' Pagan said to Judy.

Judy looked up from her laden desk and jumped to her feet, beaming with surprise. 'Mark! I wasn't expecting you until this evening. I've got a meeting in ten minutes.'

He said nothing, looked at the four telephones on her desk, picked up the nearest one, and handed it to her. 'The meeting can go ahead without you, surely?'

Judy hesitated as he walked behind her, then she felt his right arm in the small of her back, pressing her against his frayed khaki sweater. She took the telephone from him. 'Tell Tom to start the meeting without me, Annette.'

'Miss Jordan, I have Los Angeles on the line.'

Judy put her hand over the mouthpiece and looked at Mark firmly. 'Just give me ten minutes, OK?'

•

He sat down in her white leather desk chair, and Judy switched her attention to the telephone. 'Swifty? Hi, how are you? About the 1979 agreement, there are a few points I want to clear up with you before we finalize.' She dragged a heavy file towards her.

Exactly ten minutes later Judy was still discussing sub-clauses when she felt strong tapering fingers creep slowly up the inside of her thighs, stroking the petal-soft skin as the fingers moved upwards towards the neat globes of her buttocks in their covering of coffee-covered lace. Judy pressed her thighs together in discouragement. The fingers were not discouraged; instead they parted the thighs, pushing them apart so firmly that it felt almost painful; the fingers continued to stroke the pale skin, working relentlessly upwards, then two hard flat palms moulded themselves over Judy's rounded buttocks and squeezed gently, savouring the firmness of her flesh in silken covering.

Damn you, Mark, and damn your lovely hands, Judy cursed him to herself as she stood over her desk and tried to absorb the complicated point which the agent was explaining over the telephone. Right now, she had serious things on her mind – and again she wondered, a little cynically, if Mark's relish for making love in her office wasn't a way of expressing his resentment against the career which, as she had explained to this unexpected, thrilling man in her life, always would be her first love.

As she leaned forward to make another note an insinuating finger traced the crease of her buttocks and carried

•

the movement down between her legs, transmitting a caress through the screen of silk and lace. His light butterfly touches felt like flames licking her legs. Most of Judy's consciousness was now confined to that small part of her body which he was stroking, but she struggled to keep her mind on the representation agreement. She felt Mark's fingertips carefully push aside the gauzy fabric and intrude between her moist lips. Then he knelt down behind her and his warm, wet mouth kissed the inside of her thighs, lightly at first, and then more and more hungrily as his fingers reached deeper into her. He pushed her thighs further apart and she swayed in obedience to his touch, helpless to regain control of her trembling knees.

'Mark,' she whispered angrily, her hand over the mouthpiece, 'darling, this is important! I have to do it.' Judy tried to concentrate on the long-distance conversation as Mark took another nip at her thigh and said, 'I know you have to do it, darling Judy. You just go right ahead and do what you have to do, and I'll do what I have to do.' He stood up behind her, reached his hands around her, unbuttoned her dress and slid each arm out of it. The dress fell to the floor. Then Mark pressed his body against Judy's back and she realized that he was now naked and insistent. He ran his hands quickly up under the delicate brown silk and held her small breasts, slowly slipping into her as she tried to scrawl a note on the desk pad. He pulled her body back against his, rolling her small, hard nipples in his fingertips and with her

•

thighs braced against her desk, she was trapped against him, the telephone still explaining into her left ear as Mark began to nibble the right ear. Damn it, she needed to hear Swifty's opinion.

Mark's pile of discarded khaki clothes on the floor reeked of stale sweat and cigarette smoke, but his body smelled hot and musky, and she could feel him moving gently as his hips pressed hard against her buttocks.

She could no longer concentrate and there was now an inquiring silence at the other end of the telephone line.

'Swifty, may I just look through the file again and call you back?' Judy asked weakly as Mark's left hand slid down from her breast over the small curve of her stomach to plunge between her legs once more.

'OK, you win.' She dropped the telephone, twisted round, reached up with both arms and claimed Mark's sun-blistered lips. Together they fell back into her chair. 'You bastard, you'll get me fired,' she giggled.

'You liar.' He was still hard and insistent in her body, his right hand still closed around her breast. 'The directors know you do your own research.' He kissed her hungrily, sucking her pink tongue into his mouth as he pushed a pile of papers off her desk, then the page proofs of the next issue cascaded to the floor, followed by Judy's in-tray.

Later, they shared the shower in her silver office bathroom, water sluicing down his knotted brown back and her pale body. In the outside office the secretaries grinned at each other. After ten years of that two-timing stuffed shirt, Griffin, the boss deserved a bit of fun.

FOUR

2 December 1978

Judy pinned up the December cover of *Verve!* on her office wall. The latest in a long series of glossy triumphs was the photograph of Lili and Judy. Judy wore a simple, high-necked, madonna-blue silk dress and Lili wore a crisp, white piqué dress with a low, square neckline, a tight bodice, huge puffed sleeves and a full skirt. Although they were holding hands, they looked different; there was an intimacy between them that was, simultaneously, natural but apart. How can a camera pick up something between us that we ourselves are hardly aware of, Judy wondered, stepping back to study the hypnotic double portrait of mother and daughter. Judy thought, I feel closer, more loving, towards Lili than I ever have to any other person. She is my only living blood relation and, at the same time, she's a stranger, almost an alien.

Lili entered Judy's office, wearing the white piqué dress, in which she looked like a Spanish infanta; it was a ludicrous outfit for a Manhattan winter morning, but one that would show up splendidly on the monochrome page prints: *newspaper print*. If you want to jump out of a newspaper page, always wear white or black or stripes for maximum impact.

'Nervous, Lili?' Judy asked.

Lili shrugged. 'What's another press conference? Whatever we say will be taken down, twisted the wrong way and used in evidence against us.'

'I still think Kate's decision was correct.' Judy remembered Kate stuffing her underwear into a well-travelled Vuitton suitcase and advising, 'The best thing you can do, to take the heat out of the situation, is to hold a formal press conference just before the *Verve!* December cover goes on the stands. Give the papers a fair crack at the story and they won't want to buy anything from the paparazzi, who will then leave you alone.'

Lili came across the room and shyly kissed her mother on the cheek; they had never kissed on the mouth.

Judy said, 'There's something I want you to have.' She opened her desk drawer and produced a small, silver photograph frame; in it was a black-and-white, much-creased, blurry snapshot of a laughing young man, wearing a wool hat with a tassel, and brandishing a bamboo ski pole.

'That's Nick,' said Judy, 'your father.' She held out her little paw-like hands to Lili. On each central finger was a thick band of gold, mounted with a tiny, coral rosebud. 'Nick gave me these rings when we said good-bye, he said they were to remind me that I could always depend on him. I've worn them ever since. Now I'd like you to have one, Lili, so that you will feel you can always depend on me.'

'I already depend on you,' Lili said, as Judy slipped the ring on Lili's slim finger. 'Maxine was so kind to me. And Pagan and Kate were so supportive about Simon. It helped me get through the humiliation and the pain.' She hesitated, then shyly said, 'I've never really had a woman friend before, never felt this unconditional acceptance and silent affection.'

Someone yelled in the corridor, then Pagan stormed in. 'For God's sake, Judy, the security in this building is ridiculous! Some lout's just searched my purse!'

'Sit down, you stupid Limey. Lili's just telling me how warm and silent our relationship is.'

Pagan flung herself on to the cream art deco sofa as Lili said, 'I feel that I need female support to help me to learn to live on my own. After Simon, I've decided that I must live alone and learn to stand on my own two feet, or I'll never know what I'm capable of, I'll never get to know myself properly.' She looked at the endless, anonymous rows of windows in the opposite building. 'I still don't know who I really am, and I'm tired of relying on love to give my life some meaning.'

Judy looked across the room. 'A quest for identity is a journey that we all have to make.'

'Spare me the psychobabble.' Pagan propped her red leather boots on the sofa.

'Going through tough times is what forges your identity

•

so fast that you don't have time to notice it.' Judy walked to the door.

Pagan said quietly, 'I don't think Lili and I would agree with you – tough times almost pushed us under. Friends are to keep you afloat.'

Jostling photographers filled the *Verve!* board-room.

Journalists rapid-fired questions: 'How does it feel to be a mother, Judy?' 'Have you seen Lili's films?' 'What do you think of the tyre-calendar pictures?'

Suddenly, 'Who was Lili's father?' the girl from the *New York Post* asked.

'Lili's father was a British student whom I met in Switzerland,' said Judy smoothly.

Pagan looked carefully at the ceiling. No doubt there was an excellent reason for Judy's little fib, but this was not the right time to ask about it.

'Tits 'n' ass, that's all there is to Lili,' a balding photographer brayed over his shoulder as he jostled past Pagan on his way to the exit. 'None of these junior sex symbols turns me on – give me the mother. Fifty if she's a day and she still looks terrific.'

'Ms Jordan is forty-five,' the *Verve!* publicity girl said quickly.

'Oh sure, another child bride.'

Judy felt the first painful wrench of readjustment to the new status of motherhood as the press turned away from her and clustered around Lili. 'Is it really all over

•

between you and Simon Pont?' 'Are you marrying Spyros
Stiarkoz?' 'Is this true about Senator Ruskington?' 'Is it
true that you're pregnant?' 'Is it true that you're dying of
cancer of the breast?'

Lili smiled, looked sombre, turned left, turned right,
crossed and uncrossed her legs because, after a basic
clinch picture with Judy, each photographer wanted an
exclusive shot of Lili.

'Can't think why I came,' Pagan laughed at Tom.
'Nobody's interested in me or the benefit for the Institute
that Lili's promised.'

As Judy listened to them she suddenly caught sight of
her reflection in the ornate mirror. Fifty if I'm a day, she
thought bleakly. So that's it, is it? You become a mother
and next thing you know your life is over – bang – just
like that. Tomorrow I'll give away this boring dress; no
one's going to write me off just because I've got a beautiful
daughter.

The December issue of *Verve!* was a sellout.

The day after publication Tom Schwartz, Judy and the
magazine's lawyer met in Griffin's grey, suede-panelled
conference room.

Griffin rubbed the side of his nose with his left index
finger. 'Is this true or not?' He tossed the writ back to
the lawyer.

'Doesn't matter,' said the lawyer. 'Truth is no defence
in a case like this. Senator Ruskington claims malicious
libel.'

•

Judy leaned back in her grey suede swivel chair. 'Personally, I don't think we should lose sleep over this. We've had writs like this before. It happens all the time.'

Griffin looked over at the lawyer. 'What's the substance of the allegation?'

'In Lili's life story, as carried in *Verve!*, Lili states that Senator Ruskington tried to rape her when they were both staying in Spain at the seashore mansion of the Duchess of Santigosta.'

Griffin looked puzzled. Tom leaned towards him. 'Lili is quoted as saying that he looked like an ugly old tortoise and behaved like a billy goat on LSD.'

Judy grinned. 'He *does* look like a tortoise and every Washington call girl knows he's an old goat. Our readers love it when these sanctimonious jerks get their comeuppance.'

Griffin said, 'Aren't we covered by the first amendment?'

The lawyer cleared his throat. 'Not in this case, because the senator claims malice on the part of Miss Jordan. In essence, he's saying that *Verve!* magazine is repeatedly attacking him because he opposed Equal Rights legislation in his state.'

'He did,' said Judy, 'and certainly we wrote about it, and we have repeatedly criticized Senator Ruskington, with good cause.'

Griffin asked, 'How much is he claiming?'

Tom said, 'Sixty million bucks, which means about

five, but that's enough to put the magazine out of business at this moment in time. Unfortunately, we're financially vulnerable right now.'

Griffin pulled out his alligator note pad and scribbled on it.

Judy burst out, 'I can't believe that a lecherous old senator can send us sliding into bankruptcy when *we're* telling the truth, just because *he* has a smart lawyer!'

'Judy, you know perfectly well that the law isn't about truth or justice.' Griffin was irritated by her naïveté. 'The law is about obeying a certain set of rules.'

Tom said, 'Maybe if we call his bluff, we won't hear about it any more.'

'Senator Ruskington has been my good friend in Washington,' Griffin said slowly. 'I assume that Lili will back her story?'

Judy looked at the serious faces around her. 'Of course she will!' But suddenly she wasn't sure.

Two days later Judy walked briskly up Fifty-seventh Street towards Griffin's office. It was odd that he wanted another office meeting when they would be having dinner together that evening. But Griffin's recent behaviour had been strange. Or had Griffin always been odd, but she'd viewed him through rose-coloured glasses, she wondered as she waited for the lights to change at Madison. Or was his behaviour simply a masculine reaction to rejection? After ten years of explaining to her – at least once a month – why he wouldn't marry her, Griffin had been amazed,

•

•

angry, then sulky, when Judy had carefully explained why she didn't want to marry him.

From that moment Griffin had acted strangely, particularly about Lili, whose name he never mentioned, but to whom he always referred, with sarcasm, as 'your daughter', as in 'I see that your daughter's faggot boyfriend has left town.'

If it hadn't been for the new, and so far secret, excitement in her life, Judy realized that Griffin would have had her running in circles as usual, wondering what she'd done wrong. Instead of which, every time Mark suggested a date she minded less if Griffin broke one at the last minute; every time Mark laughed, Judy minded less when Griffin evaded giving an opinion; Judy sometimes wondered whether Griffin would commit himself to anything, even agreeing on the date, let alone promising to love and honour her for life. The only thing both men had in common was their concentration on their work, but, whereas Griffin never forgot his, Mark seemed willing, if not eager, when they were together, to concentrate on Judy. And what Judy most enjoyed was her increasing feeling of freedom, now that she wasn't bound to Griffin's routine of adulterous deception. So she didn't feel a bit guilty about these wonderful weeks with Mark. Well, not very guilty. Well, not guilty enough to stop seeing Mark, and feeling Mark, and feeling Mark feel her. Judy hugged her Burberry around her; the weather was almost cold enough for her new lynx,

•

she thought, as she sniffed the tang of smoke from the hot-chestnut vendor's stand on the corner of Fifth.

To Judy's surprise, there were two lawyers in Griffin's office.

After a long preamble about the corporate image of his publishing empire, and the editorial policy of *Verve!*, Griffin avoided Judy's eye as one of the lawyers leaned towards her. 'Therefore, Judy, you will appreciate our reluctance for these two concerns to be further associated, and in view of Orbit Publishing's long-standing relationship with Senator Ruskington . . .'

'What long-standing relationship?' exploded Judy.

'Naturally, we do not care to publicize our Washington connections, but you should have known that the senator is aware of our position on the quotas related to imported wood pulp.'

Judy realized that, indeed, she should have made the connection, and she also realized that it would not have damaged the story impact, had she dropped those fatal paragraphs about Senator Ruskington.

'In view of Orbit's wish to distance itself from this issue, it has been decided to sell Orbit's fifty per cent shareholding to Creative Magazines.'

'At what price?' There was a steely glint behind Judy's tortoiseshell spectacles as she realized that this was Griffin's uptown, grey suede, bum's rush.

'Two ten. Ten above market price.'

'We might offer you two twenty.' Judy and Tom each

•

held twenty-four per cent of the *Verve!* shares; Kate held the remaining two per cent.

'Judy, two thirty is a crazy price.' Tom was an experienced stock-market speculator. 'Don't make a fool of yourself for that rat fink's benefit.' Tom leaned back in his office chair. 'God, I wish Kate were here, she'd talk some sense into you. Sure, we made a wonderful profit last year, but it's not in a heap in a wheelbarrow. It's all tied up, and we're going to need all our cash to fight that scumbag, Ruskington.'

Judy had never seen Tom look so worried, and she also felt that he was holding something back; gradually she realized what it was. 'I know what you're thinking, Tom. You're thinking that if it hadn't been for my asterisk asterisk daughter, Lili, we wouldn't be in this mess.'

Tom said nothing. Judy added gloomily, 'I suppose I think that as well. But I also suppose there's no parent alive who hasn't thought that at some time or other.'

Tom said, 'Kids! You hope that when they grow up the problems will stop . . . but that's when the big ones start.'

Tom leaned over and patted Judy's shoulder. 'It's pointless to worry about what's happened or whose fault it is. We should be concentrating our energy on how to get out of this mess. But this time I don't think we can, Judy. I don't think even you can wriggle out of this one.'

Judy thought, it's one of those rare occasions when we both need moral support from each other, and neither of us is strong enough to give it. She tried to sound cheerful as she said, 'Miracles sometimes happen.'

'Such as?'

'Oh, I don't know, Tom. Give me time to think. How about you kidnapping Lili for ten million dollars, then handing the money over to me?'

Tom laughed. 'Sorry, I wouldn't know how to *start* to kidnap someone.'

'Weakling! If I can't rely on you, who *can* I rely on?'

As she lifted the telephone Tom asked, 'Who're you calling?'

'Curtis Halifax.'

'I could never understand why Curtis backed us in the first place. I know he's your old beau, but you can't expect the poor sap to be a perennial Santa Claus.'

Judy leaned back in her leather chair, grinned at Tom and started dialling.

'Get out of here!' Tony slammed his black-booted foot into the photographer's stomach to keep him out of the limousine. The man fell into the road, yelling obscenities at the back of the departing Rolls as it sped away from the airport. 'Those guys sure are persistent,' Tony said in amazement as the limousine cruised back to the *Verve!* office.

Lili ignored him, grabbed the radiophone and called the *Verve!* office. 'Judy, it's impossible,' she shouted.

•

Limo telephones always sounded as if you were calling from outer space. 'We just couldn't move – if Tony hadn't been there I'd have been torn to pieces. I had to lock myself in the cloakroom and climb out of the window to get away.'

'Did Pagan get off all right?'

'Yes. You were right, it was crazy of me to see her off. These photographers really frighten me. I think I'll have to go back to Europe.'

'Don't worry, Lili.' Judy's voice crackled soothingly. 'I've arranged for you to hide out until this fuss dies down. You can stay at Mark's apartment in the Village for a couple of days. I'll send someone to the Pierre to get your things. Tony will see you safely into the apartment and I'll come down later.'

Mark's white loft in Greenwich Village had been transformed by Judy's staff with a speed and care which Lili found touching as she noticed huge vases of white lilies, the freshly made bed with lace-edged linen sheets, ample supplies of essences and scents in the bare little bathroom beside a complete range of cosmetics, courtesy of the *Verve!* beauty editor.

Tony ostentatiously checked the bedroom windows, enjoying his role as temporary bodyguard to an international celebrity. Logs of juniper wood blazed in the fireplace, and a light but steady fall of December snow began to drift against the wall of glass that overlooked the roof garden; the faint sounds of the city were blotted out.

Lili felt that she was in a warm white nest, thousands of feet removed from any danger.

Snow swirled in spirals between the high buildings, as if a giant pillow had burst outside the glass wall. Lili felt safe. Fresh from a warm bath, wearing a white, lace-trimmed vest and shorts, she lay curled in front of the glowing fire, blinking into the heat like a comatose cat. For the first time in twenty-four hours her mind was blissfully relaxed, so she was nearly asleep, and she didn't hear the multiple soft clicks and rattles as the door locks slowly slid back.

Mark stopped abruptly in the doorway. His face was mottled with cold, and melted snow was trickling down his neck. He could see the living room reflected in the wall of bronze mirror which ran from the front to the back of his loft, linking the different rooms and levels. In front of his fire he saw a topaz-tinted picture of some mythical creature – half woman and half cat, basking in the warmth. Then he realized that this must be Judy's daughter, his temporary houseguest – the notorious Lili.

For a few moments he was stunned by the force of his own appetite as he watched her. As Lili heard him dump his camera cases on the floor she jumped up with fear, then smiled. 'I hope you're Mark.' Mark felt as if his stomach had just dropped from the fifth floor to the basement.

'Is there anything to drink?' Abruptly, he headed for

•

the kitchen, to get away from this exotic vision before he jumped on her. Judy's staff had filled the refrigerator with fruit, salad, cheese and several bottles of Chazalle champagne.

'Here.' Mark turned to Lili, who had hastily pulled on a sweater and jeans, and offered her a tumbler of champagne.

Lili smiled as she raised her glass. 'You've got ice on your eyelashes.'

Mark put a half-pound of Beluga and a loaf of rye bread on a tray, then carried it to the fireside.

'How did you meet my mother?' Lili wrenched off a caviar-laden corner of bread with her pointed little teeth. She liked the possessive ring of 'my mother'.

'It's hard for me to believe that I only met her a few weeks ago. I've never met anyone like her. I fell for her on the spot,' said Mark. 'We met when Judy came to an exhibition of my Sydon pictures. She looked like a fierce, inquisitive little terrier, dashing from one picture to the other with her eyes shining, while all the rest of the crowd was just drinking and yakking. I loved her enthusiasm. She's using some of my pictures for a feature on women as leaders.'

During the time it took to empty the caviar tin Mark talked increasingly about Judy and, if the conversation turned towards some other subject, Mark firmly steered it back to Lili's mother and the problems that might affect their relationship because of Mark's assignments in warring foreign countries.

•

'But maybe it'll be easier than if I was always around,' he said as he finished the caviar. 'It's lucky for me that Judy doesn't want the demands of a full-time relationship any more than I do; I'm pretty impossible when I'm not working; being inactive tends to make me edgy.'

'Why are you a war photographer?'

'Because I'm not a soldier.' He grinned at her in the firelight. 'I come from an army family; my father was an infantry colonel, and that's what they wanted me to be.'

'Then why aren't you in the army?' Lili poured herself another tumbler of champagne.

'If you'd grown up with my dad, you would have thought twice about the army as a profession. He was in Korea from the beginning, lost two toes on one of his feet from frostbite, but he was lucky – that was his only wound – until they were pulling out. Then a junior officer went crazy in the mess and shot seven people, including my dad. He came out of the coma with brain damage and, since then, he's been like a five-year-old child; I hardly remember him any other way.' Mark thought of the tall, stooped figure that floated like a ghost around the airy house in San Francisco, always shadowed by his mother's unspoken disappointment. 'The army ruined my father, and I disapprove of war. That's why I'm not in the army.'

'But surely what you're doing makes war glamorous?'

'No. There's nothing glamorous about killing people. I hope that my pictures show the horror of war.'

Silently they stared into the fire. 'I suppose this must

•

be what it feels like to have a brother,' said Lili. 'Let's drink to brotherly love.'

Lili realized that, for the first time in her life, she had just enjoyed a couple of hours alone with an attractive man without feeling threatened by the man's sexual interest. But, as the snow piled higher and higher on the roof outside, the normally silent Mark found himself talking about anything to fill the silence, which would otherwise have been flooded with his growing carnal desire for Lili.

FIVE

December 1978

Tom put his head round the door of Judy's office. 'First letter from Kate!' He waved the airmail flimsy. 'She says it's like the West Bank of the Jordan; it's a forced settlement operation. It's a way of invading without invading. Thousands of hill tribe people have been murdered, detained without trial or tortured. And Kate's got dysentery.'

Judy looked up and said, 'Just the holiday she needed,' then continued her telephone conversation. 'Maxine, of course I'll come. Invent an excuse for inviting me, let the situation cool for a few weeks and I'll fly over for a weekend in the New Year. Through thick and thin, remember?'

'You're crazy, Judy.' Tom looked disbelieving as she put the telephone down. 'You can't go to France now – we're up to our eyebrows in problems.'

Judy said, 'I'll only be gone over a weekend. Now, what do we have to tell the brilliant attorney who's going to wrestle Senator Ruskington to his knees?'

'Judy, I wish you wouldn't joke about this.' Tom was

exasperated. 'The fees are piling up; you'd think those guys wrote to each other on solid gold notepaper. Financially, we're on the limit of our contingency fund, and if this should ever come to court – which I pray to God it won't – and Ruskington wins, we'll be completely ruined.'

'When that day comes, promise you'll hold my hand as we take a dive together from the fiftieth floor.' Judy briskly opened the file.

'OK, you've got a date!' Tom put his hand on her shoulder. 'Look, I want you to know that if this turns out to be real trouble, we'll be in it together. I'll be with you right to the end.'

'Thanks, Tom. Now, what do the lawyers need?'

'We have to demonstrate that you, personally, have no malicious intentions towards the senator. We have to show that you are not prejudiced against him in any way. It's a tough one, Judy, because the old bird is a Bible-thumping baptist, the biggest chauvinist pig in the pen, and your daughter claims that he tried to rape her. So he's pretty much everything you hate in a human being.'

'If the senator is a bigot and a rapist, surely hating him is a reasonable attitude?' Judy argued. 'He'll never take this to court, Tom. A scandal like this would finish him in Washington.'

'What's he got to lose? The scandal's blown up already and he wants whitewash. We're the ones who'll be in trouble, Judy – a mess like this won't do our circulation figures any good.'

Judy stood up, determined to rid Tom of his doubts and boost his confidence. 'What's got into you, Tom?' she asked. 'This loser talk isn't like you at all – you know that all publicity is good publicity. We won't lose any readers by fighting this case – they'll all be rooting for us.'

Tom left Judy's pastel office feeling that nothing would make her realize how serious the situation was. More anxious than when he entered, he took away the audited circulation figures for the past quarter without showing them to Judy, because they registered a definite fall. Could Judy's judgement – for years as deadly, fast and accurate as a cruise missile – be faltering at last? he wondered. As Tom passed the boardroom he noticed a few assistant editors limbering up for the daily exercise session. Judy had never been interested in sports, unwilling to walk if she could ride, and now the spectacle of her gallantly sweating through Tony's workout, whenever her schedule allowed, was surprising. Maybe Judy was starting to feel her age at last.

An hour later Judy put her head around Lili's bathroom door. 'I thought I'd find you here. Do you mind if I come in?'

Lili was up to her nose in pink bubbles. When Lili craved comfort and security she always headed for a warm tub.

'The whole world has already seen me in the tub, I don't see why my mother shouldn't,' said Lili. 'How are things with you?'

•

'The senator is really putting on the pressure.' Judy wondered if she should tell Lili the full scale of the battle that threatened *Verve!* magazine after her fatal interview.

Lili looked over the rim of the bath at her mother. 'I've been waiting for a good moment to say this, but I don't suppose there'll ever be one.'

'Say what?'

'I'm sorry that his lawsuit is all my fault.'

'You told the truth, Lili. We took the risk. Your life story in *Verve!* boosted the circulation. We miscalculated the senator's reaction and that's all there is to it. We're still hoping that the senator will settle out of court.'

'Oh, him . . .' Lili sniffed. 'He won't be any problem to you, Judy. I told you I'll stand by what I've said and what you printed. He won't want to face me in court' – Lili reached for the shampoo – 'because he won't want his voters to discover that the man they sent to Washington is a dirty old goat.' She submerged her head in the carnation-scented water and came up dripping, big-eyed and sleek-headed as a seal.

Judy hesitated, then asked, 'Was he really as unpleasant as you made him sound?'

Slowly Lili said, 'It depends on what you mean by unpleasant.' She remembered how, a few months after Jo's death, she had been a guest of the Duchess of Santigosta at her palatial Spanish beach house on the Malaga coast. Lili had still felt her loss after Jo Stiarkoz's death, but Zimmer had suggested that she try to get more fun out of life and accept a few of the stream of invitations that any celebrity receives.

The first two days had been delightful. The twenty-two other guests were mainly European business acquaintances of the duke, who was no longer rich and supplemented his income by acting as an entrepreneur, a go-between for his business partners when they wanted to establish contact with, and impress, someone with whom they hoped, later, to set up a deal.

They swam, they water-skied, and everyone else in the party water-parachuted, including the Italian jeweller's wife who was a grandmother and trying it for the first time. It was easy, she saw; so, obediently, Lili had been strapped into her parachute harness, taken a run off the end of the jetty, then found herself jerked into mid-air, fifty feet above the little speedboat that was towing her. Lili looked down, her stomach turned over, and she thought for one moment that she was going to be sick. She knew that she suffered from vertigo, so she never stood near the edge of balconies or bridges, but she had never felt vertiginous in an airplane, so it hadn't occurred to her that she would do so now. The ten-minute ride was purgatorial, but eventually the speedboat stopped back near the jetty and Lili floated down towards the blue waters of the Mediterranean where her harness was quickly unstrapped by the boatman's assistant, who then started to gather up the parachute that was drifting in the sea water. Gratefully, Lili floated on the water with her

•

arms apart, feeling too ill to strike out for shore. It was at this moment that a nearby swimmer, a balding American senator with whom Lili had hardly spoken, swam up to her. 'Great sensation, isn't it?' he asked, then he noticed Lili's dazed expression. 'Are you all right, my dear?'

'Yes . . . no . . . I don't know . . . please . . .' A wave broke over Lili's head and she accidentally swallowed a lot of sea water. 'Please, could you h-h-h-help me back to the beach?'

'Put your arms around me, my dear.' Lili did so and felt her body drift against his, then the man was lying on top of her in the water as, dimly, Lili thought, surely this isn't the way that lifesavers do it? After what seemed an eternity the man panted, 'I think we'll make better progress if you let go, my dear, and I hold you from behind.'

A lifesaver swims backwards, kicking only with his feet, as both arms are needed – the left arm holds the drowning victim across the collarbone and the right hand cups the victim's chin above water. But this was not Senator Ruskington's lifesaving procedure. He had, indeed, swum backwards towards shore, kicking only with his feet, but he held Lili's body on top of his with both his hands firmly on her breasts.

Once ashore, Lili had lain in the shade and, within an hour, she had recovered, had thanked Senator Ruskington for helping her and had decided to go to bed early. And that, Lili thought, was the end of the incident.

Lili was awakened by a strange sensation. She opened

•

her eyes and from her four-poster bed she could see the silver moonlight striping the room. Still half asleep, Lili shivered, then realized that the covers had been drawn back from her bed. Sleepily, she felt a flood of warmth in her body that she hadn't experienced since Jo's death, then slowly she awakened, realizing one thing at a time. Her nightgown no longer covered the lower part of her body. Between her legs she felt a warm, heavy, rough sensation, like having your hand licked by a calf. Lili realized that a man was crouched by her bed, parting her lower lips with his hands and steadily licking her clitoris. As she realized what was happening, a hand slid up her body and felt underneath the nightgown for the nipple of her breast, upthrusting and hardening in automatic response to this dark stranger's stimulation.

Lili gasped in horror and tried to sit up, but the hand that was on her breast pushed her hard, back against the pillows, and suddenly the man was on top of her. He was naked, she realized with growing horror, as she felt his hardness against her. She screamed, then his mouth was on hers.

I can't believe this . . . it's a nightmare . . . no, it isn't . . . he must be a burglar . . . And then he'd taken his mouth away from hers and, in the moonlight, she had recognized his face as he arched his back and tried to thrust into her, painfully holding her by her breasts against the pillows.

'You liked me touching you in the water, didn't you?' the man panted. 'You didn't stop me, you led me on, you

•

•

little bitch.' It was that balding American senator who had helped her swim to shore that afternoon.

Lili screamed again and simultaneously reached down the bed and grasped for the balls behind his groping cock and twisted them as hard as she could. The man grunted, gasped, doubled up in pain and Lili felt thankful that she had remembered this old tart's trick from her past.

Lili managed to wriggle from beneath the gasping, fat body, then she shot across the floor to the door, flung it open and ran along the wide, silent corridors until she reached the servants' back stairs. She ran down three flights and threw open the door at the bottom. She found herself in the imposing entrance hall, silvered by moonlight. Lili raced for the guest bathroom and sat shivering on the cold seat for the rest of the night until she heard the bustle of servants starting to clean. Then Lili crept back to her bedroom.

It was hard to believe that horrible scene had really happened. The bed was in disarray but there was nothing to indicate . . . Lili ran forward as she saw a navy, red-dotted piece of silk protruding from beneath the bed. It was the tie of a man's dressing gown. Lili bolted the door and reached for the ivory bedside telephone and demanded to speak to the duchess . . . well, as soon as Her Grace was awake, in that case. It was an urgent matter.

Two hours later the plump duchess floated into Lili's bedroom wearing an embroidered, pale-grey crêpe de Chine peignoir that must have taken months to stitch.

•

Lili poured out her story, showed the dressing-gown tie, and looked into the chubby face for sympathy. The duchess took the dressing-gown cord and held it in her hands. Then she said, 'My dear, Senator Ruskington is a very influential man with whom my husband hopes to arrange . . . certain matters. This entire house party is being given to entertain him. I think perhaps you had a bad dream. And if you didn't, my dear, well, nothing has happened to you that hasn't happened to you before. A gentleman was *bouleversé* by your beauty; he had perhaps had a little too much to drink. I doubt if this morning he will remember what you say has happened. So any unpleasantness would be reduced to his word against yours. Or he might even say that you had invited him to your bedroom, in which case, what does a dressing-gown tie prove?' The duchess stood up and, in a polite but distant voice, she said to an angry Lili, who could hardly believe what she heard, 'I feel it might be best for all of us, my dear, if you left immediately.'

Judy said, 'Rape is never pleasant.' She held out a terrycloth robe for Lili as she stepped out of the bath, 'Especially if anyone suggests you were asking for it.'

Nearly five and a half miles, thought Debra Halifax, relentlessly pedalling on. Although she was in her late thirties, her silhouette was that of a girl of twelve. Each rib was visible through the candy-pink leotard as she

•

•

gazed with determination at the illuminated screen built into the bicycle's handlebar. The pre-programmed rides could be dialled on the control panel; they could increase the machine's resistance from an easy, five-minute trip to the toughest half-hour programme which, her husband complained, was like cycling over the Rocky Mountains.

Although the clock in her private gymnasium showed 8.30 a.m., Debra was halfway through the programme for the second time that day when her husband, Curtis, appeared at the door of the gym. He wore a handmade grey suit, a white silk shirt, and carried a well-polished black briefcase. There is something obscene about a woman who deliberately starves herself, Curtis thought as he saw bands of sweat spreading across the pink leotard below the areas where his wife's breasts used to be. Debra's whole appearance had become a macabre caricature of the delicate little sprite he had married; there was now a monkey-like appearance to her head, her face was deeply lined, and the outline of the skull was prominent at the temples. Curtis looked down at the bicycle dial and realized that she was pedalling the Rocky Mountain programme for the second time. 'Debra, please . . .'

'Don't say another word, I won't listen.'

'But you'll kill yourself.'

'I will do no such thing. I am promoting my health.'

'Surely it isn't necessary . . .'

'You know the way my metabolism is. I only have to look at a lettuce leaf to put on weight.'

Curtis gave up. 'I'll see you at the Peabody's tonight,

•

dear.' He said goodbye with a dry kiss on the top of her head. She did not stop pedalling.

In his car Curtis leaned back and wondered what he could do to add some meaning to his wife's life. He reached for the window control, then remembered with irritation that he must always keep the windows closed. Each day Curtis left Chestnut Hill for the bank at a different hour. Hawkins, his driver, brought the car round to the front of the house only when the butler called him on the house telephone, and both Curtis and Hawkins wore coats with a layer of ballisticproof wadding in the lining – the least conspicuous substitute for a bulletproof vest. His staff were even more exasperated than Curtis by the new security procedures. He had been obliged to call them together and explain that the insurance people now insisted on a full executive-protection programme against kidnap or assassination, and that it was his responsibility, as the bank's chairman, to follow their request.

When he arrived at the bank, Curtis, who was no longer allowed to take the mahogany-panelled private elevator to his suite, joined his employees in one of the regular cars. Alighting at the forty-eighth floor, he walked down the long corridor between two rows of early American primitive paintings to his office, where his large antique desk stood below portraits of his father and grandfather, so that anyone standing opposite Curtis looked at three generations of Halifaxes.

'Good morning, Miss Brady.' Curtis's secretary handed him the card on which she had listed his day's

•

•

appointments. 'The usual reservation at the Philadelphia Club at twelve, but make it for two people, please. And no calls for an hour.'

In these impressive surroundings Curtis had very little work to do. No matter what kind of idiot Curtis Halifax III turned out to be, the basis of the family's wealth would always remain stable. The senior managers were all clever men from old, Anglo-Saxon, East Coast families. Their loyalty was to everything the Halifax family stood for – the best, historic traditions of American life: self-reliance, thrift, hard work and Republicanism.

Curtis's grandfather had been determined that the Halifax family would, one day, provide a president for America, a wise, dignified, cautious man who would lead the country back to the old-fashioned virtues and rigorous standards of their caste. He had married both his sons into similarly minded families, and had been disappointed that his two healthy boys, between them, had managed to produce only one son – Curtis, the sole heir to his grandfather's ambitions. Grandfather Halifax had insisted that Curtis's bride should also be chosen from an ideal background and, when she was nine years old, he had selected Debra for his grandson to marry. She had been born into one of the wealthiest Philadelphia families; her pedigree, her bloodline, her studbook entry were impeccable – in fact, too much so. Curtis had grown to suspect that Debra's inherent instability stemmed from over-breeding, and ironically, this would frustrate the ambition of Grandfather Halifax.

•

Curtis sighed as he settled into his leather wing chair beneath the portraits; he knew he had disappointed them. He had failed to fulfil his family's political hopes and, because of Debra, he was becoming more of a liability than an asset to his political party. He settled his feet on the green leather-topped desk and picked up his appointment card for that day. The only name on it was Ms Judy Jordan.

Tony drove Judy to Philadelphia in her cream Mercedes 350SL convertible. He was a fast, neat driver and Judy always felt safe when he was at the wheel. During the entire two-hour journey Judy scribbled memos. She was only going to be in France over the weekend, but she wanted to leave nothing unfinished before she left. Tony never interrupted her train of thought. He now recognized Judy's moods, knew when she was feeling ebullient, knew when she wanted to work out an idea aloud, knew when she needed soothing, and he also recognized the rare occasions when she was thinking hard and didn't want to be interrupted.

When the Mercedes slid to a stop outside the Patriots Halifax Bank Tony jumped out of his seat and opened the door for Judy. Although her face looked strained, Judy was very appealing in a violet suede Calvin Klein coat and dark-violet suede boots.

But her pretty appearance made no difference in her reception. After arguing, in the most charming way, for over an hour, Curtis Halifax leaned towards her over his

•

huge, antique mahogany desk and clasped his narrow, nervous hands. Judy looked at the tall, well-built, fair-haired man and thought he'd probably never worn a store-bought suit in his entire life. 'I know we're . . . old friends . . . and because of our . . . special . . . relationship I've done as much as I could for you in the past, but this time I just can't swing it. The board won't wear it.'

'You might at least try once more.' With an effort, Judy kept calm reasonableness in her voice. 'If we show our projection figures for next year, your board will see that we only have a temporary problem.'

'Judy, don't be unreasonable. Last month I went to the limit for you so that you could buy Griffin out, and now you're asking for more.' Curtis looked uncomfortable as he fiddled with the new, automatic, gold Cartier calendar. He continued. 'No banker in his right mind would invest money in the outcome of a lawsuit. And, as I've already explained, my personal funds are committed, long term. This time the answer really has to be no, Judy.'

'No is not my favourite word, Curtis,' said Judy, a shimmer of a smile touching her lips as her dark-blue eyes looked into his pale-blue ones.

Curtis responded with a flash of exasperation. 'That's a low blow, Judy, and you know it. Stop trying to make me feel guilty.'

'I'm sorry, Curtis, but *Verve!* is my whole life and I'm desperately worried. Don't you know anyone in

Washington who could lean on Senator Ruskington?'

'I'm afraid not.' Curtis started to feel resentful. 'I haven't got that sort of clout.' The door suddenly opened and Curtis and Judy looked up in surprise to see a fine-boned blonde woman with a beautiful but gaunt face, wearing a dark mink coat with a bunch of violets pinned to it. She said, 'Surprise, Curtis darling!' Then she realized that he was not alone and added, 'Oh, I hope I'm not interrupting anything important.'

Curtis stood up automatically. 'No, Debra. Of course not. I don't believe you know Judy Jordan. My wife, Debra Halifax.'

'So glad to meet you.' Debra flashed a faint smile at Judy, then ignored her. 'Curtis darling, I'm on my way to lunch with Aunt Emily, but I just dropped by to tell you that I've changed my mind. I don't want the emeralds tonight, after all, red looks better with white crêpe. So tell Perkins to get the rubies out of the vault, will you?' She blew a little-girl kiss towards her husband. 'Must go.' She flashed another brilliant smile at Judy and left the room. 'Bye-bye then.'

There was a short silence, then Judy said enviously, 'You can always tell old money. It must be wonderful to have nothing to worry about.'

'Debra doesn't have such a carefree life as people think, and you know it, Judy.'

'What a pity that your folks were so wrong about her. Given a clever wife, you might be president by now.'

'Don't say that, Judy. Can't you ever forgive me? Can't

•

you ever forget the past? You wouldn't really want to be in Debra's place.'

'Oh, wouldn't I!' Judy's light tone conveyed that she still felt rejected by this impeccable man with his duties, responsibilities, obligations – and money. 'I wouldn't mind Debra's wonderful clothes, Debra's marvellous parties and Debra's ability to wave a wand and have anything she likes. Just because she happened to have inherited a fortune. After that the rest just followed naturally – including you, Curtis.'

'Judy, don't be bitter. I really wish that I could help you, and you know that I would if I could. And money isn't everything; Debra has her own problems, as you know.'

His telephone buzzed. His car was waiting to take them to lunch. Curtis rose. 'Let's forget money and Debra for an hour, Judy,' he pleaded. 'We've got so many more important things to discuss, haven't we?'

Judy gave him her most bewitching smile.

It was after midnight, and the servants had gone to bed, when Judy arrived at the Château de Chazalle. Maxine, wearing a lace-edged, grey silk peignoir, kissed her warmly, then said, 'Let's go down to the kitchen and make a cup of hot chocolate, like we did when we were schoolgirls.'

In the cavernous kitchen of the castle Maxine selected a small, spotless copper pan, then pushed back the sleeves of her peignoir. She laughed. 'That reminds me of the

evening before my wedding, when my mother gave me
some advice.' She poured milk from an enamelled jug.
'She told me that if I cooked chocolate late at night after
a party, I should always remove my fur coat, because
otherwise I would singe the cuffs.' Maxine whisked the
foaming chocolate, then poured it into porcelain cups.
'That was the only advice she gave me about married
life – not much use, in these circumstances.' Suddenly
Maxine put her head in her hands and her heavy blonde
hair tumbled around her face as she began to cry. Judy
put an arm round her heaving shoulders and waited for
the shuddering sobs to stop.

'What am I going to do, Judy?' Maxine sobbed in
despair. 'Charles has moved into his dressing room. He
won't look at me and he doesn't speak to me. I feel so
humiliated, so rejected.'

'What is she like?' Judy asked. 'Blonde? Beautiful?
Slim?'

'No, no. She has no style, no delicacy. She's the sort
of woman who wears a black bra under a white blouse,'
Maxine sniffled.

'She must have something that Charles wants. And she
sounds determined to have him, doesn't she?'

Maxine sat up and looked indignant. Good, thought
Judy, she won't be able to cope with the situation from
a position of complete despair – she needs to be a little
angry.

Maxine said, 'I'm sure that the bitch deliberately staged
the whole thing. I sent a telex from the Plaza, giving Charles

•

my flight time. She should have known that I was coming. I'm sure she never showed it to him. Charles can't stand rows, and he's always been absolutely discreet. I can't think how she managed to get him into bed in our home.'

'Maybe she bullied him into it,' Judy said softly. 'It's the classic mistress's move. Maybe Charles likes being bullied a bit?'

'But why would Charles . . .' Maxine began to protest, then she saw what Judy meant. Perhaps this awful woman appealed to Charles precisely because she was so domineering. She remembered that olive body writhing furiously on top of her husband, but Maxine could not recall the last time that she had climbed on top of Charles when they made love. She felt horribly exposed in such a position, showing the beginnings of a little double chin, looking fatter than she was to Charles below. Placid and easily contented, Maxine suddenly realized that she had lazily allowed Charles to assume all the responsibility for whatever had happened under the blue silk canopy; it was years since he had tumbled her wickedly in any other environment, as he had loved to do before they were married.

She pushed away her cup. 'I can't believe that he really wants to marry her – he can't possibly, she would destroy the business within a year. Please help me, Judy.'

'Maybe it's Charles who needs help,' said Judy, 'help to get out of a situation that he never wanted to be in. I've dealt with predatory women before.' She sipped her chocolate. 'Why on earth did you hire her?'

•

'We'd been asked to advise the Chinese government on the development of their own champagne industry – that bitch had a degree in Oriental studies.'

Maxine sat at her gold-columned dressing table, which had once belonged to the Empress Josephine. The light of the raw February morning, intensified by the crisp crust of snow on the grey parapet of the château, was harsh on her drawn face. The antique mirror reflected, with a dead grey radiance, the face of an opulently beautiful, but very anxious woman. She thought, I used to be a decorator, why ever did I design a grey bedroom? Why did I let good taste take the place of sensuality? What did my Aunt Hortense say? That no woman over thirty should wear grey.

A cheap office duplicate book was always near Maxine, so that she could immediately make notes and distribute them to her staff through Mademoiselle Janine, her secretary. Now she pulled a book from the dressing-table drawer and, by the time her maid came in, she had completed a new decoration scheme for the bedroom.

'Not sables this morning, Honorine, they're so heavy and dark,' she said as the elderly woman in black moved towards the fur closet. 'It's a long time since I wore the red fox. And for this evening, please lay out my pink Saint-Laurent with the red petticoat.'

With only ten guests to consider, Maxine had organized a simple programme; partridge-shooting on the estate, riding through the vineyards, cards and conversation for

•

those who preferred to stay warm indoors and, on Sunday, a stag hunt on the neighbouring estate.

Charles was the first down to breakfast in the yellow Chinese morning room.

Diffident and modest, Charles was attractive in his sheer helplessness; it was the sweet, absent-minded Cary Grant bit that the girls fell for, Maxine had explained to Judy. Now, looking guilty, he stood in his favourite position, feet astride, back to the crackling logs in the fireplace.

Next to enter was Guy Saint-Simon, yawning in his navy foulard dressing gown. 'The Louis Quinze bed needs a new mattress, Maxine.'

Guy was getting chubby, Maxine thought, and his hemp-coloured hair was starting to recede from his forehead, but the slightly hooked Roman nose and the wide, sensual mouth were unchanged. She was still amazed that her childhood friend had metamorphosed into one of the top fashion designers of France, with his own chain of boutiques, 'Limited Editions'.

Guy pulled his square-framed black spectacles out of his breast pocket, stuck them on his nose, and picked up *Le Monde*. Slowly, all Maxine's guests entered, chose their food from the heated silver chafing dishes on the mahogany sideboard and sat down at the breakfast table.

A tall man beamed good morning at Maxine as he sat down next to her. 'Maxine, you defy time.'

'So do you, Pierre,' Maxine replied, thinking that it was indeed almost true. Living in the fierce Alpine climate had tanned her first lover's face a deep, leathery brown; the etched straight lines around his eyes were white against the tan, but his tightly curled blond hair was as thick as ever and his body looked hard and strong.

Judy was the last to appear in the morning room. Her first reaction upon waking had been to telephone an old friend, now the head of *Time*'s Paris bureau. 'I can't tell you why I'm asking,' she began confidently, 'but I need to find a job for a girl with a degree in Oriental studies – something that involves a lot of travel, or even a posting abroad.'

That afternoon, while the other guests were shooting, Judy won four hands of piquet from Guy before he threw the cards at her, yelling, 'You haven't changed a bit in twenty years. A game is never a game with you. You Americans are obsessed by winning. You always want to be first. Here in France we know it's much more import-ant to be first class.' In spite of his careless pose of witty decadence, Judy knew that the secret of Guy's success was an obsession with quality and the ability to work like a dog.

Judy picked up a purple paperweight and pretended to throw it at Guy, who laughingly held his hand up to ward it off, saying, 'I know you won't throw that hunk of amethyst at me. Kate gave it to Maxine as a wedding present.' Suddenly he stopped laughing. 'It was such a pretty wedding. I can't bear to see Maxine looking so unhappy today. I always know when Charles is fooling around because Maxine dresses so badly. Lugubrious

•

colours and no jewellery. She really ought to give Charles a dose of his own medicine instead of letting him walk all over her.'

The butler appeared. 'A telephone call for Mademoiselle Jordan in the library.' Judy followed him to the panelled library where, in the rich atmosphere of hush, dust and old leather, she learned that Montpellier University had just acquired an important bequest of ancient Chinese jade and ceramics and was searching for a properly qualified curator to identify and catalogue the pieces, working in liaison with the People's Museum in Peking. Back home, a good networker can get to anyone in three moves, thought Judy, and asked Maxine if she knew anyone who knew anyone at Montpellier University. After a few minutes spent with her nose stuck in her maroon address book Maxine said, 'The best I can do is Ghislaine, my cousin, who is married to the Rector of Grenoble.'

It took four more contacts, six telephone calls and the rest of the afternoon to discover that Montpellier University had unsuccessfully advertised the curator's post for three months and were delighted by Maxine's recommendation.

At dinner Judy caught Maxine's eye between the silver trumpets of the flower-laden epergnes. Unobtrusively, she gave the thumbs-up sign.

'I can't thank you enough,' said Maxine later, as she slipped off her coral velvet dinner dress and reached

•

into one of her closets for a pale-turquoise satin peignoir.

'Other people's problems are always easier to solve than your own.' Judy grinned at Maxine in the mirror. 'Especially their amorous problems. And we all have them.'

'Do you have them with this new young man of yours? Twenty-nine years old, isn't he?' Maxine tied her sash and looked up under her lashes. 'What is love like, Judy, with a much younger man?'

'Maxine, you sound like a soap opera. There *is* a difference and it *is* important, but not in the way you think. What's important isn't that women are starting to go to bed with younger men; what's important is that age no longer smacks of terror to a woman. Women often fail to develop a strong sense of personal identity until they're into their thirties or forties; it's then that they start to find out who they really are and what sort of man they really want.' There was a thoughtful pause, then Judy added, 'Anyhow, age doesn't come into our relationship; Mark and I suit each other because we're both independent and we respect each other's freedom. What he gets is a woman who admires his talent, respects his commitment, and doesn't want to cling to him for status or affection. And what I get out of it is a wonderful lover who doesn't demand hot dinners every night.'

'As I never cook, that would be no advantage.'

'A younger man's demands and expectations are different from those of men who can remember the Second World War as well as the sexual revolution.'

•

'In what way?' Maxine fluffed up her maribou collar.

'Older men don't like a woman to spread her wings in case that might get in the way of their wings. But a younger man is adventurous, and interested in having a woman who isn't only going to boost his ego but develop her own personality; that's what they like in an older woman and that's what they respect.'

'But aren't you afraid of the future, Judy, of looking an old hag, of being abandoned, of being humiliated?'

'There's the possibility of that at any age. With any relationship you can expect suffering when it ends, plus a kick in the pants to your pride.'

Maxine said, 'Men can get away with so much more than a woman.'

'The world has always known that a man can be fascinating at any age. Now we're finding out that a woman can be as well. Women have always been exterior-oriented, but we all know beautiful women who are dull. Fascination has nothing to do with the tortoise-like state of your neck, but the unwrinkled state of your mind.'

Maxine rushed to the mirror. 'You think my neck is like a tortoise's?'

Judy grinned. 'Maxine, I'm never sure whether you're into vanity or self-improvement.'

'Take care of Lili for me, Mark,' were Judy's parting words to her lover before she left New York. He had been dismayed. While Judy was present in his life and

•

his bed, Mark could control the way that he was growing to feel about Lili but, without Judy, he was alone and at the mercy of the violent desire that Lili aroused in him. Hating to be out of control of himself, Mark found himself transferring the dislike of his own weakness on to the cause of it. Irritably, he complained to Lili that she was making his apartment untidy, and pointed to the make-up and magazines that were scattered over the living-room floor in front of the fire.

'I can't help it.' Lili looked surprised. 'I'm *stuck* here all day. I can't go outside because of the photographers.'

'Oh, don't be so dramatic; there's no reason not to go out. If you avoid the smart parts of town and stick to the places where nobody would expect to see a filmstar, you won't have any trouble.'

Lili looked sulkily defiant.

'Come on,' said Mark, 'I'll show you.'

He took her for lunch on Saturday to a tiny Oriental restaurant and listened patiently while Lili talked about the Mistinguett part that she had been offered. 'I'm not sure that I want to do it. I may be an international star but I think the part needs a brilliant dancer. There's more singing and dancing than I've ever done before, and I'm not sure I'm good enough. I'm afraid of making a fool of myself. Do you think I should do it?'

'I'm not the right person to ask, Lili. Surely your agent knows if you can do it. Why not talk to him?' As Mark passed Lili a bamboo steamer he thought that Judy never asked him to make her business decisions. He was

•

desperately looking for traits to criticize in Lili and praise in Judy.

Later Mark took her to see the Rembrandts in the Metropolitan Museum and afterwards they walked through the dirty slush of Central Park. The snow howled down again in the evening, so they struggled no further than the Italian restaurant on the corner.

'Do you know,' Mark asked, 'how to get a free bottle of wine in an Italian restaurant? No? I thought not.' So he told the waiter that it was Lili's birthday, whereupon the rotund padrone rushed out of the kitchen, kissed her wetly on both cheeks and presented them with a bottle of Italian sparkling wine – on the house.

'Have you ever tried that with Judy?' Lili asked.

'No, I haven't done it since I was a kid.' Mark poured the wine. 'Don't worry. I'll pay for it in with the tip. Happy Birthday! Judy doesn't like Italian restaurants. She says the food's too tempting. She's very disciplined, as you know. It's one of the things I admire about her.'

'What are the others?' Lili crunched a slice of fennel.

'Lots of things, not just a couple. Apart from the fact that Judy's clever and fun, I like her professionalism and her energy, her poise and her experience . . .'

'And her status, her position and her influential, interesting friends?' asked Lili cynically.

'Of course, why not? Like I said, lots of things. Some of the things I like about her are things that other people might not like. She can be sharp and tart. But that's part of being a straight-shooter. Women never understand that a man doesn't fall for this or that in a woman. He doesn't like the breasts but not the hips, like the eyes but not the nose. He doesn't like the wit but not the criticism. A man falls for the whole package, whatever it is. But women don't seem to view themselves that way. They're always worrying about the few things in themselves that they wish were different. But Judy doesn't waste time that way. And I like the way she's prepared to help me.'

'How?' Lili was astonished.

'She made me feel self-confident. A long time before I met Judy I lived with a model, but eventually I got tired of feeling like somebody else's supporting cast.' He refilled Lili's glass. 'However self-confident a young guy looks, he's probably uncertain of what he can do. It's good to get reassurance from someone whose opinion and experience he can respect – and who isn't his mother. He knows his mother thinks he's wonderful.' He laughed. 'Judy used to worry because she thought she had some sort of maternal attraction for me, but it isn't a bit like that. I already have a wonderful mother, so I don't need another one.'

'Isn't she lonely, though, when you're away?' Lili asked.

'I don't know.' It had never occurred to him that shiny, confident, poised Judy might ever feel lonely. In spite of himself, he again compared the two women. Lili ate lustily, Judy picked at food. Lili bored him with her indecision over the Mistinguett film, Judy never talked about her business when she was with him.

•

On Sunday morning Mark taught Lili to make popcorn, but it worried Mark to stand in the tiny kitchen right up against Lili and her animal magnetism. On Sunday afternoon they went to a scruffy little Chinese puppet theatre off Lower Broadway. The narrow benches were filled with noisy families. The owner welcomed Mark to his own bench and sat them between a moon-faced baby and his grandmother. In such surroundings, free from her crushing public image, Lili's natural grace flowered. Mark watched her take the baby on her knee to look at the dragons and the gods fight it out for the lily-footed maidens. The rest of the family chattered, smiled and nodded their approval as the baby threw handfuls of cookie crumbs on Lili's pink suede suit and tugged her hair over her face. So much, thought Mark, for the world's best-known sex symbol.

Maxine shivered on the high seat as the antique racing carriage followed the stag hunt through the forest. Cheeks stung scarlet with the bracing cold, she was feeling a little apprehensive. Shortly after they entered the humid forest three heavy, lumbering red deer had splashed across the muddy track ahead of the hunt. The tufters immediately leaped forward, baying with excitement. The mounted huntsmen, resplendent in gold-collared jackets, tore after the shaggy deerhounds, and the musical calls of their antique brass horns echoed plaintively through the forest.

Pierre, who was gently holding in the eager horses, turned to Maxine. As the high bench seat bounced on its curved black springs Maxine felt the stealthy pressure of his thigh against hers underneath the thick fur rug which was tucked around their knees.

'Is there a short cut? We don't want to get bogged down on this wet track.' Again Pierre pressed his hard thigh firmly against Maxine's soft leg. Message received and understood, thought Maxine as she pointed. 'If you take that track through the beeches, we can meet up with them at the bottom of the hill.'

The horses trotted swiftly as Pierre leaned closer to Maxine, and then suddenly turned and quickly brushed his lips against hers. Equally suddenly, Maxine thought, why *not*? He's been flirting with me for the whole weekend and I love it. It's especially flattering when your first lover makes it clear that he still wants to go to bed with you. I have been faithful to Charles for twenty years, and my reward was that bitch in my bed.

Maxine felt flattered, excited and a little nervous, which is the essence of flirtation. 'There's a barn a bit further on,' she suggested as they bounced past tall trees hung with tattered brown leaves.

'Perfect,' said Pierre. They both knew that an invitation had been issued and accepted.

Outside the high timbered barn Maxine now shivered with anticipation as Pierre put blankets on both horses and looped the long reins over the carriage hook. 'It's a hay barn,' said Maxine, so he brought out half a bale, grunting, 'This should keep them happy for hours.'

Then he turned and looked at her for a moment. As

•

they faced each other he cupped her chin in his hands and quickly and firmly kissed her chilled lips. 'Let's climb to the top where it's warm.'

He caught her hand and they scrambled up the prickly steps of hay to the top. Pierre threw the fur carriage rug on the sweet-smelling hay, then leaned towards Maxine. At first she was taut and trembled, but then her tension dissolved and she felt soft and boneless as a pillow. He took her in his arms and, as he pressed her to his body, Maxine felt a long-forgotten lurch of pleasure. Warm, melting desire was heightened by the fact it was forbidden. She whispered, 'I can't stand up, my knees are shaking.'

'So are mine.'

Together they fell against the tightly baled hay. His fingers felt under the glossy red fox of her coat; her trembling fingers undid the fasteners, then he was pulling up her russet sweater and pulling down the lace cups of her bra. 'Maxine, your breasts haven't changed.' He teased her nipple with his tongue, then started to move from one breast to the other, nipping the little peaks with his teeth. Maxine purred with sensual pleasure, thinking that there must be a bit of inner, magic elastic tugging from the nipples to the groin.

This is it, Maxine told herself, this is the moment when all you want is to lie back and let this easy pleasure wash over you. But perhaps that had been what had gone wrong between her and Charles. She had always expected him to do it to her; she had always been passive and timid in a way that people who knew Maxine out of bed would

•

never have believed possible. If only she hadn't been plump, if only she had been the perfect shape, then she wouldn't have been so shy and self-conscious, wouldn't have minded bouncing around erotically all over the bed. But she was, so she didn't.

Pierre pressed her breasts together and ran his tongue down her cleavage. How can I do things to him while he's doing things to me? thought Maxine. I can't concentrate on two things at once; when he's kissing my breasts and driving me out of my skull with excitement, I can't think, I can't do, I can only feel.

'My turn now,' said Pierre, as if mind-reading. He rolled over on his side and unclasped the buckle of his belt, then Maxine reached for his hard, solid body.

Later Pierre gently pushed her head downwards and Maxine licked the pink tip of his penis, which swayed as she took it between her lips. She steadied it with her cold hand, hoping that she wouldn't shrivel him. She was terrified of biting him by accident. She tucked her lips over her teeth, making a hollow monkey mouth which slid easily over the penis. No way could she get all of this in her mouth, she worried.

Pierre wriggled. 'Move your hand and mouth up and down together at the same time with the same rhythm.' Sprawled happily on the fur rug, Pierre made small involuntary movements with his hips towards her mouth. I seem to be doing it right, thought Maxine. She could feel a bump under the ridge of his penis, so she swirled her tongue round it experimentally. Pierre whinnied with

•

delight, and his hips jumped eagerly towards her mouth. Maxine lost the rhythm, panicked, and thought she was going to choke; then she felt Pierre's hands on her head, gently guiding her. Suddenly, she felt quite powerful and very pleased with herself.

Later Pierre pulled the red fox fur tenderly over her plump, white body then nuzzled underneath into her softness. 'I have dreamed of your breasts for twenty years. Did you ever think of me?'

Maxine thought this must be standard, French post-coital dialogue, so she did her best to reply in the same vein of syrup. 'Of course. Doesn't every woman always remember her first lover?' He raised the glossy fur and dropped a kiss of homage on her soft, honey-coloured pubic hair.

'What about your wife, Pierre?' she said curiously.

'Obviously you're not used to committing adultery, Maxine. Rule one is never to mention the wife but, since you ask, she is obsessed by the children and we do our duty every Saturday.'

Maxine thought, that sounds like Charles and me.

'You're not just after our sponsorship for your skier, are you?' Maxine asked, immediately wishing that she hadn't been so insensitive.

'No, I am after *you*. Seriously.' He kissed her. 'You can always find a sponsor if you're the best – and I think my pupil will prove to be the best. But I hope we sign up with Chazalle, because then it will be necessary to meet two or three times a year – at least.'

•

'At least,' agreed Maxine, carefully picking a wisp of dried grass from his hair.

'We wondered if you'd turned over,' called the huntsman as the antique racing carriage bounced across the glade.

'Took a short cut and got lost,' Pierre called back to him, his round blue eyes expressionless.

How can Maxine get lost on her own estate? wondered Judy and looked at Charles, scowling astride his slush-spattered grey as he wondered the same thing. In the circumstances he can hardly play the jealous husband to Maxine, Judy realized. But why did Maxine have to be so stupid and choose exactly the wrong moment to screw up Judy's pitch to Charles? If Judy ever got to make her pitch to Charles; in spite of her determined efforts to catch him alone, it was obvious to Judy that Charles had been avoiding her with equal determination.

So Judy was surprised when he offered to drive her to the airport to catch her Concorde flight. As they set off down the kilometre-long, gravel drive Charles surprised Judy by saying, 'I thought I might as well give you the opportunity to reason with me again, which is obviously why you hopped over the Atlantic for the weekend. How I hate women's plots!' He suddenly accelerated violently, tyres squealing round a corner, and Judy remembered what a bad driver Charles was as he continued, 'I fail to understand why Maxine expects me to behave with decorum when she fools around with her old

•

boyfriend under my nose, as everybody saw yesterday.'

Maybe Maxine hadn't been so stupid to flirt openly with Pierre, thought Judy as she said, 'I'm sure Maxine wouldn't have looked at him twice, Charles, if you hadn't hurt her so. Why do you do it? Have you reached the age where you need to prove your virility?'

'You make adultery sound like arthritis. Why don't you mind your own business, Judy?'

'Maxine *is* my business, and she's your business as well, Charles. Surely you can see that this assistant of yours hasn't the sophistication or the style or the background to run the castle and handle all the business entertaining? The public associates Maxine's glamour with your champagne. She's starred in your TV commercials all over the world. You'll find you can't switch images as easily as you can switch wives.'

Charles turned on to the highway and increased speed. 'It's not that easy to switch wives – the lawyers have already made that clear. You needn't worry, Maxine will have plenty of money.'

'That's not what she wants. She wants you.'

'You expect me to believe that, after seeing her today with that attentive oaf?'

'I don't know anyone else who's been faithful to her husband for so long. But you know that Maxine loves you. And you love her. She makes you laugh. You've got used to her, like a baby to its blanket, and she's the mother of your children. Nobody's going to spell it out to you if I don't.'

•

•

They drove in silence through the sleet. Judy thought, I've got to give it one more try, and said softly, 'I think your hand was forced. I think that what you really want, Charles, is to have the clock put back a month.'

Another silence.

'So how would I get out of it?' Charles addressed the windscreen as they turned into the airport.

'You'll have to take a deep breath and tell this woman that you have no intention of altering your life. Maybe you'll have to pay her – call it severance, of course. A year's salary should do it. And fix a better job for her, with more prestige. Make it clear that she has a choice of the cash and the job – or nothing.'

'You American women are so tough.'

'Tough means being sensible and firm, refusing to be exploited. I hope you're tough, Charles.'

That evening Judy heard the whine of a police car hurtling down Fifth Avenue, far below. 'It seemed a long weekend without you,' Judy murmured sleepily as Mark snaked his arm around her thin waist and pulled her close to him under the cinnamon silk sheets. 'What did you get up to, Mark?'

'Nothing much, the weather was foul. Took Lili to a couple of restaurants.'

'Sounds a drag.' Judy wriggled hopefully against him.

'Yes.' Mark suddenly realized that those two days had been wonderful; that after spending forty-eight hours with Lili, his first reaction of purely physical lust had

•

changed. He remembered her eagerness, her ebullience, her rages, her depression and her pathos. All now seemed violently appealing to him.

Mark felt the tip of Judy's tongue, and automatically slid his hand between her thighs. He remembered hearing her once say that when men feel guilty, they make love with especial care, because they don't want their women to guess what's happened, and because they want to reassure themselves that it really doesn't make any difference. Expertly, Mark began to caress Judy, determined that she should not realize that, instead of her neat firm buttocks he wanted Lili's ripe, rounded ass, and instead of Judy's little pink-nippled breasts he wanted Lili's golden, dark-tipped flesh, and instead of Judy's charming, button-nosed face, he wanted Lili's dark eyes, misty with ecstasy and her full lips whispering his name as he thrust inside her.

SIX

March 1979

Pagan lay awake listening to the early-morning sounds of home: the click-whirr-click of a London milk cart, the chink of bottles, a blackbird piping with indignation in the mischievous March wind, a heavy thud on the doormat as *The Times* came through the letterbox, a lighter thud as the *British Medical Journal* hit the doormat, soft swishes as the mail was pushed through the brass door flap. Downstairs her old sheepdog, Buster II, gave a token growl at each invasion of his territory by Fritz, the dachshund.

Sophia must be awake, thought Pagan as she listened to her daughter's rock music drift up from the basement. Seven o'clock in the morning and she's playing the drums already. Pagan then heard the noises she had been unconsciously waiting for, the sounds of her husband getting up. She heard footsteps on the polished boards of his dressing room, snatches of Mozart, whistled while he shaved, then stairs creaking as he thumped down to the kitchen.

With much whirring of weights and rattling of ancient brass chains, the grandfather clock struck seven. Then there was silence until Pagan again heard Christopher's feet on the stairs, then the rattle of her bedroom door-handle – and there he was, grey hair still damp from the shower, deftly balancing her breakfast tray. 'We seem to have run out of marmalade.'

'Christopher darling, I'll never make a housewife, you must have noticed by now.' He rearranged the antique lace pillows behind her head, then took *The Times* from her tray and sat on the end of her bed, saying, 'I thought the lack of marmalade was part of a plot to force me to divorce you.'

Pagan began to pour their tea. 'Grabbing the newspaper first – *always* – is practically grounds for divorce in Britain.' Her primrose cotton nightdress slipped off her shoulder and her mahogany hair fell into her eyes as she leaned forward and handed him his cup.

'I once thought you might run off with a gigolo.' Christopher bit into his butterless toast. 'When the cardi-ologist said it might kill me to make love to you again, my first thought was, how long will Pagan stand it?'

'Thank heavens that medical opinion eventually changed its mind,' growled Pagan. 'But I've always loved you for your brilliant conversation.' She never told Chris-topher how much she loved him. She was superstitiously afraid of doing so. Christopher was the mainspring of her life, the focus of her days, the theme of her thoughts. Only her husband's care had transformed Pagan from a self-

•

destructive, insecure, upper-class failure into a society figure famous for her outrageous glamour. Ironically, when Lady Swann, in some dazzling dress, swept into the room on the arm of her older, quieter husband, people naturally assumed that it was she who dominated the partnership, but the foundation of Pagan's cheerful flamboyance was Christopher's emotional stability.

For the first few weeks of their marriage Pagan and Christopher had continued their rich and, for Pagan, revelatory sex life. When his first heart attack had ended that phase of their relationship Pagan had been far more concerned about losing her husband than losing their good times in bed. 'Sex is like opera, darling,' she used to tell Christopher. 'Something that other people find fabulous, but which simply doesn't thrill me.' She hadn't really missed it that much.

'Are you ready for your joke of the day?' Christopher asked. Pagan crunched her toast and nodded.

'If you believe in the Virgin Mary's immaculate conception, then Jesus Christ must have been a woman, because the Virgin's baby could only have had X chromosomes!' He roared with laughter.

Pagan looked blank. 'Don't you remember my little lesson in genetics? Women have only X chromosomes, men have both X and Y. You can't give birth to a boy without Y chromosomes. You can't have Y chromosomes without spermatozoa. You can't have spermatozoa without a man.'

Pagan still looked blank. 'I can see you'll never win the

•

Nobel Prize for genetics, darling. Don't you remember that I was able to predict when you were pregnant that Sophia's eyes would not be brown, because the colour of a child's eyes depends on the genes of its parents? Two clearly blue-eyed parents can't produce a brown-eyed child. More toast?'

'Tomorrow morning, darling, I'd like a joke that I can understand without a Ph.D.'

Pagan leaned back in bed, sipped her tea, then reached for her letters. She grabbed the one with the New York postmark and read it. 'Half a million dollars!' She sat upright, waved the letter at her husband, then threw it to him. 'See for yourself. That's from Stash, Lili's agent. That's the profit they expect from the première and it's all for the Foundation, as well as the money we'll get from Spyros's jewellery.'

'Tiger-Lili certainly wants to try out for the team.'

'I think she does; it's rather sweet. She seems to have had such a rotten life, in spite of all the fame.' Pagan leaned back against the lace pillows. 'She's always on her guard, always wary, very conscious that people try to use her – which they do all the time. It's perfectly disgusting. Lili can be a bit imperious but, basically, she's a perfect pet.'

'She's certainly a generous friend.' Christopher kissed the top of Pagan's head. 'I'm off. Cross your fingers for the new strain of hepatitis–B. It should either do the trick, or give us an epidemic.'

As he eased his elderly Rover into the flow of traffic heading south, Sir Christopher reflected that Pagan was probably the only woman he knew who would automatically feel nothing but sympathy for a voluptuous star like Lili. Perhaps Pagan understood her because both of them were a mixture of surface shockingness and underlying insecurity, he reflected as he waited in traffic between two container trucks.

A bread van cut into the line of vehicles ahead, then swerved violently out again. Sir Christopher checked a rush of anger. Traffic snarls were a classic stress inducer; no sense in shortening his life over someone else's bad driving.

Morning mists lay in ethereal slabs over the grey river as the line of traffic started to move along the Thames embankment, then picked up speed down the clearway. He wouldn't be late, after all, thought Sir Christopher, still in convoy between the two massive trucks.

He never saw the bakery van shoot the lights, make an unsignalled right turn, then crash head-on into one of the graceful spherical street lights that stand on the stone balustrade of the river Thames.

But Sir Christopher heard the crump of metal, the thin crash of glass, then the louder impact as an oncoming automobile piled into the back of the bakery van. He slammed on his brakes at the same time as the orange truck ahead of him, which stopped abruptly, air hissing from the pneumatic breaking system.

The worn disc brakes of Sir Christopher's car were not so effective, and he realized that he would not be able to avoid hitting the lurid orange truck ahead.

•

•

The driver of the green truck behind him reacted more slowly, and crashed into the back of Sir Christopher's old Rover. The momentum slammed the Rover into the truck ahead. As if made of paper, the Rover crumpled into the back of the truck. The steering column slammed against Sir Christopher's chest like a mallet hitting steak, smashing his ribs and heart to pulp.

He was rushed to St Stephen's Hospital and hurried into the intensive care unit.

Twenty minutes later Pagan, in her primrose nightdress, held her husband's limp hand.

'I'm afraid it's hopeless, Lady Swann.' The doctor felt that he could talk bluntly to a fellow doctor's wife. 'Even if we obtained a replacement organ, there's nothing left to attach it to – the thorax has been completely destroyed.'

In a daze, Pagan signed one form giving consent for the life-support system to be switched off, another giving permission for Christopher's remains to be used for medical purposes, and a third authorizing the undertakers to proceed. She felt very cold and, to her horror, very angry. 'How could he do it?' she thought. 'How dare he leave me now?' Then she thought, 'How can I even think such a dreadful thing?'

'A mother-and-daughter conspiracy suit? What the hell is that?' Judy demanded in the *Verve!* office, wondering if she had correctly heard what Tom had said.

'Just what it sounds like,' he told her. 'They allege that

•

you and Lili hatched a malicious plot to ruin Senator Ruskington's political career.'

'But that's ridiculous,' Judy protested, her heels angrily kicking up the apricot kelim rug as she paced her office.

'Of course it is.' Tom was being patient. 'But conspiracy is a bitch, Judy. It's the vaguest, stickiest area in the whole legal code. Just talking to someone, even on the telephone, can amount to a legal conspiracy, if the circumstantial evidence stands up. The fact that Lili has now moved in with you could be disastrous if the judge decides that it's significant. Frankly, it's a pity that you've asked her to stay in your apartment.'

'Lili and I have a lot of catching up to do. God! This is all so stupid,' Judy raged. 'When Lili did this interview I hardly knew her.'

'Can you prove it?' Tom asked patiently. 'You'll have to go through all your papers tonight to see if there's anything that we can produce at the hearing on Friday which will substantiate what you say!'

So Judy cancelled her entire afternoon's programme, then read through an eighteen-inch-high pile of legal documents. After that she turned out her filing system, her desk drawers, her purse and her briefcase in search of anything at all to prove her point. She finished at eight that evening, exhausted by the effort of concentration. 'Damn that hypocritical old buzzard,' she said to Tom as she shrugged on her lynx jacket. 'Senator Ruskington has now lost me almost a day's work on top of every spare cent we have.'

•

Tom nodded. 'This case is wrecking our budget, Judy. We'll have to make fast compensation cuts, as many as possible, no matter how small.'

'What do you mean by small?'

'Do we really need an exercise instructor? Couldn't we let Tony go?'

'If we have to cut down, let's switch to a cheaper printer; that would be the easiest, quickest saving.'

'And cut the quality? You're only saying that because you're angry, Judy.'

'But it would be a really big economy and I would watch the quality like a hawk. We could make the contract conditional on quality. And what we pay Tony is a drop in the ocean compared to what we're paying the lawyers.' She jammed on her lynx hat. 'The exercise class is good for morale, and it means that I'm too tired to lie awake at night, worrying about that damned senator.'

'*You?* Lie awake?' he queried. 'What's happened to the unstoppable Judy Jordan self-confidence?'

'It was always more fragile than you thought.' Judy's voice was unusually low. For the first time Tom realized the depth of her anxiety, and immediately switched into reassurance. Playfully, he ruffled her hair. 'We've been in jams before, Judy, and you're still top of the heap.'.

'So there's farther to fall. And you get no sympathy. You're supposed to be invulnerable. Did Henry Kissinger stay awake at night, crying?'

'At least you've got Mark,' he comforted her. 'I'm finding it tough without Kate.'

●

'I don't want to burden Mark with the troubles in my life.'

'Do you mean you're frightened of doing so? Frightened that he only loves the glamorous Judy Jordan that the world sees, not the real woman that I know?'

'Mark's a lot bigger on moral issues than he is on practical ones. I can't talk to him about business because he doesn't understand it. And he doesn't understand that a lawsuit is about a set of rules, not about justice.'

Fondly Tom put an arm around her fluffy fur shoulders. 'We'll struggle through somehow.'

'Talking of struggling, how's Kate?'

'She says the problem is much bigger than she had thought. It's not just a tribal war, it seems to be systematic genocide. The Bangladesh government has tried to settle the Chittagong hills with their own citizens, and drive out the peaceful Buddhist peasants who live there. They're trying to take away Kate's visa.'

'And to think I didn't even know where Chittagong was before Kate left.'

Judy said goodnight to Tom, then walked slowly down the dark corridor. She noticed a light shining under the boardroom door and opened it. Inside was Tony, sweating in his shorts and vest as he went through a sequence of fast turns and kicks in front of the mirror.

'Still here, Tony!'

'Yeah! Working out the new routine for tomorrow.' He leaped across the floor. 'D'ya think the girls will go for it! I think they're ready for this. I think they'll manage. What d'ya think?'

Anyone who put in longer hours than she did gained Judy's instant admiration. 'Hiring you was the best decision I ever made, Tony,' she called as he whirled past her, spinning drops of sweat from his forehead each time he turned. He finished in a dramatic pose, kneeling on the floor with arms outstretched, then slowly stood up, panting. 'Getting hired by you was the smartest thing I ever did. Did ya see my picture in *New York* magazine? My mom's shown it to everyone on the block.'

'That's great, Tony. I know they'll love it. And the girls all really appreciate the trouble you take.'

Tony began to towel his dripping face. 'Do you mean it? They really dig the routines?'

'Of course. And you, too, Tony. Why's that surprising?'

'All this female attention. Goes to a guy's head.'

'Oh, come on,' Judy laughed. 'With that body, you must have had hundreds of girls after you.'

'No, I was the original Charles Atlas weakling, that's why I started working out in the first place.'

'You've made up for it since, Tony.' Judy turned to leave the room. 'Don't work too late.'

'No chance, I'm taking my mom out tonight,' he answered.

'What a lovely thought, Tony. Enjoy yourselves.'

★
●

•

'Can't we turn the volume down?' Tony's mother scowled. Carefully dressed diners were shrieking with laughter, calling greetings and gossip from table to table, while waiters clattered with laden trays across the white tiled floor.

'The fashion crowd comes here, Momma.' Tony hoped she wasn't going to make a scene. 'I wanted to take you somewhere real nice.'

'Nice! This old-fashioned stuff!' A scornful laugh indicated her opinion of the fawn leather and chromium interior, all of which had been salvaged from the liner *Mauretania*, that floating *objet d'art* of the thirties.

'So now you've got the job, you got money to burn!' Tony's mother picked up the elegant menu. 'I could cook this stuff for a tenth of the price! Papa and I never wasted a penny. Now, there was a careful man.'

Tony didn't remember his father as being careful; his earliest memories were of his father fighting with his mother, while Tony cowered beneath the cracked, checked oilcloth that covered the kitchen table.

'What'll you have, Momma? I'm gonna try the crab salad.'

'Crab salad! What nourishment is that? You like chicken, Tony, remember?'

Tony remembered the different grease stains on the kitchen wallpaper, each of which marked a spot where his father had hurled a meal against it. Roast chicken had been the easiest dish to pick off the floor. Tony hated

•

roast chicken. 'OK, I'll have the chicken, Momma. Now, what'll you have?'

Small black eyes peered at the menu, reading with difficulty. 'I'll have the hamburger. Why couldn't you let me fix something in your smart new apartment, Tony?'

She'd never stopped criticizing his apartment. Quickly he said, 'It's being decorated. Wet paint everywhere.' Tony wasn't clever enough to wonder why this small, scowling woman, who was in her forties but who looked twenty years older, should turn every pleasure offered by her son into an excuse to criticize him.

'Why aren't *you* doing the decorating?' She waved the menu at his face. Tony raised one arm and ducked as if to ward off a blow, then she continued, 'So now you're too high and mighty to paint your own apartment! You always were lazy; you always lay around doing nothing.'

They fell silent until their food was served, then Tony's mother suspiciously prodded her hamburger with her fork. 'This meat is raw!'

'It's continental style, Momma, underdone.' Tony felt an almost uncontrollable urge in his gut as his mother criticized on, on, on, and raised her voice until the other diners turned to look at her. This, too, had been the pattern of his childhood meals. She'd complain because Poppa was always late and, in return, he'd criticize the food. Then they were off, bickering about nothing. Voices would rise, fists would be raised, shouting would escalate into screaming, and then the food would hit the wall. Mealtimes were the only times that his family couldn't avoid being together, and they used these occasions to attack, undermine and casually wound, using their intimate knowledge of each other to destroy with the accuracy of heat-seeking missiles.

'Please keep your voice down, Momma,' Tony pleaded.

'That's a fine way to talk to your mother!'

'Momma, I'm only trying to give you a good time.' Once again Tony wondered whether he would ever earn adult status.

'Don't interrupt me, or I'll make you wish you'd never been born!' Tony felt sick. Inside his magnificently developed body he felt again like a small boy, a small boy terrified of his mother's unpredictable, sadistic rages, a small boy overpowered by the unreasoned guilt of childhood. Every day the small Tony had heard that savage voice and moved about the apartment in terror, lest she should pick on some trifling fault – a peanut-butter stain on his shirt, unfinished schoolwork, chores skimped – as an excuse for a beating.

Tony unlocked his front door and crushed his mother's bag of homemade cookies into the overflowing garbage bag. Another treat for the roaches. He fed a tape of *Captain Blood* into the video, threw himself on the permanently converted, never-made Murphy bed, and turned to the night table, upon which stood a signed photograph of Judy in a silver frame. 'I don't take her out, I'm neglecting her; I do take her out, I'm wasting money!'

*

•

'Isn't Spyros ever going to give up?' Lili picked the plain diamond bracelet from the newly delivered basket of butterfly orchids and tossed it on Judy's blue and mauve silk sofa. 'If I had kept his bracelets, I'd have enough to reach my elbows.'

'Lucky girl, isn't she, Mark?' Judy picked up the brilliant stream of jewels and admired it over the back of her brown hand.

Mark shrugged his shoulders and gazed at the smouldering log fire. 'That bracelet would feed an African village for years.'

'Don't be so smug!' Lili reached forward, grabbed the diamond bracelet, and flung it at Mark. '*Give* it to the Africans, then,' she said. 'I don't want it, because I know it isn't a gift, it's a bribe.' Lili snorted. 'When one of Spyros's little gifts appears in a basket of flowers you're supposed to roll over on your back and be grateful. He orders these diamond bracelets, a dozen at a time, from Cartier. To him, they're trading stock.'

'Like beads and mirrors?' Judy suggested. 'As used by the conquistadores to buy Aztec gold?'

'Exactly.' Lili's expression was offset by her bizarre make-up; she had spent the afternoon trying to copy Mistinguett's make-up; her guide photograph lay among scattered cosmetics on the low, red marble table.

'You'd better get that stuff off your face or you'll be late for the concert.' Judy picked up the brass poker and prodded a falling log back into place.

'True.' Lili stood up, stretched and headed for the

•

bathroom. 'Won't you need this make-up?' Judy called after her, meaning get this mess out of my sitting room.

Mark said, 'She likes being untidy, you should see the state she left my place in.'

'So what does a little mess matter? The reason Lili wanted to move in with me was so that our relationship could develop.' Softly, she touched Mark's long, tapering, brown fingers. Gently Mark pulled his hand away.

'Tom told me that having Lili living here with you, Judy, could be playing with fire; it might prejudice the lawsuit.'

Judy neatly replaced the poker on the poker stand. 'We're never going to get to know each other properly over restaurant tables and in hotels.' She turned as Lili appeared, glorious in dark-green shot silk and opal ear-rings. 'I'm off.'

Lili's carnation scent lingered in the sitting room as the front door slammed. Mark wished that he, too, could leave. It's a classic double bind, he thought miserably: if I leave, then Judy will take it as rejection, and if I stay, the whole thing will shortly explode in our faces. Here we sit, sipping Perrier on top of an emotional time bomb. Surreptitiously he sniffed the carnations and couldn't help imagining Lili's gold-skinned body as she emerged from the tub.

Lili let herself into the apartment and unclasped her green velvet cloak. They hadn't gone to bed yet – she could hear Judy's earnest voice saying, '. . . But why,

•

Mark? Why have you tried for four hours, in various indirect ways, to get me to ask my daughter to leave this apartment?'

'For Chrissake, don't you understand, Judy?' Unseen, Lili heard Mark's weary pleading, and her hands halted on the gold clasp.

And, suddenly, Judy did understand. 'Of course! I must have been blind! You're in love with her, aren't you, Mark?' Her voice was hard. 'I must have been blind!'

'I don't want to hurt you, Judy.'

'Too bad, sweetheart, you just did,' she flashed back at him. 'Men always say they don't want to hurt you, when they've just dealt you a death blow.'

'I don't want to hurt Lili, either. She trusts me. I don't want to upset her life, or your life, or your life with Lili, or my life.' Mark tried not to raise his voice. 'To Lili, I'm the only man she knows who isn't trying to get into her pants.'

'Except that's what you want to do, isn't it?' Judy demanded.

There was a pause, then Mark said in a low voice, 'If you want the truth, I don't think any man could resist Lili's extraordinary sexuality.'

Lili caught sight of her reflection in the dim, silver depths of an elaborate Louis Quinze mirror. What is it, she thought, what is it that I have in me that casts this spell, this curse, on almost every man I meet? What is it? I can't see it. Why can't I switch it off?

As if echoing her thoughts, in the living room Judy

•

shouted, 'I can't see it, and neither can any other woman. That's why it's so maddening to see you men all making fools of yourselves over Lili.'

Gazing at her reflection, Lili realized that she was tired of being a sex object, tired of being considered a male plaything, tired of being idolized by both sexes – unknown men because they desired her and unknown women because they desired to be like her. Lili realized that her fatal attraction was, above all, fatal to herself.

'Does Lili know you feel this way about her?' Judy was trying to control her voice, because she had to know the answer to her question.

'No,' Mark answered, 'and I don't want her to know.'

'What does she feel about you?'

'I think she trusts me.' He paused. 'I think she sees me as a brother.'

'Are you and I living in the same century?' Judy suddenly yelled. 'Brother, indeed!'

'I'm not going to threaten the only shred of family security that Lili's ever had.'

Judy interrupted him bitterly. 'Well, that just makes it perfect.' Her voice was vicious. 'I'm losing my magazine, my money, my job; then you try to fix things so that I'll lose my daughter and my lover into the bargain. And to top it all, you're full of sympathy for *her*, not me.'

Mark shouted back, 'Look, I don't want Lili. I want *you*. But I want you like you used to be.'

Judy heard the pain behind his words and realized that

•

Mark was telling the truth when he said that his passion for Lili was something that he didn't want.

'You're difficult to sympathize with, Judy.' Mark finally found an exterior focus for his anger. 'You've changed since I met you. You were such fun. Ambitious, hardworking, successful, and tough – sure. But fun. You were kind to people and strong. You gave me support and self-confidence.'

'Now I'm the one who needs support,' Judy wailed, suddenly out of control and frightened.

Suddenly Mark was able to crystallize his feelings and put them into words. 'You seem to have lost your own self-confidence.'

'What do you mean?'

'I don't recognize you any more. You taught me that real self-confidence isn't put on every morning like a silk shirt to impress the outside world. Self-confidence is something that's built on knowing what you can do and what you can't do. Now you seem to have forgotten that. What's got into you?'

'What's got into me?' Judy was suddenly quiet. 'I'm terrified that I'll end up like my mother, feeding the cat and watching the neighbours and waiting. I don't want to be powerless like she was, just sitting helplessly in the middle of her own life, waiting for it to end.'

'There's a lot to be said for that sort of life.' Now Mark was angry. 'At least that sort of woman isn't jealous of her own daughter.' He was unable to resist the urge to hurt the suddenly vulnerable Judy. 'You used to say that

•

jealousy was the penalty of thinking only about externals. You used to say that there would always be younger, more beautiful women in the world. You used to say that jealousy never troubled a self-confident woman.'

'So now I know I was wrong!' Judy shouted. 'Do *you* want to know how it feels to become a mother when you're my age and then suddenly find that your baby is one of the most beautiful women in the world?'

In the hall Lili didn't want to hear any more but she didn't want to leave. Mesmerized, like a frog in car headlights, she felt unable to move.

'Do *really* want to know what it feels like to be Lili's mother?' Judy continued. 'It feels as if I'm slowly becoming nobody! It feels as if I'm becoming the Invisible Woman! Little by little, I'm losing my identity! Very quickly, I'm losing the business that I spent twenty years building up. So I'm losing my job, my status, my money. I'm facing financial and professional disaster and disgrace. And I'm desperately afraid of failure – all because I'm Lili's mother.' Her voice cracked. 'Everything's slipping away and I'm frightened, Mark.' Too late she was finally telling her lover what was on her mind.

Lili stood up and tiptoed to her room, tears running down her face. She didn't want to listen any longer as the two people she cared for tore their relationship to pieces – because of her.

Judy perched in front of her breakfast counter sipping her high-energy drink – the juice of an orange, a

•

teaspoonful of honey and a whole, raw egg; it was blended every morning for her breakfast, and tasted nicer than it sounded. Force of habit had compelled her to get up at her usual six o'clock, but this morning there had been no reason to linger because Mark had moved out the night before with his clothes stuffed into a khaki duffel bag. He had been exhausted and angry because Judy couldn't understand his predicament. As Mark saw it, he was being falsely accused of disloyalty, when he had tried to be truthful and faithful.

Gallant, confident Judy, the brave little drummer boy, had suddenly crumpled into a clutching, distraught female, and Mark simply didn't know how to cope with her; he wished he could help her but he couldn't. He could see that his presence upset her. So he had left. It seemed better than having an all-night row, which is what they had been obviously heading for. He had said, 'Take care of yourself, Judy,' then walked out of the door, leaving Judy bitterly to wonder why people always say, 'Take care of yourself,' when they mean that *they* don't intend to take care of you. She'd never needed a man in her life so badly before, and now, when she needed Mark, he was leaving her. He thought he'd be able to get an assignment in Nicaragua. It might as well be the moon.

As Judy finished her drink Tom called from the *Verve!* office. 'Not good news, Judy,' he warned.

'Hit me, I can take it,' she replied, dully, their joke formula for riding a crisis.

'Judy, I can't keep up this juggling act much longer.

•

I've held the creditors off for as long as I can, but they won't take our-cheque-is-in-the-mail any longer. This is now more than a cash problem. We'll have to pull something out of the hat, fast, Judy.'

There's nothing left in the hat, Judy thought to herself as the other phone rang and she picked it up. It was Lili's agent, Stash. A phone clasped to either ear, Judy said, 'Morning, Stash, d'you want Lili? I think she's still asleep.'

'No, I want you.' His silky voice held a trace of middle Europe. Judy turned to the left telephone and said, 'I'll call you back, Tom,' then turned to the right and said, 'Why, Stash?'

'Would *Verve!* magazine like to be one of the sponsors of the International Beauty Pageant this year?' the world-weary voice inquired.

'Sounds interesting.' Judy's voice was guarded. 'What does it involve?'

'They want you to be one of the judges in Miami, and then you would chaperone the winner to Istanbul and Egypt on the start of her world tour.'

'Our policy on *Verve!* is to soft-pedal the beauty contests. We like to think that our readers have more on their minds than lipstick.' Judy's response was automatic. 'In any case, our sponsorship programme is allocated for this year.' Years of experience had taught Judy never to say no outright, even when people approached her for money.

'This isn't the normal deal; you won't have to put in a

•

cent. They're offering you a big slice of equity in return for coverage in the magazine and identification with yourself. They want to reposition the beauty contests so that no woman would feel them degrading.'

'I appreciate your offer, Stash, but I couldn't leave New York.'

Stash said, 'These days New York is only twelve hours away from anywhere, and your magazine works on a six-week schedule; it's not as if you were running a daily newspaper.'

Judy paused. Stash mentioned the money involved. Judy gasped. Carefully backpedalling, she said, 'We've always made a point of staying in touch with the average American woman and her ambitions, and there's no doubt that the beauty queen is one of the most fascinating figures of our age. Providing the terms are right, I think it would be in all our interests, but I may have to fly back if there are any . . . business problems.'

After discussing further details with Stash, Judy exuberantly called Tom. 'Hi, this time we really *are* about to mail the cheque.'

'She bought it right away, just like you said.' Wearing his usual vicuna coat and black leather gloves, Stash walked into Lili's bedroom without knocking. Judy had long since left her apartment and gone to the office. Stash knew that there was no chance of being overheard.

Lili gasped rhythmically as the Japanese masseur made delicate crisscross movements up and down her spine with his thumbs. 'Are the International Beauty people happy?' she asked as she was rolled over.

Stash's glance at her flesh was that of professional appraisal. Knowing how much Lili could eat, he vigilantly checked her weight and, when he did so, also made a covert inspection for needle tracks in her arms, crêpe skin that would indicate diuretic abuse, puffiness that might be due to drink. That was part of an agent's job. As usual, Lili was amused by the lizard-like, quick appraisal.

Stash said, 'Frankly, they took a lot of persuading. They said they didn't need a woman's magazine.'

Lili yawned, 'If they want me as a judge, then they've got to have *Verve!* as a sponsor.' The Japanese masseur started to attack Lili's left thigh as she continued, 'Oh, Stash, I've decided to do the Mistinguett film after all.'

Stash was surprised. 'I thought wild horses couldn't drag you away from your mother at the moment!' He looked serious. 'It's about time you got back to work again, Lili. We both know that I get no percentage if you don't work for six months. But you can't afford to be out of view for that long. *You* know how fast they forget, and how fickle the public can be.'

'Yes, but I thought that learning to love my mother was more important than money or fame; now I know that the best thing I can do for my mother is leave town.'

'OK, I'll set up meetings with Omnium.' He was delighted. Not only was it a great dramatic part, but it was the best vehicle yet for Lili's considerable singing

•

and dancing talents. She'd have to get fit fast, but that was the only problem.

Lili sat up on the massage table and pulled out the tortoiseshell pin which held her silky hair clear of the massage oil. 'It'll be fun to spend the summer in Britain,' she said, without much conviction. 'Though I can't understand why they want to make a film about a French vaudeville star in Britain.'

Stash shrugged. 'Maybe they got a tax situation; maybe Omnium has some money blocked somewhere; maybe a reciprocal deal . . .'

SEVEN

March 1979

Sir Christopher's coffin was carried out of the chapel at Trelawney; on top of it was a single red rose from Pagan and a nosegay of white daisies from their fifteen-year-old daughter, Sophia.

In spite of the dreadful weather Pagan had insisted that the funeral party walk to the private chapel from the stone manor house. A fierce Cornish wind blew from the cliffs, thrashing the blooming thickets of rhododendrons, whipping at Pagan's black veil and threatening to blow the sodden, black umbrellas inside out.

Pagan had insisted on an old-fashioned burial, and there had been an explosive family row when Selma, her mother's partner, had remarked that, as most of Sir Christopher's organs were now in the deep freeze waiting to be dissected by medical students, it hardly seemed worthwhile to bury what was left.

Pagan knew what had prompted her vicious remark. Selma had helped Pagan's mother to convert the debt-ridden manor house into a profitable health farm. Selma had almost succeeded in cheating Pagan of her inheritance, and Selma could never forgive the younger woman for the fact that one day the entire estate and the entire business would belong to Pagan.

'Darlings, don't come, I want to be alone,' Pagan had firmly told Judy and Maxine. So now Pagan stood alone at her husband's graveside, and the rain beat down on the big black umbrellas as the box that contained Christopher was lowered into the rich, red Cornish earth.

Pagan still couldn't believe that Christopher was gone and that, after her sixteen years of care because of his serious heart condition, her husband could have been wiped out by one careless driver's one careless moment. After long years of cancer research Christopher's team had been on the verge of a triumphant breakthrough, but now success had been snatched from him, and he had been snatched from her.

Pagan felt far away, as if she were watching the entire scene from the top of the tiny seventeenth-century church. Everyone present, including herself, seemed doll-sized as they huddled in the graveyard. As the priest intoned 'ashes to ashes, dust to dust' in the teeth of the gale Pagan wondered if there was a sinister reason why the grass in grave-yards was always so thick and green; she could hardly see the little yellow aconites which studded the turf.

Beside her, young Sophia cried silently into one of her father's enormous handkerchiefs. 'I'm sorry, Mummy, I can't stop crying.'

·

'It doesn't matter, my darling. Daddy won't mind you howling your eyes out.'

Why aren't I crying? Pagan wondered. She blinked her eyes to try to make tears come, but nothing happened. I *should* be crying, Pagan told herself, I've lost the only man who ever loved me. She tried thinking of all the tenderest moments that she had shared with Christopher, but still no tears came. Mortally wounded men on the battlefield often cannot feel pain. Similarly, some widows cannot cry, and although they often seem to be amazingly collected – almost unfeeling – they are anaesthetized by shock.

Suddenly a blast of wind blew Pagan's umbrella inside out and tore off her black velvet hat and veil. Blast God, she thought, for taking Christopher before his work was finished. How dare God do this to me! How *can* He? I did all I could. It's not fair. I can't be expected to put up with this. Why should I? I've done so much good. (Well, I haven't done much bad . . . Well, I've done less bad than most people.) What *more* does *He* want? Why did *He* have to pick on me?

After the mourners had left Pagan walked to her favourite cliff-top.

Her old sheepdog, Buster II, wheezed at her side through the dead bracken. Pagan sat on the weather-beaten wooden bench and recalled Christopher's black figure sitting here, hunched against the grey sky, when first they had met. Suddenly, Pagan no longer felt sheltered, like a big baby. She felt nothing: no misery, no

•

pain, no grief. Her body felt numb. Inside her head there was chaos but no feeling; her thoughts bolted crazily in all directions, like a herd of panic-stricken animals. Unwelcome pictures slid into her mind, and she remembered, with distance, her husband's knobby feet, the way his bald head freckled in the sun, and his irritating habit of loudly crunching peppermints. Pagan thought, how dare Christopher leave me alone? She felt bewildered, disoriented and frightened by her own feelings. She felt as if she were in a never-ending black tunnel – the Valley of Despair.

During the following three weeks Pagan was unexpectedly calm as she held meetings with lawyers, trustees and accountants. Then she began to forget things. Christopher's secretary quietly took over the organization of his memorial service at St Bartholomew's Church in Smithfield after she discovered that Pagan had forgotten to invite most of her husband's closest friends.

Every morning Pagan heard the newspaper thump through the letterbox and waited hopefully. She always thought, it isn't true, it hasn't happened. God wouldn't let it happen to me. I haven't done anything to deserve it. It must have been a bad dream and Christopher is really shaving in the bathroom at this very minute.

'I wish that I wasn't so terribly tired all the time,' Pagan complained to Sophia, 'and I wish it wasn't so cold in this house.' She sat, swaddled in her old Persian lamb cloak, in front of a roaring log fire, and added, 'Christopher was

·

so mean about the heating installation.' Sophia decided not to mention that, while the rest of London enjoyed an unusually balmy spring, Pagan's sitting-room thermostat registered 78 degrees.

Two days later Sophia came home from St Paul's school to find her mother pale but dry eyed, briskly digging a hole at the bottom of the garden. Buster's dead body lay under the plane tree. 'I forgot his lead, and the stupid dog ran off after a cat – straight under a motorbike. God knows what we've done to deserve two road deaths in one month. But Buster's time was up, he was almost twenty.' To Pagan, life was unreal. It was a nightmare from which she hoped, shortly, to wake up. Actions were meaningless. People were meaningless. Nothing in life made sense. What *was* the point of life?

The following day Pagan's old MGB was stopped by the police, doing almost 100 mph down the crowded streets of Ladbroke Grove, and she could not remember the registration number of her car. 'I have all these huge, black holes in my memory, officer,' she explained, but he didn't seem to understand. Bloody man.

'I do think, darling,' Pagan told Sophia that night, 'that your father might have picked a better time to leave us. I've no idea how he wanted to allocate the money from the première, and there's nothing in any of his papers to tell us whom to appoint as the new director of the Foundation. Why on earth should I be expected to put up with all this? Just what am I supposed to do now?' She prowled around the pink, hydrangea-patterned drawing room, thinking, who can I talk to now? Who can I do things with? Who can I share things with? Who knows my past, my jokes, my fears? Who am I supposed to spend Christmas with? Aloud, she said, 'Just what am I supposed to do now?'

'You sound like Grandma,' said Sophia bluntly, hoping that this unforgivable insult would shock Pagan into becoming, once again, her erratically adoring mother instead of this whining automaton. Pagan took no notice. She switched on the television, picked up a box of chocolates and watched a raucous game show until Sophia burst into tears and rushed out of the room. Then a black pool of cold panic started to rise in Pagan's body as she heard that Mona, from Chipping Norton, had won a hostess trolley, a facial sauna and a giant Donald Duck. What's happening to me? Pagan wondered. Why can't I control what I'm thinking? As she watched Mona scream with unbelievable joy and hug her husband, Pagan thought, why can't I behave as I want to? Why can't I remember things? As Mona, who couldn't think of the name of a peanut farmer who lived in a white house, was ignominiously bundled off the stage, Pagan thought, perhaps I'm going mad. Perhaps I'll go to the doctor tomorrow. She did not know that she was suffering from the classic symptoms of bereavement, that she was groping her way through the tunnel of death.

But the next day she looked around her kitchen and decided not to visit the doctor. There's no point in saving

•

a worthless person like me, thought Pagan, swinging from shock to depression. Doctors are for people who are really sick, not women who haven't enough self-discipline to pull themselves together. She looked around the cosy kitchen at the bunches of rosemary and thyme from Trelawney which hung from the ceiling, the well-used pans, the hand-thrown terracotta pots, the baskets of brown Cornish eggs and fresh vegetables. The delicate, pink-rimmed Minton dinner service she had inherited on her marriage was ranged along the ashwood shelves of the country dresser. Whatever is the point of trying to make a kitchen attractive? she wondered. It's just a food-processing plant, dolled up by pretty china. Plates always break in the end, however much you like them. Everything breaks in the end. Pagan took one of the Minton tea plates off the dresser, opened the window, threw the plate out and watched it smash in the basement area. That's what happened to me, she thought. My life is smashed like broken china.

Half an hour later Sophia stood in the kitchen looking at the empty shelves of the dresser. She had already noticed the pile of smashed china when she opened the front door. 'Mother, I'm going to stay in Tuscany with Jane for the holidays.' Defiantly she flicked spikes of auburn hair back from her face, silently daring her mother to care for her, daring her mother to say, 'Oh, no, you won't! You'll stay here with me.'

'Whatever you like, darling,' Pagan replied, absent-mindedly.

•

'Mummy, I can't stand seeing you like this any more. I'm leaving now,' Sophia shouted. Pagan took no notice as Sophia ran to her bedroom, stuffed two shirts and her tape-player into a tote bag, then rushed out, slamming the door.

Suddenly the house seemed quiet and empty. Pagan picked up the bottle of cooking brandy from the kitchen shelf and put it to her lips. She felt an emptiness within her. I am worth nothing, nobody cares about me, and nobody ever will again. I don't want to live. Life is my enemy and death is my friend. The future is black and pointless and threatening.

By midnight she had also drained the gin, whisky and vermouth in the drinks cabinet, followed by the Drambuie. She threw up in the kitchen sink.

Then she thought, I'm not going to let it happen to me again, and telephoned Alcoholics Anonymous to find out the date of the next meeting in the crypt of the church in Trafalgar Square.

'Now the openings – push against me, harder . . . harder . . . goddammit, will you take that away?' He poked a finger into Lili's stomach.

Lili shut her eyes and clenched her abdominal muscles with all her strength to pull her belly concave. 'It won't go any flatter,' she gasped between clenched teeth.

'Too much tension in your neck. Relax.' Again the Pilates trainer folded Lili's knees against her chest and leaned on them with all his weight. 'You'll have a back like Makarova by the time I'm finished with you. OK, that's enough. Now the weights.'

Lili moved across the studio to the fixed bed. Outside the rain lashed against the skylight; God, she was sick of this New York winter.

'Are you doing better in class, yet?'

'My ballet teacher's using me to demonstrate.' Lili strapped the black leather weight belts around her ankles.

The trainer believed her. Lili had been badly out of shape a month ago, and he had been surprised by her fierce concentration and tenacity. Accustomed to training professional dancers, he had seldom met with such a capacity for discipline in an actress. He knew that he could be tough with her, because she would fight back and try harder, whereas most actresses would burst into tears and he'd never see them again.

'You're not *Folies Bergère* standard yet, Lili.' He pushed her on to the exercise bed, where she lay on her right side, bending her right leg and extending her left leg straight in front of her.

'OK, up and down fifty times,' said the trainer. 'You still need more strength in that left leg.' He corrected her pelvis position and watched carefully as Lili slowly grunted to the fiftieth lift.

'Look – you're changing.' He pulled her upright, and in the mirror he pointed out to Lili the sleek, long muscles that were appearing on her thighs, the hollows in her buttocks, the flat, taut area below her breasts, where

•

•

her stomach muscles were developing. It was OK. By May Lili would be in shape for *The Best Legs in the Business*.

The old London cinema had been especially decorated for the rock concert. It now looked like a giant scarlet parcel topped with a silver ribbon bow. The red plastic wrapping bellied in the wind, straining dangerously at the nylon ropes that held it together. Each time the wind gusted, the ropes slapped loudly against the giant yellow sign which announced: ANGELFACE HARRIS: GIFT-WRAPPED. BRITISH TOUR BEGINS TONITE. APRIL 5 SOLD OUT.

Eddie thought life had been a lot easier for a publicity agent back in the good old days of punk, when everybody was broke but believed in what they were doing and all you had to organize, publicity-wise, was getting one of the band arrested at the start of the tour, then the ballyhoo took care of itself.

As he approached the star's dressing room, the door was flung open, and a girl was thrown out into the corridor, blood streaming down her lower face.

'You fucking cow,' she yelled, shoving tufts of black hair back from her pallid face. She struggled upright against the grimy wall, pulling the black leather miniskirt over her chicken-skinny thighs. 'You fucking fat London tart!' One hand checked the silver chain that pierced her left nostril, looped across her left cheek and hung from her ear. 'Who the fuck d'you think you are?'

•

•

A cheap, orange plastic toolbox was flung out of the dressing room. As it crashed to the floor the box burst open, spilling greasepaint, wads of dirty cotton, glittering powders and gels in a dozen crude colours.

'I'm his wife, darling, and nobody better forget it!' A tiny woman, wearing a white fox, floorlength coat, appeared in the doorway. 'Now get your skinny arse out of here before I do you an injury.'

'Now would that be this week's wife or the one before?' spat back the girl in the miniskirt. 'Or is this one of Angelface's special relationships and you're going for a whole month of wedded bliss? Someone ought to organize a grand reunion for Angelface's old ladies – at Wembley Stadium.'

There was a moment of electric silence and then Maggie, the fourth Mrs Angelface Harris, stepped forward on her six-inch-heeled, silver cowboy boots, and raised her tiny hand to the other girl's face. But instead of slapping her Maggie hooked two fingers through the silver chain that ran from ear to nose and yanked it hard. The girl screamed as blood spurted from her nose and streamed down the length of her body, like rain down a windowpane.

Eddie, the publicity man, muttering 'For Chrissake' as he ran forward, pushed Maggie aside, then hurried the bleeding, screaming girl upstairs to the box-like room behind the stage where the two Red Cross volunteers were reading paperbacks.

Eddie reached for the radio in the back pocket of his

•

jeans. 'Kev – the make-up girl's had an accident. Get a car round to the stage door and take her to the hospital. And there's a bit of a mess outside Angelface's dressing room. Get someone to clear it up.'

He walked into the dressing room and waved at Angelface Harris, who was standing at the counter, finishing his make-up. He wore only a dancer's support, the small black elastic pouch kept in place around his genitals by a G string running between his hollow-cheeked buttocks.

'Everything under control?' Angelface raised his cherubic eyebrows, widened his innocent blue eyes and put down the *Daily Mail*. Even with red greasepaint streaked down his cheeks, his face had an appealing urchin impertinence. Eddie looked at the white, sinewy body and wondered what was the secret of Angelface's legendary, evergreen youthfulness. Whatever he's on, I'd like some, too, Eddie thought to himself, as Angelface squirmed into a red-and-silver striped leotard and then clipped on a massive, winged silver collar, studded with rhinestones, which swept out beyond his narrow shoulders. Angelface now had a V-shaped silhouette of a body builder.

Of course, Angelface's musical secret was that he had always stuck, leech-like, to the spirit of rock 'n' roll, which was a mix of black American blues and American country music. Angelface had been one of the original rockers of the fifties; then in the sixties he'd re-invented himself, with a band, as a lead singer of the Dark Angels. Every time rock 'n' roll rushed up a blind alley, Angelface's career had wobbled. In 1967 he had been buried by psychedelic rock, but by 1977 Angelface was top of the heap again, and *Rolling Stone* magazine was wondering how many times this lovable old strummer could be recreated as Angelface relaunched himself in black leather and studs on the crest of the punk-rock wave.

It was simple, really, Eddie thought. Every time a new generation of fans rediscovered rock 'n' roll, they also discovered Angelface; two years older than Mick Jagger, he still looked as cute and skinny as the day he first stepped into the spotlight.

Maggie buttoned rhinestone-covered silver gauntlets around her husband's wrists, then fitted silver wings around her husband's Flash Gordon boots. Angelface peered into the dressing-room mirror and made a few, tentative passes at his eyebrows with the black grease-paint.

'I hate doing me own make-up, Maggie,' the singer grumbled to the bundle of white fox that covered his sulking wife. 'I wish to God you'd kept your hands off the make-up girl until she'd finished my face. You know I'd never touch a nasty scrubber like that.'

'Filthy bitch bled on me,' muttered his wife, sponging a spot of blood from the white fox. 'Right, I'm off to get me hair done for tonight.'

After she left Angelface sucked in his small beginnings of a belly and leaned towards the mirror again. Sometimes he wondered if Maggie wasn't a bit of a nutter. Chicks always got uptight when they thought it was expected of

•

them, but Maggie sometimes went over the top with jealousy. Last week she'd set fire to that chick's hair, just because he'd touched her bum as he came off-stage; one click of Maggie's cigarette lighter and the girl was a hospital case. This week she tears the make-up girl's nose in half. What the hell was he in for next? Angelface wondered as he picked up the telephone and dialled a New York number. 'Judy? Yes, it's me again. Gotcha at last. Listen, don't hang up on me or I'll reach for me lawyer . . . I'll *tell* you why I'm phoning. Says in the *Daily Mail* that Lili's due to film in Britain next month . . . I've told you before, I don't believe you . . . You know bloody well that the reason I couldn't help you when the baby was born was because I was as broke as you were, but that ain't the case today, Judy. Today I'm worth eleven big Ms and I want to get to know me daughter. I want to meet Lili . . . what d'ya mean, I *can't*. I'm entitled to . . . don't you tell me I'm entitled to nothing . . . it's a bit late to tell me that I'm not her father, and I don't bloody well believe you, Judy . . . don't give me that line again about being irregular and getting your dates wrong. I gotta *memory*, Judy, and I remember you was crazy about me . . . Judy, I'd hoped that you'd be nice about this, but since you aren't, I'm *telling* you. First, I know I'm her father. She gets her looks from me, don't she? Second, I'm gonna meet her without telling her . . . because I'm gonna make sure she likes me for meself before springing the big surprise. And you can't stop me, Judy, so don't bitch it up from your

end, or you'll be sorry. That's what I wanted to tell you!'
Angelface slammed the phone back in its cradle.

In Manhattan Judy slammed the phone back in its
cradle.

And somebody in the adjoining room quietly, carefully,
replaced the extension telephone.

May 1979

Lili stalked furiously across the café, ripped the lighted
cigarette out of the man's mouth and slapped him across
the face. Energized with fury at her insolence, he grabbed
the cigarette back from her pouting lips. Again Lili
snatched it from his mouth, so he flung her to the floor
by the old, upright piano, then spat insults at her as she
scrambled to her feet. Then he grabbed her arm and
savagely whirled Lili into Mistinguett's famous apache
routine. Lili kicked the man and he dealt her a brutal
blow to the head. She fell to the floor again, and again he
dragged her upright. She spat in his face as he ripped her
skirt off, and so they danced on, portraying a lover's
quarrel, at the end of which Lili grovelled at the man's
feet in an ecstasy of masochistic passion.

'Cut!' Zimmer shouted. The technicians and the watching dancers softly applauded. Lili's magnetic animal sensuality effortlessly supplied the passion that was needed
for the apache number.

•

'Zimmer!' Lili called, still on the floor of the French café set. 'Do I really have to hit him so hard?'

'But of course,' Zimmer shouted back. 'The apache number has to be savage and sadistic. It's about the eternal battle for supremacy between a man and a woman. You *must* hit him hard; you are hitting back for all the oppressed women of the world, remember! That's it for today, everyone.'

Zimmer nodded. 'Action!' The clapboard snapped.

Thirty-six showgirls in flesh-coloured fishnet tights, holding up their ten-foot-long, white ostrich-feather trains, paraded down the glittering staircase, their tall feather headdresses nodding as they walked.

At the top of the staircase Lili stepped forward. She was wearing a few square inches of spangled gauze, a spangled chastity belt and a huge, blue peacock tail.

'CUT!' bellowed Zimmer. 'What is this on your legs?'

'Tights,' Lili shouted back into the dark emptiness beyond the pool of bright light.

'Get them off – I want shiny legs!' the director hollered. 'Take five, everybody!'

Back in her dressing room Lili peeled off the fishnet tights and said, 'I should have listened to you, Guy.' Guy Saint-Simon was Lili's personal wardrobe designer for *The Best Legs*.

'He's edgy because he's so anxious,' Guy explained. 'This is the biggest budget picture that Zimmer's ever made. He merely wants your legs to have that smooth,

•

shiny, twenties look. Let's get you into the silk tights.'

Carefully they eased three pairs of silk tights over Lili's legs. Lili replaced her spangled chastity belt, the designer fixed the huge blue peacock tail behind her, and they looked in the mirror. Lili wailed, 'My legs look like sausages!'

Guy nodded sorrowfully. 'Mistinguett must have had legs like sticks to get away with three pairs.'

Lili started down the staircase again.

'CUT!' yelled Zimmer. 'Your legs look like *saucissons*.'

'You wanted Mistinguett's authentic costume,' Lili shouted back. The technicians let out a mass sigh of ennui as another break was called. Lili released her cumbersome feather tail and ran down to the footlights, her breasts bouncing under their crust of glass jewels. 'Where are you, Guy?' She searched the darkness for the designer. 'Quick, I've had an idea.' The footlights flung dramatic black shadows over Lili's face and silken legs as she leaned over and peered into the dim stalls.

'Doesn't she look like an early Toulouse-Lautrec?' murmured Zimmer, who collected French music hall paintings, to his visitor.

'Yeah,' said Angelface Harris, 'that dwarf painter.'

Angelface had dropped his well-brought-up English accent. He no longer spoke correctly and enunciated clearly. Like so many pop stars, he dropped his h's and adopted a pseudo-working-class accent with a mid-Atlantic twang.

Angelface sat unusually still and silent as Lili pushed

●

back her cloud of hair and called again for her costume designer. She was the most beautiful, amazing chick he'd ever laid eyes on. And she was the sexiest chick he'd ever seen, he thought as he watched it all spill out of the spangles.

'Anyone screwing her?' Angelface asked suddenly.

He can't wait to get in there, thought Zimmer as he shrugged his shoulders. 'No idea. You can't meet her today. She's not to be distracted.'

But Angelface had not felt lust; he had suddenly felt a burning desire to flatten whoever was screwing his daughter.

Twenty minutes later, plumes once more in place, Lili again started down the staircase, her legs gleaming under a thick application of oil.

'Perfect,' said Zimmer as Lili reached the front of the stage, the microphone swung over her head and she began to sing. *'C'est Paris . . .'* Lili's confident, throaty voice rang through the empty theatre as the chandelier twirled and the thirty-six showgirls twitched their feather tails and stepped forward.

'She can *sing*.' Angelface sat up in surprise. 'Her phrasing is great. She's got a sort of harsh quality in her voice that chicks can't usually get. It's a strong voice and a sexy voice, but not a sweet voice.' Angelface hadn't expected Lili to be able to sing. But he knew who she got her voice from.

'CUT!' Zimmer yelled. 'Mike in shot.'

And so it went on. Unlike the rest of the cast, Lili was

•

in almost every scene and, when shooting finished at nine o'clock that night, she was too exhausted to absorb further criticism and her left eye had started to squint slightly, as it always did when she was tired. Nevertheless, Zimmer appeared in her dressing room with a sheaf of notes. 'About your singing, Lili.'

'I'm sorry I missed that top G,' she said quickly. 'I lose my range when I'm tired.'

'*All* your singing is wrong, Mistinguett, she had a voice like a cement mixer, you are singing too *well*. I want you to *rasp*!'

Three months with the Met's voice coach. Why did I bother? Lili snapped, 'If you want me to sing like Louis Armstrong, why not dub my voice with a cement mixer?'

A month later they were shooting in the countryside and Lili no longer had to try to roughen her voice because it was hoarse with overuse. A scarf was wound around her neck to protect it against the damp air of the May evening as Lili strolled by herself through the field.

Her calf muscles ached and her battered joints protested as she climbed over a five-barred gate.

Physically, Lili was exhausted, but mentally she was content. Halfway through the shooting, Mistinguett looked very promising, although Lili knew that you couldn't consider a film successful until you saw the final print. A film could be spoiled in the editing, badly dubbed or lost in a film industry vendetta, never to be screened. But the dailies were good and so was the atmosphere on

•

set. There was a hopeful buzz about the whole production. Zimmer was no longer tense and had even grunted, '*Pas mal*,' today. He was rapidly turning back into the charming, supportive colleague who had been the first person to treat Lili as a serious actress, and who could coax a better performance from her than any other director.

Swallows cruised against the iridescent pink of the evening sky as Lili sauntered into a muddy lane. On either side of the road rainwater chuckled down the ditches, bluebells gleamed in the hedgebanks and raindrops dripped softly from fern fronds. England was very pretty when it stopped raining, Lili thought as she paused in the middle of the lane to re-tie her headscarf. Listening to the faint call of the swallows, Lili was hardly aware of a thin, insect-like whine in the distance, until suddenly the whine became a roar and a black shape leaped from the corner in front of her, mud and water spewing from under its wheels. Lili shrieked as she threw herself against the hedgebank.

The car howled past her, then screeched to a halt further up the lane. A man in dirty mechanic's overalls flung himself out of the car and raced back towards Lili, calling, 'Are you OK?'

'Of course not!' yelled Lili angrily as the man reached her. This reckless fool could have killed her.

'I'm most awfully sorry.' He helped her to stand upright. She winced with pain and started to pull the brambles from her hair as he continued, 'I never expected anyone on this road, because it's private. And this part of the country is always deserted in May – even in the holiday season it's only used by ramblers. Are you on holiday?'

'No, I'm working and I can't afford a broken leg. Why don't you look where you're going?' Lili took a few steps and winced again as pain shot through her left knee. She took another step, felt sick with pain and staggered. The man in dirty overalls steadied her arm. 'I'd better give you a lift back,' he offered.

'No, thanks, I can manage.' Lili set off, limping, down the road, hoping that this idiot hadn't blown the film for her.

He caught up with her, running his fingers through his sandy hair, streaking more grease on his already dirty face. 'I'm so very sorry. I promise you, I'm a safe driver. I was just seeing how fast I could corner her, because she still needs a couple of adjustments to the gears.'

He'd be quite good-looking if he washed, Lili thought, in spite of her pain. In fact, he might be *very* good-looking if he cleaned the grease and mud off his face.

'Please let me drive you home – it's the least I can do.' Nice grey eyes, long straight fair lashes, big freckled nose . . . Lili agreed. The low cockpit of the beetle-black car was little more than a shell of raw metal with wires taped in different directions across the interior.

He drove very fast. 'Doesn't this car do less than seventy mph?' Why had she agreed to be driven by this lunatic? Omnium's insurers would probably cancel on the spot if they could see her.

•

•

'She's not very good in the lower gears yet,' the gawky, good-looking Englishman apologized. 'This is the prototype. We're still working on it, and I shouldn't have taken it out of the garage. Would you mind not mentioning to anyone that you've seen it?'

As the car stopped in front of Lili's hotel (a famous eighteenth-century coaching inn) her driver asked, 'How long are you staying at the Rose and Crown?'

'Another four weeks. I've got a part in the film they're shooting at the manor house. What's your name?'

'Gregg Templeton. What's yours?'

'Um . . . Elizabeth Jordan.'

He made no move to help her out, and Lili made no move to open the door. It was that awkward moment when two people who have only just met are both reluctant to make the first move and invite rejection. Eventually Gregg offered, 'So shall I see you again, Elizabeth?'

'It's difficult, we never get any time off,' she said truthfully. 'Why not give me your number and I'll phone you when I'm next free. What garage do you work for, Gregg?'

'Eagle Motors in Whitechurch. I'll give you the workshop number.' He scribbled it on the back of an envelope, then helped her out of the car. She winced again. 'You need a shoehorn to get out of that thing.'

'Please forget you ever saw me in it.'

'OK, your boss will never know.'

Gregg looked faintly surprised, then grinned.

★

•

LACE 2

•

On Sunday afternoon Gregg collected Lili in a beat-up Jaguar XK 150 drop-head coupé, which was as grubby as if chickens were kept in the back. After another fast drive they swept over the brow of a hill and saw Lyme Regis lying below them, the distant cliffs glowing gold and white, the pretty circular harbour cluttered with fishing boats.

'Can we go out to sea?' Lili pointed to the small fleet of clinker-built craft at one end of the ancient, stone harbour wall.

'Why not? We'll take a motor boat.'

After an hour ker-chugging over sparkling water they walked back to the town and, in a bow-windowed Regency tearoom, ate fresh-baked scones with strawberry jam and clotted cream. When Gregg passed his cup to Lili for a refill he noticed her noticing his grimy fingernails. 'My mother's always complaining,' he grinned. 'Drink up, time to take you home.'

And, to Lili's disappointment, he drove her back to her hotel, then waved a cheery goodbye without making another date.

Lili gazed around the cream, oval reception room at the London Ritz. Elegant women drifted across the pink carpet, greeting each other among the small tables and large palm trees. Behind them a fountain trickled over a naked golden giantess with a strangely prim expression.

'I'm almost enjoying my Merry Widow act now that I've started the good works part.' Pagan's cheerfulness

•

was brittle, Lili thought as the Englishwoman rattled on. 'Organizing your gala keeps me busy and stops me brooding. We can have Drury Lane Theatre on the last Sunday in July, if that suits you, Lili?'

'I'll have to check with Stash, my agent. He's coordinating with the choreographer, who's directing the show, and they'll check the date with the singers, the dancers and the musicians.' Lili poured out more tea; this weird British custom was habit-forming. 'Remember, Pagan, that we split up at the end of filming *The Best Legs in the Business*, and it's a complicated job to get everyone together again just for a one-night live show for charity.'

'I've got a terrific committee together to organize the evening,' Pagan enthused, thinking that Lili looked preoccupied. Again Pagan felt that pain in her chest. The doctor had said that it was merely another manifestation of grief; he had reassured Pagan that her depression, memory loss and strange behaviour were not unusual after a bereavement. He'd also hinted at another delicate matter and asked her if she'd been, as he phrased it, 'missing her husband at night'.

'If you can't sleep,' he suggested tactfully, 'tune your radio to the BBC World Service.'

He thinks nice women don't wank, Pagan had thought. But the following night at 3 a.m. she had remembered his advice, twiddled the radio dial, found some pleasant Mozart, then settled back and let black night wash velvet over her. Suddenly a cheery, dynamic voice had urged her to buy tickets for a rock concert in Croydon. Crossly,

•

Pagan had twiddled the dial, got what sounded like some soothing Sibelius, and recomposed herself just in time to hear the news in Dutch. As dawn blocked in the shape of her bedroom windows, feeling depressed and unsexy but wanting to sleep, Pagan had reached for Sheila Kitzinger's book on female sexuality, which fell open at the masturbation chapter.

In the Ritz tearoom Lili fidgeted in her gilt chair. 'What am I going to do about it?'

Pagan blinked. 'But we've already decided what you're going to do for the gala – a show based on some of the numbers in your Mistinguett film.'

'No, I don't mean that,' Lili waved aside the gala with one hand. 'I mean, what am I going to do about Gregg? Do you think I shouldn't have noticed his filthy hands? Do you think I embarrassed him? Do you think I came on too strong, Pagan? Do you think that tomorrow is too soon to telephone him?'

'Lili, you can't start an affair with some village mechanic, just because he's the only man you've met in the last five years who isn't dying to make love to you.' Pagan sipped her Earl Grey. 'Don't you think that perhaps you want this man so much simply because he doesn't want you?'

'I'm not sure what to think.' Lili sounded wistful. 'Except that Gregg behaves as if I'm normal.'

Pagan raised her mahogany eyebrows. 'Were you wearing that kit when you met him?' If so, Pagan couldn't imagine any man *not* wanting Lili, who was swathed in layers of pink-and-white knitting. All Lili's clothes

•

seemed to be made in Paris by Japanese men who had never heard of skirts, blouses or frocks.

'No, I wasn't wearing this.' Lili was defensive. 'I was walking through the mud in an old raincoat without any make-up and with a scarf around my hair . . . Pagan, *how* can I see him again?'

'You have his number – telephone him.'

'Oh, I couldn't do that! I don't want to look too . . .'

If you don't care about someone, Pagan thought, it is perfectly easy to pick up the phone and dial his number; but if you care, then all you can do is sit and watch the telephone and silently *will* it to ring.

'If he's a mechanic, why don't you get yourself the sort of car that demands attention?' Pagan suggested.

'You mean something like a Porsche?'

'No, not at all like a Porsche.'

'Naturally, you can't expect everything that you would get in a new model, but our own guarantee accompanies every car we sell,' said the fat salesman in ginger tweed. 'How about this MGB GT – a collector's item now, Madam.'

'No,' said Lili, looking around the showroom at the array of battered agricultural vehicles, decrepit sports cars and ancient saloon cars that had been carefully maintained by old ladies. 'I want the cheapest car you've got.'

'That would be the Riley, then.' Just another lady customer; they never laid out on a car. 'Totally reliable model, this one, Madam.'

Lili shook her head.

'We're expecting a very fine Ford Granada in to-morrow.' The salesman sucked on his pipe to imply trustworthiness.

'No, this is my only morning off.' Lili's make-up call was at 5 a.m. 'How about that?' She pointed to a tiny Morris painted with pink and orange flowers, cabalistic signs and the words LOVE and PEACE, none of which disguised the rust on the doors.

'Frankly, Madam, you would be taking your life in your hands. That's a trade-in we accepted from the hippy commune in Uttoxeter and it's only fit for scrap.' No profit on that one, the salesman thought; he'd better scare her. 'We could not give it our guarantee, Madam.'

'Perfect,' said Lili. 'I'll take it.'

Ten miles out of town the little Morris gave a despairing clank, shuddered and stopped. Delighted, Lili walked another mile to the nearest telephone booth.

Within an hour Gregg was fiddling under the battered hood. 'We'd better give it a run.' He pulled a dirty rag out of his pocket and wiped his hands. 'But I don't think this clutch will last much longer.'

They jerked in silence along wet country lanes until Lili saw a painted sign swinging in the breeze at the roadside beside a white, thatched building. 'The Magpie and Stump! We don't have pubs in France.' Dropping a hint was a new experience for Lili.

•

Picking up a hint was a new experience for Gregg. 'Want to go on Sunday?'

Next Sunday, after visiting the pub, they sat in the tin-roofed country cinema and watched *Spartacus*. It was raining and there was nowhere else to go. On the following Sunday Gregg hired a fishing boat and they caught two evil-looking black lobsters. 'Let's take them back to my hotel and have them cooked for dinner,' said Lili. She found it uphill work. At this rate they would not be holding hands before Christmas. But she sensed that, surprisingly, this gawky Englishman did not know how to make the next move.

'Your leg OK now?' Gregg asked as they drove past high, honeysuckle-entwined hedges.

Lili pulled up her chamois skirt and thoughtfully felt her thigh. 'Almost.'

'Good.' He did not take his eyes off the road.

They crossed the hotel lawn and approached the kitchen door. As they reached it a shower of pink-tipped white petals fell around them. Lili stopped and looked up into the lichen-covered branches of the apple tree.

'Oh, the poor thing – it's trapped!' She pointed up to a terrified ginger kitten stuck on the tip of a fragile branch.

'Stupid moggy. Shouldn't have climbed up there in the first place.' Gregg, like most country people, was not sentimental about animals. 'Can we get into that room?' He pointed up at the mullioned window close to the struggling kitten.

'Yes, it's the staircase window. I pass it every morning,' said Lili.

They clattered up the uncarpeted oak staircase and Lili opened the window, but Gregg could not quite reach the kitten. Every time he leaned out the window a little more the kitten retreated a little further back on the branch, then mewed more loudly. 'Cats always back off if you grab at them.' Gregg thought he was damned if he was going to risk his neck for such a dumb animal.

Slowly he twiddled his fingers as he withdrew his hand from the branch.

Slowly, the kitten followed the fingers.

Then Gregg grabbed.

'There, there, kitty, panic's over.' Holding it by the scruff of the neck, he handed the ginger scrap to Lili, who plonked down the eerily-moving bag of lobsters on the staircase and cuddled the kitten to her breasts, where it promptly hooked its claws into her white cotton sweater.

'Stroke it,' she said, pulling Gregg's hand to the kitten. His hand was much bigger than the little animal. Lili stood on tiptoe, shut her eyes, and kissed him full on the lips.

After a bit she said in a wobbly voice, 'My suite is just along the corridor.'

Lili's bedroom had an oak-beamed ceiling which sloped down towards the diamond panes of two small, stone-framed windows. The chintz curtains matched the yellow-flowered rug on the dark, polished floorboards; a copper warming pan hung on one side of the stone

•

chimneypiece, while a row of hunting prints hung on the other. All this tourist-trap, Manderley kitsch was spoiled by the cheaply made, flimsy, standard British hotel bed, covered by a slippery, green satin quilt.

Gregg pushed Lili's lips apart with his tongue and explored her mouth. She felt the muscles move in his back as she slowly slid her hands down his spine, and an ache of desire tugged between her legs. Gregg's soft dry lips brushed her throat, then Lili heard him murmur her name as his lips moved downwards.

Once in bed, Lili noticed, Gregg lost his awkwardness, but he wasn't very experienced, she thought, gasping as he nibbled a little too hard. I mustn't come on too strong, she thought. She felt the tremor in his fingers as he parted her pearl-pink lips and moved his fingers softly, cautiously inside her.

Ought I to be doing this with firm thrusts, or three fingers? Am I going to hurt her? Gregg wondered as, with small purrs she moved slowly against his hand. Where the hell is it? wondered Gregg, groping hopefully for the tiny seed-pearl lump. The tips of his fingers found a firm tip, like the point of a pencil under the soft, slippery skin. Lili arched like a leaping trout as he touched it. Got it, he thought with relief; no need to ask for directions.

After a bit Lili gasped, 'Now, now,' and he rolled carefully on top of her. With a sigh of joy, Lili welcomed him into her body and he began moving with slow, deep thrusts. The bed swayed and creaked with every thrust, releasing little clouds of dust from its chintz flounces.

•

Lili felt as if she were floating, falling, slipping unconscious, into a new incarnation as Gregg thrust steadily,
his lips brushing the pale-blue veins of her neck. The
erotic smell of his fresh sweat grew stronger as Lili pulled
him into her at every stroke, clenching her muscles around
his shaft to suck him into her body. The gasps and groans
and odd little bird-like cries grew louder in the quiet
room.

Then, suddenly, Gregg arched his back and shouted,
'That bloody cat!' he roared.

The frightened kitten had first hidden under the bed,
then adventurously it had jumped on to the night table,
where it had purred like a little sewing machine. Then,
with bared claws, it had dived on to Gregg's naked back.

Gregg swatted at the kitten and half fell off the bed.
The green satin quilt slid to the floor, and the kitten
skittered under the carved oak linen press.

Lili sat up and licked the tiny spots of blood on Gregg's
back. 'Forget Ginger,' she murmured. Sensuous and
eager, their bodies joined again. 'Lili, Lili, oh, Lili,'
Gregg breathed as the rhythm of his body became urgent
and inexorable. Lili realized that he was gone, he could
not stop, he could not hear her, he was unaware of
everything except that he was cresting that wave
which . . .

With a crash, the bed fell apart.

'I think the earth just moved,' said Gregg from among
the wreckage.

*
•

•

The sea was gunmetal, the sky was purple-grey, and black clouds collided overhead as they battled through the rain towards the end of the jetty. 'No chance of taking a boat out today,' shouted Gregg through the lashing rain and sea spray.

'Why is it that all the things Englishmen like to do make you cold and wet?' Lili yelled above the gale.

'Be fair, there are some things I'd rather do in the warm.' Gregg hugged her and their raincoat buttons tangled as he kissed her salty, wet lips.

'OK, I can take a hint. Let's get back.'

They turned and, heads down, battled against the shrieking wind towards the rocky beach.

There was a curse as the photographer slipped on the seaweed-covered rocks. 'Over here, Gregg,' he shouted. 'Just one shot – who's your ladyfriend?'

EIGHT

Early June 1979

Lili's face tensed as she looked at the photographer, but Gregg calmly turned to pose, his arm still around Lili's shoulders. 'Better make it just one shot, Eric,' he said pleasantly, 'I'm off duty today. This is Elizabeth Jordan.'

'How's the Spear coming along, Gregg?' The man reached inside his grubby duffel bag for an even grubbier notebook.

'Pretty good. We'll be racing at Silverstone next week.'

'I expect Sir Malcolm's over the moon, then. Are you going to run at Le Mans?'

'He's very pleased, yes,' said Gregg. 'But whether we qualify for Le Mans depends on how we run at Silverstone.'

To Lili's amazement, the man picked up his camera case, stowed his notebook and floundered back up the beach as Gregg said, 'Sorry, darling, I'm afraid I'm the only celebrity in town most of the time. That photographer was from the Dorset *Echo*.'

Then Lili remembered that on the hotel bed he had called her Lili.

'Gregg, you recognized me!' she said accusingly, her secure happiness starting to crumble like a child's sand castle washed by the sea. He had been lying to her.

'Of course, Lili. You're a household face. Anyone would recognize you, in spite of the headscarf.'

Lili sighed. 'I thought we might have more chance of a relationship if you didn't know who I was. Any nice guy runs for cover when he sees me coming, and the creeps come out of the woodwork.'

'I guessed it was something like that, because in a minor way I have the same problem myself.' Gregg helped her scramble back to the beach over the slippery, seaweed-draped rocks. 'I lied to you as well, for the same reason. My name is really Eagleton, not Templeton.'

'Oh,' said Lili. 'So you own the garage?'

'Yes.'

'What did he mean by the Spear?'

'I nearly ran you over in it. I'm a racing driver and I also design cars.' They tramped up the pale, pebble-covered beach to the car park, where he helped her into his battered black XK 150. 'I took over Eagle Motors last year, when my father retired. The firm was headed sharply downhill, but we're managing to turn it around.' He drove out of the rain-grey town and headed into the open country. 'The Spear's the first new car that we've launched for a long time. We're producing a racing model first, in order to attract the maximum publicity. Then

●

we'll go ahead with the road version; that was the car
with which I nearly ran you over.'

'But that was just a tin can on wheels!' Lili remembered
her first, bone-shattering ride with Gregg. A look of
annoyance flashed over his face as she hastily continued,
'What's it going to be like when it's finished?'

'That "tin can" will perform better than a Porsche and
have more prestige than a Mercedes.' They were driving
through a gloomy, dripping beech wood. 'She's basically
a four-litre, V8, turbo-charged engine which can produce
800 horsepower with four-wheel drive. She'll do about
210 mph.'

There was a pause. 'What colour is it going to be?'
asked Lili.

'Black, because the sponsors like it.' Gregg swerved to
overtake a cattle truck. 'When I appear on the track, I'm
just a human advertising board. Sponsorship finances our
entire operation.'

The car darted through heather-covered countryside.
'In the fifties Eagle Motors was one of the leading European
specialist manufacturers.' They swooped round the bottom of a sugar-loaf hill. 'My dad was once the European
Sports Car Champion, but you can't eat fame, Lili. I must
have been about three years old when Pa went bankrupt.
My first memory is of the bailiffs taking my tricycle away
from me; they took everything we had.' Gregg slowed down
behind a hay truck, then added, 'I'm determined to take us
to the top again – only this time the accounting system will
be as up-to-date as the maintenance log.'

•

They shot ahead of the hay truck. 'Once I've re-established our name on the racetrack, I'm going to launch our new sports car on the market. It looks as if we can get financial backing from the government. But first I've got to prove that I can deliver the goods.' The rain stopped as they turned into a gravel drive that wound between tall elms.

'Where are we going?'

'My home,' said Gregg. 'I live over the shop.'

The Eagle development workshop was a converted stable block at the rear of a large, ugly Edwardian house built of red brick. Inside the spacious workshop a number of black sports racing cars, in various stages of assembly, were lined up against the whitewashed brick walls. With careless pride, Gregg waved a hand towards a wedge-fronted, sinister machine. 'This one was sprayed yesterday.'

'It looks far more glamorous than the one you nearly killed me in,' said Lili as he opened the door of the glossy, panther-black car.

'It has a very special feature.' He patted the hood. 'It can manoeuvre sideways, crab-wise, for parking in town.' He ran his fingers lovingly over the black gloss gull-wing door and opened it for Lili. As she lowered herself into it Lili thought, cars are really sexy for men. Women don't understand this, because cars aren't sexy for women, they're just conveyors or status symbols.

'Not bad, is it?'

LACE 2

•

Lili recognized the Englishman's understatement. She also realized that she was falling in love with a man who was in love with a car.

They spent the next ten minutes growling round the laurel-edged drive and parking the Spear sideways. The car had a hydraulically operated fifth wheel and computer-controlled four-wheel drive. Gregg was as proud as a new father.

'Would you like a quick spin? We've got a practice track.' Like a big black panther, the car swooped, swerved and slid around the small circuit, spurting gravel and rainwater under the wheels. Eventually Gregg pulled the Spear up, neatly, in front of the workshop door.

Lili's knees were trembling, and again she felt sick as Gregg helped her out and said, as if to himself, 'The big question is, will the Spear be ready for the Silverstone Five Hundred Kilometre Race? If she performs well at Silverstone, it's been secretly agreed that we'll be allowed to race her at Le Mans next month. So keep your fingers crossed.'

'Why is Le Mans so important?' asked Lili, stretching her bruised legs.

'Because it is one of the toughest possible tests of a car. Le Mans is a twenty-four-hour endurance race, it goes on day and night. We'll need at least twelve pit stops to refuel and make minor adjustments,' Gregg explained. 'I have two co-drivers and we take turns at the wheel. The car hardly ever stops for more than two minutes and it's put under a fantastic strain. So you see' – he flicked a

•

wisp of grass from the wing – 'if the Spear finishes well at Le Mans, it will immediately be taken seriously by the racing world – and by the government.'

Back in the workshop, mechanics in grubby, once-white overalls were crawling around and under half-completed cars. Lili shook rain from her headscarf. 'Why are you working on Sunday?'

'They'll work around the clock if they have to; we're in this business to win,' Gregg said as they passed a mechanic who was bolting a power tool to the workbench. 'When I'm on the grid at Le Mans in the Spear, fifty people will have put us there, a lot of them volunteers.' They stepped over a pair of overalled legs sticking out from under a chassis. 'The support team does everything, from handmaking the parts here to buying my sandwiches at the track.' They passed a third pair of dirty overalls, bent over an engine. 'The team will drive through the night to get us to the race. There's never enough time, but they'll even work on the dockside at Boulogne if necessary.' Gregg stopped at the end of the workshop and looked fondly at a pimply lad in spectacles, who was filing down a bolt. 'And most of them do it for love, because I can't afford to pay them. Because they want to see Eagle on top again, just as it was when Pa was champion.' Gregg gently kicked a pair of overalled legs that stuck out from under yet another black chassis.

From beneath the chassis a voice said, 'Psychologically, the first race is the hardest, Gregg.' The legs wriggled out. They belonged to a small, stout man with an amiable red face and a beak-like, Mr Punch, nose. 'Gad, it's chilly under here, my feet are freezing. Let's go up to the house for a glass of sherry, and you can introduce me to this charming young lady.' Sir Malcolm held out his blackened hand to Lili.

Inside, the mansion was almost colder and clammier than outside, thought Lili as she reluctantly took off her white raincoat and enviously eyed the thick, shapeless, mauve knitted jacket worn by Gregg's mother. As they sipped sherry, conversation centred around the Silverstone race circuit. There were constant telephone interruptions from drivers, sponsors, volunteers and, finally, a London newspaper that wanted a quick quote for the diary page on what Gregg wore in bed. Lady Eagleton's serene grey eyes, a faded copy of her son's, did not register annoyance. 'In thirty years of marriage I've learned never to come between a man and his car,' Lady Eagleton said to Lili as Gregg was called back to the workshop, his father again called to the telephone. 'It's a pleasure to meet you, my dear. Gregg seemed to be keener on engines than girls. I sometimes think that motor racing is a disease, not a sport.'

'Don't you worry about him?' Lili tried to stop her teeth from chattering with cold. As it was June, the British considered it to be summer, no matter what the thermometer read.

'You learn to live with the worry. Eventually. My husband lived through a 180-mph crash.' Lady Eagleton

•

shrugged. 'Gregg's chances of dying on the circuit are one in seven. But they improve each year. I simply don't allow myself to think about it.'

'WHAT DID YOU SAY?' Silverstone was the noisiest place ever, Lili thought as Gregg, in a baggy white fireproof suit, climbed into the driving seat of the Spear. The Silverstone circuit looked like a cross between a filling station and a supermarket, set in a dusty, urban park. Behind the teeming crowds that streamed on both sides of the wide tarmac track, the dazzling billboards howled their messages like bright washing-powder packets. Every racing car, every racer, every mechanic, every ice-cream van was also plastered with advertising.

Lili could not imagine a more total assault on her senses than this riot of noise, colour, and stink, as Gregg shouted, 'I'LL SEE YOU IN THREE HOURS.' His lips poked through the balaclava which protected his face from fire. Then Gregg turned to his crew and Lili knew she was forgotten.

Two minutes later Gregg settled his helmet over his head, and the white overalled team pushed the Spear towards the starting grid.

The Spear, with most of the cars, roared off behind the pace car, then belched flame at a corner. 'IS THAT NORMAL, JOHN?' Lili asked Gregg's psychological advisor, a lean, bearded man with a mid-Atlantic accent.

'YES. DON'T WORRY, IT'S GOING GREAT, EVEN BETTER THAN AT LAST WEEK'S TESTING.' He led her

•

up to a glass box above the pits, where the noise level was lower. 'We shouldn't have any trouble this time.'

Lili did not understand why the car had previously given trouble. After all, it was an expensive car and, for the past few weeks, sixteen mechanics had crawled all over it, testing every nut and bolt, nurturing the car in every way short of breast-feeding it. She had not wanted to ask stupid questions of Gregg, but she didn't mind looking dumb in front of this kindly, ginger-headed Viking. So Lili asked, 'Why do so many things go wrong with these cars?'

John tried to explain in words of one syllable, such as could be understood even by a woman. 'A racing car is a sophisticated, complex mechanism. It always performs at the absolute limit of its capability. A lot of our problems are due to things like stress, high temperatures and fuel management microprocessors. Any human error is on top of that.' He turned as a Lancia limped into the pit next door with a plume of acrid, black smoke rising from its exhaust pipe. The mechanics scrambled to their posts like fighter pilots. John nodded. 'That Lancia went out on the track as perfect and precisely assembled as the team could manage, but it is being driven at speeds up to two hundred miles an hour for hundreds, perhaps thousands, of miles nonstop. Like a racehorse, the entire machine is designed for performance and nothing else. In order to get the speed that's necessary to win, the car has to be constantly pushed to its limit. So, inevitably, you get trouble.'

•

As the lead car passed the pits in a blur of green and orange Lili asked the last of the questions that she'd been dying to ask for weeks. 'What makes a good driver, John?'

He wiped his hands on a rag. 'Hair-trigger reactions, concentration and control. It's a young man's game; a driver starts to slow down when he's about thirty, but you also need an older man's mature judgement and steady nerves. While those guys are burning around the track, their minds are running like computers, and their bodies are sensing feedback through the car's level of performance and its speed. And, of course, they're violently competitive blokes, so they're always revising their own tactics to beat the rest of the field.'

'And does the biggest daredevil win?'

'There aren't any daredevils on that track. A good driver never takes an unnecessary risk. They aren't foolhardy boy-racers, they're cool professionals with a deep respect for danger; they don't fool around.' He handed Lili a pair of black ear-protectors and they turned back to the pit where Lili sat for two and a half hours, deafened by the snapping exhaust roars as she inhaled the stink of hot rubber and fuel fumes. The howl of engines drowned the loudspeaker commentary as the cars spread out round the circuit. The noise was all enveloping, relentless and extremely exhausting, like a discothèque under gunfire.

'Gregg's just made the fastest lap speed ever recorded by a trial car in its first big race,' John yelled in Lili's ear. 'ONLY ANOTHER TEN LAPS TO GO.' Lili felt her

•

headache lessen as the cars snarled into the last half-hour of the race.

Suddenly Gregg's team grabbed their tools and looked expectantly to the left.

The Spear appeared, cruised silently down the pit lane, then stopped.

Mechanics crowded round the back of the car as Gregg climbed out of the gull-wing door.

Ten minutes later Gregg noticed Lili. He stomped over to her, resigned exasperation on his face. 'Bloody gearbox blew up,' he yelled. Then Jack, the mechanic, who was doing calculations on a clipboard, held his thumb up. Slowly, Gregg grinned as a TV sports reporter shoved a microphone under his nose. 'So it's Le Mans next stop, Gregg, for the twenty-four-hour endurance race?'

'Yes, that's always been my ambition.'

'Are you going to celebrate this evening? Lili's giving a surprise party for you, isn't she?'

'If so, you've just spoiled the surprise, mate.'

'I don't understand why we had to come, Angelface, especially when no one invited us.' Maggie Harris looked round at the noisy party. The fresh-faced young racing crowd all wore Armani jeans and Cerruti silk shirts, with acquiescent Farrah Fawcett Major clones hanging on their arms. Nothing to worry about there, Maggie thought, as she dismissed her opposition with one flick of her eyelashes and glanced down at her white satin jumpsuit. From armpit to ankles, on either side, the suit

•

had a two-inch gap, crisscrossed by white leather thongs over her naked flesh.

Maggie stamped one of her silver cowboy boots. 'I don't know any of these boy-racers, Angelface, and neither do you.' She turned on her silver heels. 'Let's go. I feel uncomfortable. It's not as if you were singing.'

As she started to elbow her way through the ebullient crowd Angelface grabbed her by the shoulder. 'Oh, no, you don't! I expect my old lady to stick beside me, even when I'm gatecrashing.' His face had the taut, sunken-cheek look of a sixties-generation rock star. Angelface Harris was tough, as only twenty years of rock 'n' roll tours can toughen you, thought Maggie as the famous blue eyes glared from the halo of wild black hair. His voice was a deceptively mild, throaty growl as he said, 'Shut up, darling, and have fun.'

'Take your hands off me!' Maggie gave a quick look around the room and decided not to cause a scene; it was too early and too crowded. Besides, even if he was a promiscuous bastard, even if he was getting a bit over the hill, Angelface was still the best-looking man in the room, and if she stormed out . . . well, she wouldn't want him to stay behind, not with all this spare talent, fresh from the hairdresser, and him in his best leathers. Angelface's studded, black leather suit was moulded to his body and wrinkled around the joints like an iguana skin.

'You stay here and behave yourself,' Angelface growled to Maggie. 'I'll get us a couple of drinks.'

He plunged into the crowd towards the bar, where Lili

was greeting her guests. Angelface shoved his way past everyone until he stood in front of Lili.

He adopted his standard, lights-up pose – legs straddled, head on one side, hands clutching the neck of his leather jacket, which was unzipped to the waist. Lili blinked with the usual puzzled look of a hostess who can't recognize her friends when they're cleaned up. 'Er, hello.'

Angelface continued to give her the old, jean-creaming, lovable, lopsided grin, the look that had launched forty albums.

'Why are you staring at me?' Lili stepped back, and her pink taffeta dress rustled. 'Did my teeth just fall out? What's wrong with my face?'

'Abs . . . olute . . . ly nothing.' Angelface pitched his sixties cockney-sparrow charm, then started to croon softly, in a camped-up voice. 'You must have been a beautiful baby . . .'

Everyone stopped pretending they were not looking, and the party turned into an audience. Again Angelface pitched the crooked smile at Lili.

> *'When you were only startin'*
> *to go to kindergarten,*
> *I bet you drove the little boys wild . . .'*

He put his arms around Lili's shoulders, crushing her taffeta ruffles, and together they faced the crowd, moving rhythmically together, Lili smiling, but still puzzled. She hadn't realized that Gregg knew this famous rock star.

•

•

At this point Maggie started to shove through the crowd, muttering, 'So that's the reason we came, he's got the hots for that stuck-up bitch.'

She reached her husband as Angelface finished the song to a spattering of laughter and applause. Angelface introduced her to Lili in a silky, amiable voice which Maggie correctly interpreted as a threat.

'Pleased to meet you, I'm sure, Lili.' She smiled brightly, then whispered in Angelface's ear. 'Let's get out of here – and I mean it. Now.'

Angelface ostentatiously kissed Lili goodbye and swaggered down the staircase, his tiny, blonde wife hanging grimly on to his black leather arm.

'If my wife acted like that, I'd send her back to the works for modifications,' Gregg whispered to Lili. 'If looks could kill, you'd be six feet under by now.' Lili shrugged her golden shoulders, and turned back to her guests.

'You're obviously doing well, Teresa.' Lili leaned across the Parisian restaurant table and flicked the pleated chiffon collar of the other woman's purple Saint-Laurent suit.

'Not too bad,' Teresa agreed complacently, 'and the work isn't as draughty as making porn movies used to be. D'you remember how cold it was in Serge's studio, Lili?'

'He did it on purpose, to make our nipples stand out.'

'Sssh!' The waiter served two silver plates of ice-bedded

•

oysters to the glossy-haired, immaculately groomed women. Lili leaned forward conspiratorially.

'What's it really like, working for Madame George? Do you still go for the old guys, Teresa?' Lili was dying to catch up with the only female acquaintance she'd had in her youth. Teresa had been kind to Lili, and had taught her the rough, street wisdom of a high-class call girl.

Teresa said, 'It's a pity you can't stay overnight, Lili, and have a look at the office. Très chic, alors, to fly to Paris just for lunch.' She slid an oyster down her throat with a flourish. 'Working for Madame George is like working in a well-organized model agency. There are six girls in the office; they sit at desks, taking telephone appointments. We wait behind the office, in the pink salon, chatting, playing backgammon or watching television until we're booked out.' Another oyster vanished between her glossy lips. 'Madame George's drivers are all built like tanks, so you never get any trouble, and the accounts are computerized, so we always get paid on the seventeenth of the month. There's a fixed-fee scale for our services, and the girls are graded in categories.' Teresa carefully dripped Tabasco on the next oyster. 'Ever since that business with the minister, they all ask for me, so I'm in Category A – own chauffeur, own apartment, own maid and a Saint-Laurent credit card.'

'What are the men like?' She was genuinely curious.

Teresa gulped her last oyster, checked her lip-gloss, grinned and called for a second dozen. 'Madame George is a French institution, like the Louvre or the Crillon.

•

Any cultivated man knows about Madame George, whether he's a filmstar, a politician, a general or a nuclear physicist. We see them all.'

'But are they any different from the johns off the street?'

'A john is a john. Some are clean, some are dirty, some are trouble, some are not, some are fast, some are slow.' Teresa shrugged. 'So long as they have the cash, they all get the same treatment – the best, and the most discreet – from Madame George's girls.'

'You weren't very discreet when the minister snuffed it. What exactly were you doing to him, you naughty girl?'

'Poor Maurice always needed a little . . . assistance.' Teresa gave an explicit gesture and Lili choked with unexpected laughter. 'Madame George said it served him right, he always paid late. If we hadn't all been at a hotel, she could have hushed it up. However, every cloud has a silver lining. Did you see my picture in *Le Figaro*?'

'Yes.' Lili leaned over the bowl of cream roses and lowered her voice. 'That was why I wanted to see you.'

Lili couldn't think why she had ever been frightened on the small Eagleton practice track, as Gregg drove round and round it in the commercial prototype Spear, muttering to himself nonstop. 'Bit of understeer there . . . still running a bit lumpy at 7300 on the straight . . . don't like the sound of third gear . . .' The high-pitched scream of the engine hurt Lili's ears, the oily stink of fumes clung to her hair and clothes and the bucket seat gave her cramp. Lili did not care for the life of a racing groupie and could not understand why Gregg seemed to prefer driving round and round this track to being in bed with her. There was always some excuse. He wouldn't do it for two days before a race, he was too exhausted the night after, and he seemed to spend every second night in the workshop, bent over some greasy hunk of malfunctioning machinery.

'Why can't I drive it?' Lili suddenly suggested.

Gregg laughed.

'No, I'm serious, Gregg. I can drive sports cars. I've got a Porsche in Paris.' She leaned across and lightly raked her fingernails down his inner thigh. 'I'll tickle you to death if you don't let me.'

Gregg wriggled and grinned. Lili added, 'After all, the commercial Spear is supposed to be driven by ordinary drivers like me!'

Eventually Gregg agreed. 'Go easy on the gas, the acceleration's pretty fierce.' He demonstrated the controls and then they changed seats. Gingerly Lili put the car in first gear. The machine leaped forward like a hunting leopard, then bounded down the drive and swooped into the green-fringed lane. At first Lili felt as if the machine were a savage, living thing that was running away with her, but once she became used to the power beneath her foot she felt exhilarated by the sense of danger and mastery that it gave her, as they hurtled between the pink-campion-sprinkled hedgebanks and wind tore through

•

the prototype's glassless side windows. Ostentatiously Lili double-declutched as they plummeted down the sugar-loaf hill.

Gregg yelled, 'Go easy, this is a blind corner!' They were on it and round it before he had finished speaking; then, simultaneously, they saw that the road ahead was blocked with languid black-and-white cows.

Lili swung the wheel over and boldly headed for the open gateway through which the cows had just passed. She hit the brakes too hard. The car skidded on the muddy road surface, hit the bank with a sickening crunch, turned on its back, skidded along the slippery road, then slowed to a halt within inches of the terrified, stampeding cattle.

'Are you all right, Lili?' Gregg yelled as they hung upside down from their safety belts in the crumpled wreck of the Spear.

'Lili, you can't be serious!' Maxine protested. 'My butler tells me that you need another bedroom. Don't you and Gregg . . . er . . . I mean, aren't you . . .'

'Not for two days before a race.' Lili pulled a face, picked up a silver hairbrush and turned to the mirror. 'And as it's Le Mans, I'm to live like a nun all week. I had to promise not to seduce him, otherwise he seriously told me that he was going to share a trailer with the Spear team.' Gregg was affectionate, passionate, considerate and inexhaustible – but he spent almost every waking moment in that damn garage, passionately absorbed by those damn cars.

•

Men! thought Maxine, oddly comforted as she looked at Lili's beautiful, resigned face. Charles was just as bad. It had been weeks since that bitch Simone had left, but Maxine's husband still slept in his dressing room. Her bedroom had been redecorated in voluptuous shades of claret and a group of dishevelled Fragonard beauties hung provocatively on one wall. But Charles had not yet seen them, and Maxine did not know what to do next; she and her husband were on speaking terms – overpolite, in fact – but the air was still unfriendly.

'It's because of the Spear that I met him and because of the Spear that I hardly see him,' Lili gloomed. 'I just happened to turn up at the wrong moment in his life. Right now he needs every ounce of energy and concentration and effort for my rival, the Spear. And he's still got the big excuse.' Lili slowly started to brush her black hair. 'He's still bruised from our car crash, and he's supposed to rest his ankle. As the whole thing was my fault, I can hardly kick up a fuss, not when his whole future depends on this race at Le Mans.'

A distant engine snarled over gravel; from the terrace below rose a cloud of agitated doves. Lili jumped up and dropped her hairbrush. 'That must be Gregg!'

'What's their verdict on the fuel, Jack?' Gregg asked anxiously. Bleary-eyed from lack of sleep, the chief mechanic had just returned to the trailer after presenting the Spear in Le Mans town square for scrutinizing. He had been there for eight hours.

•

'Last thing they worried about, but there was a long wrangle over the driver's footwell measurements; bloody Frogs spent an hour crawling over her, taking measurements. In the end it came down to an interpretation of how the measurements were taken.'

'They're bastards about the regulations. Did you send in Johnnie Walker?' They didn't want to be disqualified on a technicality before the race started.

'Two cases. It did the trick.' Jack slapped him on the shoulder. The Eagle team's equipment included three crates of Scotch whisky with which to smooth the Spear's path through the maze of pettily enforced French regulations.

'Better not risk disqualification,' Gregg decided. 'We can reshape the footwell overnight.'

Lili drove back to the Château de Chazalle alone and Gregg worked through Wednesday night with his mechanics. By the following morning the Spear's wheel bearings and gearbox had been stripped down, checked and reassembled.

On Thursday panic threatened after lunch, when the clutch was discovered to be a millimetre off-centre, which was enough to lock the system. The men worked fast, but not fast enough. At dusk they wheeled the car out. 'Nothing to be done about it.' Gregg's freckled skin was pale. 'We'll have to do the qualifying laps as she is, then work on the clutch overnight.'

Lili managed to persuade Gregg that another broken night in the trailer with his team would leave him unfit

•

to race, and reluctantly he agreed. So Maxine's chauffeur delivered him, white and tired, to the château steps just before midnight on Friday.

'We did it!' Gregg called triumphantly, plodding up the staircase towards Lili. 'Whatever happens now will be a bonus – we've qualified the Spear, we're in the race and that's the main thing.'

'What did you do about the clutch?' Lili asked as they both sat in the small yellow morning room. Gregg fell on the little pot of hot beef casserole and crusty French bread.

'Jack realigned it,' he said, between mouthfuls. 'He's a rare bird, works for sheer love of precision engineering. So much garage work nowadays is being a fitter, not a mechanic. They don't *make* anything and no real skill is needed. If something is wrong with a car, they simply take off one unit and put on another. But every nut and bolt on the Spear must be tightened to exactly the right torque. Do you know, I can take my hands off the steering wheel on the Mulsanne Straight at two hundred miles an hour and hardly feel it?'

Lili picked up one of his big, grease-stained hands and kissed it. 'Why would anyone want to take his hands off the steering wheel anywhere at two hundred miles an hour?'

The moon cast black, calm shadows over the undulating silver sand. Beyond the flames that leaped from the huge campfire King Abdullah could see the necks and swaying,

•

supercilious heads of the camel herd, silhouetted against the sky. They had been couched for the night and their knees had been tied to prevent them straying. In spite of jeeps, helicopters and light planes, the most reliable desert transport was still the camel, Abdullah reflected. A camel ate very little, only needed a drink every five days, could survive twenty waterless days if it found grazing, and could carry 600 pounds of freight strapped to its back.

The Hakem tribe had spent much of the day racing camels in the desert and Abdullah had won the main race. The King's camel race win was now being celebrated by the poet of the tribe, a greybeard in black robes, who invented the verses as he declaimed them around the leaping yellow flames of dried camel dung and dead wood. Whenever Abdullah's name was mentioned, the men yelled and fired their rifles into the air in salute.

Opposite the King the firelight shone on the excited little face of twelve-year-old Prince Hassan, the King's nephew and his heir. Abdullah had brought Hassan to the Hakem mansef to present the boy to the tribe over whom, one day, he would rule. It was the fourteenth mansef that Prince Hassan had attended this month. Abdullah made these formal visits to only the most important sheikhs in his domain and it was on these trips that he recruited his soldiers. The freedom of his country depended on the loyalty of the army. Fighting was the price one had to pay for being a small, backward, oil-rich country that was strategically important to the Western powers.

•

The poet finished and harsh, guttural voices barked loudly in the night as the warriors started to reminisce of past fights, past camels, past hunts. The yellow flames cast shadows up into the men's lean faces, long shaggy black hair and black eyes that glittered like the star-spattered, black sky overhead. Tonight they would sleep on the sand around the campfire, protected only by their black cloaks from the chill night. Bedouins such as the Hakem tribe scorned comfort.

Thinking of his normal routine, the paperwork, the meetings with ambassadors, ministers, department heads and commanders, Abdullah felt a deep satisfaction at being among these tough, simple, courageous men who lived in the satisfying emptiness of the desert, where one day was pretty much the same as the next, and where time was not the master of men.

The feast was announced and the desert warriors followed their sovereign into the thirty-metre-long, black goatskin tent. At the entrance Prince Hassan stumbled and nearly fell. Abdullah glanced at the tired child as a white-robed bodyguard helped him to regain his balance. Inside the luxuriously carpeted tent young boys bowed and offered dishes of sticky dates and speckled figs. Bitter, black coffee, flavoured with cardamom seed, was poured from intricately worked brass pots into miniature cups with no handles. Gravely, King Abdullah allowed his cup to be refilled thrice, as was customary, and then they brought him the ceremonial bowl of camel milk, still warm from the udder and tasting slightly salty. When

•

SHIRLEY CONRAN

•

Abdullah had drained it, the sheikh of the Hakem tribe sprang to his feet and launched into the traditional welcome speech, spattered with overstated compliments, honey-flowered flattery and showy superlatives. He thanked Allah for the mighty Slave of God, which was the Arabic meaning of Abdullah, he praised all his deeds and wished him everlasting life. This took some time.

King Abdullah looked across the tent at Prince Hassan. The boy never complained and obediently performed all his royal duties, but obedience was not a useful virtue in a future king. Will Hassan have the spirit to control men such as these? Abdullah wondered as he glanced around him at the fierce, desert-hardened tribesmen.

Abdullah did not love his nephew. Since the death of his beloved son, Abdullah had loved no one and trusted no one. Abdullah had committed himself to no one and nothing except his country, the cause of his people, and his army. Abdullah's mother had died when he was born; he felt her death as a wistful lack. The murder of Abdullah's father provoked in his son only ice-cold anger. The knowledge that his own life was in constant danger left Abdullah feeling that deep involvement with any living person would render him too vulnerable to assassination.

Inside the tent richly-patterned carpets had been laid on the desert sand and heaped with tasselled cushions. Abdullah's watchful eyes moved warily from side to side, although he held his head still; arrogantly self-assured, with tawny skin stretched tight over the bone, his winged

•

black eyebrows met above a nose that curved like a falcon's beak over the wide mouth.

Boys in white robes carried huge silver trays into the tent, each one piled with a bed of rice, surrounding a whole lamb which had been roasted over a wood fire and stuffed with a mixture of cinnamon rice, plump raisins, pine nuts and almonds. Eight men sat cross-legged around each tray, pulling off bits of lamb and dipping them in the silver bowls of yogurt, rolling the rice into small balls with their fingers, always using only the right hand, because the left hand was used for sanitary purposes.

The boys served silver trays of kanafa, sweet cakes filled with white goat's cheese and served with hot syrup. The harsh wail of a primitive clarinet, the pipe of flutes, the insistent rhythm of the drums started; it was a prelude to the dancing and singing of traditional songs that were quavering ululations with no pauses, no rhythmic or harmonic variations, only repetitions of the wailing tune pattern.

Across the tent General Suliman Hakem caught Abdullah's eye, nodded and quietly moved behind Prince Hassan, ready to escort him forward for the presentation to the Hakem tribe. Gazing at Suliman's lean, hard face, Abdullah suddenly realized how extraordinary it was that Sheikh Hakem's son had accompanied Abdullah to the Royal Military Academy at Sandhurst. Together, he and Suliman had sat at those long, highly polished mahogany tables, sparkling with crystal, silver and candelabra, with everybody togged out in full mess kit and the strings of

•

the regimental band sawing through a selection from
Oklahoma! Suddenly Abdullah was sharply aware of the
dichotomy between his Eastern life and his Western life
as he remembered bicycling with Suliman from one class-
room to the next and drilling endlessly on the parade
ground in heavy, black boots. Together, he and Suliman
had learned how to handle an infantry platoon. Fully
dressed in combat clothes, they had together jumped into
rivers, bumped in Land-Rovers over mountains at night
and hurled themselves out of airplanes by day. Together,
they had been acknowledged the best horsemen and the
best shots at Sandhurst, which was hardly surprising as
they had both been riding and hunting in the desert for
as long as they could remember. Both, at full gallop,
could shoot a partridge on the wing, as could most warriors sitting tonight in this sumptuous tent.

The music stopped abruptly when Abdullah stood up
and made the ritual speech that asked the Hakem tribe
to pledge their lifelong loyalty to his house and his heir.
Abdullah then motioned Hassan to stand. As the boy got
up his eyes lost their focus and he tumbled forwards on
to the antique carpet.

There was an instant cry of alarm. General Suliman
pulled the boy upright, but Prince Hassan lolled against
him, unconscious and moon-pale. Abdullah's face was
expressionless as he ordered General Suliman to accompany the prince to the women's tent.

Sheikh Hakem flung himself at the feet of Abdullah to
protest his loyalty.

•

Nobody moved in the tent for ten minutes, until General Suliman hurried back to the King's side and whispered reassuring news in his ear. Prince Hassan had merely fainted, worn out by the incessant travelling and ceremony of the past month.

There was an immediate hubbub of relief.

As Abdullah washed his hands in the proffered silver bowl none of the tribesmen around him could have guessed how profoundly anxious the King felt. Prince Hassan had been constantly ill at Port Regis, his English school. Either the child was the victim of slow poisoning or else he was unfit to be a future king.

It was a blazing hot June day and the sun beat down on the concrete grandstand at Le Mans as gendarmes made periodic sweeps to control the crowds of hangers-on who swarmed over the track. The roars and snarls of the finely tuned engines could be heard far away, in the flat forests beyond the circuit, as the cars took their places on the grid. In the noisy, crowded grandstand an exuberant group waved Union Jacks and the black Eagle flag.

'Where's Gregg?' Maxine strained her eyes in the bright smoke-tinged air, but couldn't see the Spear in the line-up.

Lili wriggled out of the spectators' box and ran to the pit, where mechanics worked fast and silently on the Spear.

'Throttle's jammed. It's this bloody heat,' Gregg

•

shouted over the roar of starting cars. 'We're going to lose a lap.'

Lili watched as the cars tore off, hugging the ground in formation behind the pace car for the pre-start lap. Then, with a howling crescendo, they began the race. Before the end of the first lap the Spear slipped on to the track.

By the end of the second hour the Spear was lying in tenth position. Triumphantly Gregg jumped out of the car, shouting, 'God, that car's so beautiful!'

'Who's leading?' Lili yelled, as Gregg's co-driver shot off in the Spear. The confusion of heat, the fumes, the cheering crowds and the distant cacophony on the fairgrounds made it impossible for her to keep track of the race.

'Nannini in the Lancia; he's really giving it stick,' Gregg bellowed as the Spear slip-streamed past the green BMW Sauber C7 and gradually nosed up to overtake it.

Five minutes later the Canon Porsche spun out of control, hitting Jacky Ickx's Rothman Porsche, which spun briefly on the grass, then rejoined the race, having lost a place.

By the end of the fourth hour the Spear was lying sixth. Lili watched the car shudder into the pit with damaged balance weights on the front right wheel; the mechanics worked frantically to replace the whole wheel in twenty-five seconds. 'See why we need so many spares?' Gregg prepared to take over from his co-driver. 'This race really puts a car through it.'

And it puts the drivers through it, thought Lili as, for the first time, she found herself desperately anxious about someone else's safety. Suddenly the race was not dull, it was not exciting; it was frightening. Lili felt only cold terror for Gregg as she saw a Mazda 717 briefly balk the Spear, then both cars veered apart as they tore under the Dunlop bridge.

At the end of the fifth hour a double pile-up on the Mulsanne Straight took both Aston Martin Nimrods out of the race and left Gregg lying second, behind the leading Porsche.

In the grandstand Lili heard the name Eagle Spear in the crackle of noise that was issuing from the commentary loudspeakers. 'WHAT'S HAPPENING?' she screamed to Charles.

'HE'S IN THE LEAD,' Charles yelled back excitedly. 'THE PORSCHE HAS GONE!'

Gregg knew that eight more Porsche 956s were snarling up behind him. Porsche always dominated all the endurance races, thanks to the excellent German engineering. At Le Mans a car could self-destruct under its driver; metal would shear, rubber would wear away, plastic would melt; in twenty-four hours' hard driving, a car could simply fall apart around and beneath its driver. Only the toughest survived Le Mans.

The third gear felt ominously sticky as Gregg changed down, anticipating the slow right-hand turn at the Tertre Rouge. Andretti, in the Kremer Porsche, was closing up behind him. Gregg's left ankle started to throb and,

•

suddenly, he found it difficult to concentrate all his energy on the corner.

Then Gregg felt a stab of white pain, he heard a gnashing, mashing of metal, saw the world spin in front of him and fir trees rush towards him as the Spear shot off the road.

'Luck of the devil!' Charles threw his long, thin body into a velvet armchair. 'He crashes at two hundred and fifty kilometres and all he suffers is a sprained ankle.'

Outside the French windows of the château the bubbling song of a nightingale and the tart scent of lime trees drifted into the library. Exhausted by the emotion, the excitement and the anxiety, Maxine shrugged off her voile jacket and collapsed on to the blue brocade sofa. 'Ouf, it's a hot night!'

They were silent for a moment. The servants had gone to bed and the library was dark except for a dim, brass reading lamp. Maxine sighed. 'Charles, I'm exhausted. D'you mind waiting up until Lili gets back from the hospital? She was making a lot of fuss, but her concern was genuine. I'm getting fond of her. Maybe she really will settle down with Gregg.'

'He seems like a nice enough fellow.'

'And very suitable for Lili.' Maxine yawned. 'If he becomes the European Sports Car Champion, he'll have nothing to gain from Lili's success. He doesn't need to hitch on to her fame and, as he's not in the same business, their ambitions won't clash.'

Charles nodded. 'He won't feel threatened by her.'
Slowly he stretched his arms and legs.

'I can never understand why men find a successful
woman a threat.' Maxine eased off her white sandals.
'Women don't find a successful man a threat.' She lifted
her toes and wriggled them. 'Women think success is
sexy.'

Maxine stretched her tired legs out and rotated her
ankles. Even after twenty years of marriage, Charles
couldn't take his eyes off Maxine's long, pale, rounded
legs. Maxine knew this perfectly well, and so continued
to twirl them slowly in the dim, amber light.

Eternally pragmatic, Maxine realized that seeing someone you know nearly die really sorts out your priorities
fast. Charles had been nicer to her than he had been for
months as they drove back from the hospital where Gregg
had been taken. Delicately Maxine massaged her left calf,
thinking, our situation won't be resolved until he says
he's sorry, and he's never going to say he's sorry. But
Charles will always *show* that he's sorry, if I give him the
chance and don't rub his nose in it. She pulled back her
voile skirt and started to massage her left knee. Softly she
said, 'Charles, I'm sorry.' It was better to put yourself in
the wrong and get your own way, than to stubbornly
insist on being right and continue to be miserable.

'What are you sorry for, Maxine?'

'Everything.'

Charles pounced. 'Successful women are always over-
dressed,' he whispered in her ear as she squirmed happily

•

beneath him. Charles plunged his hands inside the filmy fabric of Maxine's dress, ripped off her peach satin camisole, and started to flick his tongue, lizard-like, over his wife's creamy body.

NINE

Mid-June 1979

Outside the Sydonite Embassy the June sun sparkled on the distant Potomac. A picket line of dejected feminists in jumpsuits carried placards that read ARABS OPPRESS WOMEN, ISLAM EQUALS MUTILATION and CUT IT OUT!

Wearily the cops cleared a path for King Abdullah, who flashed out of the maroon Rolls and through the imposing front door, followed by General Suliman.

'Mark Scott's exhibition is a great success.' His Majesty peeled off white gloves and thwacked them on to the silver salver proffered by a robed servant. 'And that leader in the *Washington Post* about the circumcised child was exactly what I'd hoped for.'

'If the World Health Organization really got behind us, such atrocities would be forgotten in ten years,' said General Suliman. 'Tomorrow Your Majesty will meet the Coptic woman doctor who led the campaign against female circumcision in Egypt. I have put the United Nations report on your desk.'

'What's the summary?'

'Only the Sydonite women themselves can stop this practice. A man may agree that a virgin bride need not be proven so by mutilation but the women do not believe that, when it comes to the point, a man will accept such a girl. Because of their fear, no progress can be made.'

Abdullah sighed, then asked, 'What's next?'

'The child specialist is waiting in the audience chamber, Your Majesty; then this evening you will preside at a banquet which is being held here, in the embassy.' The general stood aside as Abdullah strode into the audience chamber. Two neat, grey-suited men were waiting for him. Abdullah looked surprised. 'I was expecting you alone, Doctor.'

'My colleague, Dr Margolies, specializes in the psychiatric problems of adolescents.'

The King raised his eyebrows. The doctor elaborated. 'After examining Prince Hassan, I find that there is nothing physically wrong with him, Your Majesty. He is a healthy boy.'

'Then why is he constantly ill at school? He's missed so many lessons that the headmaster's warned me that my nephew may not be accepted for Eton. Yet two years ago he was a perfect student.'

'Perhaps too perfect, Your Majesty,' the psychiatrist suggested. 'Prince Hassan seems to be a quiet, well-behaved and studious boy, but he is abnormally docile for a twelve-year-old, and shows little sign of aggression or curiosity. He is exhibiting the classic behaviour of a child reared in an overly authoritarian home environment.'

'What has that to do with his illness?'

'Prince Hassan seems to . . . prefer being ill to being healthy.'

'If my nephew is malingering because of idleness, then he must be disciplined.'

For nine months of the year Prince Hassan attended Port Regis, a British boys' boarding school in Dorset. During the holidays Prince Hassan was tutored in twentieth-century history, military strategy, tactics and modern statecraft. For one hour a day he was permitted to play. This meant training his falcons with the keeper of the Royal Mews. Prince Hassan was not encouraged to play with children of his own age, because it was thought that this would make him vulnerable to kidnap and assassination attempts.

Dr Margolies said, 'Prince Hassan is not malingering, Your Majesty. His bronchitis and sinus problems are genuine, the physical symptoms are unmistakable.'

'Then I don't understand what you're telling me. Is my nephew ill or is he not ill?'

'Psychosomatic illness is a physical illness in every respect, but the underlying cause is not physical. In Prince Hassan's case, his lengthy periods of sickness meant that he was confined to the school sanatorium, where he was cared for by the matron, who seems an exceptionally gentle, affectionate woman.' His Majesty

•

looked perplexed as the psychiatrist continued, 'We suspect that your nephew's illnesses are merely nature's way of ensuring that he gets something he lacks, but which is vital to the well-being of a twelve-year-old. That is, the love and care of a woman.'

'Naturally, my nephew misses his mother.' Abdullah was puzzled. 'Sadly, my sister died five years ago, but there are women in the prince's household.'

'I don't mean female servants, Your Majesty,' Dr Margolies explained. 'Prince Hassan is lonely, and he is at the threshold of puberty. Normally, a mother encourages and supports her son as he grows to manhood. Ideally, an adolescent boy makes his first, inevitable mistakes in a nonjudgemental environment of encouragement and shelter. Without this, a lonely child might well lack the urge towards curiosity and aggression, two qualities that are necessary to any adult male.'

And especially so to a king, thought Abdullah. No Bedouin tribe would be ruled by a weakling.

At midnight a depressed Abdullah, followed by General Suliman, strode from the banquet hall, through beautifully carpeted corridors, towards his bedroom. He had not been able to secure the help he needed to defeat the Fundamentalist guerrillas, who now controlled one quarter of Sydon. American diplomats were being held hostage in Iran, and the United States did not want another overt involvement in Middle Eastern politics at such a sensitive time.

This evening's banquet, designed to smooth the nego-

•

tiations, had been a disaster. The old ambassador must be retired. Immediately. Clearly the wine had been ill-chosen, because the American guests had barely touched it; neither had they eaten the over-elaborate nomad feast. In fact, Abdullah had heard one guest remark to another, 'Greasy rice and tough mutton is bad enough, but, by the end of those damn speeches, it was cold as well.'

The three American women guests had looked ill at ease among the many silent Sydonites, who were not used to making conversation with women. The atmosphere had not been one of all-male joviality, neither had it been one of graceful hospitality. Abdullah resolved that his next ambassador to Washington would have a cultivated, intelligent wife who could properly organize, entertain and administer the social side of his embassy, like the wives of the Western diplomats. He had heard that the wives of German diplomats received salaries for supporting their husband's work, and, after this evening, Abdullah understood why.

Earlier in the week Sheikh Yamani of Saudi Arabia had given a banquet in honour of Abdullah. Yamani's chef had been flown in from the Paris Crillon, the white truffles came from Italy and the string quartet from Vienna. Tonight, by comparison, the Sydonites had looked like prehistoric savages. Without being told, Suliman knew how Abdullah felt; he was the only person who understood why the carefree, promiscuous Abdullah had turned into this grim-faced ascetic. After years of bravery and patience, struggling to preserve his country from

•

Communist infiltrators, after years of attempting to drag his reluctant subjects into the twentieth century, Abdullah was, quite simply, tired. He was also lonely and isolated, he trusted no men, and most women bored him.

Abdullah said goodnight to General Suliman, then lifted the red scrambler telephone. After arranging to replace his ambassador in Washington he opened the day's box of State Papers and began to work through them. At the bottom of the pile he found an engraved invitation with, attached to it, a three-line file update from Intelligence on Pagan, Lady Swann. Abdullah's black brows compressed in a puzzled frown as he recognized the handwriting on the invitation.

Behind her untidy desk, piled with brochures, gala programmes, opened envelopes, silver-framed pictures of her family, a moth-eaten rabbit's foot and old copies of *Horse and Hound*, Pagan looked puzzled as she worked her way through the morning mail. Again she read the thick, cream page, embossed with a crimson crest.

His Majesty, King Abdullah of Sydon, has asked me to reply to your invitation to the Royal Gala in aid of the Anglo-American Cancer Research Foundation on 31 July. His Majesty regrets that he is unable to be in Great Britain on that date, and will therefore be unable to attend.

His Majesty has further asked me to request the pleasure of your company at Ascot Racecourse on Ladies' Day to watch his filly, Reh al Leil, run in the Chesham Stakes.

•

It was signed with a squiggle, by an equerry.

But I didn't invite Abdullah to the gala, Pagan thought, checking the guest list again as the telephone rang. 'Yes, this is Lady Swann speaking . . . Oh, does he? . . . Hello? . . . Of course I'm surprised to hear from you . . . yes, I've just received it.' She turned over the letter. 'Of course I'd love to see you again, Your Majesty, but I'm afraid it's not possible . . . No, I'm no longer in mourning, but I can't go racing next week.' Pagan's automatic response to every invitation since Christopher's death had been to refuse it. '. . . not at all. I'm very busy, organizing a charity gala . . . A widow's life isn't as empty as you seem to think . . . it's just . . . it's just . . .' Flustered, she offered a final, weak excuse. 'Well, I haven't got the right clothes. You know how everyone dresses up for Royal Ascot . . . Oh, all right, Abdullah, I'd love to come.'

Pagan put down the telephone, thinking, that's the first time I've called myself a widow. It didn't sound so bad. She stood up and peered into the mirror over the mantelpiece. Anxiously Pagan counted her laugh lines.

Ever since she and Abdullah had first met, when they had been students in Switzerland, Pagan had possessed an almost magic power to make him discard his wary, formal attitude. Pagan could make Abdullah relax and laugh. In an odd way he had always regarded Pagan as a woman who belonged to him. She had been his first love and he had been her first love. He had never stopped trying to seduce her, even throughout her marriage to Sir

•

•

Christopher, and Pagan had never stopped refusing him; although the relationship was only a friendship, Pagan never told her husband when she was meeting Abdullah; although it was only a friendship, she always dressed with uncharacteristic care before racing off to the Dorchester; although it was only a friendship, Pagan knew that Abdullah could only think of a woman in sexual terms, so their friendly meetings wafted along on an undercurrent of unmentioned eroticism. As she stared at her reflection in the mirror Pagan felt hopeful, flattered and afraid.

An hour later, the doorbell rang, and outside stood a messenger from Fortnum and Mason, carrying a tower of dress boxes. Beside him stood the deputy fashion buyer, ready to bring a further selection if nothing was to Lady Swann's liking.

Pagan dithered between a green-and-white flowered chiffon dress and a pale-primrose silk suit. Then the deputy fashion buyer opened the hatboxes. Secretly Pagan thought that she looked wonderfully romantic when she wore a hat but, invariably, as soon as she found herself wearing one on the street, she felt overdramatic or silly. So she picked the smallest hat. The buyer looked doubtful. Pagan snatched off the little white sailor beret. The buyer confidently handed her a large-brimmed floppy straw, which folded back like a fisherman's sou'wester. The rich ochre straw framed Pagan's pale skin and mahogany-coloured hair. The buyer nodded. Every woman looked good in the straw sou'wester.

*

•

'Isn't she getting overexcited?' Pagan asked Abdullah as Reh al Leil curvetted sideways round the paddock, her chestnut neck stained with sweat.

'Isn't it natural for a girl to get excited on her first outing?' Abdullah smiled. 'I seem to remember that when you were a débutante, you were sometimes quite hard to handle.'

Pagan laughed, then again looked doubtfully at the filly. 'Look at her, she's running the race in the paddock.' The filly was dancing in circles around her groom, a telltale white lather of perspiration building up around her girth.

'Aren't you going to bet on her?'

'Not if she carries on like that. She'll be exhausted before the race begins,' Pagan teased him. 'Young horses are pretty much the same over a short distance, so I always bet on the jockey, like the rest of the punters. I'm putting my fiver on Lester Piggott, on number seven.'

'Golden Gondola.' Abdullah checked the race programme. 'The favourite. So you want to play it safe, Pagan?' She became aware of his soft black stare and the warmth of his hand on her arm.

'You know I've always been a coward, Abdullah.'

He smiled at her and clicked his fingers. An equerry stepped forward. 'Lady Swann wishes to place a five-pound bet each way on the favourite.'

'Abdullah, don't be silly, I was only teasing. Of course I'll put my money on your horse.'

•

As soon as he had mounted Reh al Leil pitched her jockey on to the velvet turf, and the odds lengthened to 100-7.

As the other horses cantered sedately down the course to the start Reh al Leil tore off at a gallop, her once-glossy flanks thickly plastered with white foam and her nostrils gaping wide and red.

She reared in terror at the starting stalls, again unseated her jockey, and delayed the race a further ten minutes.

When the starting gate finally flew open, Reh al Leil was twenty feet behind the other horses and heading in the opposite direction to the race.

'Wherever did you find that filly?' Pagan asked Abdullah as Golden Gondola set a businesslike pace in the lead.

'Kentucky,' he said pleasantly. At the first furlong Reh al Leil was the last horse in the race.

At the third furlong post she was halfway up the field of eight young horses, and showing extraordinary speed.

By the last furlong Golden Gondola had dropped back to third place and Reh al Leil, cheered on by the roar of the packed grandstands, was out in front, then triumphantly won by a neck.

'I'm glad I didn't bet on the favourite, she's lost a lot of money today,' laughed Pagan as they made their way to the winner's enclosure. 'She couldn't have gone slower if she'd been a real golden gondola.'

'Most modern gondolas are motorized.'

'How unromantic. Were there ever golden gondolas in Venice?' Pagan asked Abdullah as they watched Reh al

•

Leil, draped in sweat rugs, being walked steadily up and down.

'Yes. In fact, there still are, Pagan. Haven't you ever been to Venice?'

'No,' said Pagan. 'What's your tip for the next race? Oh, watch out, here's the Queen Mother.' With difficulty, Pagan curtseyed in her tight primrose silk skirt.

Afterwards Abdullah and Pagan walked slowly past the paddock to the sun-dappled half-circle of white rails at the end of the racecourse grounds. 'This is my favourite part of Ascot,' Pagan said dreamily as she watched the horses being prepared for the journey home. The farrier removed the light racing plates from Reh al Leil's oiled hoofs, and Abdullah rewarded the horse with a couple of peeled, scrubbed carrots.

'His Majesty is upstairs,' the ancient doorman told Pagan the next day, after directing her to the back staircase. Women – or lady guests, as they were known at Black's – could only enter certain parts of the club and they were forbidden to use the main staircase.

In the shabby dining room the walls were covered by gold-framed pictures of bloodstock. Elderly waitresses moved slowly from table to table. 'I see nothing's changed,' Pagan said to Abdullah.

'Nothing has changed.' Abdullah smiled back at her. 'The food is as bad as ever.' He nodded amiably at the Minister of Defence as he passed their table. The part of Abdullah that had been educated at Eton and Sandhurst,

•

the lover of field sports and a respecter of tradition, was extremely comfortable in Black's. The part of Abdullah that was proudly Arab detested the claustrophobic atmosphere of privilege and prejudice in the dim panelled rooms, where judges, politicians, churchmen and diplomats drank fine champagne from silver tankards, snoozed in old leather chairs and, although polite, really wanted nothing to do with dirty wogs.

In the early days of their friendship, when lunch at Black's had been a frequent event, Pagan and Abdullah had realized that the only way to eat well in the club was to order food that had been purchased from the members' own estates, which meant river fish, game and esoteric vegetables such as salsify and samphire.

Abdullah watched Pagan as she dipped slim green asparagus spikes in melted butter, then ate plain salmon trout with new potatoes, fresh peas and cucumber salad.

When the raspberries arrived, Abdullah ate them with his fingers, picking up each small red fruit, one at a time. Why should such a harsh man have such a soft mouth? Pagan wondered, watching him; his lips look as soft as Reh al Leil's nose. Pagan felt the elation of flirtation. She realized that not once, since they had sat down, had Abdullah taken his dark eyes from her face.

When the waitress removed the silver raspberry dishes, their hands were half an inch apart on the white damask tablecloth. Abdullah slowly stretched his fingers and Pagan felt the warmth of his fingertips.

Speaking very slowly and pinching her fingertips very

lightly between his, he said, 'I don't want to play games with you, Pagan, and I don't want us to mess it up this time. I want you. I want a real relationship.'

'I didn't realize that you have real relationships in Sydon,' Pagan babbled, speaking too fast in her nervousness. 'I thought you had political marriages.' She immediately regretted her words.

'Darling Pagan,' Abdullah said, thinking he'd like to thump her, 'we are not in Sydon now.'

'Will you be having coffee, sir?' the waitress interrupted.

'Why not have coffee in my suite at the Dorchester?' Abdullah suggested.

Pagan sat silent for a full thirty seconds, her lips parted, her legs trembling and her mind frozen with alarm.

Abdullah said a word he very rarely uttered, and he said it quickly, with force. 'Please, Pagan.'

'Why not?' Pagan heard herself agree.

What on earth am I doing? she asked herself as she glided down the back staircase, listening to the fears in her head. 'I'm a widow. I haven't made love for ages. I'm only used to Christopher. I must be out of my mind. I'm no longer the girl he remembers. He won't want me once he sees me with my clothes off. Arabs treat women like donkeys, and Abdullah's hurt me so much already. He's dangerous for me. If I get involved with him again, he'll hurt me again.' All her old feelings rushed back to frighten Pagan, the fear of private humiliation or, even worse, of public humiliation.

•

Internal red lights and warning sirens continued to blare at the back of Pagan's head as she reached the bottom of the threadbare staircase. Abdullah stepped forward, caught her in his arms, and pulled her out of sight behind a pillar. 'Don't you dare change your mind, you little coward,' he breathed, brushing her lips with his. She felt the tip of his tongue touch her lips, erotic and inviting. She melted, then clung to him. Abdullah said, 'Let's get out of here.'

At the doorway of the club they were stopped by a policeman. 'Sorry, sir, we can't let anyone leave the club. Another bomb scare. Please return indoors, and keep the lady as far as possible from the windows.'

Outside they could see that the road was crisscrossed by white tape; a police transporter was slowly towing away all cars except for a blue Ford on the right-hand side of the road. At the end of the empty street a small group of policemen chatted beside an ambulance, its door ominously open.

'What are we going to do?' Pagan asked Abdullah, almost crying with disappointment, but at the same time relieved. A group of club members, noisy with drink, was turned back at the door. Led by a rubicund bishop, they clattered up the staircase, back to the bar.

Abdullah led Pagan away from the door. He took her hand, quickly pressed the narrow, pale palm to his cheek, then kissed it and licked each finger with his warm tongue. 'I've wanted you for years, and I'm not going to be stopped by an IRA bomb.'

•

•

'Abdullah, stop starting, when we haven't anywhere to go. A bomb scare could trap us here for hours, you know.'

He kissed her palm harder, crushing his lips against it. 'Run up the ladies' staircase,' he whispered. 'I'll meet you on the top floor, in the billiard room.'

The billiard room on the top floor of Black's was as quiet as a cathedral. The windows were permanently covered by green velvet, so only a few motes of dust floated in the occasional ray of sunlight. In the green gloom stood two billiard tables. Larger than pool tables, they were made of smooth, heavy slate, covered by green cloth. Pagan eyed the polished boards of the floor, the narrow black leather bench that surrounded the room, and then the tables. 'Abdullah,' she whispered, 'we can't! Not on the table!'

'We can,' he said as he locked the door in the half-darkness and pulled her towards him. He kissed her slowly and gently. Then he crushed Pagan's body against his, and she felt the side of the billiard table press against the back of her thighs.

Slowly Abdullah took off the green-and-white dress, kissing each exposed area of flesh as he did so. He looked at Pagan in her plain, white satin slip, picked her up in his arms and laid her long, white-satin-wrapped body on the green baize table. The slate felt hard and cold beneath the cloth. Soft, slow kisses traced Pagan's collarbone, then she felt his lips on the delicate skin below, where the faint shadowy outlines of her ribs appeared. As his warm lips touched her skin she thought dreamily, I'm

•

lighting up, like the sun rising over the Swiss Alps, when the mountain peaks get that living pink glow that spreads slowly down to the valleys. Suddenly she realized that it had been years since her body had felt so alive.

Pagan's slip slithered off the table as Abdullah started to kiss her breasts, then moved downwards, beyond her ribs, his warm breath clinging like mist to the rise of her belly. Pagan suddenly thought of the dark velvet of a horse's nose, and the potential power of that animal's strength for danger and destruction. The tip of Abdullah's tongue traced round her navel and slowly trickled over her lower abdomen. Then, maddeningly, his lips returned to kiss her on the mouth, and Pagan felt the harsh fabric of his uniform, the hard metal of brass buttons against her bare flesh.

'But suppose we spoil the table?'

'Then the table will be spoiled.' He unbuckled his belt.

'Abdullah – please! What if somebody comes up?'

'They will find the door locked, that's all.' Slowly he undressed, and Pagan thought, why, he's treating me like a young horse. Act confident, make no sudden movements and never let them know you're scared. Having shed his clothes, Abdullah leaned over the table and kissed her body again until Pagan quivered, moaned and forgot about the table and the bishops and discovery as a warm brown arm encircled her long white waist. Abdullah's velvet-brown eyes looked into Pagan's pale-blue eyes, then his full lips moved forward as he bent to kiss her again. Then he pulled back, lips smiling, eyes dancing.

Pagan tried to kiss him, but he ducked his head. Giggling, they struck at each other like snakes, then finally surrendered in a long erotic embrace as they both felt the strange hard chill of the slate that lay below the bright green baize covering the table.

As she became increasingly conscious of the lazy warmth and sympathy of their entwined bodies Pagan felt her self-consciousness evaporate. The comfortable friendship, which had endured since they were teenagers, now wrapped them in cosy intimacy as Abdullah's fingers slowly caressed her body as softly as his lips had done before. He kissed the arch of her mahogany eyebrows, the fine bridge of her nose, the long line of her jaw. He began to kiss her breasts, nuzzling her right nipple with his lips, sucking, first gently, then more insistently. He's taking the whole afternoon to get to know my body, thought Pagan, tingling with ardour.

As Abdullah slipped his hand inside the back of her white cotton panties Pagan wished with all her heart that they were apricot satin and lace from Keturah Brown, and didn't have a safety pin on the side. She felt another flash of vulnerability as light warm kisses fell on her soft mound, and the hot tip of his tongue wriggled into the opening under the curls. Then she felt nothing but yearning, crushing pleasure as his hands slid under her buttocks and pulled her to him, so that he drank from her, like a cat lapping cream.

Repeatedly Abdullah swept Pagan to the edge of orgasm, then moved up to kiss her mouth again. Then,

•

slowly, he mounted her and began to enter her quivering flesh, pushing inside her a millimetre at a time. This deliberate, careful slowness made Pagan feel as if she were moving in a dream. When they had first met, Pagan had imagined what it would be like to let Abdullah make love to her. After her teenage decision not to let him Pagan had never allowed herself to regret it, or even to admit that there was anything to regret.

But she'd never imagined anything like this.

'Open your eyes, Pagan,' he breathed. As she looked at him, inhaling her own musky odour on his mouth, he pushed slowly on and Pagan felt as if she was being swept away on a foaming Hokusai wave. She gave a weak cry as her climax gathered, then broke over her. Abdullah held her body tightly to him, cherishing the communion of their flesh.

She did not cry, as he had expected, but lay quietly in his arms, mouthing gentle kisses with her narrow lips. Abdullah considered taking her again to climax, but decided to wait until he knew the long, pale body better, as gently he returned her light kisses and began to satisfy himself. He knew that he could sensually dominate the timid Pagan, but he wanted her to love him and to come to his arms with confidence. Later he would show her how to caress him, teaching her, as he had been taught, the art of love.

Afterwards they lay together in the green quietness of the billiard room, her long pale body and his brown one side by side. Faint bursts of tipsy laughter wafted up from the bar on the floor below, where the bishop and his friends still quaffed champagne from silver tankards.

With his lips against the mahogany hair that spread over the green baize, Abdullah whispered, 'When I first met you, I tried to imagine you naked, but I never could. I think that's when I discovered that, for me, you were different from other women, because I couldn't do what I wanted with you. I couldn't even undress you in my own imagination.'

Pagan pulled him towards her and felt the room recede, together with her sadness and confusion and timidity, as she felt the flesh upon flesh of their lips.

Then the bomb went off.

The explosion shook the entire building, including the heavy, slate-bedded table on which they lay.

There was an instant of silence. It seemed to last for ever. Then, glass began to fall in deadly waterfalls from the windows.

Snake swift, Abdullah scooped up Pagan and pulled her naked body beneath the billiard table. A cacophony of voices rose from below them. 'We should perhaps get dressed,' Abdullah suggested.

The telephone call from a call box in Kilburn to the *Daily Mail* news desk was semicoherent. A voice announced that the bomb had been planted outside Black's Club, and that they hoped the Minister of Defence had enjoyed his last lunch.

When the anti-terrorist squad discovered King Abdullah

•

•

playing billiards with Lady Swann, they realized how much more serious the terrorist attack might have been. This time, instead of the senseless, pulped-flesh carnage of the usual IRA bomb attack, there had been no casualties except for a superficial cut on the cheekbone of the uniformed doorman, who was reluctantly escorted to St Thomas's casualty ward, muttering that he didn't know what London was coming to, what with the Irish killing old women and children, the Iranians holding Americans hostage in their own embassy, the Lebanese machine-gunning each other, the Syrians hijacking airplanes and the Nigerians kidnapping their diplomats and crating them up for export. Sometimes he wished he was back in the trenches, he grumbled to the paramedic; at least on the Somme, you knew who your enemy was and where Fritz was hiding.

Abdullah turned to Pagan, who was huddled in the corner of his Rolls. 'Next time we must go somewhere quieter,' he suggested.

'Abdi, your driver will hear.'

'No, he won't. That's a permanent, bulletproof, glass partition.' He noticed that, for the first time, she had called him by his old pet name of Abdi.

'Will you spend the weekend with me? We could go where nobody knows you.' Abdullah's hand was insistent on her thigh.

Pagan gabbled, 'I couldn't do that. People would talk. It's only been five months since Christopher died and I was very fond of him, you know.'

•

'That is exactly why you need a few days away from life. A weekend in Venice. We could be there and back before anyone noticed.'

Pagan hesitated. 'What do you mean by a weekend?'

She felt his forefinger trace her calf, then her knee, then her thigh again. Pagan wished that she wasn't wearing chainstore pantyhose. She wished that she was wearing black, sheer silk stockings with black satin garters and lots and lots of lace. She'd better nip round to Keturah Brown before this trip to Venice.

Pagan walked slowly up the stairs. It seemed a very long climb to her bedroom. Once inside, the drawers of the Queen Anne tallboy were difficult to open. Where did I put my bathing suit? she wondered. Aimlessly she began to pull out clothes and throw them on the floor. Suddenly she felt something hard and knobby in her hand. She looked at it for a few moments before realizing what it was. The old red dog collar was worn and curled at the end; a few of Buster's coarse hairs were still caught beneath the metal studs.

Suddenly Pagan saw Buster lying dead on the road, then this was replaced by a different mental picture. Pagan saw the hospital sheet draped over her husband's mangled body. She felt her mouth open in a distorted scream. At last she felt tears in her eyes. 'Christopher!' she shouted to the empty room as sobs tore at her chest. Why am I crying? she asked herself. I shouldn't be crying.

•

Christopher died months ago. This is ridiculous. I must stop it.

One of Mark Scott's war photographs flashed into Pagan's mind. She saw a bombed building, exposed like an open doll's house to the outside elements. The flowered wallpaper was hanging in strips from the walls, the pictures were crooked, a chair and a smashed television set were piled on top of the rubble. Coats still hung from the hooks in the hall, but the end of the hall was missing. It wasn't meant to be like this, the building mutely said. That was how Pagan felt about herself and her altered life. One minute it was there, whole and complete, and the next minute it had been smashed. Half her life was missing, like half that building was missing.

Suddenly Pagan was able to accept that the life she had known was a thing of the past. It was gone for ever. She was able to accept that her situation had changed, that she had to make her own way in the world. She realized that she was not alone in the world, that she had known good times and bad times before Christopher died, and she would do so again. Life would never be the same again, but she would make a different life. Life would go on, and so would she.

Pagan could not stop crying. When Sophia returned home from school, she found her mother curled up on the bedroom carpet, still clutching Buster's collar in her hand and sobbing noisily.

'Mummy, what is it? Why are you crying?' Sophia

•

stroked Pagan's head and wondered what to do, who to call.

'I don't know,' Pagan howled, 'but I can't s-s-s-s-stop.'

Sophia sat down beside her and also started to bawl.

At last, together, they were able to share their grief.

TEN

Late June 1979

'They'll just have to wait for their money, my blood isn't bankable.' Judy wearily shoved a pile of bills off her knees; they slid down the fox-fur spread of her brown velvet bed with a menacing little shoosh to Tom, who was seated on the end of the bed. 'At least switching the printers paid off. We've saved a slice of this month's budget.' Noisily she blew her nose; her bout of summer flu just made everything that much worse.

Tom shook his head. 'I didn't want to discuss it until you were back in the office, but the colour reproduction of our July issue is way below standard.'

'The printers swear that they'll do a better job next month. Teething troubles, they said.'

Again Tom shook his head. 'Next month is too late. Lady Mirabelle Cosmetics has withdrawn the new fall campaign because they say our colour reproduction is no longer good enough.'

Judy's already pale face went white. 'When did that happen?'

'This afternoon. That's why I had to talk to you. A lot of advertisers have been griping; we've already lost a few of the smaller ones, but Lady Mirabelle's a body-blow.' Judy knew perfectly well that the Lady Mirabelle Christmas Gift campaign accounted for a big chunk of their revenue from September to Christmas. 'We can't replace that money,' Tom emphasized.

'Does anyone else know?' asked Judy.

'No.'

'Are you sure no one knows?' she persisted.

'No.' Tom gave a short laugh. 'Not even Tony knows about the Lady Mirabelle problem.'

Judy flopped back wearily on her cream silk pillows. Tom looked at her and thought, it's not like Judy to act so spoiled and sound so sorry for herself. And she hasn't got that much to be sorry about. Just because you were born poor doesn't mean that the world owes you a living at some later date. Parts of Judy's life had been hard, but they'd nearly all been interesting, and she'd had some really lucky breaks on her way to the top. Maybe she'd become over-ambitious, maybe they both had. Tom knew that was Kate's opinion. Trouble was, Judy wasn't used to losing. And they were both under great strain. Tom said, 'Judy, we took a gamble on the printing and we lost the gamble. But winners always take risks and sometimes they lose. Failing sometimes is a part of long-term winning. You can see their point, Judy. They aren't going to

•

•

spend millions developing plum colours, then run ads for them in a magazine that prints them light purple. Switching printers was a false economy.' Tom's usually cheerful face was strained. 'And there's another thing that you may have forgotten. All our business loans are guaranteed against each other. The PR company is still doing fine, and so is the property company, but they guarantee the magazine, which, in turn, guarantees our stock market investments . . .'

'Losses, you mean!' snorted Judy.

'. . . which means that we can't liquidate one part of our business without the domino effect. They'll all start crashing.'

'Tom, this is like a nightmare. A crash is what I've always dreaded, and you've always told me my attitude was overcautious. You always said that we were borrowing in order not to miss business opportunities. Why, only nine months ago you told me that we were worth two million dollars *more* this year. What about the Hoffmann-La Roche profits that you stuck in Swiss francs?'

'That was before our copper futures problem.' Tom looked uncomfortable. Judy had always hated him playing the futures market.

Judy said, 'I wish we'd sorted out the *Verve!* portfolio and separated the investment business from the rest of the company, as Kate suggested.'

'We just never got around to it. I wish you'd never run that interview with Lili! Let's both stop wishing and think positive!' He handed her the box of Kleenex. 'Our

•

financial situation is a house of cards; we've borrowed from Peter to pay Paul for months now and we can't go on much longer.'

'Sometimes,' Judy's voice was flat, 'I'd just like to take a plane and leave it all behind me.' She looked at the space on the wall where her treasured silk painting of a Manchu noble had hung until it had followed the jade collection to Sotheby's a few weeks earlier. Despite the warmth of the apartment and the thick fur spread, Judy felt cold and bone-tired. Why hadn't the *Verve!* lawyers picked up the danger in that fatal interview with Lili? Why didn't the First Amendment apply to magazines as it did to newspapers? How could one lousy paragraph of print have sabotaged her entire life's achievement? If I could wipe out five minutes of my life, Judy thought, I'd choose the time it took for Lili to tell me about Senator Ruskington.

Tom stood up, then picked up the heavy file box that contained their depositions for the hearing on the following day. 'I want you to read your statement once again before you sign it, Judy,' he said gently. 'We've got to get this absolutely right.'

Judy sighed, took the document from him and began to read it. 'At least after we win this hearing we'll wring a few thousand in damages out of the senator when we counter-sue for libel.'

'Nobody wins a lawsuit, Judy, you know that. Even if we win, we'll still be thousands of dollars in hock.'

'Not "if" Tom, "when",' Judy stressed, with weary

stubbornness. She hadn't achieved what she had by giving up easily. Tom said nothing and looked at his scuffed Gucci loafers. To change the subject he asked, 'Want to hear what's happened to Kate?'

'Of course.' Judy brightened as Tom pulled from his pocket an airmail envelope covered with neat, small hand-writing, with no loops or flourishes.

'"The hill-tribe guerrillas are getting stronger," she says. They've raided banks, attacked the Bengali settle-ments and the army garrison and she thinks they're secretly planning an assault on the oil companies. That will be Shell, I suppose. Her typewriter's been stolen, but she hopes to buy a new one on the black market, and she says she'll sleep with it chained to her wrist.'

'You don't seem very worried about her, Tom.'

'You know Kate. She hates a dull life, so I go along with what makes her happy. Of course I'm worried about her.'

'Hasn't anyone got any good news to cheer me up?' Judy picked up a second legal document from the pile.

'No news of Mark?'

'I've already told you, that's over. Mark and I were finished months ago.' She buried her head in her hands 'I can't take it any more,' she whispered. 'Why is it that the minute you're off balance, the vultures close in, trying to bring you down? Mark's in Nicaragua, and he's in Nicaragua because he doesn't care to be around unsuc-cessful, old me.'

Tom silently offered her another tissue from the box

on the rosewood table beside her bed. 'Judy, I can't imagine that anyone would leave you just because you're vulnerable or depressed or not sixteen any more. You're a complete woman, Judy, and an honest woman. I think you're the most honest woman I've ever met, and any man could love you for that alone.'

She shook her head and slowly wiped her reddened eyes. 'All that Mark really liked about me was the fact that I *didn't* need him. As soon as I needed him, *really* needed him, he ran away in the most destructive possible way.' Again the tears started trickling from the sides of her eyes. 'The crisp executive in me was irresistible so long as she was giving her attention to Mark's brilliant career and his home comforts. He was very pleased to live off my emotional strength when I had enough for two, but when I needed someone to take care of *me* for a change, he couldn't take it.' Judy's voice crackled with misery and she sobbed silently behind her hands.

Tom said, 'It's normal to suffer when a relationship ends. You get a few kicks in your pride, your dignity gets a bit dented, it's a diminishing experience for everybody,' he soothed. 'But Judy, you've only got to compare the divorce rate and the marriage statistics to know that people can split or hitch up any time, at any age. You're still attractive . . .'

'That's great, Tom, just great – that makes me feel like Methuselah's mother. "You're still attractive" means that when people look at me they can see the day coming when I won't be attractive any more. It means that time's

•

running out.' She blew her nose again. 'This isn't the way I want to end up, Tom, alone in bed with my work. This wasn't the rosy vision I had in front of me when I first ran away from Rossville to make my fortune.' She scraped her face with a tissue, leaving red weals on her cheeks.

'Don't be too hard on Mark,' Tom pleaded. 'I don't suppose either of us is the easiest person in the world to be with when we're under this sort of strain.'

'That's not it.' Judy pushed her fingers through her hair with a gesture of anguish. 'I'm not easy to be with because everybody's got the wrong idea about me. Mark's no different from any other man. To him, a woman in a top job is tough, self-possessed, independent – all the things he has to be to stay at the top of his profession. What he doesn't understand is that, just because I am those things at work, it doesn't follow that I want to be the same way at home. Like all you men, Mark thinks a successful career woman isn't interested in kindness, or caring and sharing, and he thinks I don't need it. But I *do*. I'm just as thirsty for love as any housewife running a couple of kids and a recipe club; the only difference is that I run a corporation.'

'Finish these papers, Judy, and then I'll take them all away,' Tom coaxed her. 'Crying won't get us out of the hole we're in.'

As Judy dried her tears and finished reading her statement, Tom turned on the TV in time to catch the late news. As he had anticipated, Senator Ruskington was interviewed with his loyal wife at his side. Her face

•

was serious and indignant. The senator answered the interviewer. 'This is indeed a most unpleasant case, which is why my wife and I feel that it is my duty to the public to expose this situation for what it is.' Expertly Ruskington turned to face the camera head-on. 'An unpleasant attempt to sell an unpleasant magazine through salacious innuendo and un-Christian lies. Any money which comes to us through this lawsuit will be donated to a charity which will be chosen by my wife.' The senator was glibly pious.

'But you are claiming ten million dollars in damages,' the reporter reminded him.

'Whatever the court sees fit to award us will all be given to charity,' the senator confirmed. 'My wife and I wish it to be known that there is not a shred of evidence to support the vile accusations printed in *Verve!* magazine. We feel it is appropriate that the people who publish this dishonest magazine should see the rewards of their evildoing.'

Judy shook her fist at the TV screen and gathered up the scattered papers on her bed. 'I'm going to go through these once again, Tom,' she said.

The woman TV reporter suggested, 'Some people find it hard to understand why you are pushing this case against *Verve!* magazine with so much vigour.'

'Attagirl!' Judy cried, sitting up in bed. 'I bet she reads *Verve!*'

The senator again turned to the camera. 'My wife and I feel that, until some person in our situation makes a stand, any so-called actress can draw attention to herself by linking her name with that of a prominent public citizen.' The senator paused for breath. 'I want everyone to know that our family is united in fighting this attempt to blacken our good name and to brand me as a fornicator and an adulterer.'

'But, Senator, isn't this also an attempt on your part to obtain a great deal of money?' the reporter prodded him.

'My personal reputation is worth more to me than any sum of money,' said the senator. The interview ended and Tom switched off the TV.

Tom left her apartment shortly after midnight, saying, 'Take care of yourself, Judy.'

That's what I've been trying to do for the last thirty years, she thought.

Judy remembered how depressed she'd felt in Switzerland, where she'd worked all day at the language laboratory and every evening and weekend as a waitress at the Chesa. She'd never learned to ski, she'd never gone to dances and she'd never had pretty clothes like Maxine and Kate. She still remembered her sudden bitterness when the young Pagan had, without thinking twice, returned the diamond necklace that Prince Abdullah had tried to give her; that necklace would have paid for Judy's entire year in Europe.

Judy never permitted herself to remember what it felt like to be really poor, because she panicked when she recalled having only one pair of shoes and one repeatedly

•

patched dress. But when she remembered her mother's hopeless face and the strained, tense atmosphere in their home for the two years during which her father was out of work, then Judy felt grim determination to succeed – at no matter what cost to herself.

Tom told me to take care of myself, she thought bitterly, picking up her ebony bedside mirror and looking at her face, which reflected the tension of the past few months.

Judy worked through the night on her deposition and finally finished it at six in the morning. She heard the maid's key in the lock, and called, 'Forget about breakfast, Francetta, and call me at eight o'clock. I'm off to Philadelphia again.' Then she drifted off to sleep.

'What time will you be home, Curtis?' Debra Halifax asked her husband.

He walked to the sideboard and lifted the silver entrée dish for a second helping of scrambled eggs. 'Usual time, I expect.' He wondered how it was possible to feel so worn and jaded at the beginning of a new day. 'What are you planning to do today, Debra?'

'I'm not planning to do anything.' Debra managed to make the statement sound like an accusation. At least, thought Curtis, she was eating again, although she did not seem to be gaining any weight. Dr Joseph thought that her infertility had been linked to her anorexia.

'Don't forget what Dr Joseph said. If you want to make a full recovery, you must start leading your own life and you begin by structuring your day. Why don't you go shopping with Jane?'

'You don't get over a nervous breakdown by going shopping. That's all I've ever done with my entire life. That's the trouble!'

'Now, Debra, Dr Joseph explained that it wasn't exactly a nervous . . .'

'Oh, yes it was!'

She's almost proud of it, Curtis thought wearily; it's her one achievement in life, the only thing she ever managed to do entirely on her own – have a nervous breakdown.

'Dr Joseph also said that what I needed was the love and support of my husband.'

'I do love you, Debra, and I try to support you,' Curtis said once again.

'Then why don't you spend more time with me?' she demanded. 'If you're not at the bank, you're at the Philadelphia Club or off playing golf or fishing with your friends.'

'Now that's not so. I spend a lot of time with you, Debra.'

'Not alone.' Her voice was vinegar. 'We give parties, and we go to parties; we meet the same people over and over.'

'But they're our friends,' Curtis protested.

'Would you say we have friends, Curtis? I wouldn't. We have your business people and your political people and our families, but we don't have any real friends, do

•

•

we? And I never have a spare minute, but I lead an empty life.' Again her accusatory tone flicked at her husband as Debra started her weekly moan. Curtis never knew what to say or what to do or what to suggest. 'Look, I've got to leave, I'm late. Why not take Jane to a museum?'

'You know very well that museums depress me. A museum wouldn't solve *my* problem. Not now that I know what my problem is.' Debra's voice trembled. 'There's someone else, isn't there? You're in love with someone else, aren't you, Curtis? That woman I saw in your office. I know she lunched with you yesterday, I saw it in your appointment book. She's always coming down to see you. You're having an affair with the famous Judy Jordan, aren't you, Curtis?'

'No. I see her on business!' Curtis felt exhausted as his wife's persistent questions continued. Debra had started to stage jealous rages over his imagined infidelity almost immediately after they married. Dr Joseph had explained that Debra's jealousy was the classic result of paranoid delusions. Curtis had bowed his head under the onslaught of accusation. After all, he had a reason to feel guilty, although he was pretty sure that Debra didn't know about it.

Gradually Curtis recognized that Debra said little which was founded on reason, and then, slowly, he had come to realize that his wife was not entirely . . . well. Dr Joseph used the phrase 'borderline psychotic'. After twenty years of marriage Curtis Halifax knew that his wife's grasp on sanity was easily loosened; her family had always known of this and now the Halifax family knew

•

of it, but the subject was never discussed. Debra was nervous, that was all.

Now she said, 'If Judy Jordan was only in your office to discuss business, then why was she crying?'

'I don't recall that she was crying.'

'Yes, she was. Or she had been. I saw her eyes.'

'I simply haven't got time to rerun this scene today. I promise you, there's nothing personal between us.' Curtis rose from the damask-covered breakfast table, gave his wife a quick, impersonal kiss on the forehead and left, late for his meeting.

Once her husband had left, Debra Halifax went up to her pink bedroom where, leaning over the hand basin painted with apple blossoms, she stuck two fingers down her throat and vomited up her breakfast. To disguise the telltale odour of her stomach juices on her breath, she swilled eau-de-Cologne around her mouth, then spat it out; the repellent taste was a punishment for having eaten two pieces of toast at breakfast. No wonder Curtis no longer loved her, she thought as she pinched her thigh. I'm fat, I'm self-indulgent, I've got no self-control.

Every time Debra looked up at her reflection in the mirror she really believed that she saw a lumpish, frowsy, fat woman, instead of a small, skeletal figure. She panted through her morning session on the exercise bicycle, dragging her body through the Rocky Mountain pro-gramme twice, then worked out with weights to punish what she believed were her too-plump thighs and well-cushioned stomach.

•

•

Afterwards, Debra aimlessly wandered through the quiet house. A lot of her day was passed in an uncoordinated mental state, in which she was never fully aware of the time, of where she was or what she was doing. She flicked through magazines, read a few sentences and left them. She picked up a piece of petit point which had lain on her worktable uncompleted for several months, sewed a few stitches and abandoned it. She watered a handsome Clivia plant, which the gardener watered each week in any case. Debra's luxuriant house plants often died because of their owner's erratic attentions.

For the fourth time that morning she picked up the telephone to call Jane, but the effort of talking was too much for her. Besides, Jane only liked being with her because Jane had no money. Perhaps Jane had her eye on Curtis. That would make sense from Jane's point of view. But Jane was a Catholic and she was married with two children. Always running through Debra's head, like the sound of a distant river, was the idea that Curtis was unfaithful to her with some woman. By midday, when the maid brought her lunch on a tray, Debra had formed the image of a faceless seductress who was stealing her husband away from her. By the middle of the afternoon, when the shadow of the magnolia tree was lengthening across the lawn outside, she hated this anonymous woman with murderous ferocity.

It was too hot in the garden. Debra drifted into the library and sat in her husband's chair behind the green leather-topped partner's desk. She imagined Curtis on

•

the telephone to his faceless mistress, while she, Debra, slept innocently upstairs. She imagined her husband whispering hot words of love and saw his features soften with affection and sensuality, as she remembered them during the first few weeks of their marriage. By the end of the afternoon the vision of her husband's infidelity was far more real to Debra than any real experience she had encountered that day.

One by one she opened the drawers of the desk and rilled through the papers she found in them. There must be love letters, but where were they? Sure enough, the small top drawer was locked. Debra scattered the pens from the pen tray, found the silver paperknife and forced the little lock.

Inside the drawer were some black-and-white photographs of a small girl, a pile of press clippings and a curl of dark hair tied with a white ribbon. Debra's claw-thin hand pulled out a few recent clippings and turned them over. 'Lili to star as Mistinguett', she read. So Curtis was fooling around with an actress. Debra shivered with rage. You may be young, beautiful and famous, Lili, but let's see if money can hurt you.

The Spear flashed by, unmistakably black among the white, green and orange bodywork of the other competitors at Brand's Hatch. Inside the hot cockpit Gregg sat in a pool of sweat; a driver could lose over five pounds in a long race. Ahead of Gregg a white BMW went into Stirling's Bend too fast, lost adhesion, ploughed straight

•

on to hit the bend hard and, as Gregg passed it, burst into flames.

Gregg suppressed the vision of his own body enveloped in flame as the Spear streaked past the grandstand for the fifth time. He listened to the high-pitched whine of the engine as he dropped two gears to set the car up for Druid's, the hairpin bend. Coming out of the bend, he saw the Dinetti-Mazda not far ahead. He's in trouble; I'll pass him on the Cooper Straight, Gregg thought.

By the end of the first hour of the 1,000-kilometre race Gregg was lying seventh, but the gaps were small and that meant nothing at this stage; a bit of bad luck could knock you right out of the race in a second.

He rounded Stirling's Bend, and accelerated away down to Clearways. He projected his mind ahead to Clark Curve, which always looked deceptively gentle, but which demanded extra concentration for a car with the power of the Spear. Gregg was now close enough to take the Aston Martin Nimrod on the top straight. He blinked sweat from his eyes as, three cars ahead of him, the green-and-white Jaguar shed a rear wheel with no warning, swerved into the barrier, then shot backwards on to the track amid a shower of sparks.

The Porsche behind it pulled out fast; the two cars touched but the Porsche managed to straighten up and hurtle on. The Nimrod driver miscalculated the Jaguar's continuing path across the track, and crashed into the spinning Jaguar. The two cars twisted together with a sickening crunch of metal, then the force of the impact hurled them both off the track, two seconds before Gregg would have hit them.

Now bathed in cold sweat, Gregg's legs involuntarily shook, and it took a fierce effort to turn his mind to the road ahead and away from the burning destruction behind him – of which he had so nearly been a part. Suddenly Gregg felt a thread of pain shoot up his left leg and his foot jumped on to the clutch. Must be that ankle. Thank God he got off the throttle in time. He'd hand over at the next pit stop.

Four hours later Gregg was lying close behind the leading Porsche, a position that, for the previous twenty-seven laps, he had grimly clung to, but had been unable to improve. Then the gap between the Spear and the car ahead began slowly to close as Gregg, sandwiched between two Porsches, crept closer to the lead car, and they braked for Paddock Bend.

Just ahead, Gregg calculated, a group of slower cars were bunched together. Gregg decided to make an immediate bid for the lead on the inside of Druid's, beyond which they would catch two of the slower cars. On Hailwood Hill he pulled out and left his braking to the last moment. The Spear shot past the Porsche as they entered the corner.

Gregg held the tight inside line, but slid out wide on the exit. The Porsche stayed behind; this was no place to retake. Then Gregg was weaving between the back markers in front of the South Bank stands, aware of a

•

crescendo of spectator cheering as he roared past with sixteen laps to go.

His ankle ached but the pain was easily bearable. It was really just a bloody nuisance. Inside the noisy cockpit Gregg could not hear the mounting excitement of the PA commentator. '. . . and with three laps to go, it looks as if Gregg Eagleton in the Eagle Spear is increasing the lead over the Porsche . . .'

As he hurtled into Dingle Dell Corner for the hundred and fiftieth time that day Gregg struggled to keep his eyes on the track. The pain in his left leg was increasing. Suddenly his sight became misty and he thought, dear God, stop me blacking out before the race is over.

The turbo-charged engine belched flames as Gregg missed a gear before the grandstands. Suddenly each movement of his injured foot produced an excruciating wrench of agony. He heard the voice from the Eagle pit over the radio link that was built into his helmet. 'Stick with it, Gregg, you're well in the lead now.'

'How much lead have I got?' Gregg's stomach was beginning to churn with pain.

'Fourteen seconds.'

No chance of pulling into the pit and handing over to his co-driver for the last few laps. Nothing for it, he was in this race to the end.

The next time he left Paddock Bend Gregg again fumbled the gear change. His injured foot was now so swollen that he could barely move it.

'Porsche is creeping up, Gregg,' the voice warned in his ear.

The Spear flew on.

As he pushed the Spear out of Hawthorn Bend his left foot had only just enough pressure for the clutch pedal, and Gregg felt vomit in his mouth. For a moment he lost his concentration.

Passing the Aston Martin Nimrod, the Spear swerved frighteningly close to the other car, and got off line.

The Porsche slipped through at Dingle Dell.

Through a rising mist of pain Gregg registered the delighted howl of the crowd, then the Eagle flag, to signify the last lap, was flourished at the side of the track.

Another mouthful of bile and Gregg lost concentration for another fatal second. The radio voice registered no emotion. 'Stephenson in the BMW is creeping up as well. Will the foot hold out?'

'Yes.' Gregg's voice cracked with the effort of controlling the pain in his body. For the last time, and in a maze of pain, he took the car around the tree-lined circuit; he could feel an internal grating pain in his ankle at every movement. He barely noticed the BMW pass him.

'Yes, the Spear is definitely in trouble. This is going to be a great disappointment to the Eagle team,' gabbled the commentator as they turned into the Brabham Straight. 'And, as the flag drops, it's first place to Werner Hentzen in the Porsche,' announced the PA, 'followed by Stephenson in the BMW and Eagleton just manages to scrape

•

third place in the Spear from Dinetti with . . . and something is happening to the Spear! . . .

From the viewing area above the pits Lili saw Gregg flash past in third place, then the Spear lost speed dangerously fast and began to weave towards the side of the track. The drivers crossing the line swerved to avoid the black Spear. One did not.

Lili screamed in terror as the white-and-orange Lancia obliquely hit the back of the Spear. Both cars spun off the track and the Spear slammed into a barrier. Ignoring Jack's shout of warning, Lili set off, running behind the pit area towards the twisted wreckage of the Spear, from which a column of smoke was now billowing upwards.

'Get back, get back, you stupid bitch – she could blow at any second.' A paramedic picked Lili up and half threw her behind the barrier.

The other paramedic yanked open the door of the Spear and pulled out Gregg's inert body. Within minutes the medical helicopter, with Gregg aboard, lifted towards Sidcup and St Mary's Hospital.

The PA blared, 'Eagleton is definitely injured . . .'

'A stress fracture in these bones, that's the cause of the trouble.' The doctor waved his pen over the X-ray plate. 'As your first accident was several weeks ago, and the injury wasn't diagnosed at the time, I'm afraid it's possible that the associated swelling and distortion may have affected the other joints.'

•

'So how long before I can drive again?' Gregg's face was bleached and strained.

'Difficult to say. We'll give you painkillers, of course, and a series of injections to reduce the swelling, but healing the fracture itself is something that we can't do much about. Only time will put it right.'

'But how *much* time? I've got to race in France again in three weeks.'

'The best advice I can give you is to forget all about racing for at least two months.' The doctor slipped the X-ray back in the buff file. 'Complete bed rest for a minimum of six weeks, and no hard exercise of any kind until you are one hundred per cent fit. With this kind of injury, nature must take its course.'

After the doctor had left Gregg began to work through his letters with his secretary until Jack arrived with a detailed report on the Spear's condition. 'She's looking good, Gregg – the fuel pump was as clean as a whistle this time. What about you? Shall we get Pete to stand by for Richard?'

Lili waited patiently at the end of the line of visitors. Then, as she bent to kiss Gregg, a young blonde nurse popped her head around the door to say, 'Time's up for today, everyone. Doctor's orders. Mr Eagleton has to rest!'

As the others moved towards the door Lili said sadly, 'I've hardly had a chance to talk to you, Gregg.'

'Sorry, darling, but I'm trying to run my business from a hospital bed. I've got to see Jack, my secretary, the

•

sponsors and Dad as well as you, and I'm only allowed
visitors for an hour a day. I know you haven't seen much
of me since you met me, but I don't want you to get the
wrong idea. You've met the team, Lili, and you know
what my responsibilities are.'

Lili looked down and sighed as Gregg said, 'I'm not in
business on my own, darling. Everyone in Eagle Motors
depends on me and I depend on them. I have to meet a
pretty large payroll every month to feed families. There
are men in the Eagle team working for me, for my father
and for the idea of a British privateer outfit in saloon
racing, who put in twenty-four-hour days on their
vacations. I can't let them down, Lili.' He reached for
her hand and pulled her to his side. 'I can't do what I
want, or go where I want when I please, or step into
that car at less than my best. It would be unfair and
irresponsible. You've got to understand that the business
comes first in my life, and I can't let anything divert me
from it, not even you, darling.'

Silently Lili bent and kissed him. 'I can wait.'

Debra Halifax leaned back against white broderie-
anglaise pillows and aimlessly turned the newspaper pages
until she reached Liz Smith's column. Suddenly an item
caught her attention and she read it aloud. 'Lili to star in
charity benefit . . .' Debra looked up, instantly alive, and
said softly, 'This is what I've been waiting for.'

ELEVEN

Early July 1979

The pink hydrangea wallpaper matched the heavy, chintz curtains, which were swagged back by tasselled gold ropes. A maple-framed portrait of Lord Byron hung above Pagan's desk. The back of the high satinwood desk was lined with tiny drawers and cupboards; silver-framed photographs, small bowls of potpourri, an antique silver calendar, jostled for space with a pile of letters that were weighed down by her long-dead grandfather's lucky hare's foot. It looked like a royal desk, the sort of desk upon which there was no space to work.

'Any other business?' Pagan looked around her drawing room at the eleven other members of the fund-raising committee that was planning Lili's gala for the Anglo-American Cancer Research Institute. They had discussed the rehearsal costs and the extra time demanded by the stagehands' union for working on Sunday; they had approved the programme design and the seating arrangements for the Royal Box. Pagan had joyfully announced that the theatre was sold out, and now her chewed yellow pencil was poised above the last item on the agenda.

'One final matter.' The organizing secretary passed her a letter on the blue writing paper of the Grosvenor House Hotel. 'Someone has offered to give a pre-theatre party for us.'

'How very thoughtful. Who is it?'

'Another anonymous benefactor, Lady Swann.'

Pagan skimmed the letter quickly, 'A champagne reception for two thousand guests! That's wonderful news.'

'Someone must think a lot of the Foundation.'

'Or of Christopher,' said Pagan, momentarily sad.

'Or of Lili?' the wife of the chainstore millionaire suggested. 'Perhaps it's one of her admirers?'

'He must have a bob or two to lay on champagne for two thousand people,' said the grey-haired merchant banker, who was smoking a cigar.

'We'll send the invitation out with the tickets.' Pagan leafed through her file.

'But is there time to print invitations?' The Scottish duchess looked anxious.

'Yes,' said the secretary. 'I've already checked with the printer.'

Pagan, notorious for the tight financial control with which she organized her fund-raising events, flipped through her file. 'Have we got the cheque?'

'The Grosvenor House Hotel has been paid direct, by banker's draft.'

'How *very* thoughtful,' Pagan said. She stood up and

opened a window, because she hated a room to smell of cigar smoke and it took at least two weeks to get rid of the smell. She walked back and leaned against the rather ugly, black marble fireplace, which was covered by a jumble of blue chinoiserie plates, a ginger jar, a Regency biscuit box and a small blue-enamel clock with a diamanté-encircled face that had been given to her grandmother by Queen Alexandra.

Pagan smiled at her committee. 'I'm sorry we've run a little over time, today, but this unexpectedly generous offer had to be discussed. Now, if you'll excuse me, I must dash or I'll miss my flight to Venice.'

The wind whipped at Pagan's hair as the high-powered speedboat raced across the lagoon towards Venice. In the distance she could see the grey domes of the cathedral, the imposing belltower in St Mark's Square, the candy-striped mooring poles sticking at crazy angles out of the water, and clouds of pigeons fluttering in the hazy blue sky.

Abdullah's private jet had flown them to Marco Polo Airport, and they were now heading for the Cipriani Hotel. In the launch behind them travelled Abdullah's four bodyguards and a great deal of luggage, most of which belonged to Abdullah.

Pagan looked at the enticing city rising straight out of the water. She was excited. 'Oh, Abdi, it's so beautiful. It's floating in the sea like a shimmering, gold mirage!'

'Don't expect too much romance,' Abdullah warned her. 'A lot of people loathe Venice.'

•

'Why, for heaven's sake?'

'The smells, the crowds, the claustrophobia and that dreadful, vulgar glassware.'

Pagan laughed. 'In that case,' she said, 'I won't expect any golden gondolas!'

'The golden gondolas only come out once a year, for the gondoliers' festival races.'

The battered, green crocodile suitcase that had once belonged to Pagan's grandmother was deposited on the pale-coral carpet of the suite. The walls looked hand painted with an airy green forest, which blended with the green sofas and the green-and-silver Fortuny curtains. Pagan rushed through glass doors that led on to a terrace lined with miniature cypress trees; it overlooked the orange trees that surrounded the hotel swimming pool and, beyond that, the entire panorama of Venice.

'Do you like it?' She heard Abdullah's voice behind her.

Pagan looked embarrassed and uncomfortable. She didn't know whether Abdullah was planning to share her suite.

Abdullah grinned. 'I shall be in the next suite . . . if you need me. Sadly, there is no billiard room in this hotel. Space is at a premium in Venice.'

The following morning, as Pagan waited by the two black-and-white-striped mooring poles of the Cipriani jetty, she clutched at Abdullah's arm. 'Look! You were

•

wrong!' A golden gondola bobbed towards them over the scummy green water.

Abdullah said, 'As a matter of fact, it's yours. I hope it's not too ostentatious for you.'

Under the golden, arched canopy, sitting on the faded, purple cushions, Pagan gazed up at the naked, golden backside of Neptune as he wielded his trident over the poop of the boat. To her disappointment, this glorious vessel was motorized, with a spluttering engine more appropriate to a fishing smack than a ceremonial barge.

The gondola chugged down the Grand Canal between boats delivering coal, Coca-Cola, Japanese tourists and gangs of workmen to their appropriate destinations. They passed pink-and-ochre baroque palaces, tidemarked by water, with ferns twisting their bricks apart and cobwebs veiling their patchy, peeling plaster.

'Don't ask the gondolier to sing Santa Lucia,' murmured Abdullah, 'because it is a Neapolitan song and he will grind his teeth.'

Pagan sniffed happily. 'I love everything about this place, even the smell.'

'The smell is decay and water rot, which smells fascinating so long as it is not in your home.'

Later they landed and explored a little of the town on foot, but as soon as they left the large, crowded streets for the narrow, winding alleys behind them, Pagan looked puzzled and stopped. 'All these alleys look the same. I'm confused.' One of the bodyguards stepped forward and muttered a few guttural words to His Majesty. They followed the man until they again found themselves at the small wrought-iron bridge where the golden gondola awaited them. Abdullah said, 'Although Venice is such a small town, it's very easy to get lost here. It's a well-known hazard. All the bridges and buildings look different according to whether the tide is in or not. The streets are a twisting maze, so you can't look back and get a sense of direction.'

Abdullah then insisted that Pagan do some shopping in the shops round St Mark's Square. She was measured for a pair of silver snakeskin shoes and then chose a classic shoe in red. Abdullah said, 'They're very elegant. Order them in every colour they have.' He waved his hand at the excited young shoemaker and strolled out of the shop as Pagan mused, 'What on earth will I do with twenty-seven pairs of pumps?'

By the time they were drinking their lunchtime Bellinis (the mixture of champagne and peach juice that was invented in Venice) the bodyguards were also guarding a second launch, laden with a complete set of calf luggage with golden clasps, twenty metres of handsome lace, which Pagan planned to keep for Sophia's wedding dress, and more clothes than Pagan had ever possessed in her life, including three antique Fortuny dresses, in coral, brown and dark green, and an opera cloak in canary-yellow silk.

They spent an unforgettable afternoon in bed.

★

•

'Your Majesty, this is the Sala del Maggior Consiglio, the very cradle of Western democracy, where the Great Council of Venice met to elect representatives to the governing committees.' Pagan and Abdullah obediently followed the curator's finger with their eyes as he pointed up to the painted ceiling, where the nacreous light from the lagoon outside played on the rich colours of the panels. 'Notice the frieze of the seventy-six Doges, the painting of Paradise by Tintoretto, and here the Apotheosis of Venice by Veronese.'

'Cradle of democracy!' muttered Abdullah, amused. 'How can they make such a claim when Renaissance Venice was a corrupt state, run by spies and assassins, with dungeons, daggers and poison.' He and Pagan were both tired after hours of pacing through the richly ornamented palace, followed at a respectful distance by Abdullah's two bodyguards. Pagan's neck ached from looking at the sumptuous stuccoed ceilings and her feet were sore from the hard marble floors.

'At least only the Venetians elected their rulers,' Pagan argued.

'They elected them from the aristocratic élite. That is not a free election in the democratic sense,' Abdullah corrected her.

Stung by his patronizing voice, Pagan retorted, 'Five hundred years ago Venice was still more democratic than Sydon is today. Your Council of Five isn't elected by a free ballot of all your citizens.'

'Pagan, don't be stupid. Democracy can only operate

•

•

in a country with literacy, a good standard of living and no endemic corruption. The average citizen of my country would vote for anyone who promised him two goats and a bracelet for his wife.'

'Then why don't you do something about it?'

'You know that I'm trying.' Abdullah's voice was frosty.

'I think you're happy as a benevolent despot,' Pagan snorted.

'Democracy doesn't insure a healthy state. Good government does that.'

'In a democracy, wealth isn't in the hands of a few tribal clans as it is in Sydon.'

'That is a foolish remark.'

'Oh, don't be so bloody pompous!' Pagan snapped, turning crossly on her heel. She strode through a doorway into yet another immense room. Hearing footsteps behind her, she turned to see that one of the royal bodyguards was following her, while Abdullah, as if nothing had happened, was talking to the guide. Being a royal tourist was worse than being a schoolgirl, Pagan thought irritably; you were never allowed to walk alone. After only one day she found it oppressive. She started to walk faster. She was damned if she was going to be nannied.

As the Doge's Palace had been closed for their visit, Pagan moved with increasing speed through the empty rooms to the staircase which led down to the courtyard. But, as she dashed under the triumphal arch of the palace and out into the crowded Piazza San Marco, she could

•

hear the bodyguard clattering down the steps behind her.

Damned if I'm going to let Abdullah's bloody sheepdog round me up, she thought angrily, darting through a small herd of German tourists.

Seeing the restaurant where, that morning, they had drunk Bellinis, she ran blindly into the back and opened the washroom door. But it turned out to be the kitchen door. Pagan hurried past astonished waiters and cooks, past crates of fruit and vegetables, to the exit at the end of the room. Outside, she found herself in a small, smelly alleyway where the rosy evening sunlight reached only the highest balconies that overhung the dustbins of the restaurant.

Pagan darted into a doorway and peered round it at the restaurant kitchen door until she was sure that the bodyguard had not followed her. Then, jauntily, she set off down the alley, intending to go back to their hotel.

But, although they had explored the city by gondola that morning, Pagan suddenly realized that she had no idea where she was or the address of her hotel. No problem. Venice is a small town. When she found a canal, she could walk until she saw a water-taxi, then ask him to take her to the Cipriani.

Getting lost had never worried Pagan. However far she wandered as a child, she had always been able to find her way across the Cornish moorland, back to Trelawney. In fact, she rather liked not knowing where she was, Pagan

•

thought as she turned into another alleyway; life seemed full of delicious, unexpected possibilities when she was lost. I wonder why I like surprises and hate routine, Pagan mused as she considered whether to cross a carved stone bridge to her left or to plunge into the maze of alleys on her right.

At the top of the arched bridge Pagan stopped and watched the dirty grey canal below, crowded with boats of every kind. She could also see the landing place, where the little launches – taxis of the town – were taking on passengers. She moved towards it, but when she had nearly reached the landing, Pagan changed her mind. An hour of freedom in Venice was not something to be squandered, just because your feet hurt. She turned and strolled in the opposite direction.

Seeing an enormous wooden door ajar, Pagan walked inside, and found herself in an incense-scented church. Unlike the magnificent churches that she had visited with Abdullah, which were more like picture galleries than places of worship, this was a working church. Dressed in black, several old women were praying; the statue of the Saint, Anthony of Padua, was encircled by half-burned votive candles. An array of gold and silver tinfoil images were pinned to the wall, messages of thanks to the saint who had granted the prayers of worshippers. The tinfoil hands, feet, arms and legs, were for healed injuries; tinfoil babies were from once-childless couples; tinfoil hearts with crowns, roses or ribbons around them were from newlyweds. These people don't hide what they want,

·

thought Pagan. That's one of the differences between the English and the Italians.

The huge door creaked as she squeezed through it into fading daylight. As Pagan turned around the corner she heard the door creak again, then light footsteps behind her. Pagan suddenly realized that those steps had been much too quick for the arthritic old ladies in the church. The pearly light of the Venice evening was fading fast as Pagan hurried back towards the canal. Only she hadn't been walking towards the canal, she discovered. She stood in front of a narrow waterway with houses rising straight out of the dark water. Suddenly she recognized a fall of asparagus fern from a first-floor balcony down the path on her left. Aha, she'd noticed that this morning; she was on the correct route.

Again she set off confidently. Again she heard the light, stealthy footsteps behind her.

She stopped and looked over her shoulder, her heart starting to thump as she realized that it was some time since she had passed anyone in these narrow alleys.

The footsteps also stopped. Pagan started to hurry between the high, crumbling walls.

She stopped again and listened. The light pitter-patter of footsteps behind her stopped again.

Pagan spun round. The road curved behind her and she could see no one, but she was certain that someone was following her and, suddenly, Pagan was frightened.

Darkness was falling and, as she began to run, Pagan thought, it's not Abdi's bodyguard, I'm sure I lost him.

•

Perhaps it's a mugger? I'll go back to the church and ask one of the old women to help me. No one will mug me in a church. She ran faster.

As she scuttled down empty lane after empty lane, blindly turning corners at any faintly familiar sight, Pagan realized that she had no idea where she was. And, as she ran along the crisscrossing labyrinth of dank alleys, the footsteps behind her grew louder and closer. Pagan stopped helplessly at yet another crossroads.

Suddenly a powerful hand grabbed her by the shoulder and spun her around.

It was Abdullah.

With relief, she threw her arms around him. 'I thought you'd never catch up!'

'Why were you running?'

'I thought someone was following me,' she said, unwilling to admit that she had been frightened.

'Do you know where you are?'

'No. Where are we?'

'I haven't the faintest idea.' He put his arm around her. 'You know you're in the most confusing city in the world.'

'I think we're near the fish market.' Pagan wrinkled her nose.

'The whole of Venice smells of that watery, rotting smell,' Abdullah dismissed her suggestion.

Around the corner they found themselves in the deserted fish market.

·

'At least we know where we are.' Triumphantly Pagan pointed. 'There's the canal! Now, all we have to do is find a water-taxi!'

Abdullah looked at her tired face, drew her to him and kissed her.

'I've been hoping you would do that all day.' Pagan wound her arms around his lean body. 'It's so nice to be without your bodyguard chaperones.'

'You should be used to them by now.' Abdullah brushed her eyebrows with his lips.

'I don't think I'll ever get used to them; they make me feel claustrophobic. I'm so glad I managed to throw them off.'

Abdullah pulled back, alarmed. 'I sincerely hope you have not thrown them off.' He quickly looked around. 'If they aren't behind us, then we must return to the hotel immediately.'

They hurried on. As they crossed the wet market cobbles Pagan heard the stealthy noise of following feet. Again she felt a twinge of panic. 'Abdi, I think someone is following us. Maybe the bodyguards are catching up, after all?'

'Nonsense, Pagan, it's just the echo of our own footsteps. You always hear that in Venice, the sound ricochets around all the little alleyways.'

'Yes, of course.' Pagan's voice was doubtful. There were footsteps behind them, coming from the deserted market buildings.

Pagan and Abdullah had almost reached the canalside,

•

•

when, from a side street, two young men stepped out and blocked their path.

Abdullah pushed Pagan into a doorway with one hand and, with the other hand, he seized one of the men around the neck, grappling for the pressure point, through which he could make the man unconscious.

There was a dull glint of metal as the second youth opened a switchblade and circled the two struggling men, looking for his chance to attack.

'Run, Pagan! They've got knives!'

Abdullah slipped on the slimy stones and fell, losing his grip on his opponent, who fell with him.

Pagan was no longer frightened. She felt calm and almost elated as she whipped off her high-heeled shoes and flew at the attacker on the ground, when he tried to get up. With her metal-tipped stilettos, Pagan lashed at his head. As the second man lunged forward Abdullah seized his knife hand, and then, with an agile heave, he threw both the attacker and the weapon into the canal.

As Abdullah whirled to help Pagan the second youth managed to dodge her blows and started to run along the canalside, chased by Abdullah. The mugger ran fast, but he was unlucky. As he rounded the next corner he blundered straight against the broad chests of Abdullah's bodyguards.

'You're carrying a knife as well!' Pagan gasped to Abdullah. 'Goodness, you fight dirty.' She pushed her hair out of her eyes.

•

•

'All kings fight dirty,' Abdullah panted. 'When you are a king,' he added, adjusting his tie, 'you must always fight to win.'

That evening they had dinner on the terrace of their suite, looking at the blazing lights of the Piazza San Marco across the lagoon. Abdullah waited until the silver tray of coffee had been removed, then he leaned forward to Pagan, who was wearing her dark green Fortuny.

Abdullah said, 'Shut your eyes.'

She heard his chair scrape against the stone flags as he rose, then she sensed that he was standing behind her. She felt his hands lift the hair from the back of her neck and place something warm and heavy on her collarbone as he murmured, 'I hope that by now you're old enough to accept a necklace from me.'

Pagan rushed to the huge Venetian glass mirror in the salon. A necklace of platinum links, scattered with emeralds, lay against her pale, freckled chest.

In the mirror she saw Abdullah approach and hold her shoulders. He started, 'We worked well as a team this afternoon . . .'

'You're not just a pretty face,' Pagan allowed.

'You aren't as tough as you think you are.' Abdullah grinned.

'You really were protective.'

'You really were aggressive,' Abdullah said. 'Can't we be together for longer than two days?'

•

Pagan suddenly felt nervous. 'I don't know.'

'Would you spend the rest of the summer at my place in Cannes?'

'I don't know,' she stalled.

'If I invited Maxine and Charles, would you come?'

'I've never thought of Maxine as a chaperone before.' Abdullah's insistent black gaze made Pagan feel as if her guts were dissolving. 'I think that would be . . .' She had intended to say impossible, but heard herself say, 'Wonderful!' As she said it, bursts of falling green and pink stars were reflected in the water from a firework display on the other side of the lagoon.

Abdullah held Pagan's bare shoulders and turned her towards him. She closed her eyes and turned her face up to him, expecting a kiss, but instead, Abdullah said earnestly, 'Listen to me, Pagan. I have to explain to you about Sydon. The Fundamentalists are getting help from the Communist bloc, and if I can't defeat their guerrillas soon, I'll have a full-scale war on my hands. I can't defeat them without American arms and aid, and at the moment I can't get help from the Americans.'

Pagan hadn't expected a political lecture. 'I know that modernization has brought you problems,' she said, hiding her disappointment.

'Another of my problems is the women of my country.'

'In what way?' Pagan asked, without much interest at that moment in the problems of other women.

'In every way. It has been far harder for the women than for the men of my country to become part of the

modern world. In the old days, when they lived behind
the veil, they were completely dependent on their men,
but also completely protected. Independence frightens
them, but they cannot cling to the old ways for ever.' A
burst of golden sparks cascaded across the sky as he
added, 'They pity Western women, struggling along without male protection . . .'

'But they don't!' exclaimed Pagan.

'Under Koranic law, a man is obliged to support all the
women of his household. A Western man can discard his
wife, with very little responsibility. So a Western woman
does not always have the absolute security that she thinks
she does.'

Thinking of her divorce from her first husband, Pagan
could only nod as Abdullah continued, 'Nevertheless, the
younger women of my country are starting to question
some of our traditional ways.'

'Such as?'

'As you know, female infibulation is still practised.
And a woman's body belongs to her father or her husband,
like their goat's.'

'I know all that, Abdi, you've told me over and over
again. Why are we discussing it now?' Pagan was puzzled.

'Because unless women play an active part in my country, we can never be part of the modern world.' A screaming green rocket flared briefly and fell into the sea. 'I need
an experienced, diplomatic, sophisticated woman with
organizational ability at my side. That is what my country
needs.'

•

•

'You sound as if you're drafting a want ad,' Pagan told him. 'Gynaecological experience an advantage.'

Abdullah released her shoulders and walked across the terrace to the balustrade, then turned to face her. 'I need someone who understands Western ways, and Western women, and the need for our women to assert themselves.'

'Why not propose to Gloria Steinem?'

Abdullah's mouth twitched with anger. 'I swore to myself that I would not lose my temper. Pagan, I will *not* allow you to misunderstand me again.' He shook her by the shoulders. 'I realize that you're headstrong, impulsive and . . .'

'Self-conscious?' Pagan interrupted him. 'Mustn't forget that. That's why we used to have so many rows when we were young. You were nervous and pompous and I was just nervous.'

Behind Abdullah's back the white filigree façade of the Doge's Palace gleamed in the floodlights at the far side of the lagoon. Abdullah said, 'We are no longer young.'

Pagan laughed. 'You're so tactful. But, Abdi, I still feel young and nervous and uncertain when I'm with you.'

'You would get used to me.'

Suddenly Pagan realized the reason for the political lecture.

Abdullah said, 'Yes, I want you to marry me!' Earnestly he said, 'Let's not mess it up again, Pagan.'

'I can't believe it.'

'I knew you'd say that.' He rose again and strode away to the edge of the terrace again, silhouetted against the

•

•

gold flares of the fireworks as they whistled over the sea.

Pagan rustled across the terrace and laid her hand on his arm. 'You don't understand . . .' she began.

Abdullah interrupted her. 'Yes, I do understand, Pagan. You're afraid of being humiliated again, you're afraid that I'll reject you again, as I did when I was nineteen.' He sighed. 'Please remember that was a bloody long time ago!'

Pagan said, 'It's true, I don't want the pain of hoping again, Abdi. I don't want the uncertainty and then possibly . . . the realization that, at my age, I've allowed myself to hope for too much, that I've made a fool of myself again – but this time with the whole world watching.'

Abdullah took both her hands in his. 'But I *really* need you. *Especially* you, Pagan, because you have also been hurled from a life of ancient tradition into the modern world, so you will understand my people.'

Pagan still felt as if she were being recruited for a particularly unpopular diplomatic post, rather than being courted by a man who wanted to marry her. She thought, here we are in this beautiful romantic place, the moonlight is trembling on the waves and the gondoliers are poling around down there, singing love songs, and Abdi's talking to me as if he were hiring a Middle-East liaison executive.

'I can see why you need a queen,' said Pagan, 'but I'm not sure I understand why you need a wife.'

There was a pause. 'For the usual reasons.' He looked away from her.

•

'Abdi, in the centre of her heart every woman is always seventeen, and this seventeen-year-old wants to hear it.' I'll make him say it, if it kills him, Pagan promised herself. Every woman wants to hear it, and men never understand why.

Finally, Abdullah looked at the floor and muttered, 'I love you.'

Gently Pagan said, 'And I love you.'

'Can I assume then that your answer is yes?'

Again Pagan caught the odd, brisk note in his voice. Was this the notorious lover? The romantic playboy, the man who had spent a fortune on red roses? She said, 'There are a couple of subclauses that we really should discuss.'

Nuzzling her neck, he said, 'I don't want to hear that you're not young enough or unsuitable in any way. Let's brush these insecurities aside.'

'No, let's pull them all out in the open, *now*, Abdi. First of all, I think I'm too old for you.'

'Kindly let me be the judge of that.'

Pagan touched the green ribbon of the order of Semira, which hung over Abdullah's white dinner jacket. 'I know this isn't the traditional moment to bring this up, but it's very important to me. I must know. Do you intend to be a faithful husband, Abdullah?'

'Why must you Westerners confuse sex and love? Sexual fidelity has little to do with marriage.'

'*Do you intend to be faithful to me?*' Pagan felt as if she were walking on eggshells, but she was determined that Abdullah should answer her question. 'After all, in the

●

East, sexual fidelity has a lot to do with marriage –
for the wife. Adulterous women are still occasionally
beheaded, aren't they? So what are your intentions,
Abdullah?'

'When one knows that one can have any number of
nubile young women by snapping one's fingers, one feels
less inclined to snap them.'

'Abdi, don't evade my question. Will you be faithful
to me?'

'I cannot say.'

'We're being honest,' she reminded him.

He paused. 'Then I doubt it.'

'You might feel inclined to snap the fingers?'

'We're being honest.'

Pagan felt a dull ache. 'Then my answer must be no,'
she said with dignity as her ache turned to pain. She
pulled away from him, disappointed and angry. 'Why are
you so impossibly arrogant?'

'You asked me to be truthful. But once again you put
your pride before reality.' He looked at her, trying to
control his anger. 'I swore that I wouldn't let you lose my
temper again.'

'Me – lose your temper!' Pagan shouted.

Abdullah grabbed her hand. 'We must stop this,
Pagan.' He controlled himself with difficulty. 'We're
having a quarrel about something that happened thirty
years ago.'

'Something that didn't happen, you mean.' Pagan's
tone was bitter.

•

'Something that could happen now,' he insisted gently, pulling her towards the couch.

Pagan thought, he's just demonstrated the perfect way not to propose to a woman. She said sadly, 'Abdullah, I don't think such a marriage would ever work. I couldn't bear it if you started being the Playboy of the Western World again.'

The last of the fireworks spluttered out and the sea seemed darker than before. Abdullah accepted temporary defeat. 'But you will still come to Cannes?' he asked quietly.

'Are you sure you want me to come?'

'I think we should both consider what we may be missing.'

Does he mean it or doesn't he? Pagan wondered. It was like listening to those pursuing feet earlier and trying to work out where the sound was coming from; every indication seemed deceptive.

But I'll never know if I don't dare to find out.

'I'll come to Cannes,' she promised him. 'After my Drury Lane gala.'

TWELVE

July 1979

'We've made a lot of extra money on the drinks fee and the raffle.' The Scottish duchess looked around the ballroom. Bare-shouldered women in bright taffeta gowns talked to men with pearl-studded shirt fronts, on their best behaviour.

Pagan, whose face ached with smiling at her guests, was hardly listening as she anxiously wondered whether the hotel had allocated enough waiters.

'It's a long time since I've seen so many real tiaras,' said the duchess. 'Hardly anyone wears their real jewels today. Nicole Birmingham said that the last time she wore her aquamarines, it cost five thousand dollars for the insurance and the bodyguards, so the next morning she went straight round to Kenneth Lane.'

Pagan anxiously eyed the clock set in the wedding-cake plaster moulding above the door. Another five minutes and she'd have to make her speech, then marshall the 2,000 guests to the Theatre Royal, Drury Lane.

Suddenly the banquet manager was at Pagan's side. 'May I have a word with you, milady?'

'What's wrong, Mr Gates?'

'I've just spoken to Mr Zimmer, who telephoned from the theatre. He told me to tell you that they've had a slight technical problem, something to do with the fire curtain. So Mr Zimmer asked if you would announce that the gala will take place an hour later than scheduled, at eight-thirty. He told me to tell you not to worry, everything is under control, the engineer just needs time.'

'What a nuisance, Mr Gates,' said Pagan, thinking *bloody* fire curtain. 'I'd better tell everyone straight away.'

She made her way to the podium, climbed up the steps and took the microphone. 'My lords, ladies and gentlemen . . .'

'The curtain should have gone up ten minutes ago, but there isn't one person out front.' There were tears in Lili's eyes as she peeped through the red velvet stage curtains. Beyond it were 2,000 empty theatre seats.

The stage manager, his bow tie askew, nodded tensely. 'There's still no sign of anyone in the theatre. Not one person.'

Behind her heavy stage make-up Lili's eyes looked scared. Nervously she pulled up the long black glove which covered her right arm. 'I can't believe it.' She shook her head, scattering spangles from the three white Prince-of-Wales ostrich feathers that hung from her skullcap. 'What the hell has happened?' She bit her bottom

•

lip to control her agitation, then nervously smoothed the skintight black velvet dress which left one shoulder and one leg bare.

'I don't know.' The stage manager ran his hands through his greased blonde hair. 'They should have poured through the doors at least half an hour ago. The theatre is absolutely empty.'

Lili tapped her silver shoe, her leg elegant and taut as that of a polo pony in her gleaming silver tights. 'Please check the tickets again. Please check that they printed the correct date!'

'We've already checked. There's nothing wrong with the invitations.' The stage manager looked helpless. Charity benefits – run by amateurs – were always a nightmare.

Zimmer put his arm around Lili. 'Don't cry, darling, or you'll have to re-do your make-up. Best thing is to get back to your dressing room, like everyone else. Stash will find out what the hell's happening.'

Lili's agent nodded, patted her spangled shoulder, then hurried to the stage-door telephone.

Zimmer knew that this was not a run-of-the-mill theatrical disaster; there must have been some colossal street accident near the hotel, maybe a 707 had crashed in Piccadilly, but his job was to calm the leading lady, so he said, 'Toughen up, Lili. You're a professional remember? Worse things have happened in the theatre. Nobody's dropped dead on stage. Abraham Lincoln hasn't been assassinated out front. The Phantom of the Opera is still in Paris.'

Lili gave him a weak smile. Zimmer was at his best

•

when things were going wrong; the worse the crisis, the calmer he became.

Stash reappeared in Lili's dressing room. 'Mystery solved,' he said. 'They're all still at Grosvenor House because someone announced that we had backstage problems, and that the opening had been postponed for an hour. I managed to speak to Lady Swann and she's going to get everyone here within fifteen minutes. They're radioing for every cab in London.'

Zimmer said, 'It'll take fifteen minutes to seat everyone. So, Lili, you've got half an hour to calm down, to think yourself into your role and keep your legs warm.'

He was right. Lili reached for her grubby purple leg-warmers.

'And check your make-up, darling,' said Zimmer. Tears had smudged her thick black eyeliner. 'Then concentrate on your part, Lili. Forget everything else. Leave it to me.'

Zimmer knew that any actor is in a fragile state of mind before going on stage. Often the half-hour before curtain-up is spent quietly sitting in a chair and thinking himself into his part, concentrating only upon what lies ahead and blocking out any extraneous thoughts. During that time an actor hates to be spoken to, or interrupted. A good actor produces his performance from inside himself, which is an unconscious process; he's learned his lines, he's studied, he's rehearsed with the rest of the cast, and before curtain-up time is when the part takes over the actor. The conscious mind is suspended as the subconscious takes over, transferring all rehearsed input into a living performance.

Twenty minutes later there was a tap on the dressing-room door and a distraught Pagan appeared in a tulip-skirted cream satin dress, and Abdullah's emerald collar.

'I don't know what's happened, Lili, but I know that someone's tried to ruin our benefit and *we're not going to let them*. You'll have a full house in fifteen minutes.'

'It's all very well for you, Pagan,' said Lili, sounding exhausted. 'You don't have to go out there and smile and knock 'em dead, as if nothing had happened.'

'Lili needs to be alone, now,' Zimmer said firmly. He led Pagan out of the dingy dressing room and up to the backstage area, where the crowd of dancers were sweating in the hot July night. Zimmer tiptoed across the stage, peeped through the spyhole in the centre of the curtain, then tiptoed back to Pagan.

'They're coming!' he confirmed, then turned to the theatre manager. 'Please get your security men to search the entire theatre. Tip up every seat, check the flies and the scenery storeroom, empty the lavatory cisterns, clear the street outside.'

'We can't possibly do that; it'll delay the performance even longer!' The house manager promised himself that he'd never let the theatre owner give another charity event, so long as he still worked at that theatre.

'We know that someone out there doesn't like Lili,' Zimmer said. 'So we must insist on a full security check.' He turned back to Pagan. 'This is a terrible thing to

•

•

happen to a performer. The opening is going to be very tough for Lili.'

'I know. That's why my opening speech is going to be different from what I'd planned.'

Pagan found that her legs were shaking as she walked out to the centre of the stage. A stagehand pulled the red velvet curtain aside for her. She took a deep breath and stepped through the opening. The spotlight temporarily blinded her. She held up her hand for silence and saw the upturned faces in the front row seats. Beyond them was blackness, although Pagan knew that they had a full house, as she beamed at her audience and started.

'Many things can disturb a star's self-confidence, but the one nightmare that every performer knows about is that no one will come to watch the show. Because, without an audience, there can be no performance.' Pagan was aware of the hush in the theatre as she went on. 'Tonight, for almost an hour, it seemed as if that nightmare had become a reality, for Lili, our star . . .'

After Pagan ended her speech a few scattered handclaps quickly grew into a roar of applause. Pagan hurried into the wings as the curtains drew back and the lights dimmed, leaving the stage black. Then a single spotlight picked out the silhouette of Lili's small, silver-spangled figure at the top of the elaborate staircase.

The applause became a standing ovation as the audience clapped and shouted their approval for a full five minutes before Lili could start to sing. 'C'est Paris . . .'

★
•

'". . . can only praise her jaunty courage", that's the *Mail*.' Lili's agent tossed the newspapers on to Lili's bed, pulled off his black leather gloves and unbuttoned his vicuna coat. '*The Times* says you're the natural successor to Piaf and Garland, and the *Sun*'s given you the front page – "Sex Goddess Lili Drama". They've all run it as a news story. You've got great coverage.'

'And you still have no idea who planned this horrible joke.'

'All we know about him is that he must have plenty of money. It was an expensive operation.'

'Talking of expenses, did you send the money to Teresa?'

On the nightstand lay a delicate pair of gold handcuffs from Van Cleef in Cannes. An empty bottle of Bollinger and a lipstick-smeared champagne glass stood beside a plastic bag of cotton balls and a small pharmacist's box of amyl nitrate capsules. The other glass lay smashed on the floor beside a purple satin, black-fringed négligé.

Teresa was wearing an elaborate, black leather Barbarella costume with four-inch spike heels on her black leather thigh boots. She was lovingly cooing scatological insults into the ear of the stout man who lay on the bed beside her.

'Please stop,' he begged. 'Don't be so cruel, I didn't mean it.'

'You mean you lie to me as well.' She shoved him away from her and he fell over the side of the bed to the floor,

•

yelping as his body hit the broken champagne glass.

He crawled away from the bed on his hands and knees. Nimbly Teresa jumped off the bed, kicked his wobbling, hairy backside with her high heels, then, with a practised hand, she flourished her thin black whip over her head, just missing the plastic chandelier.

He whimpered, 'Don't kick me, don't kick me, please.'

'These boots are filthy,' she snarled, 'you haven't cleaned them properly!' She took another neat jab at his rear, thinking, I'd better be careful, I don't want to mark him.

As expertly as a rodeo cowboy, she lightly flicked his ear with the whip. 'Turn around,' she commanded, thinking she'd better get this over fast, she didn't want to be late for her tennis coach this afternoon at Washington's prestigious Potomac Club. She jabbed at the fat man's pendulous stomach. 'Now, lick my boots!'

As the man did so Teresa could see that at last his claret-coloured private parts were responding. Thoughtfully she tickled his spine with her whip, then threw it on the bed and leaned backwards towards the cotton balls and the capsules.

She kept up the litany of abuse and, from time to time, she gave him an encouraging whack with her hairbrush as she deftly wrapped the capsules in cotton, then twisted them in a handkerchief.

'Ah . . . ah . . . ah,' he groaned in ecstasy. Teresa looked down. The john was nearly ready for her. He wasn't a bad old boy and he was generous. She'd give

•

him an extra kick or two, on the house. After all, she *was* getting paid twice over.

'You'll never learn to do it properly, you filthy pig.' She pulled her feet away from his tongue and reached for the whip. Briskly she kicked him flat, turned him over with an economical jab of her toe, and straddled the whimpering plump body. With her left hand she reached for his penis. Her right hand grabbed the empty champagne bottle, smashed it against the lumpy handkerchief, and then briskly held it under the fat man's nose. A purplish-red flush suffused his face and neck; Teresa heard inarticulate noises, gurgles, and groans as he turned purple and his pop-eyes looked up at her in ecstasy.

How much more can this old bastard take? wondered Teresa. By the time she got back to Paris, her backhand would be invincible.

'Would you please stick this in a red file before you leave for the night?' said Judy. In her personal office all productive work which had an end aim – and a deadline date – was put in a red, transparent plastic envelope. These red files had their own 'in', 'pending', and 'follow' tray. All 'in' red file work was always done first thing in the morning, before any other work was discussed, even before the telephone was lifted. This meant that priorities were painlessly sorted out and the achievement work was dealt with before the routine work.

The secretary left the office and Judy picked up the projected advertising figures for August. Next month

•

looked as if it was going to be even more depressing than July; summer was always a thin period for advertising revenue.

There was a knock and Tony entered. 'You left this file in the car, Judy. Gee, I'm sorry we've lost Lady Mirabelle.' Judy looked up in surprise. Tom had said that nobody knew they'd lost that account. As Tony left the office he almost collided with Tom, who was entering. Tom waited until the door had closed, then he said, 'OK, Judy, we're ready to go belly up, if it has to be. I've prepared for everything except hocking our watches.'

Night after night, after the staff had gone home, Tom had secretly worked to prepare *Verve!* magazine for closure. Bit by bit, Tom had transferred every asset owned by *Verve!* magazine into the names of two holding companies which had been set up for the purpose. Now everything tangible, from the office lease to the messenger-boy's motorbike, might be saved from the wreck so that they might start again. Tom had checked through all the staff contracts and, without Judy's know-ledge, quietly negotiated for two of the longest-employed editors to be offered good jobs on rival magazines, thus saving their compensation payments from his company. He had set these strategic savings against the disastrous projected loss. He no longer felt any regret for the years of business triumph, only the calm determination of self-preservation. Tom's clear head and inventive busi-ness brain would, he hoped, save the roof over both his

•

families; Kate didn't know of the impending crisis, but now she owned their apartment and their country house. His ex-wife and two sons had a trust fund that could be touched by no one. Tom had always been more realistic than Judy. Although he took high risks in business, they were always carefully calculated. A good gambler always knows bad luck when he meets her, knows that when he's on a losing streak he has to toss the cards on the table, stand up and say goodbye.

'I'm afraid they'll have to be shot, Suliman, as quickly as possible. Give the orders at once.' General Suliman saluted and left the room. Abdullah leaned back and allowed his eyes to close for a few moments. He pinched the bridge of his sharp aquiline nose, where a knot of tension had formed between the winged black eyebrows. Then he rose, walked slowly to his London embassy, over the green grass of St James's Park and looked up the Mall towards the severe grey stone of Buckingham Palace. He'd returned from Venice the day before to find a crisis waiting on his desk, of course.

His ancestors had not known the comfort or the complications of civilization. Their life was simple because there was very little to clutter it up; neither possessions nor sentimental attachments; but what his Bedouin ancestors possessed was the ultimate luxury of freedom; their lives were circumscribed by the cruel physical environment and pitiless discipline of the desert, but their spirit was free. Suddenly Abdullah felt the old, familiar urge for the

•

•

harsh peace of the desert. He sighed and moved towards the drawing room.

'Well?' Pagan pushed her heavy mahogany hair back and looked at Abdullah with concern. He seemed to have grown ten years older in the two days that he'd spent anxiously considering the fate of those three terrorists.

'Execution.' Abdullah took the chair next to her, his sombre face and khaki uniform contrasting with the blue silk cushions. 'My father was right. Forget the smell of mercy when dealing with your enemy.'

You don't have to teach a cat to sit by the fire, Pagan thought, and you don't have to teach a Bedouin to be cruel. The desert is cruel, and so is anyone who survives in it. Desert life is so harsh that punishment has to be even harsher. Pagan could understand Abdullah's Bedouin nature, but she wondered if she could ever get used to it. 'Your father never had to deal with the Muslim Fundamentalists,' she said doubtfully, privately thinking that the old bugger had only had to deal with the traditional gang of power-crazed second cousins trying to stab each other in the back.

'No, but he had his own fanatics to put down,' said Abdullah.

'Will the priests find out?' Pagan knew that if the terrorists were executed, Abdullah risked making them martyrs.

'Not immediately. When they get no news of their men in prison, then they'll know, but too late. It's hard to make martyrs months after the event. And if these men

•

had been popular in their own village, there would have been a greater outcry when they were arrested. The priests were unable to whip up much of a demonstration. I think their power is weakening, at last. The priests exploit the ignorance of the people. In Sydon we've had to achieve centuries of development in thirty years. It's the same for every nation on the Gulf; I don't want my country to go the way of Iran. I will not see Sydon hurled back into ignorance and superstition. My job is to guide my people into the twentieth century.'

He jumped up and prowled around the room, remembering his dusty country, neatly wedged between Oman and the United Arab Emirates on the Persian Gulf. He thought of the camels and Cadillacs side by side on the desert roads, the extremes of feudal poverty and half-assimilated modern sophistication.

'I've disposed of eleven revolutionary groups since I became King.' His voice was sombre. 'Each one of them was led by one of my own blood relations, and they were all executed.'

Pagan thought, no wonder Abdi has only one heir.

'They all want the same thing – power. The priests are no different, except that they use the sacred name of the Prophet to justify their betrayal. They confuse and frighten my people, who, like all people, hate change. It's difficult for them to change from our traditional ways to the modern way of life that's been developed in the West. They prefer to rush back to the Middle Ages.'

'It's the same choice for you, isn't it?' ventured Pagan.

•

'What do you mean?' Abdullah looked at her in surprise.

'You're also stuck between two worlds, aren't you? You can't be an absolute ruler like your father . . .'

Born in the East, Abdullah had been deliberately educated in the West so that he would be capable of dealing with the rulers of the West. Through his Western ego he had learned to criticize his own people; he had dropped one culture and not been accepted by another. So he felt an isolation in his life and Pagan had spotted this long ago.

Abdullah perched on the arm of Pagan's chair and kissed the tip of her freckled nose. 'My father's problem,' he said, 'was persuading the nomad to build a house. Then his problem was persuading the nomad to build a lavatory in the house. After that, when I became King, the problem was to teach the nomad to stand in front of the lavatory instead of climbing on the bowl. Now, if the priests are not controlled, the nomads will convert their cisterns into camel-troughs because the priests tell them it is not the way of Allah to piss indoors.'

Where other women felt an urge to rearrange the furniture, Maxine rearranged the now priceless treasures of the de Chazalle family. Years ago she had saved them from mildew and moth when she had saved the château by opening it to the public as a beautifully presented, historic showcase which also promoted the family champagne business.

•

LACE 2
•

When Pagan arrived at the Château de Chazalle she was shown to the wide, Chinese-yellow picture gallery on the first floor, known to the public as the History Walk, although the family called it Ancestor Alley.

Maxine, in her stockinged feet, was standing on a chair and hacking at a gold picture frame with a kitchen knife.

'Whatever are you doing, Maxi?' Pagan blew her a kiss. 'Why are you ruining that picture frame?'

'I'm not ruining it, I'm distressing it,' Maxine smiled down at her. 'I'm making it look old and worn, as if it has been hanging here for at least one hundred years, instead of three days.'

'What's the point of that?'

Maxine jumped off the chair and kissed Pagan on the cheek. 'It's the essence of shabby chic, the way that aristocratic houses should look. Anyone with money can have everything new, but it's far more difficult to achieve this slightly worn, not-perfectly-matched, artlessly charming look of a room in which a priceless painting hangs next to a watercolour of Sorrento by your grandmother.'

'But what's chic about having a chipped picture frame?'

'Anyone with money can buy that glossy magazine look. You need generations of family history to feel comfortable with an Aubusson carpet that's worn on one corner, chintz curtains that are faded because they've been hanging at the same window for over one hundred years and Chinese hand-painted wallpaper that is, perhaps, a little dim because it was painted in the eighteenth century by Chinese

•

artists whom your ancestors imported from China to do the job.'

'But what's the point?'

'Snobbery, darling Pagan. It's the new decorator look. The point of shabby chic is that you can't achieve it unless it is authentic, or unless you have a very clever decorator.'

'Don't you ever stop working, Maxi?'

'If I enjoy work more than pleasure, then is it work or pleasure?'

'Crumbs, don't ask me. I hate decorating. If the shops have what I want in the right colour, then it's the wrong size. Always. Sophia wants her bedroom redone for her birthday, and I really can't face it. She wants stripped pine furniture and a Victorian brass bed.'

'I'll do it for you, if you like,' Maxine offered, 'but not in stripped pine and brass, that's too passé.' She took Pagan's arm. 'Now let me show you to your room, and then you can tell me why you have to see me so suddenly. What's so important that you can't talk about it on the telephone? What is it that can't wait until our holiday in Cannes?'

'I want to ask your advice. But first I want to talk to Charles.'

'Charles! What on earth do you want to discuss with Charles?'

'Politics. Eastern politics.'

After dinner Pagan steered Charles to a green leather sofa in the library. She knew that Charles had Middle

East associates, and he had known Abdullah as an acquaintance since he had married Maxine.

'Charles, I want to talk about Abdullah,' she started,
then felt embarrassed. 'You know – Abdi, Playboy of the
Western World.'

Charles twirled the brandy in his glass. 'It's only in the
West that people regard him as a playboy, Pagan. In his
own country, and among the Gulf states, he's considered
a brave, devoted leader.' He sniffed his brandy. 'Abdi is
the most skilful of all the Gulf rulers at dragging his
country into the twentieth century, although he's in such
serious trouble at the moment.'

'What do you mean?' Pagan, accustomed to listening
with only half an ear while Abdullah talked of his state
affairs, suddenly wanted Charles to tell her more. Now
that Abdullah and she were apart, Pagan managed to drag
his name into every conversation, no matter how odd the
context.

'Like every other oil-boom people, the Sydonites are
bewildered by the modern world, and confused about
their national identity.' Charles took a sip of his Napoleon
brandy. 'You really want to know more?'

Pagan nodded,

'The Fundamentalist guerrilla army is getting help
from the Communists, Pagan. If Abdullah can't handle
that situation, not only will he lose his country, but the
red flag will shortly be flying over one of the most strategic
positions on the coast.'

'I had no idea . . . I didn't realize . . .'

•

'Combine that with the Iranian situation and the Ayatollah on the other side of the Persian Gulf and you might end up with Muslim fanatics controlling eighty per cent of the world's oil – and taking their orders from Moscow.'

'No wonder Abdullah's so grim about it all,' Pagan murmured.

'Sydon is a grim place and it's a crazy place. In fact, the whole Gulf area is crazy. I've done business with Saudi princes who wear silk shirts, drink whisky and speak better English than I do. But at their homes, their mothers and wives wear long black traditional robes. Then, underneath the robes they wear the latest Paris fashions, and the most wonderful jewellery, Christian Dior and Cartier. The women are never seen in public and only wear these beautiful clothes to drink tea with each other. And that's about all they're good for.'

'What do you mean?' Pagan asked, intrigued.

'Because they've always been excluded from public affairs, most Arab princesses have no sense of social responsibility. They don't do a thing to help the poor of their country.'

'How do *you* think a Gulf princess should behave?' Pagan tried to sound casual.

Aha, thought Charles, so that's it.

'She shouldn't be spending her time watching video tapes, gossiping and eating cakes. She should organize help for the young, the old and the poor. She should do the sort of work you do for the Research Institute, Pagan.'

•

•

'Do you think so?' Pagan didn't sound as casual as she had intended. She jumped up and fidgeted with a bowl of pink peonies. The library was filled with peonies and pink hydrangeas in blue chinoiserie bowls.

The following morning Maxine suggested a walk in the park. 'I want to get you on your own, Pagan,' she said as they strolled over the grass behind the bounding, pink-grey Weimaraners. 'Now, what's up?'

Pagan burst out, 'Maxine, why do men find it so difficult to say "I love you"?'

'Ma chère, they say it, but not in those words. They say, "I wouldn't be here if I didn't, would I?" or "But I married you, didn't I?"'

Pagan stomped across the grass in silence.

'Words don't matter,' Maxine encouraged. 'It's the actions that count. Any Latin con-man can say "I love you". You must judge men by what they do, not what they say.'

Pagan was silent until they reached a little arbour. They sat down under the lichen-covered statue of Apollo. Pagan said, in an off-hand voice, 'What do you think the world would say if I married Abdi?'

Maxine jerked her head around so suddenly that her sunglasses almost fell off. So Charles was right. 'You mean – he's asked you, Pagan?'

'Yes, but I haven't said yes. That's why I wanted to talk to you. You remember how he behaved . . . when we were young. That's why I haven't said yes.'

'Why not?' Maxine couldn't believe her ears.

•

'Because if I married Abdullah I'd also be marrying his country, his people, his oil fields, his seat at OPEC, his Communist guerrillas, his backward people and his oppressed women.' Pagan bit her bottom lip. 'I can't *cope* with all that, it scares me to death.'

'Rubbish! You coped with that audience at the Theatre Royal all right. You coped with Christopher's illness, you've raised thousands of dollars for the Cancer Institute. You have a positive genius for coping – except when you're in love.' Maxine took off her sunglasses and stared at Pagan's worried face.

'But suppose he dumps me, like he did before?'

'So few women realize that there *is* life after humiliation. And why should he dump you?'

Pagan jumped up nervously. 'Let's keep walking.'

They sauntered in silence along the seven-foot-high box hedge that bordered the estate. Eventually Pagan burst out, 'I asked him if he intended to be faithful. The rotter said . . . well, he indicated . . . Maxi, the silly bugger said, "I cannot promise you fidelity because I do not know if it is possible, I simply don't know."'

Maxine laughed at Pagan's imitation of Abdullah's most pompous manner. 'But that's very sensible of him. It doesn't mean that he's going to dump you. It means just the reverse. He's being very honest.'

Pagan looked anxiously at Maxine, as if asking a fortuneteller to read the future. 'But I don't think my pride would let me turn a blind eye to a crowd of young

•

blondes with big tits. In theory, perhaps, but in fact, I'm pretty sure I couldn't.'

'Pride has always come between you and Abdullah. Abdullah's fierce pride and your stubborn pride. You'll learn that one of the good things about getting older is that one learns to compromise, to give and take.'

'So I've noticed with you and Charles. You give and Charles takes.'

Reaching the curlicued, wrought-iron gates, they turned to walk back on the grass at the side of the drive. 'Charles is very careful of my dignity,' Maxine said, with dignity. 'Well, nearly always. He has his little affairs, but he is very discreet, he never humiliates me. Well, hardly ever.'

'That's what *you* settle for – your dignity and a quiet life. What is the difference between your dignity and my pride, Maxine?'

'I have decided to settle for ninety per cent of the cake instead of fifty per cent of the alimony.' Maxine crossly removed her sunglasses.

'You see, here we are talking about divorce and I haven't even got married yet,' giggled Pagan. Maxine began to understand how Abdullah might sometimes be exasperated by Pagan's flippant charm.

'Oh, Pagan,' she sighed. 'Abdullah is what you've always wanted. I can't understand why you don't jump at the chance of marrying Abdi, when you've been in love with him for years.'

'Being in love is different from loving!' Pagan said. 'I

•

•

can't imagine loving Abdi in the way I loved Christopher. Christopher really cared about all of me; we trusted each other, so we could expose our vulnerability. I wouldn't like to risk exposing my vulnerability to Abdi. And he'll never trust anyone.'

In the distance the eighteenth-century turrets of the château shone purple in the sun.

'But what about all the wonderful things that the hakim taught him when he was sixteen?' Maxine reminded Pagan.

Pagan hesitated. 'When we're in bed, it's physically wonderful, but Abdi's not emotionally involved. That love doctor in Cairo taught him everything about eroticism and nothing about love. I don't want only a sexual relationship. I want warm intimacy and mutual concern.'

'Perhaps you can change him?' Maxine made the female's fatal error of believing this to be possible.

'At least I'm not stupid enough to think that!'

'But if he's asked you to marry him and you're not certain, why not ask for a six-month engagement, a secret engagement that the world will never know about, to give you time to get used to the idea? You have nothing to lose with a secret engagement.'

On the distant stone building row upon row of windows glistened in the sunshine. Pagan turned the idea over in her mind. The most attractive aspect of Maxine's suggestion was that Pagan would now be able to put off her decision.

'Maxine, I think you've solved the problem,' she said,

•

LACE 2

•

looking at the row of fountains in front of the château terrace, where the July sun formed rainbows in the dancing water.

THIRTEEN

August 1979

Layer upon layer of swan-white lace swayed softly as Sandy moved her hips, and the half-hidden diamanté brilliants twinkled like the stars in a Walt Disney sky. Sandy crossed her wrists in front of her, which pushed her breasts together and upwards. The flounces helped as well, she thought, but she sure wished her tits were bigger.

'How much is it, Ken?'

The dress manufacturer's plump pink hand carefully smoothed the satin petals of the ice-pink rosebud between her breasts. 'Let's not talk about the price, Sandy. Just tell me what you think of it.'

Sandy knew that when a man said, 'Let's not talk about the price', the deal was going to be very expensive. However, the circuit gossip was that Ken liked it straight and came fast.

'Why it's just beautiful, Ken,' she cooed, right into her southern belle act. No girl got to be a beauty contest finalist in a dress run up by her mother, in spite of the rule that no evening gown could cost more than two hundred dollars. Which is why Ken Sherman loaned his dresses for publicity value, if he thought a girl had a good chance of winning the beauty pageant. And, of course, a girl had to be nice to Ken.

'I could not imagine a finer ante-bellum gown in the whole world.' Sandy smiled her gleaming, wholesome smile. In the gloom of the deserted showroom Ken twitched the pink satin sash into place, stood back from the spotlight and slowly nodded. No girl could lose in that dress. 'Right,' he said briskly. 'Care for a cocktail at my place?'

'Why Ken, I would be honoured,' Sandy breathed. The bullshit level had to be higher, the closer you got to the top.

The bedroom floor and walls were covered by white fur. The lamps were Lalique crystal seashells and the circular bed was covered with a white leather spread, upon which lay Ken with his legs apart while Sandy cheerfully sucked his stiff little cock. The girls were right about Ken, this was the cheapest dress she'd ever acquired. But Sandy was merely making her down payment; Ken wanted more for his money, and he knew that he wouldn't have another chance after tomorrow's contest.

'Let's take a look at you.' Ken pushed a white fur bolster behind her head and spreading out her waterfall

•

of pale blonde curls, he felt for the zipper of her silver lamé boiler suit and yanked at it. 'Listen, baby, you got nothing to worry about, tomorrow.' He took a look and thought they'd hardly make a 34B as he ripped off the silver lamé. 'Like some music?' He pushed a couple of buttons on the bedhead console that looked capable of flying a 747. Dolly Parton started to wail 'Stand By Your Man' and, overhead, the remote control videocamera started to roll as Ken purred, 'Why, you're as bald as a baby down there,' and pushed Sandy on to her back.

Who did he think he was fooling with that mirrored ceiling, thought Sandy, as Ken squeezed gobs of body lotion over her breasts. Obediently, she massaged the translucent white goo over her breasts; no wonder the bedcover was easy-wipe white leather. 'Honey, you are amazing,' she breathed as she thrust one immaculately manicured finger inside her pink gauze panties, then stuck her rump in the air and pulled at the bows which held the pink gauze in place.

Half an hour later Sandy had been squeezed and shoved and pulled, pushed and arranged in a hundred different poses. She realized that the videotape must be running out, because Ken squeezed her breasts together, felt around her clitoris for a few moments, missed it, poured body lotion on his penis, shoved it inside her, gave ten very careful thrusts, gasped, rolled off, felt around for his cigarettes and said, 'What happened to the thatch, honey?'

'Electrolysis. Hurt like hell. Worse than having the

•

teeth capped. They should give you an anaesthetic.'

Ken dragged on his cigarette. 'So do we have a deal?'

'What sort of deal?'

'If you win the Miss International Beauty Pageant tomorrow, you'll need more gowns, at three thousand dollars a throw.' He pushed his cigarette end into a built-in ashtray on the bedhead. 'You get the gowns from me for ten per cent of the prize money. And don't try to bargain, that's the going rate.'

'Why, honey, whatever you say. I have no head for business.'

Ken leered at Sandy. 'You don't need a head in this business.'

Sandy slid off the bed and smiled. 'Honey, I've got to take a shower and get home for my beauty sleep.' In the shower she ran through her plans. When Ken showered, she'd jump on that bed and push at the mirrored tiles until she found the one that concealed the camera. You certainly *did* need a head in this business: only last year the California Citrus Princess had been forced to resign when a boyfriend published split-beaver pictures of her in a stud magazine.

By the third day of the Miss International Beauty Pageant, the Clarence Plaza Hotel in Miami overflowed with females of every age and shape. Like grown-up children playing with their Barbie dolls, pudgy professional mothers, often obese, chaperoned their still-slim, professional-virgin daughters. Looking as whole-

•

some as strawberry yogurt, these girls had learned to be as tough as infantry boots, but the rules insisted on one chaperone per entrant, and a mother added greatly to the clean-living, all-American apple-pie atmosphere. The unspoken, uncodified and unstated agreement was that this image should be preserved, unsullied. This was why, however jealous, desperate, cynical or vicious a competitor felt, she never let it show. The currency of conversation was always candy-coated. The myth was that all the girls were loving friends.

Sandy's mother, wearing a peach polyester pants suit, sat on the terrace overlooking the swimming pool. Ostentatiously she stitched the ice-pink rose on the front of Ken Sherman's extravagant gown; you scored extra points if your gown was homemade. Lying beside her, Sandy sunbathed in a swimsuit that was carefully cut to match her competition costume, so that her tan marks would match up. Sandy was certain of being one of the three finalists, and knew that she had a good chance of winning the title.

So did the other contestants. On the next lounger Miss Canada propped herself up on one elbow and asked, with honeyed friendliness, 'Are we going to see you use those wrenches today, Sandy?'

Sandy immediately dived into her tote bag and produced a pair of nickel-plated plumber's wrenches. 'Why, honey, I never go *anywhere* without them. Good conversation point. Good defence weapon. And you'll see me use them in the talent section.'

•

SHIRLEY CONRAN

•

'How did you figure out your neat act?' marvelled Miss Canada, who was sick of seeing Sandy giving her frank, freckle-nosed, virginal grin as she brandished her gleaming wrenches in contest after contest, to the delighted surprise of the crowds.

Sandy allowed herself a moment of complacency. 'It's easy if you've got personality.' She put the wrenches back in her tote bag and reached for the suntan oil. They both knew that personality was the winning trick. It was what the judges were looking for, because they needed a girl who could speak up on a talk show or at an opening ceremony. Personality meant the ability to define your own chosen character in three words, and in Sandy's case it was SOUTHERN PLUMBER'S DAUGHTER.

'Sandy's always had personality.' Her mother bit off the cotton thread and held up the seafroth-white gown for inspection. 'Just as well, because she cracks the windows if she tries to sing, she can't dance worth a dime and the only thing she was ever any good at was baton.' Proudly she stroked the satin rose again. 'Sandy, honey, your dress is all finished.'

'That is the most adorable dress I have ever seen,' Miss Canada said, sitting up and curiously looking at the delicate lace. 'I can hardly believe it only cost two hundred dollars, honey.'

Sandy sauntered on stage in overlarge denim coveralls, with a red-and-white spotted handkerchief in the pocket, plumber's wrenches in each hand; she looked refreshingly

•

346

•

wholesome. She began to twirl the wrenches as if they
were batons, whirling them up in the air, then catching
them with panache. As the banjo music slowed Sandy
mopped her forehead with the red handkerchief, gave it
a flourish and pulled a bunch of flowers from it. After her
little conjuring trick, the tempo of the music quickened as
Sandy produced three giant metal washers from the back
pocket of her faded blue coveralls and deftly juggled the
metal circles to a crescendo of applause. Sandy thought,
fuck you, Miss Canada.

On the following evening Sandy dripped blue drops
into her eyes to make them sparkle; she cleaned her
teeth with red toothpaste to make them extra white; she
checked the thick tan make-up on her shoulders; she
looked at herself in the mirror.

Perfect.

Then she squeezed into the tight white satin corselette
and hooped petticoat which went under Ken Sherman's
gown. 'Hook me up, honey,' she murmured to Miss
Canada, who was sticking on her left eyelashes. Carefully
Sandy stepped into the middle of Ken's white lace master-
piece. Miss Canada felt for Sandy's zipper, then paused.
'Hey, Sandy, something's wrong with this zipper!'

Sandy instantly sensed disaster. She grabbed a hand
mirror from the make-up counter, spun around and examined the rear view in the mirror. The zipper down the
back of the gown had been slashed in a dozen places and,
as she touched it, the zipper fell away from the dress.

•

●

What Sandy wanted to say was 'Holy fucking shit'. What she automatically said was 'Jeepers creepers'. Using unladylike language was a sure way to get thrown out of a beauty pageant on the spot.

Goddammit, I told Mama not to let the dress out of her sight, Sandy thought as she shrieked for the pageant supervisor. It was not abnormal for the best dress in the pageant to be sabotaged with a razor blade. It only took thirty seconds.

'OK, you're on last,' said the pageant supervisor, taking in the situation at a glance.

'Mama, go get the hotel maintenance man here with his toolbox,' Sandy ordered.

When the bemused janitor arrived outside the dressing-room door, Sandy dived into the toolbox for the roll of waterproof adhesive used to make temporary repairs in cracked water pipes. It was wide and strong and sticky on both sides. Swiftly Sandy cut twenty inches of the tape and ordered her mother to stick it down her back. Without a word, Sandy's mother spread a dust sheet on the floor, then held the dress as Sandy stepped into it. Clutching the white flounces to her breast, Sandy carefully lowered herself on to the dust sheet, face down. Then, while her mother held the edges of the dress in place, Miss Canada walked daintily on Sandy's spine, her bare feet pressing the dress firmly on to the double-sided strapping. Then both of them helped Sandy to stand up. She thought, thank Christ I really am a plumber's daughter as she said, 'Thanks. Guess I mustn't breathe

●

too deeply, but I reckon every cloud has a silver lining, because now I've got the last number.' The last girl in the parade had the best chance of making a strong impression on the judges.

Sitting at the judges' table, Judy and Lili watched the endless stream of girls, glassy-eyed and stiff, walk down the catwalk towards the cameras, the host and microphone. Their smiles were peppermint-fresh, their faces were peach-perfect and their flesh was the colour of peanut butter

'Can't think why they chose Miami in August,' muttered Lili to Judy.

'Politics, politics,' Judy murmured back to Lili, who had flown over from Europe for the judging. Both women had agreed not to stay in Miami for one minute longer than was necessary. The humid, tropical heat blasted them every time they left the over-elaborate lobby of their gaudy hotel, and within minutes their clothes would be soaked with perspiration, and the energy drained from their bodies.

The final parade, in formal gowns, was the first time that the audience had heard the girls speak. Each girl was interviewed to determine whether or not she had personality. Translated, that meant whether she would be able to stand up for herself on talk shows in the appropriately charming, self-deprecatory manner.

Suddenly the hot, tired women in the theatre gasped as Sandy glided down the wide staircase. Sandy looked

•

as if she had been sprayed with lace foam that was slowly slipping down from her shoulders and about to reveal her body.

'Tell us about yourself, Sandy,' encouraged the white-suited host as he handed the microphone to Sandy.

Sandy gave the judges her most brilliant smile. 'I am majoring in social science and then I plan to be a teacher because I just love children.' Pause at that point, thought Sandy.

'This is a beautiful dress you have on,' the host prompted, holding the microphone under the tip of her nose.

'I usually make all my own clothes,' Sandy confided, thinking, keeping the answers short, 'but my Mama helped me with this.' She blew a kiss to her mother in the audience.

'And what do you do in your spare time, Sandy?'

'I like to water ski, I go dancing, and I'm taking an evening course in domestic engineering.'

'*Domestic engineering?*' The host glanced briefly at his prompt card. 'What is that, Sandy?'

'I guess it's just a fancy name for plumbing,' Sandy repeated her confident laugh. 'My Daddy's a plumber and he taught me all I know. When I get married, I'll be able to fix the washing machine.' Roars of applause.

'May I ask if you are courting at this time?'

'Do you mean, do I have a boyfriend?' Sandy moved closer to the microphone so that her voice sounded

•

breathy. 'Well no, I do not. Right now my life is just so full of opportunities that I want to get on and enjoy it to the full.'

'And now, Sandy, for the final question,' the host finished. 'Tell us why you are proud of your country.'

The beauty queens had all rehearsed their answers, but Sandy's reply sounded enthusiastically impromptu. 'Because America really *is* beautiful, America really *is* friendly, and America really *is* free! I believe that America is the land of opportunity and I am the living proof of that. My Mama was a dancer from Sweden and my father came over from Ireland, when he was just a kid. Why, if it hadn't been for America they would never have met up.' Sandy deliberately turned away from the host and waved to the close-up camera. 'Hi, Mama and Daddy, I am so glad *you chose America!*'

The theatre erupted in a storm of cheering and clapping. Many in the audience dabbed their eyes or wiped away tears as they stood and applauded. Sandy mentally evaluated her chances. Sudan was statuesque, almond-eyed, and the Third World girls always got sympathy votes. Sri Lanka might be an added threat because she had been a stunning sight in her national costume, ultramarine silk, with tinkling bracelets on her tiny, high-arched feet.

As the ten nervous girls clattered up the backstage stairs Sandy wondered why, for Chrissake, Canada had been selected. According to Sandy's research, Canada and the United States were never chosen together, since it was considered undiplomatic to pick neighbouring countries.

•

Maybe Canada has something going for her that we don't know about, maybe someone down here owes someone up there one big favour, Sandy decided as, carefully, she pulled her full skirt clear of her high heels, and walked across the dirty backstage floor, crisscrossed with electrical leads.

While the audience was entertained by a team of dancers in azure chiffon and sequins, the judges withdrew to a side room and considered their decision. Judy unpinned the lurid purple orchid from her cream silk lapel and pondered the three nordic, three hispanic, three black and one oriental finalist; she realized that the colour mix for the final line-up was as predictable as the colours in an ice-cream sundae.

The international photographer offered first opinion. 'I want Sudan,' he said firmly. 'She's marvellously photogenic; she's got terrific presence and she's unattached.'

The Mirabelle man interrupted quickly. 'Sudan would be of limited value to us.' He meant that the Mirabelle range was not designed for a black skin. 'Our vote goes to United States; her microphone manner was professional.'

Lili asked, 'What about Sri Lanka?'

Several judges shook their heads. 'She'll never make it on talk shows.'

'My vote goes to Italy,' said the Hollywood agent.

'Italy is just a little bit adult for us.' The Mirabelle man meant that, at the age of twenty-three, Miss Italy's skin had already lost the childlike smoothness that made mass-produced cosmetics look good in a high-definition colour

•

photograph. He added, 'And United States has the look that Mirabelle will promote next year.'

After another twenty minutes of argument the judges marked their prepared ballots and tossed them into the wire basket held by the organizer, who announced with satisfaction, 'United States it is, with Sudan second and Italy third.'

When the pre-recorded trumpet fanfare blasted and the host announced that Miss International Beauty of 1979 was Miss United States, Miss Sandy Bayriver from Louisiana, Sandy looked suitably astonished and elated, then wiped an imaginary teardrop from the corner of her eye, and allowed the host to lead her to the winner's throne. Gotcha, she thought, as yet another diamanté crown was placed upon her head.

Judy signed the hotel bill for two glasses of freshly squeezed lemon juice and turned over on her yellow sunbed to let the Florida sun toast her back. Lili sat up and poured both packets of sugar into her glass. Lili's sweet tooth and Judy's taste for bitter drinks were both satisfied if they ordered two freshly squeezed lemon juices and Lili used all the sugar before adding water to both glasses. In ten months, this was the nearest they had come to a family custom.

Lili wriggled on her sunbed. 'This heat! I'm going for another swim.' She jumped up and ran towards the blue sea.

After a bit Judy noticed that Lili's small red snakeskin

•

purse lay between their two yellow sunbeds. The catch
wasn't closed and the contents were spilling over the
sand. Judy leaned forward and carefully shook sand from
the lip gloss, the tissue and the unwritten postcards. Then
she picked up the airmail envelope and froze as she noticed
the Nicaragua stamp, Mark's familiar handwriting and
his name on the back.

The envelope was still sealed, but it was badly sealed
and only stuck down at the tip of the flap. Furtively Judy
started to raise the side of the envelope. She couldn't help
herself. Peering into the envelope, she could just make
out the words 'love' and 'helpless', then she heard Lili's
voice behind her. Quickly she stuffed the letter back in
the purse.

'It's no use. You'd think they'd leave me alone when
the place is stuffed with beauty queens. I'm going inside
to the air conditioning.' Lili picked up the red snakeskin
purse, stuck her sunglasses on and walked towards the
hotel.

Judy turned on her stomach and buried her face in her
beach towel to hide the tears which prickled her eyelids.
Thank God Lili was flying back to Europe tomorrow.

Thank God this race was only 500 kilometres thought
Lili as the Riviera sun blazed down upon the raw, white-
painted concrete of the pits, and hurt Lili's eyes with its
savage glare.

This sun was almost as fierce as Miami's had been, last
week. The only difference between the Paul Ricard circuit

•

and the British tracks seemed to be that the grandstands were flanked with dusty tubs of oleanders, the French spectators were not quite so badly dressed as the British ones and the car park was littered with empty wine bottles, rather than empty lager cans. Apart from these points, the tawdry souvenir booths sold the same tasteless BMW baseball caps, Ferrari bomber jackets and Lancia T-shirts as they did in Britain; the competitors were the same, they drove the same cars, the noise and the smell were exactly the same. Only the wording on the billboards was different – Michelin instead of Dunlop and Elf instead of Mobil.

Wistfully Lili looked at the purple-smudged hills in the distance and longed to be in the dappled shade of the pine forests instead of by this stinking, sunbaked racing circuit.

The low black Spear snarled past, hugging the ground like a sinister giant insect. Lili checked her stopwatch. Two seconds faster than his best practice time. With any luck, they'd be back in time to have a swim before dinner.

The PA droned on. 'And halfway through this four-hundred-kilometre race, it's Werner Hentzen's Porsche in the lead, followed by the Dinetti, then Gautier in the Lancia . . . and the Spear has just overtaken the Lancia and it's pulling ahead . . .'

Lili yawned, stuck her ear protectors back on and pulled the script for her next movie out of her leather hunting bag. It had arrived that morning from Omnium Pictures. She would have some terrific outfits as Helen of

·

Troy and, after the Mistinguett role, she was in good shape for another musical.

A blue airmail letter fell from the leather hunting bag. Lili sighed. She'd stuffed it in there this morning before Gregg saw it. Mark knew and used the secret code that was used to bypass Lili's fan mail, so she always received his letters. And she always tore them up, unread. It was the least she could do, she thought sadly as she tore the pale blue envelope into strips, and threw it away. Then she turned her attention to the script.

By the time King Agamemnon had pitched his tent in sight of the walls of Troy the Spear was challenging the Porsche for the lead as the PA shrieked '. . . and, with only three laps to go, the Spear is lying behind the Porsche and Werner Hentzen is fighting off the challenge . . .'

By the time Paris wished that he had listened to Cassandra's prophecies the PA was ecstatically screaming, '. . . and now the Spear is neck and neck with the Porsche . . . and Eagleton has passed the Porsche! With only one lap to go, the Spear is in the lead . . .'

Insulated from the noise by her earmuffs, Lili did not know that Gregg had gained the lead. Neither did she know, as the triumphant Hector wearily unstrapped his gleaming breastplate, that Gregg had lost the lead and fallen back behind the Porsche.

But after the giant wooden horse, its belly full of soldiers, had crossed over the plain towards the walls of Troy, the other spectators started to jump up and down and this distracted Lili from the script.

•

Lili pulled off her ear protectors, to hear the PA gabble
'. . . and the Spear has taken the Porsche on the inside
. . . now they're coming down the final straight towards
the flag and it looks as if . . . yes . . . IT'S THE SPEAR
. . . with the first win for Gregg Eagleton!'

Gregg was hauled out of the car, weighed down with a
laurel wreath, soaked in champagne, kissed by half a
dozen girls promoting a new cocktail mix, carried
shoulder high to the grandstand, awarded a silver rose
bowl, then more champagne, then photographed with
his arm round Lili in a crush of champagne-drenched
admirers.

Gregg posed for one last picture, then they stumbled
away to the trailer park. The Spear, its wings coated
with red dust, was being wheeled into its trailer by two
mechanics. Gregg climbed into the driver's cab to change
and shower in the tiny compartment behind the seat. The
mechanics walked back to the pit to pack up their tools.
Lili sat on the edge of the transporter, swinging her legs
and waiting for Gregg.

Five minutes later he climbed into the back of the
trailer, his hair still damp from the shower.

'Give her a rest, darling!' Lili jumped up and picked
her way into the dark, petrol-smelling interior, knowing
that Gregg could not pass the Spear without wanting to
lift the engine housing and fiddle with something. She
didn't notice the elated gleam in his eyes and the urgency
in his manner as he pulled the lever that closed the back
doors of the trailer.

•

•

'Gregg. Stop playing around! It's dark in here.' Lili crossly felt her way forwards in the dim, hot trailer and blundered into his arms. He kissed her hard, then pulled her up the ladder to the driver's bunk above the seats.

'Stop it, Gregg. And it's as hot as hell in here!'

'Can't stop, I want you now.' He kissed her harder as he pulled off her white linen shift, under which Lili was naked. The stink of oil and petrol normally made Lili feel faintly sick, but now it seemed erotic. Sweat poured from Gregg's body as their flesh met and Lili felt a hot rush of warm pleasure.

'What's got into you?' murmured Lili.

Gregg said, 'Winning. That's the real turn-on.'

'This is such a wonderful view!' Pagan jumped on to the parapet of Abdullah's turreted château, and waved her arm at the lavender hills of the French Riviera. Her loose, red cotton dress blew behind her like a flag in the breeze as she turned to Maxine and said, 'Aren't you glad you came? Who'd have thought, all those years ago in Gstaad, that we'd still be friends today.'

Maxine shrugged. 'Perhaps we wouldn't be such friends if we all lived next door in each other's pockets. As it is, we're not round each other enough to demand more closeness or support than we are able, or want, to give.'

'Maybe the secret of friendship is not being too friendly.'

They left the roof and started to walk down the elabor-

•

ate wide staircase of the sumptuous château, passing richly coloured tapestries, suits of moorish armour and crimson brocade curtains. What a pity, Maxine thought. The tapestries were nineteenth-century fakes, lacking the delicate colour, the rat-nibbled charm of the real thing.

Pagan wondered what the servants would think if she slid down the banister, then said, 'It was easy to be friends at school, when all our lives were pretty similar but, later on, friends travel down different roads, and some of them are marked "No Entry".' She lifted the elaborate metal visor of a medieval helmet, and said, 'Boo!'

'I don't know where Abdi got the decorator,' said Maxine, 'but he's gilded everything from the light switches to the banisters. All the furniture legs have claws, and look as if they're about to stagger across the floor.'

'I knew you'd hate it,' said Pagan as they passed a green malachite table edged with ormulu and supported by two overweight gold cherubs. 'It gets worse.'

For once, Maxine was speechless as they walked through the salon and out on to the terrace.

Abdullah waved from the side of the pool. How much older Abdullah looks, Maxine thought, noticing the frosting of grey hairs among his strong black curls, and the deeply etched lines in his forehead.

That evening, in the darkness, on the terrace, Abdullah pulled Pagan to him and kissed her. She could smell the vanilla-scented bougainvillaea bushes and the old-

•

•

fashioned cologne Abdullah wore and the faint odour of his Turkish cigarettes and the starch of his shirt.

'Have you decided, Pagan?'

Nervously, she said, 'I need time to get used to the idea. I'm worried because it could be so difficult, not only for you and me, but for your country – if it didn't work out. I wondered, that is . . . would you mind if . . . we have a six-month secret engagement?'

He released her so abruptly that she almost fell over the parapet. 'Secret! Are you ashamed of me?'

Pagan's mellow happiness dissolved, leaving her with a stomachful of anxiety. 'No, I'm afraid of the future, Abdi.'

'You can't be ruled by fear in life. Who doesn't dare, doesn't win.' Abdullah was an angry silhouette against the blue-black sky. 'I'm sorry, Pagan, but you can't have me on approval.'

'But I want to be certain.' Pagan thumped her knee with her fist.

'Oh, Pagan, you can never be certain.' Abdullah sounded exasperated and sad. 'Life is a series of risks, Pagan. You either open the door marked "risk" or you stay in the cabbage patch for ever.'

'But, Abdi, you're asking for a lot. You're asking for my whole life.'

'Yes, Pagan, I am asking a lot. I am also offering a lot. I am sorry that you can't accept it.' He strode away, leaving Pagan alone on the empty terrace.

FOURTEEN

1 September 1979

In his Philadelphia office Curtis Halifax watched his family attorney read the telegram. Telling Harry hadn't been as hard as he'd expected; in fact, Harry hadn't batted an eyelash as, haltingly, Curtis had told him of the long-kept secret; but attorneys were accustomed to hauling family skeletons out of the closet. Curtis leaned back in his leather wing desk chair, feeling relieved. At last he had told somebody.

'Dear Daddy, unless you pay them ten million dollars within fifteen days, they will kill me. Stand by for payment in Istanbul. Directions will be sent to Mommy at the hotel. Love – Lili,' Harry read and then raised his eyebrows. 'Curtis, this telegram reads like something from an Andy Hardy movie.' He read the telegram aloud. 'Are you sure this isn't some crazy joke?'

'No, I've already spoken to her mother.'

'And this Lili is the *movie star*?'

Curtis nodded.

'You're *sure* . . . that is . . . there's no doubt in your mind that you are the father?'

'No doubt at all, Harry.' Curtis shook his head. 'I've known about the child since she was born. She lived with foster parents in Switzerland, and her mother and I were told that she'd died at the age of six.'

Slowly Harry sipped his highball. It wasn't unlikely that a childless man of Curtis's age should be proud of fathering an illegitimate child, but the Halifaxes were an illustrious Philadelphia family and everyone knew what Debra was like; a scandal like this might push her over the edge.

'Curtis, are you sure you want to go to these lengths? You're really prepared to fly to Istanbul? How are you going to explain that to Debra?'

'No problem. I fly to Europe on business quite often. Debra won't mind, unless I'm not back in time for Ceezee's Thanksgiving party.'

Harry glanced up at the portraits of Curtis's father and grandfather hanging against the panelled walls. 'My advice would be to consider that other issues might come to light, as well as your paternity of an illegitimate child.'

Curtis knew that his attorney was hinting at the long series of loans the bank had made to Judy Jordan's group of companies, as Harry continued, 'Curtis, it all happened a long time ago. Why not just forget it?'

'It may have been a long time ago, Harry, but I've always regretted the way I treated her mother.' Curtis reached across his desk and held out his hand for the

•

telegram. 'It's simple. My family raised me to be responsible, and I'm going to be responsible for my daughter, who's in danger.'

'But you say you've never even met this woman!'

'I wanted to meet Lili.' Curtis remembered the previous October and his meeting with Judy in the dim, discreet, New York restaurant. Angrily he had brandished a copy of *The New York Times* and pointed at the story of Lili's search for her mother. Wrathfully Curtis had asked Judy why she had invented the story that Lili's father was a dead soldier when he, Curtis Halifax, was the father of Lili. Reproachfully Judy whispered that she had lied to protect Curtis's marriage. How would Debra feel, if told that Curtis had an illegitimate child? How would an ex-porn star fit into Debra's social life in Philadelphia? How would such a beautiful stepdaughter affect Debra's anxiety about her external appearance; if she didn't starve herself to death, Debra would be in constant surgery having her body and face restructured and lifted.

'You must protect Debra.' As usual, Judy had gently played on his guilt. 'Leave Lili alone.'

Curtis had hesitated. 'But she's my . . .'

Judy had interrupted, 'After all, you once left me alone, didn't you? You made *your* choice twenty years ago. You didn't know that you were choosing loneliness when you married Debra, but I knew that loneliness was what you were choosing for *me*.'

Curtis's attorney looked at the silver-framed photograph on the banker's mahogany desk and, as if reading

•

his client's thoughts, he said, 'Well, you know what'll happen to Debra, if any of this leaks out.'

'Look, Harry, I asked you to drop by to check my legal position, not to hand out marriage guidance.' Suddenly Curtis looked like the portrait of his grandfather.

'Curtis, if you admit paternity of this child, you could lay yourself open to . . .'

Curtis impatiently cut him short. 'Harry, I hear what you're saying, but I've made my decision. Now, can we get on with the logistics? How can I raise the money?'

'Even if we could raise that much fast, Curtis, there's no way you could pay kidnap ransom, because it is against government policy to pay kidnap ransom. So, for a start, remember that you'll be up against the law if you transfer the money out of the country.'

Again Curtis showed his grandfather's drive. 'What about our Bahamas operation, Harry, what can we raise there? And we've got the properties in Rio, as well as the Tokyo development. There's enough security there. You're not going to tell me that we can't raise a lousy ten million bucks outside the country!'

Harry looked doubtful. 'My advice is to play this one for time. Both Lili and her mother are influential people with influential friends. By the time you get to Istanbul you may find that the Turkish police have already found her.'

Curtis propped his neatly groomed grey head on one hand. 'I hope you're right, Harry, but in case you're wrong, I want you to raise as much as you can on those

•

Brazilian leases and transfer it to Istanbul. Nothing you say is going to stop me flying out there tonight. I feel so fucking powerless, sitting behind this fucking desk when my daughter is in danger.'

In twenty years Harry had never heard Curtis swear. 'OK, Curtis.' The attorney stood up. 'But try to stay within the law. I don't want to be part of your defence team.'

2 September 1979

'Stop throwing plates, Maggie. I'll explain!' Angelface Harris ducked behind the closet door of the all-black kitchen as his wife hurled another handful of expensive, handmade pottery at him.

'I've had enough of your bloody lies,' Maggie screamed as she grabbed a yellow Italian soup tureen from the black worktop and threw it at her husband. A pile of ceramic shards was building up in front of his hiding place, and the gleaming black kitchen shelves were almost bare. 'You've lied to me every day of our marriage, why should I believe you now?' A scarlet meat plate followed the yellow tureen.

'It serves you bloody right for going through my pockets!'

'I was only looking for grass. And if I hadn't been, I wouldn't have found that telegram.' Maggie flung a Carol

McNicholl teapot. 'Dear Daddy, unless you pay them ten million fucking dollars within fifteen days, they'll kill me.' Maggie picked up the food processor, then changed her mind and went for the coffeemaker. 'You ain't going to Istanbul, Angelface, and you ain't sending any money to that fucking porn queen.'

'Maggie, I told you, I've no idea what this is about.'

'I never knew you *had* ten million dollars,' Maggie shrieked, 'or I'd never had signed the fucking premarital agreement.' Maggie had now thrown everything she could lift and the kitchen shelves were bare.

'Maggie, be reasonable!' Angelface looked round the closet door. 'Of course I don't have ten million dollars! What's more, I intend to hang on to every penny I got.'

With difficulty, Maggie picked up the food processor and pitched it. The machine hit the door, scraped the paint off and flew apart as it crashed to the floor.

Angelface knew that Maggie had no ammunition left. Warily he stepped out. 'I got no intention of paying ransom for Lili *or* going to Turkey *or* getting involved with the fucking Turkish police.' He picked his way across the seventh set of crockery to be broken since their marriage. 'Now, will you swear not to tell about that telegram?'

Maggie scowled at him. 'I might and I might not.'

'You better not, you stupid bitch.' Angelface looked down at her and glared. She reached up and slapped his face. He grabbed her hand and pushed her back against the black worktop. Maggie was not intimidated, she was gasping with excitement, and Angelface's eyes were glittering as he tore her shirt open and lunged at her breasts. 'I'll teach you a lesson,' he panted, feeling his cock start to harden. Maggie tried to knee Angelface in the crotch, flailed frantically at him with her free hand, then she pulled a heavy cast-iron saucepan from the sink and smashed her husband over the head with it.

With a roar of rage, Angelface smacked her face.

Maggie's head cracked against the wall, and she collapsed into a screaming heap on the floor.

Angelface jumped to the far side of the black table, as if he wanted a solid barrier between himself and his wife.

'You shouldn't have bopped me with that iron pot, that wasn't playful,' he muttered.

Maggie continued to weep, blood streaming from her split lip.

'It wasn't funny, Mags.'

Piteously Maggie looked up; mascara, blood and lipstick streaked her face.

'Oh, shut yer face and come 'ere,' Angelface ordered out of the side of his mouth. He wasn't going to pick her up.

Maggie picked herself up and tottered towards his grudgingly opened arms. Angelface licked the blood from her split lip and whispered hoarsely, 'I'm sorry, baby, but you shouldn't provoke me that way.' He gently pulled off what remained of Maggie's silk shirt and used it to wipe the tears from her red-and-black streaked face.

•

•

Cheekily he pinched one of her nipples and she gave a mollified sniff.

'For all I know, Maggie, I might have hundreds of kids around the world,' said Angelface reproachfully, 'but I'd be daft to own up to any of 'em.' He thought, I am tickled fucking pink to think that my kid's turned out to be one of the most beautiful chicks in the world, but I'd better not tell Maggie, or she might really try to hurt me.

Slowly Angelface pulled down the zipper of her jeans. 'You know how the chicks come after me, Maggie. Knickers off and legs up in rows outside me dressing-room door. It was before you come along, darling.' He slid his hands inside her jeans and comfortingly squeezed her ass. Maggie was so tiny that one of her buns was hardly a handful. 'You know I got me appetites, Maggie.' He grabbed her hand and thrust it down his pants, where she could feel his growing affection. 'And you know you love it, baby.'

Entwined, they tottered upstairs to the bedroom, then hurled themselves at each other on the unmade, black-sheeted bed.

Two hours later, when their Filipino houseman had cleaned up the kitchen and Angelface had locked himself in the recording studio with his band, Maggie leaned back against the black sheets, lit a joint, reached for the Mickey Mouse telephone and called her best friend. 'I dunno what I'm going to do, Joanie,' she moaned, with no preamble. 'He busted me lip again and I'm sure he's broken me wrist. D'you think I should leave him this time?'

•

Joanie asked what had started it, after which they discussed the ongoing tragedy, and the proper etiquette for an upgraded groupie when faced with an illegitimate stepdaughter who was far more beautiful than Maggie, and famous.

By eight o'clock the next morning, when Angelface crashed out on his bed, reeking of brandy, and Maggie was deep in barbiturate-assisted sleep, Joanie had called the rock column of London's evening newspaper. By eleven in the morning the editor had decided to splash the story and, by one o'clock, billboards all over the city screamed: LILI – KIDNAP SENSATION.

La Divina stretched her ripe, red mouth as wide as if she were projecting a perfect high C to the dome of La Scala, then firmly clamped her lips around the penis. Slowly she pushed her mouth over the smooth flesh. With satisfaction, La Divina thought that no younger woman, however beautiful, could do this as well as she. Twenty years of practice kept the rhythm steady and helped her to sense if she was going too slow, too fast or too gently (the most frequent male complaint) as Spyros rubbed against the roof of her mouth. Oops! Spyros twitched and La Divina nearly gagged as her uvula made an involuntary movement. That's what happened if you lost your concentration. It should feel, to the man, as sensuously satisfying as having a hand sucked by a newborn calf.

Suddenly the thought of calves and kittens and puppies came into her mind, and La Divina seemed to see a view

•

•

of herself on the bed from a corner of the ceiling. Oh, Heavens, why was she doing this? It really wasn't an act of love, mouthing this bratwurst with such care. It was a well-practised, pathetic act of desperation, a sensual bribe, her last resort, inspired by despair at the thought of losing Spyros and all that he stood for. Her love was no longer love, it was fear; the fear of being abandoned, of public humiliation, of being alone. La Divina sucked harder. How much longer was he going to take? She would start counting the thrusts. Ten . . . twenty . . . forty . . . She started to get cramp in her jaw.

The fey young men who had formed La Divina's entourage when she was the world's most adored diva now sniggered that her mellifluous voice had failed because of the damage done to laryngeal tissues by her bedroom practices. But La Divina no longer cared about the gossip, which rustled through the opera houses of the world, about her affair with the Stiarkoz brothers. She was deathly tired of that demanding circus, the adoring audiences who would shout for blood as readily as for the thirtieth curtain call. Buenos Aires had been a nightmare. She had adequately performed the first half of the recital, then halfway through the aria from *Norma* she had failed to reach high C and an almost crow-like harshness had crept into her lower notes.

There had been catcalls, jeers and howls of laughter. On the following day, when she read her notices, La Divina had cancelled the rest of her tour and fled back to Europe and the sanctuary of the yacht *Persephone*, which

•

was cruising the Greek Islands. Last night she had been reunited with Spyros. Now, all that she cared about was hiding from the world with this man in one of their private places – on his island or his yacht. She wanted to forget that she had ever been a *prima donna*, to forget the anxiety, the responsibility, as well as the honeyed applause. She wanted only to pass her days in sensual reverie and her evening hours feeling him move into her hungry body, thrusting a reason for living back into her immaculately maintained shell.

'I had forgotten how good it feels to be with you.' Spyros slowly drew his blunt fingertips down the fullness of her left breast until he reached the hard dark peak.

But I have forgotten nothing, thought La Divina. She remembered living in a mist of unhappiness after Jo Stiarkoz, as if hypnotized, had abandoned her for that bitch, Lili. It had happened overnight, and La Divina had at first felt numb with misery, then suspended in a miasma of pain and loss. For weeks that grew into months, La Divina lived in a trance of shock, sorrow and humiliation. Finally, she became apathetic; she couldn't be bothered to get out of bed, to get dressed, to go out or to see anyone. When Jo Stiarkoz had been killed in a car crash, La Divina did not (as everyone expected) become hysterical upon hearing the news, because she had been mourning Jo for years.

And then, one day, shortly after Jo's death, her maid had brought to her bedroom a willow basket planted with spring flowers. Twisted between the miniature cyclamen

and wood anemones La Divina had found a delicate
eighteenth-century diamond collar of rose-cut stones
linked by fine bows of smaller brilliants. The card read
'Spyros Stiarkoz'. She smiled. This would only be the
beginning, she knew. He would not expect her to thank
him, but to wait for his next move.

The next morning she had unwrapped the warm croiss-
ant on her breakfast tray and a pair of matching diamond
earrings fell from the pink napkin. As she held one,
dangling to the light, her bedside telephone rang. 'I've
just finished my calls to Hong Kong – may I see you?'
asked Spyros Stiarkoz, without introducing himself. La
Divina guessed what Spyros meant, because his older
brother, Jo, had always preferred to make love in the
early morning, after the Hong Kong trading had finished
or late at night, after the American markets had closed.

Two hours after receiving the earrings La Divina had
been standing on the deck of the *Persephone*. The tang of
the sea had mingled with Spyros's faint odour of starch,
cigar smoke and clean, warm flesh. That night, before
she had a chance to undress, he had quietly appeared in
her stateroom. Without a word, he had moved forward
and silently held her against him for a long time.

Then, with care, he had softly pulled at the shoulder
of her topaz satin gown. She had not moved as he pulled
the dress down to her waist, then bent his lips to her
large, dark nipples and kissed them lightly, feeling the
buds grow hard. Then he had sucked hard at them,
and fierce stabs of pleasure had shot, almost painfully,

•

between her legs as he held the tips of her breasts softly
between his teeth, then teased them with his tongue, and
La Divina had shuddered as life washed into her body
once more. Although she had scarcely begun to moisten,
she had pulled Spyros close to her, hungering for his vital
hardness, feeling the warmth of his erection through the
thin silk of his navy dressing gown.

They had fallen back on the bed and she had felt his
hand softly, slowly, stroking her inner thighs, higher and
higher. Still he made no sound but, as he reached her
mound of Venus and started to softly stroke it, she rose
eagerly against the rhythm of his hand, feeling no anxiety,
no necessity to hurry, just the certainty of her eventual
orgasm. When she climaxed, her whole body arched in
ecstasy, then she felt for the head of his penis and guided
it into her; their mouths were together and their fingers
entwined.

Later she had sobbed with gratitude as Spyros held her
to his hairy damp chest.

Slowly La Divina's confidence, career and greedy appetite for life had revived and now, six years later, she knew
the responses of Spyros Stiarkoz's body better than the
power of her capricious voice.

Yes, I have forgotten nothing, La Divina thought, as
she lay against the body of Spyros Stiarkoz. She would
always remember what he had done for her. Why, when
she had telephoned two days ago from Buenos Aires, after
cancelling her tour, he had comforted her and told her to
fly straight back to Athens.

•

•

She had only arrived this morning but his helicopter had been waiting to carry her to the *Persephone*, which was anchored off Aegina.

That afternoon they had made love for over an hour, until both were exhausted and sweating, but Spyros had been unable to have an erection. Afterwards La Divina had, silently, considered all the possible reasons. Of course, Spyros would never see sixty again. Perhaps he had a health problem; ten different sorts of tablets and capsules stood on the tray beside the gold dolphin faucets in his bathroom.

This evening La Divina was determined to arouse him. Now, as her throat accepted the flesh she loved so much, she ran her fingers lightly up his thighs, softly raked his buttocks with her fuchsia nails, then plunged her fingers into his dense pubic hair. But, as she massaged the sensitive area behind the base of his testicles, she felt his balls begin to slacken away from his body and realized that she was not getting the usual response.

La Divina hollowed her cheeks and sucked harder. But it was no good. Spyros's erection had faded.

Finally she pulled away, and looked at him, her eyes filling with anxious tears. Spyros seemed completely unconcerned as he said, 'It will be fine later, darling, I promise you.'

'No, no!' She broke into noisy sobs. 'It's different, isn't it? What have you done with that creature, that now you can't make love to *me*?'

•

Spyros did not reply, because there was no point in saying anything to her when she was determined to make a scene. And, in fact, he was extremely worried about his lack of response. Nothing like this had happened since he had started taking the serum.

'It's not enough for you to have Zeus Air! It's not enough for you to have more tankers and bigger tankers than Jo had in his fleet!'

La Divina started hitting the cream linen sheets with her clenched fists, and crying louder. 'It's not enough that the *Persephone* is ten metres longer than Jo's yacht! It's not enough that you have *me!*'

Spyros sighed. The first tantrum after twenty-four hours of peace. Ashtrays would be flying within five minutes.

'It's not enough that I love you, Spyros, more than I ever loved your brother! Don't you realize that *nothing* will ever be enough to make you feel you've beaten Jo?' La Divina started to hit his hard, grey-haired chest with her clenched fists. 'But now I know what you want. I didn't think it was true, but it is. *You want Lili as well.* Don't try to deny it. I saw that photograph of you two in the *New York Post*, last November, at the opera. *Dozens* of kind friends sent me the clipping. You remember, I was singing in Sydney. The press was on my neck the next day. Had I any comment, they wanted to know? I had to smile pleasantly, say no, no comment, *and then step out on that stage!*'

So she *had* known about Lili. And for ten months she

•

had not mentioned it. Such emotional self-control was rare in La Divina.

'I promise you, darling, I haven't spoken to Lili for months.' No, Spyros thought, but Lili had been on his mind every day since he had touched her. La Divina's instinct was uncanny.

Spyros had wanted Lili's succulent body for added reasons that he did not care to acknowledge. Certainly, Lili had rejected him, but Spyros never gave up. When anyone opposed him in business, Spyros single-mindedly concentrated on destroying that person. When Spyros wanted something for his collection of Greek antiquities, he was prepared to wait for it – sometimes for years – and he was prepared to pay far, far above the market value for something he really desired. He was very rich and, because he was growing old, there was very little in life that he wanted.

But he wanted Lili.

Now, he briefly kissed the hand of La Divina and returned to his cabin, pausing to admire the purple silhouette of Aegina against the darkening Greek sky.

Back in his own suite Spyros telephoned for the ship's doctor and then showered. Afterwards, one millimetre of serum was injected into his muscular left buttock, which was then respectfully swabbed. The serum was provided by the Swiss clinic that Spyros attended every winter for a week. The precious drug was cultured from the gonadal tissue of embryo pigs; within an hour it would make the sixty-eight-year-old as virile as a fifteen-year-old, Spyros hoped as he dressed. By midnight La Divina would have dried her tears; she would be exhausted and contented and, he hoped, as his valet fastened his platinum cufflinks, she would also be quiet. Thank God she didn't know about the telegram, which had arrived that morning.

There was a knock at the door and a white-uniformed aide entered, holding a paper. 'Just came over the radio, sir. They've located Judy Jordan's hotel in Istanbul. Mr Menecik at the Turkish Foreign Ministry has radioed back to you, offering his services, and Mr Vlassos of Interpol will be available in twenty minutes.'

3 September 1979

Across the road from the Sydonite Embassy the ducks sailed serenely on the pond in St James's Park. Abdullah stared at them, then looked up in surprise as Pagan, wearing a blue Japanese kimono and no make-up, burst into his library, brandishing the *Daily Mail*.

'Abdi, this is terrible!'

Abdullah, who had already signed a thick folder of decrees and state instruments, used the peaceful morning hours to read the most important reports. Now he put down the précis of his Intelligence Department's Washington report.

'Look what it says in the *Daily Mail*!' Pagan read aloud, '"Angelface Harris and Lili, kidnap drama".' She looked
•

up at Abdullah. 'Lili's been snatched in Istanbul! Judy's still there. I must telephone her straight away.'

Abdullah waved his bodyguard out of the room. 'Does anyone know the identity of the kidnappers or what they want?'

'No idea who they are, but it says here that they've demanded ten million dollars from Angelface Harris. Judy will be frantic!' Pagan loped around the large library, her untidy hair unbrushed, her kimono flying out behind her. As she passed Abdullah's desk she caught her kimono sleeve on a silver tray and impatiently tugged at it. The filing tray fell to the floor, scattering a pile of papers and a telegram. Abdullah jumped up, picked up the telegram and stuffed it in his pocket, then started to shove the papers back on to the silver tray. Pagan was so distraught that she did not notice this strange action. Normally, Abdullah would have pressed a button on the floor beneath his desk, whereupon a black-robed secretary would have entered and picked up the papers.

'I'll get home and pack my bags straight away, Abdi. I'll have to go to Istanbul as soon as I can get on a plane. Judy will need friends around her at a time like this.' She flung a Burberry raincoat over her kimono as Abdi rang for the car.

An hour later Abdullah appeared at Pagan's front door. She had just hurled open a newly packed suitcase, hunting for her passport.

'I don't like the idea of your going to Istanbul alone,' Abdullah said. 'I think I'd better go with you. My people

•

have never trusted the Turks, so we have a good intelligence system there. So we might be able to help in some way. We have a very pleasant little palace in the diplomatic quarter. My dispatch boxes can be sent there. Suliman has arranged everything, our plane will leave in two hours.'

Pagan jumped up and kissed him. 'Darling Abdi, you *are* so kind!' It did not occur to Pagan to wonder why Abdullah should be so willing to make this uncharacteristic gesture of support. 'Now, where the hell is my passport?'

Patiently Abdullah said, 'Your passport is of no consequence when you are travelling with me. I suggest, however, that you ask your maid to find you something more suitable to wear.' Pagan looked down and realized that she had been about to depart in her blue kimono.

'Miss Jordan is expecting me,' Pagan explained to the desk clerk for the fourth time, demonstrating the universal habit of raising the voice to uncomprehending foreigners. The next moment she was almost knocked off her feet as the plump and sweaty manager of the Harun-al-Rashid bustled forward with two assistants and bowed to the thin man in uniform, who was standing behind Pagan.

The marble lobby of the hotel was alive with journalists of every nationality. Television cables crisscrossed the rich rugs on the floor, tripping the flustered bellhops as they carried messages. The telephone switchboard was lit

•

up like Las Vegas, and one of the operators was quietly weeping. Everyone was sweating, shouting to make themselves heard, and confused by the hysterical rumours which swept through the press corps every half-hour or so. Photographers jockeyed for position at the entrance on the side street; one intrepid lensman had climbed on to the roof of the hotel annexe and was hopefully fitting telephoto lenses to his cameras in order to pry inside Judy's suite.

Finally Pagan threw up her arms in despair and, having been told that Judy was on the first floor, she bolted up the staircase to the first floor, shouting, 'Judy, it's Pagan, tell them to let me through!'

Judy heard her, flung open the heavy cedar doors of her suite, and Pagan tumbled into the room, and the two friends hugged each other.

'It's like World War Three out there,' Pagan gasped when she got her breath.

'We're waiting for the police chief,' Judy explained. 'I hope he's got some news.' There was a knock at the door and she whirled towards it. 'That'll be him now!' But Gregg Eagleton, looking pale and crumpled, stood in the doorway. 'I couldn't get an earlier flight, Judy. What the hell is happening?'

Ten minutes later the hotel manager escorted into the room a small group of Turkish policemen, headed by the tall thin man who Pagan had seen in the lobby.

Colonel Aziz had round, heavy-lidded eyes and a melan-

•

choly expression. He wore the beige uniform of the Turkish police but spoke perfect English with a slight American accent, having done his basic training in Miami. He
reassured Judy that everything possible was being done
to find her daughter. 'We have involved Interpol, the
Sûreté in Paris and the FBI; we have never had a case
such as this. You, Miss Jordan, have informed the police
of three ransom demands that sound like jokes, all beginning "Dear Daddy", sent to a Greek shipping magnate,
an American banker, and a pop singer. But I understand
from Miss Jordan,' he inclined his head to Judy, 'that
Mademoiselle Lili's father died before she was born.' He
spread his long, narrow hands in a gesture of surprise.

He thinks this is a publicity stunt, Judy realized as she
handed over the telegram that Curtis had given her that
morning, before disappearing to sleep off his journey.
The British police had already sent out Angelface's telegram. And Stiarkoz, when he spoke to Judy via the ship's
radio, had promised to deliver his cablegram when the
Persephone docked in Istanbul.

Colonel Aziz examined the three pieces of paper. 'There
is little we can discover from these, other than that the
messages are identical. We found no sign of force or
struggle in Mademoiselle Lili's suite, and our informants
in the Grand Bazaar report no unusual disturbance yesterday.'

What would he describe as an unusual disturbance?
Judy wondered, gazing up at the dusty chandelier as she
remembered the noisy, sweaty crowds that jostled in the

•

smelly booths of the Bazaar: you could have garrotted twenty people in that chaotic place and nobody would have noticed.

'So we are left with the possibility that whoever has abducted Mademoiselle Lili may be someone whom she knew, someone whom she would trust not to harm her.' The colonel sat back in his green velvet armchair and looked from one strained face to another in turn. Gently he asked, 'Who does Mademoiselle Lili know in Istanbul?'

'No one, as far as we know. She's never been here before.' Judy took off her tortoiseshell glasses and rubbed her tired eyes. 'Miss Bayriver, the Beauty Queen winner, and I are the only people that Lili knows in Turkey, apart from the hotel staff, our driver and the guides. I can't imagine any friend of Lili's being capable of this.'

Gregg was slouched in a corner of the sofa, one ankle resting casually on the other knee. 'Surely this is either a straightforward criminal case or a terrorist kidnapping?' Gregg had only ever before felt this anxiety fill his chest when his father was racing. He wished to God he hadn't treated Lili as an ordinary woman: that was what she wanted, so he had tried to hide his bedazzlement behind a façade of unconcern. But she couldn't be treated as an ordinary woman, because she wasn't one. If only he'd looked after her more carefully. He wanted to accompany her on this trip, but Lili had insisted that she wanted to travel in the smallest possible group in order to get to know her mother. Gregg couldn't stop accusing himself of neglecting Lili. If only, if only, if only, he thought.

•

'I'm inclined to rule out terrorism,' said Colonel Aziz. 'Certainly, in Turkey, we have our fair share of these groups – AMLA, the PLO, some Kurdish separatists. What modern capital city is free of these parasites?' Colonel Aziz shrugged. 'But when terrorists kidnap a person, they have two aims. They want a substantial sum of money to buy arms to use against people such as myself.' Colonel Aziz gave a tight smile. 'And they want the maximum publicity for their cause.' He coughed. 'Kidnapping an international celebrity is a highly effective way of insuring worldwide maximum press coverage, but it's unusual for the terrorist group not to make themselves known immediately. Anonymous kidnapping is not terrorist style.'

Gregg said, 'Are there any other alternatives?'

'Regrettably, yes.' The colonel hesitated, looked at Judy, then continued. 'We cannot rule out the possibility that this is an elaborately disguised murder. It's not unknown for a murderer to lay a false trail, and the peculiar nature of the ransom notes suggests that this is not an authentic kidnap. Do you know whether Mademoiselle Lili had any enemies?'

'Why, I've just remembered something!' Pagan jumped up and knocked an engraved brass tray off its stand. 'Lili's just done a charity benefit in London and the performance was almost sabotaged. The man who did that is undoubtedly an enemy of Lili!'

Colonel Aziz made a note on his pad. 'Did you make any inquiries at the time?'

•

•

'Yes, of course. Someone threw a big party for the entire theatre audience at a smart hotel. That party was an expensive, well-planned, weird operation, like this kidnap.'

'Who paid for the party, Lady Swann?'

'The hotel staff were far too discreet to tell us who paid the bill. As nothing illegal had been done, they had to respect their client's wish to remain anonymous.'

'We have no proof that whoever paid for the party made the hoax telephone call,' Gregg reminded Pagan.

'Now that something illegal *has* been done, the hotel will have to tell us all they know, and so will the bank which paid the draft.' The colonel tore off a sheet of note pad and handed it to one of his assistants.

'I think it was a nutter,' said Gregg. 'Just another sicko, with a bit more loot than most of Lili's crazy fans. Lili gets a regular stack of hate mail. Any one of those creeps might have flipped his lid and decided to grab her.'

'I doubt that the person behind this operation is the sort of person who pesters filmstars.' Colonel Aziz looked from one face to another. 'The obsessive fan is usually an inadequate, pathetic personality who can't form relationships with real people, and so lives in a fantasy world. Any reality usually defeats such people.'

'But they still manage to assassinate the occasional rock star or head of state,' Judy observed sourly. Having seen Lili besieged by obsessive male admirers, none of whom appeared inadequate or pathetic, she was exasperated by the colonel's bland psychological explanation.

•

'Such acts are generally accidents, rather than carefully planned crimes.' The colonel dismissed Judy's point. 'But we are treating this as a carefully planned, clever crime. Whoever has kidnapped Mademoiselle Lili took great care to investigate your background, Miss Jordan. And he knew that Mademoiselle Lili would be in Turkey at this time.'

Gregg jumped up angrily, and started to pace around the room. 'Anyone who can read a newspaper knows that Lili was on tour in Istanbul with Miss International Beauty.'

Colonel Aziz ignored him. 'An obsessive man might want to possess Mademoiselle Lili as an art collector desires a painting.'

Gregg stood still. 'Do you mean that the point of kidnapping Lili might not be to get money, but to get Lili herself?'

Simultaneously Judy and Pagan thought of the same man.

Slowly the yacht *Persephone* sailed past the Leander Tower Lighthouse, then the vast white craft anchored in the middle of the shallow bay. Within a few minutes, the Harun-al-Rashid private launch, with one solitary passenger, was gliding across the blue-green water towards the yacht.

From the white linen cushions of the aft salon Spyros Stiarkoz rose to greet Judy. No wonder this man frightens Lili, she thought as she looked at the blunt hands, massive

•

shoulders and acquisitive, Levantine eyes of her host.

'My lawyer says that it's unwise for me to be here.'
Spyros waved Judy towards a white couch, and she sat
down. A white-uniformed steward brought a brass pot of
sweet Greek coffee as Spyros handed Judy the much-
fingered sheet of buff paper. 'Here's the telegram.' Judy
twisted her hands together in her lap, then pressed them
against her thighs to steady the trembling. Wordlessly
her face asked Spyros a question.

Spyros shook his head. 'I will not pay the ransom.'

'Then why invite me on your yacht?' Judy tried not to
sound as hostile as she felt.

'Naturally, I'm concerned for Lili's safety or I wouldn't
have sailed here. But my advisers have made it clear that
if I accede to one single kidnap demand, I will be paving
the way for every member of my family and every em-
ployee of my organization to be kidnapped. I cannot
afford to be as soft as Getty, and see my grandchildren
threatened by kidnappers for ever.'

Judy jumped to her feet. 'Then what exactly does your
concern for Lili amount to, Spyros?' Her voice shook.
'Floating around on the Bosporus, wishing us well, while
these bandits start cutting off Lili's fingers in order to
motivate us?'

'I'm here to make sure that this affair is properly
handled.' Spyros sipped his syrupy black coffee. 'Police
are the same all over the world – incompetent, mediocre
bureaucrats.'

'But . . .' Judy stopped as Spyros held his hand up.

•

'I wonder if you are aware, Miss Jordan, how easily a situation such as this can be mishandled?' He stressed the 'Miss' lightly, but with contempt. 'If the kidnappers' hiding place is found, the local police might be trigger happy and attempt to storm the building.' He put his cup down and motioned to the steward to refill it. 'If so, they would probably kill half the bandits, get killed themselves, and perhaps be responsible for the death of innocent onlookers. And by the time they found Lili, she would also be dead.'

Judy hated him for being right. 'Do you think the kidnappers are bandits?'

'Perhaps. My people are making inquiries, but we haven't had any firm news yet. It could be the Kemaiat – like your Mafia – or it might be AMLA, which is, as you know, a group called the Asia Minor Liberation Army. So far they've funded their activities only by robbing small-town banks and by hijacking lorries, but perhaps they're getting more ambitious.'

Half an hour later Judy had repeatedly, unsuccessfully, pleaded and begged Spyros to pay the ransom. She stood up, intending to leave, because there seemed no point in staying.

'I'd like to make it clear, Spyros, that I think the most useful thing you can do is pay the money. Somehow, between us, Lili and I will be able to pay you back.'

This damned yacht had cost far more than ten million dollars. The *Persephone*, for all its glittering white luxury, seemed sinister and claustrophobic to her, and Judy was

•

•

afraid that if she stayed any longer, listening to Spyros's patronizing refusals, she might lose her temper and alienate a very powerful man. Judy was also afraid because Spyros Stiarkoz was a rich man, a careful, clever man, an obsessive art collector, and he was besotted by Lili. His other passion, as every gossip writer knew, was to acquire whatever and whoever had belonged to his dead brother.

Certainly, Stiarkoz had received a ransom demand, but wouldn't it be the move of a clever man to send one to himself in order to throw the police off the scent? With a heavy heart, Judy realized that if Stiarkoz had abducted Lili, then his presence there could only be for one of two reasons. Either he had the gall to openly check on police progress, or else he had arrived to gloat at their unsuccessful efforts to find Lili. Either possibility would mean that Stiarkoz could not be entirely sane. And either possibility meant that Judy was unlikely to see her daughter again.

Later that night, before dinner, Judy and Sandy waited for Pagan in the comforting darkness of the domed, carved balcony that hung over the Bosporus like an enormous birdcage.

'That Colonel Aziz shouldn't have questioned you for hours.' Sandy's voice was sympathetic, but she couldn't help wondering what was going to happen to Miss International Beauty's world tour. After all, they were now supposed to be in Egypt, but the Turkish police wouldn't allow Sandy to leave.

•

LACE 2

•

'He was only doing his job,' said Judy, 'and in very difficult circumstances.' The world's press had descended upon the hotel and Sandy's picture had been flashed around the world. The press couldn't believe their luck: one international beauty kidnapped, and another one available for photographs.

Sandy and Judy were now virtual prisoners in their hotel suite. All day one or other of them had been barked at by the police and eventually the telephone had been disconnected, because the Turkish operator could so easily be fooled by lying journalists, who assured her that they were returning Judy's calls.

'I could have spat in the eye and stamped on the foot of that colonel,' said Sandy. 'In fact, when I think of what he put you through, I feel like kicking him in the balls.'

Judy was astonished to hear Sandy drop her genteel speech. 'Why, Sandy, that's the only criticism I've ever heard you make.' Judy was eager to divert her mind by talking about anything rather than the kidnap.

'Honey, in my business, a girl learns to watch her mouth,' said Sandy.

Judy looked at Sandy; she was pretty, bright, shrewd and deftly practical, but all that cleverness and capacity for calculation was carefully used to give the impression that she was foolish and incompetent.

'Sandy, what made you decide to be a beauty queen?'

'Honey, that's only the first step up my ladder. In

•

a few years I aim to be hostessing my own TV show.'

'But why start on the glamour circuit? No one will take you seriously after that.'

'What about Bess Myerson? She was Miss America and now she's in consumer affairs. Anyway, being a pretty girl is the only start you can get in a place like Baton Rouge.'

'Pretty is OK, Sandy, but what about your southern belle act? Sure, the guys love it, especially the old ones, but you'll have to stop being . . . acquiescent . . . if you want to host a talk show.'

'Honey, I guess I was brought up to be agreeable.'

'Sandy, it won't work when you get older, and it won't work when the going gets tough. There's nothing more gruesome than an ageing Blanche Dubois, simpering with girlish charm.'

Sandy was suddenly stung by the comparison to a Tennessee Williams version of a washed-up, neurotic southern belle.

Boldly she said what she'd been dying to say for days. 'Judy, what I can't understand is how Lili's father can pay the ransom, when Lili told me that her father died long ago?'

'I have no idea, Sandy, how this kidnapper could be so crazy or so cruel.'

Sandy remembered the ransom note that had been delivered in the bunch of red roses. It read: 'Wait in your hotel suite to hear from Lili's father. He must pay the ransom.'

•

•

Sandy said, 'I wonder how much longer we'll have to wait?'

Judy's nerves snapped. 'For heaven's sake, can't we talk about something else?'

Sandy said, 'Why, yes, Judy, there is something else I have been *longin'* to talk to you about, something I really want to ask you, Judy.' Sandy took a deep breath, then burst out, 'Just which one of those bastards *is* Lili's father?'

FIFTEEN

3 September 1979

'It's none of your business!' Judy's voice echoed across the dark water and rang around the still room behind them. 'How dare you ask a question like that!'

'Honey, I'm not the only one who's asking,' said Sandy. 'Colonel Aziz gave me a really hard time in his office for two hours. After all, you told the world that Lili's father was dead, then suddenly all these guys got telegrams.'

'For all we know, Sandy, ten other rich men may have received that telegram. Next week the lunatic who's writing them is probably going to send one to John Travolta and President Carter!'

Sandy persisted. 'Who was it, Judy?'

'Lili's father was a British soldier who was killed by the Communists in Malaya.'

Sandy said, 'They'll check.'

Judy jumped up from her seat and leaned over the balcony, with her back to the other woman. Sandy added, 'Colonel Aziz said they'd do blood tests. He's spoken

●

to Lili's doctor in Paris and he's getting Lili's medical records. A modern blood test can really narrow down the field, it's not like one of those old maybe-he-is tests.' Sandy's voice was soft but warning. 'They're going to find out, Judy.'

Judy turned around to face Sandy. Beyond the darkened balcony, just inside the sitting room, moths were dancing around the fringed, pink silk shade of a table lamp. As Judy watched, one of them swooped too close to the hot light bulb and fell, fluttering in agony, on the tabletop.

Sandy stood up and put an arm around Judy's shoulder. 'Honey, *I'm* rooting for you. We've got a lot in common, after all. *I'm* a small-town girl. *I* know what it's like to be no one from nowhere, and how tough it is to get started. I'm sure that there was a good reason for whatever you did or said.' She patted Judy's shoulder comfortingly. 'But I'm a card-carrying twister of the truth, and it takes one to know one. I'm sure it wasn't pleasant to hear Colonel Aziz ask if you'd slept with all these guys. But watch what you're saying, because I can see that the colonel doesn't believe *anything* you're telling him.'

In the cool, soothing darkness only the lapping of water under the elaborate balcony could be heard. Since Lili disappeared, Judy had been in a state of almost unbearable tension; she hadn't slept for two nights and, even before that, she had been exhausted by months of anxiety, due to her multiple business problems.

●

Suddenly Judy cracked under the strain, buried her face in her hands and started to cry.

Sandy stroked Judy's hair and softly reassured her. 'Don't fret, honey, you're not the first girl to screw more than one guy in a month.'

Through her sobs Judy snuffled. 'It wasn't the way you make it sound, Sandy. They weren't all in one month and besides, I've never been regular.' She gulped, snuffled again and blew her nose. 'The whole trouble started when I was a fifteen-year-old student in Switzerland and working as a waitress. For the first six months I had to work too hard to have any fun. One of the waiters, Nick, had a crush on me but, physically, the chemistry just wasn't there, for me. Then, one night, I was raped. It was on my mother's birthday, February the seventh. It's silly, the things you remember. He was one of the guests at the hotel.'

'Poor baby. What a stinking, rotten way to lose your virginity.'

'When I saw the bastard in the hotel afterwards, he didn't even recognize me. I meant nothing to him, but that experience changed my life. It made me feel degraded. So I never told anyone what had happened. It was my dirty secret.' She blew her nose again. 'Then I met Curtis Halifax, and he made me feel clean again.'

Like people who confide their secrets to a complete stranger on a train because of the unbearable urge to unburden themselves to someone, and because they feel that never again will they meet that stranger, the over-

•

•

wrought, despairing Judy told Sandy the story that she had never told anyone, the secret that only one person had guessed, the tale that had started so long ago in the small, Swiss luxury resort of Gstaad.

14 February 1949

Judy remembered the stars on the ballroom ceiling as the Swiss accordian band played 'La Vie en Rose', at the St Valentine's Day Ball. She had just carried a heavy tray of glasses at top speed up from the kitchens. Without a word, a hard-pressed barman grabbed the tray from her thin, childish hands, and crashed it on to a bench. '*Aidez-moi, paresseuse!*' he snapped.

Judy picked up two of the still-wet glasses. The barman quickly loaded glasses from the tray on to the rack above his head. '*Vite, vite!*' he shouted again. Judy stood on tiptoe as she tried to push the glasses on to the high wooden rack, but she couldn't reach it.

'*Mademoiselle n'est pas assez grande.*' It was the worst French accent Judy had ever heard. From the customer side of the bar a bow-tied American boy smiled at her.

Judy grinned. 'That sounds like an East Coast accent.'

'Philadelphia. I'm Curtis Halifax. Listen, I'm tall enough to put those glasses away for you, if you'll pour me a bourbon?'

Periwinkle-blue eyes crinkled, a bright, frank smile

•

dimpled his cheeks. He looked the sort of tall, clean cut, wholesome guy you saw on Coca-Cola ads, thought Judy as she swiftly stacked the dirty glasses.

From their little table by the dance floor, Kate in cream moire and Maxine in pale-blue silk waved at Judy, who explained to Curtis, 'They're my friends.' Curtis turned and looked at them, gave a brief glance to the other rich, pretty girls sitting round the dance floor, then firmly turned his back on them, clearly fascinated by the tiny blonde American waitress behind the bar.

There was a sudden roll of drums. All heads turned to the glass ballroom doors, where the guest of honour, Prince Abdullah of Sydon, stood stiffly by the side of Pagan, in a sparkling, grey tulle ballgown. Curtis gave them a brief glance, then turned back to Judy. 'Do they ever let you out from behind that bar? How about skating on Sunday?'

Judy didn't have time to reply, as a waiter dashed forward with an order for the royal lemon juice.

'Nick, I can't read your bar slips,' Judy called. 'The head barman will have your head on a platter if you don't write more clearly, sweetheart.'

Curtis looked worried as Nick dashed off with his tray of *citrons presses*. 'Sweetheart?'

'A figure of speech. We're just good friends.'

Curtis was no better at skating than he was at speaking French. While Judy whizzed around the crowded rink, Curtis struggled to stand upright but, every time he let

•

go of the barrier, his long thin legs went gliding out from under him. Eventually he gave up, and sat with Judy on the terrace, sipping hot spiced punch. Curtis said, 'Rumour has it that you have a fiancé back in West Virginia.'

Judy wasn't sure that she wanted Curtis to know about her nonexistent fiancé: she had invented Jim as a smoke-screen, behind which she could escape from involvements she didn't want. Judy's goal was to learn fluent French and German in a year, then head for Paris to make her fortune. Her days were spent in the language laboratory and her evenings as a waitress at the Imperial Hotel, in order to pay for her year in Switzerland. There was no place in Judy's schedule for a man.

But Curtis took no notice of Judy's good resolutions. Every day, as soon as the sun left the valley and the shadows lengthened across the narrow, snow-packed streets, Curtis appeared in the hotel coffee-bar. Once, when her supervisor started to give Judy sharp looks because of the time she wasted talking to Curtis, he apologized to the man with Ivy-League charm, then tucked a big tip into the beer stein by the till, where the staff tips were pooled.

The following day, as Curtis slid into his usual seat with a bright-eyed smile that was simultaneously knowing and innocent, the supervisor winked at Judy and jerked his head. 'Here's your rich boyfriend again.'

Judy was thoroughly charmed. The boys she had known back home in Rossville were awkward and gauche;

•

they preferred beer, football and fishing to girls. But Curtis had beautiful manners, which was why Judy felt completely at ease with him. Curtis treated Judy like a lady, and, shell-shocked by the peculiar, alien atmosphere of Europe, she enjoyed being with a fellow American who was as homesick as she was. They told each other what they missed about America: Hershey bars, thick milk shakes, steaks that were not leathery flat slices of *bifteck* which stuck in your teeth. 'And what I wouldn't give to go to an undubbed American movie,' said Curtis wistfully. 'I can't understand films in French.'

Curtis first kissed her after they'd been moonlight skating, and were watching a torchlit display on the ice. As Judy felt the rough, male touch of Curtis's fur-lined, camel-hair coat, she felt no longer homesick, but safe, warm and happy in his arms. She also felt a delicious melting-inside sensation. 'It's too cold to kiss outside,' said Curtis. 'Let's go to my place.'

Three weeks later Curtis sat on the edge of her bed, pulling on his white socks. 'Of course I love you, Judy. Ever since St Valentine's Day, remember?'

Judy sat up in bed, pulling the quilt round her shoulders. 'Then why are you going back to Philadelphia to marry someone else?'

'I've explained it over and over. This was all planned a long time ago. Debra and I were pinned on her seventeenth birthday and everyone expects us to get married, especially Debra. My father, and my grandfather before

•

•

him, built up the business with the aim that one day a Halifax would become President of the United States. That's what they both live for, and I'm the only heir, so I have to try for them. It's my responsibility.'

And I'm not your responsibility, thought Judy sadly as Curtis earnestly continued. 'To get a crack at the presidency, I need money; politics is an expensive business. And I need the right wife.' Curtis looked uncomfortable as he reached for his snowboots.

'You mean a rich wife.'

'I've grown up with Debra. I'm very fond of her and I couldn't possibly hurt her. The whole of Philadelphia has known for a year that we planned to marry at the end of her débutante season.'

'But why didn't you tell me?'

'When I first saw you being bullied by that Swiss barman, something happened to me. I just wanted to put my arms around you, take you away, and look after you for ever.' Curtis couldn't look her in the eye, but he was trying to be honest. 'I can't figure out how a guy can love two women at once, but one minute I was drinking bourbon and the next minute I couldn't think about anything but you. You're so different from the girls I know back home, you've got so much pep and go, you're so full of life. I guess I just fell for you.'

'But how can you love me and marry someone else?' Judy scrubbed away her tears with the corner of the quilt.

'I can because I must,' Curtis said miserably. 'Anyway, you're going to marry that guy in Rossville.'

•

Judy said nothing. Once again she wished that she hadn't invented that goddamn Jim in West Virginia.

The little scarlet cable car swung in eerie silence, suspended from one taut metal rope, high above the sparkling white valley. Doll-sized skiers swooped soundlessly over the ski *piste* below as Maxine listened to her Aunt Hortense's scurrilous Paris gossip and hoped that the two smart Italian woman and the boy in the black ski suit couldn't understand English. The two Italian women were middle-aged, pear-shaped, and wore mink-lined parkas. They were immaculately made-up and coiffured and, despite their pristine pairs of Head skis, they obviously had no intention of skiing when they arrived at the top of the mountain.

In her gravelly voice Aunt Hortense confided to Judy, 'Of course, everybody likes to think that Roland is *tapette* and so when Zizi found him in the . . .' She stopped abruptly as the cable car gave a frightening lurch, halted, then started shaking from side to side as the couplings up above ground noisily.

There was a moment's sickening silence. Judy felt helpless and trapped, as if the walls of the car were closing in on her and growing smaller; she wondered how long the air supply would last, and whether they'd freeze to death before help arrived as claustrophobia started to set in.

'*Dio mio!*' cried one of the Italian women, and she lunged to the end of the car. Her shifting weight made the cable car bounce, as if it were about to uncouple itself from the cable and plunge on to the rocks far below.

'Don't move!' Aunt Hortense said sharply in Italian, but the woman ran back to her original place.

'*Santa Mamma Mia!*' Pink mink parka started to beat her breasts. 'My children! My husband! What will they do?' She threw herself into the arms of her friend. The cable car, which was the size of a small elevator, lurched under the sudden movement, then swayed sickeningly.

Aunt Hortense's craggy face looked mildly regretful as she briskly cracked the back of her ski mitt across the woman's face. 'Your husband and children would not want you to get hysterical, Signora.' Aunt Hortense's wide purple mouth softened. 'There's no danger, so long as we don't move. We should all sit down on the floor very carefully. Down there, they know what's happened to us, and the mechanics are working on it. What we must do is think about something else. I suggest a game of poker.'

Mauve parka whispered to pink parka, who was blazing with rage as she watched Aunt Hortense flip up the back of her white fox coat, then carefully arrange herself, cross-legged, on the floor of the cable car. She opened her large, crocodile Gladstone bag, groped inside and produced a silver hip flask of cherry brandy, which she handed round to the five other passengers as they carefully sat on the floor.

'I know there's a pack of cards in here somewhere.' Aunt Hortense searched in her bag. Her emerald eye

•

•

shadow matched her Pucci après-ski outfit and, in spite of her shaggy white fox hat, her beaky nose was red with cold as she searched for the cards. She pulled out a Swiss army penknife ('So useful for the corkscrew'), a menu from Maxim's ('Bébé Bérard drew this picture of me the night before I left Paris'), and a battered hand-rolled cigarette, which she hastily put back; then she discovered the cards and turned her wide, enchanting smile on the boy in the black ski suit as he held out his hand to take the cards and shuffle them; obviously, he was the only other person present who could play poker.

Half an hour later, by the time the cable car shuddered into life again, the cherry brandy flask was empty, the Italians had lost all their money, and Aunt Hortense was kicking herself for not having called this English boy, Bobby Harris, on a pair of twos.

The restaurant was perched on top of the mountain. Maxine bit into a meringue as she leaned over the wooden rail of the sundeck and looked around at the shadowed peaks, jagged against the sapphire sky. 'Maman wrote that you've chosen me some lovely summer clothes from Christian Dior,' she said. Aunt Hortense blotted her purple lipstick and smiled indulgently. 'What are god-mothers for?'

Judy felt angry and rejected, humiliated and crushed as she looked at Maxine. Thank heaven she'd never told the others just how involved she had been with Curtis. Curtis would never have dared dump a girl like Maxine,

•

Judy thought. Dumb girls from poor families in small towns are always going to get screwed by hypocritical rich bastards with fancy manners, because they had all the power and all the know-how, they could use plain folks like Kleenex, then throw them away when they'd served their purpose. Feeling like a depressed sparrow, huddled in her old navy pea jacket, Judy momentarily envied Maxine more than her wealth and social position; unlike her, Maxine was happily in love and the sight of her complacent, sensual satisfaction made Judy feel that twinge of envy. 'That's your third meringue, Maxine,' she said. 'Pierre won't love you if you get fat.'

'But I'm still starving,' Maxine objected. For a moment Judy felt violent resentment. Judy's reluctant memory of the painful poverty that she had endured as a child was triggered when she heard anyone cheerfully say, 'I'm starving!' Suddenly Judy's knees would tremble, her guts would shrivel and she would feel as if she wanted to pee.

She felt a gust of rage as she thought, Maxine has no idea what she's talking about. Until she left home, at the age of fifteen, Judy had been gnawed by hunger almost every day. Her family in West Virginia had been painfully poor, and the shame had been almost worse than the hunger. Judy remembered the sniggers of the kids at school, because they knew that she would be forced to refuse anything that cost money; Judy also remembered the giggles as she appeared in the same threadbare winter coat, year after year. At first the kids sniggered because her brown coat was far too large for her, an obvious

•

hand-me-down; eventually they sniggered because, when she outgrew the coat, her mother had sewn on cuffs and a false hem, cut from an old grey blanket. 'Listen to Judy's coat!' the kids would shriek with the cruelty of youth; her coat rustled because her mother had sewn newspapers behind the lining, to make the threadbare coat warmer for winter.

What Judy most remembered about poverty was the humiliation.

'And how do you intend to avoid starving? Or do you intend to play poker as a profession?' Aunt Hortense waved her gold bracelets towards Bobby, who was standing next to Maxine and shading his big blue eyes from the sun.

'My father wants me to be a stockbroker and join his firm.' Something in Bobby's voice made it sound unlikely. 'That's why I'm a student at the business school.'

'But what do you really want to do?'

'I want to be a singer.' He gave Aunt Hortense a crooked grin.

'A singer? Like Frank Sinatra?' asked Aunt Hortense as Maxine licked her fingertips, stretched her arms to the glittering sun and then unzipped her jacket, thinking that nice boys from good families do not go into show business.

'Not like Frank Sinatra; not like anybody you know!' Bobby threw her an impertinent, urchin grin.

'Then do you play the piano, like Cole Porter?' Aunt Hortense persisted.

Bobby gave Aunt Hortense a cherubic smile. 'I play

•

•

the piano, but not like Cole Porter.' Still modest at eighteen, Bobby could also play the guitar, the flute and the organ; if they intended to take music scholarships to Oxford or Cambridge, the most gifted music students at Westminster school were allowed to practise on the massive, seven-keyboarded organ in Westminster Abbey. Bobby Harris's stockbroker father had firmly told him that any kind of career in music was out of the question, but Bobby wouldn't and couldn't stop playing, any more than he could stop breathing.

'Where do you sing, Bobby?' Aunt Hortense demanded.

'I don't sing in public, I just sing.' Bobby scratched his curly dark hair and felt uncomfortable; he didn't want to make polite conversation about music to someone's aunt.

'So what are you going to do about your future?'

'I don't know.'

Aunt Hortense had no children, but was still, at heart, a child herself. She enjoyed doing whatever it was that young people were doing that week and (unlike them) she had all the adult goodies – the cars, the cash, the credit cards and the credibility – to make fact of the fantasies of the young. Now Aunt Hortense leaned forward and said, 'No one will throw you into jail if you don't become a stockbroker, Bobby. And if you don't like it, you'll probably be a bad stockbroker. People generally perform best at what they like doing best. So what do you like doing?'

•

'I write songs. I play a bit.' Bobby shrugged and lifted his high-arched eyebrows even higher.

'So why don't we go this evening to a nightclub, and ask the band if you can sing with them for a few numbers?'

'*We* can't,' said Maxine, crossly, 'because Monsieur Chardin, the headmaster, would never allow us out of school for the evening.'

'I can't.' Bobby was obviously embarrassed. 'Because my allowance has run out, and I've just paid for our lunch with my poker winnings.'

'Aunts are for when your allowance has run out. Would you like another meringue, Maxine?' Aunt Hortense waved her purple-nailed hand at a waiter. 'Myself, I have not much money, but I have enough for serious frivolity. I will ask Monsieur Chardin to make an exception for you tonight, Maxine, and I will beg your supervisor to free you for one evening, Judy. Then we will all dance all night together.'

'She will, too, she's as strong as an ox,' Maxine said to Bobby.

Unfortunately, Bobby did not sing the kind of songs that provided good rhythm for dancing, and he was embarrassed by Aunt Hortense's insistence that he perform in the small, dark, pine-panelled nightclub. Reluctantly he went into a huddle with the band – four middle-aged men, wearing lederhosen and green felt jackets. There was much head-scratching and explaining, then Bobby said, 'Forget it, fellows, just forget it. Give me the

•

guitar and I'll get this over with.' He dragged a stool up to the microphone and started to play.

Judy was surprised to hear this diffident English boy open his mouth and holler two blues numbers as, under his agile, skinny fingers, the tired old dance-band guitar produced tortured wails and hot rhythms. Then Bobby jumped off the stool and replaced the guitar on its stand as the audience, sitting at candle-lit tables, gave a cheerful round of applause. But Aunt Hortense sent him back to the microphone saying, 'The band has taken a half-hour break, so it's your job to entertain us.'

Judy soon found out that Bobby only liked black American music. Under the bed in his chilly bed-sitting room he kept a heavy portable record-player and a suitcase full of American records. All the records seemed to be by blues singers with three names: Blind Lemon Jefferson, T-Bone Walker, Sunny Boy Williamson. Bobby treated his 78s as if they were made of spun glass; he dusted the records every time he played them, and he changed the steel needles in his record player almost every day, to make sure that the discs weren't damaged.

'I suppose you couldn't write home to one of your friends, Judy, to get me some records?' Bobby threw her his angelic smile. 'It's terribly difficult to get blues records, even in London, and it's downright impossible in Switzerland.'

So that's why he's being so cute, thought Judy, who now found it hard to believe that any boy could be nice

•

•

to her simply because he liked her. But Judy soon found
out that she was wrong about Bobby Harris. He genuinely
liked Judy because she was nothing like the twinset-and-
pearls, protected, fluttery girls of whom his parents
approved. Bobby liked Judy because she was brash,
independent and – above all – because she was American.
Anything American was magic to Bobby. Little blonde
Judy, in her pedal pushers and navy pea jacket, seemed
as glamorous and alluring as his new pin-up, Marilyn
Monroe.

Judy liked Bobby because he made her laugh, and
because she was flattered by Bobby's comparing her to
the blonde in the potato sack who was pinned up on his
wall. Bobby's friendly attention helped to rebuild Judy's
demolished self-esteem and, with the puppy-like resili-
ence of youth, she quickly started again to look forward,
hopefully, instead of backward, regretfully.

Bobby's courtship strategy was to play his most sexy,
suggestive songs late into the night. However late Judy
finished work at the Chesa, Bobby would always be awake
and waiting for her, ready to throw open the big, double
windows of his room and help her scramble up from the
street below. His fat, sulky landlady would not have
allowed it but, luckily, she was a sound sleeper. One
night, as Bobby played to her, Judy went to sleep, sitting
on the floor with her back against the wall, and didn't
wake up until morning. Soon, Judy couldn't see the point
of crunching back to the Imperial through the starlit
streets at four in the morning, when she would have to

•

be up again at six. Somehow, she managed to survive on hardly any sleep, muttering that if Napoleon only needed two hours a night, then she had better cultivate his habit.

One evening, when Judy was sitting cross-legged on the threadbare rug in Bobby's room, she said, 'Maxine's boyfriend, Pierre, says you're going to get thrown out of the business school, Bobby, unless you start working. He says you're rude to the lecturers and never write any essays.'

'At least I'm not so dumb as that ski-bum, Pierre.' Bobby fixed a capo on the neck of his guitar to alter the pitch. 'The head had me in for a wigging but, as a matter of fact, I hope that they do chuck me out.' He readjusted the capo. 'Anyway, if I get expelled I'll be unemployable, and then I'll be *free!*'

'But you'll never get a good job,' Judy worried. 'You can't waste all your time playing these songs. You ought to be studying in the evenings.'

'I wish you'd stop telling me what to do.' Bobby was annoyed.

'It's for your own good, Bobby. I'm only thinking of you.'

'I wish you wouldn't.'

'What do you mean?' Judy thought, not another one, getting ready to walk out on me. She said anxiously, 'Why shouldn't I think of you? You love me . . . don't you? You've told me so often enough.'

Bobby said nothing.

★
•

'Telephone, Monsieur Harris, from Paris!' He could hear the disapproval in his landlady's voice as she shrieked up the stairs after breakfast.

It was Aunt Hortense, with a surprising suggestion.

'You're a frivolous, irresponsible old woman,' he happily shouted into the black receiver.

'And I miss you, too.' Aunt Hortense's mellifluous voice floated out of the trumpet-shaped ear-piece.

'You have told them I like to sing the blues, not le hot jazz?' Anxiously Bobby raised his high-arched eyebrows even higher. This was too good to be true.

'They are delighted, delighted. It's a very *louche* little club, they love the idea. And, when they see that angel face of yours, they'll love you on sight.'

Bobby scrawled Judy a note, then caught the next train to Paris.

'Two men in two months – that doesn't make you a fallen woman,' said Maxine, comfortingly. 'It's not your fault.' She passed Judy her handkerchief, looked around Judy's narrow servant's bedroom and thought, growing up seemed to need a lot of handkerchiefs. Again Maxine read Bobby's crumpled note: '   I didn't tell you I was going because I knew we'd have a row . . . know you don't really like my songs or my music, but I'm determined to give myself a chance . . . hope you'll understand . . . hope you'll come and see me at the Hep Cat Club when you come to Paris. Don't be mad. Lots of love. Take care of yourself. Bobby.'

•

•

'But what did I do wrong?' Judy threw herself on her bed, lay on her stomach and buried her face in the big square pillow. Her muffled voice demanded, 'Why do they all leave me, Maxine?'

'Maybe you're a bit too . . . bossy?' Maxine suggested. She was not sorry to see the collapse of this unsuitable liaison, but she was sad to see Judy's misery. 'A boy does not like to be told what to do, he gets all that from his mother.'

'I'm not bossy, I'm decisive,' wailed Judy. 'Why can't I be how I am? All I want is a direct, honest relationship with a boy. I want to be loved and trusted. I want to be his friend as well as his girlfriend. I can't be a flattering, calculating, clinging vine.'

'Then you're in for a hard time, Judy, because most boys do not want an independent girl.' Maxine shrugged. 'Why not be clever, Judy, and pretend to be a little helpless sometimes?'

'I don't think it's possible for me to play a part. I want to be an honest person.' Judy sat up. 'But if that's how things are between men and women, I guess I'll just have to try being devious.'

In the darkness Sandy was only a curly-haired shape against the Istanbul skyline, but Judy could hear the warm sympathy in her voice as she said, 'So that's why you never knew which one was the father of your baby.'

'Bobby left for Paris in early April. By the end of April I thought I might have missed two periods, but then

•

I've never been regular, so I didn't worry much. And somehow, I never thought that God would let it happen to me. After that I wasn't really interested in men for years.'

'Why didn't you get an abortion?'

'You're young, Sandy, you've no idea what it was like for a woman only a few years ago. We were only schoolgirls, we had no idea how to get an illegal abortion, and the doctor was Catholic, in Switzerland.'

'Did any of those guys help you, when the baby was born?' Sandy would never have got pregnant in the first place and, had she done so, she would have gotten rid of it, in the second place. And, on the way, she would have milked any man for any money she could derive from the situation.

Reluctantly Judy said, 'At first I didn't want to ask either of them, but then I remembered what Maxine had said. Why didn't I try a little female manipulation? Kate, Pagan and Maxine had been so supportive – they had each agreed to help pay for the baby – but I was the only one who couldn't manage to scrape the money together – although Lili was *my* baby.'

The Turkish balcony lit up briefly as the beam of the Leander Tower Lighthouse swept over it. Judy added, 'It was easy for Maxine, because she had an allowance from Aunt Hortense. It was easy for Pagan, because she had an allowance from a family trust fund. It was easy for Kate, because her father was rich, but I was a fifteen-year-old waitress.' Judy remembered that long-ago day,

•

when Dr Geneste, her gynaecologist, had let her use his telephone to place the international call. She remembered Curtis's reaction. Even at that distance, his voice had sounded frightened as he said, 'But, Judy, why didn't you tell me earlier?'

'How could I?' she had hollered down the receiver. 'You'd just been married, Curtis. You were somewhere in the Virgin Islands, on a yacht.'

There was a pause. 'Don't worry, Judy. Let me have the details and I'll send you money for the baby's care. But promise me that Debra will never know about this.'

'Of course,' Judy shouted gratefully. 'I promise that she'll never find out.'

In the empty Hep Cat Club, just off the Champs-Elysées, the silver-foil fringe around the stage looked tawdry with the lights up. The smell of cigarette smoke and old cooking fat lingered in the air as Judy said, 'Look, Bobby, do you want to see your daughter?' She looked straight into his innocent blue eyes as she handed him the photographs. Bobby flipped through them once, then more slowly, then he stopped at the close-up of the pudgy little face with blackcurrant eyes. Slowly Angelface grinned. 'Yeah, she looks like me! Cute smile, isn't it?' He pulled out his notecase and carefully tucked the photographs away. 'Just one thing, Judy, we must keep quiet about this, and there's no question of marriage, understand? There never was, and I told you that all along. So let's

•

keep this just between you and me, and I'll let you have as much cash as I can.'

Judy felt weak with relief. She didn't care who was the father or how she got the money, so long as her baby was properly looked after. It looked as if things were fine for the moment, but you never knew what would happen next. She'd save any extra money for a rainy day, in case the baby was ill or something. She felt guilty because she hadn't told Curtis about Bobby, or Bobby about Curtis, but then, had she done so, probably they would both have refused to help her.

The moon came out from behind a cloud and lit up the distant domes of the Topkapi Palace. On the balcony Sandy turned to Judy and said, 'You did the right thing, honey. Life is tough for a small-town girl, once she's left home. We have to do whatever we can, to get wherever we can.'

Judy decided not to continue. Even Sandy might not understand the full story.

SIXTEEN

4 September 1979

The building which Abdullah had described to Pagan as 'a pleasant little palace' was an eighteenth-century, imposing, pale building with an Arab garden, through which Pagan and Abdullah were walking in the early morning sunlight, along an avenue of lofty palms, towards an elaborate fountain. The palace gardens, scented with rosemary, roses and jasmine, were purple with falls of bougainvillaea. The soft splashing of water came from the interlinked streams, fountains and pools among the verdant foliage and bright flowers.

At the end of the avenue was an octagonal, white-marble pool with fountains jetting into it. Pagan sat on the edge of the pool and trailed her hand in the water.

Abdullah sat beside her and gently caught her hand underwater. He said, 'Pagan, I know I'm a difficult man and I have a difficult job to do. I have been involved with many women but you were my first love, and it seems that you have always stayed in my heart.' He looked at her, in her lavender gauze, loose, long robe, with her hair streaming down her back. 'Let's not waste any more of our lives, Pagan. I love you and I need you, and I'm only going to ask you once, and I must request a positive answer. Will you marry me?'

Pagan looked at him and, slowly, she nodded. Abdullah took her in his arms and held her against his heart. Together they laughed with relief.

They felt that they shared a secret that the world did not yet know. Abdullah seemed to drop his worries, and, gleeful as a schoolboy, excitedly started to plan their future.

Much, much later, Pagan said, 'We can't announce it now. We'll have to wait until this business of Lili is . . . resolved.' She added, 'I can't bear to see Judy so distraught.' Hesitantly she looked at Abdullah. 'Are you sure that it's not possible to help her raise the money, Abdi?' Privately Pagan was thinking that ten million dollars wouldn't amount to more than one day's output from Sydon's oil fields.

Pagan, sitting on the low surround of the marble fountain, said, 'Couldn't you possibly . . . help Judy directly, Abdullah?'

Abdullah thought, I shouldn't have come here. When first he had read that weird telegram, he had thought it some drunkard's joke. He had once loved Lili, but she had walked out on him and it was no affair of his. He had intended to stay uninvolved, to ignore the telegram. Then Pagan had read the newspaper report, and Abdullah

•

realized that Lili's disappearance was genuine. They had arrived in Istanbul to discover that identical telegrams had been sent to other rich men in Lili's life. Abdullah had decided to keep silent about his telegram, rather than attract undesirable publicity. That wouldn't help the situation.

Pagan trailed her hand in the fountain pool. '*Please help, Abdi.*'

'Pagan, I've already explained that one should never give in to kidnappers; many more lives might be in danger if ransom is paid to terrorists, because they'd use the money to kill innocent people.'

He seems so detached, thought Pagan. She was uneasy about the objectivity with which Arabs view women, particularly Western women. Suppose I had been kidnapped, Pagan wondered. Would Abdi talk like this? Maybe women are expendable to him.

Abdullah added, 'Paying the money wouldn't guarantee Lili's safe return. Once she'd served her purpose, as soon as they got their money, the kidnappers might kill her; it would be safer for them.'

A red-uniformed servant approached the fountain to announce Abdullah's next appointment, so Pagan went into the conservatory. Pagan had always loved conservatories. Waiting among the scented orange trees and the dripping fern fronds calmed her anxiety. She was feeling her usual optimistic self by the time she saw the grey Mercedes slowly drive from the palace entrance and pass the conservatory. In the back of the limousine was a small, slim figure who seemed familiar but, although

•

Pagan strained her shortsighted eyes in the bright sunlight, she could not see the face of the passenger.

Mark Scott, wearing his usual crumpled khaki shirt and trousers, carried his battered, silver camera case into the lobby of the Harun-al-Rashid and asked for Miss Jordan. The clerk at the check-in desk was unhelpful; Miss Jordan and her party had left the hotel. Mark asked for a room, and was told the hotel was full.

Mark tucked a fifty-dollar bill in his passport, handed it to the desk clerk, said he was sure that there was a free closet somewhere and which suite did Miss Jordan occupy? The clerk said he would try to find a room, kept the money, handed back the passport and delicately rested his hand on the pigeonhole numbered 104. Mark dumped his bags and ran up the marble staircase to the first floor.

Somehow, Mark had expected to find Judy alone, not sitting with a group of people that included Gregg, Sandy and two policemen. His rehearsal speech forgotten, he simply looked at Judy and said, 'I came as soon as I could.' Judy seemed smaller, sadder and older than he had ever seen her look, thought Mark, longing to take her in his arms. 'Can I help in any way?' Mark asked.

'No, there's nothing you can do, Mark,' Judy said quietly, 'the police are handling the problem. Would you please go.'

Mark looked at the group. 'Judy, can't we speak alone? I want to tell you why I've come here.'

She longed to touch him, to smell him, to hold him.

•

But she knew that she dared not invite humiliation. 'Mark, I know why you've come, but I want you to go. Please.'

Mark said, 'In case you change your mind, I'll let you know where I'm staying, as soon as I know.'

Back in the lobby Mark sat down and checked his cameras. After thirty minutes the desk clerk discovered that two German tourists were leaving, because they couldn't stand the pandemonium of police and photographers. So Mark had a room. Again he climbed up the marble staircase (no elevator), but Gregg, who had been watching him from the floor above, stepped out and barred his way. 'No you don't, chum. Find somewhere else to stay. Judy doesn't want you here.'

Angrily Mark shoved Gregg aside, saying, 'What's it to you?'

Gregg shoved Mark. Mark lost his footing and grabbed Gregg's arms, then slipped on the smooth marble staircase. Together the two men tumbled down the stairs, shouting accusations as they fell, and then continued their fight in the hotel lobby. As Mark struggled to rise Gregg grabbed Mark's foot, and again he lost his balance.

The two men were strangers. Gregg only knew from Lili that Mark fancied her. Mark didn't know who the hell Gregg was, but knew that he was frustrating Mark's attempts to see Judy. Had it not been for the tension they both felt because of the kidnapping, they would not have been fighting, but the fight enabled them to externalize their feelings.

•

As the two men kicked and punched, grappled and yelled, the pressmen who were hanging around the lobby formed a noisy circle, then started taking pictures, shouting, cheering on their buddy, Mark, and betting on the result of the fight.

Suddenly there was silence as Colonel Aziz and his escort entered the lobby.

'Who is Mr Eagleton fighting?' the police chief demanded of the nearest cameraman.

'Mark Scott – a freelancer who works mostly for *Time* magazine,' the man replied. Colonel Aziz immediately remembered that Mark's name had been included in the long list of men who were, according to Judy, obsessed by Lili.

Colonel Aziz pointed to Mark. 'Get that man off the floor and arrest him,' he ordered his men.

Accustomed to being jailed by hostile police officials, Mark knew that he had only to bide his time until his fellow journalists, who had seen the arrest, were able to telephone his editor at *Time* magazine. His editor would then telephone their man in Washington, who would have a word with the appropriate government department on Capitol Hill; he would send a note, via the US Ambassador in Turkey, to the Turkish Foreign Ministry and, at that point, some Turkish civil servant would lean on the Police Department and secure Mark's release. It would take less than twenty-four hours in a trivial case such as this.

Mark still thought he had been arrested for brawling, and not as a kidnapping suspect.

•

LACE 2
·

At about 3 a.m. Colonel Aziz decided to interrogate Mark. He was brought from his cell and told to sit in front of the police chief's table.

Colonel Aziz said, 'You have been arrested for causing a disturbance at the Harun-al-Rashid Hotel, and I am holding you to help us with our inquiries into the kidnapping of the French actress, Lili. Tomorrow a lawyer will be appointed for you by the court. You are not obliged to say anything but I strongly advise you to cooperate.'

'How long am I being held here?' asked the astonished Mark. 'I want to telephone my embassy. You have my passport, you can see that I only entered the country yesterday. Surely that's enough evidence? I can hardly have arranged a kidnap from Nicaragua.'

'Passports can be falsified. Nobody has accused you of being a kidnapper, but it's interesting that you should jump to that conclusion. How long have you known Mademoiselle Lili?'

'None of your business.'

'Oh, but it is. Be careful, Mr Scott. You are perfectly qualified to have committed this crime. You are accustomed to procuring illegal services in foreign countries, and you are accustomed to conducting clever, lengthy research investigations. And I am informed by Miss Jordan that you were involved with the victim.'

'And I'm probably the only suspect you've got?'

'Be careful. You are a long way from home, Mr Scott. You are clearly capable of being involved with this crime, and you have a motive.'

·

•

'A motive? Why would I do it?' Mark laughed and put his hands behind his head.

A policeman stepped forward and prodded Mark painfully in the ribs with a truncheon. Sharply Mark brought his arms down.

'Your motive might be vengeance. You might have kidnapped Mademoiselle Lili because she would have nothing to do with you.'

'What a crazy idea! There was never anything between us.' Mark wasn't worried, but he was irritated and knew he had to hide his irritation. The best thing to do was not to refuse to talk to Old Bootface here, but to say as little as possible, and just put up with the situation for a couple of days.

'But perhaps you *wish* there was something between you, Mr Scott. You are under suspicion because you know Mademoiselle Lili. We have reason to believe that she was abducted by someone she knew. If you had told her a plausible story, she might have left the hotel, accompanied by you, without struggle.'

'If you look at my passport, Colonel, you'll see it would be very difficult to fake.' Mark looked at his thick, much-stamped, many-visaed, often-confiscated, dog-eared passport, which was now laying on the colonel's table. 'You'll soon receive news of me from your superiors, Colonel. As you also confiscated my accreditation, you're aware of my connections.'

Colonel Aziz jerked his head and said to the policeman standing behind Mark, 'Take him back to his cell.'

•

•

The next morning Mark was released and his property was returned. With resignation, he signed for it, knowing in advance that it was unlikely to include most of his cash and his most expensive camera.

In a small park by the edge of the Bosporus Curtis Halifax was walking with Judy, who wore large dark glasses. Judy said, 'So now you know as much as I do about these weird telegrams, and I've told you as much as I'm prepared to tell you about my affair with Angelface Harris, but remember that I only became involved with Angelface because you left me.'

After so many years of guilt, believing Judy's child to be his, Curtis had been stunned by the news of Angelface's ransom telegram, which he had read about in the *International Herald Tribune* as soon as he stepped into the Istanbul Hilton.

Honest himself, Curtis found Judy's deception difficult to understand. Now he said, 'But you let me think that Lili was my daughter. You asked me to pay for her care as a child.'

'Curtis, I'm sorry. I can't bear to hear myself say this but at the time I didn't know which of you was Lili's father. You paid twenty-five per cent of the cost of her care, and there was more than a twenty-five per cent possibility that Lili was your child.'

'She still might be my child.'

'No.' Judy was sorrowful but firm. 'The grown-up Lili resembles her father, in temperament more than looks.

•

I'm truly sorry that I involved you, but at the time I thought I was doing the best thing for my daughter. You and Angelface both helped to pay for her care until she was six, when I was told she was dead. There was some surplus money, but not by the time I'd finished searching for Lili in the refugee camps. That trip cost a small fortune and left me in debt.'

'Nevertheless, I've paid for someone else's child. And why did you lie on TV? Why did you say that Lili's father was a British soldier?'

Judy spun round and faced the angry Curtis. 'Just be grateful that I didn't say it was you, Curtis.' Suddenly Judy was equally angry as she demanded, 'Do you understand what desperation is, Curtis? You've never been poor, you've never been desperate. You've never been tempted, you've never had to survive by yourself!'

Judy remembered that bleak winter day in 1956, after the Hungarian uprising, when she had returned to New York from Europe after her unsuccessful search for Lili in those chaotic refugee camps on the Austrian border.

Returning after a fourteen-hour, overnight flight, Judy had staggered into the hallway of her apartment house on East Eleventh and dumped her shabby suitcase in the hall. She felt desolate and alone. After Lili's birth, after breast-feeding her for three months, Judy had been forced by poverty to hand her baby daughter to somebody else, and Judy had never seen her again. Now her daughter was dead; Judy would never know her. Judy felt as if the world had turned against her. Everything seemed

•

•

pointless. She would never achieve anything. Life was going to be one endless struggle, and there was no reason to continue it. Everyone wanted to take, take, take. No matter what talent she had, however hard she worked, Judy was never going to get her head above water in this tough jungle called New York City.

She checked her mailbox. Bills, bills, bills. And on top of those, she owed Pat Rogers the plane fare. Pat Rogers was the department head of Judy's office. Pat knew that Judy hated to borrow money, because it made her feel humiliated, but Pat also understood that Judy couldn't exist in New York City on only stamina, ambition and one hot-dog a day, cut into three pieces.

Standing beside the dark waters of the Bosporus, Judy could still remember what it felt like to be hungry, not to be able to afford bus fares, not to be able to afford shoe repairs. Even though she lived and worked in luxury, Judy would always be that young girl who had lived on a hot-dog a day and, at heart, her sympathies would always lie with hopeful young girls who had not yet been kicked in the teeth by fate, or dumped by rich boys with no problems.

Judy looked at Curtis and suddenly didn't mind giving him her next bit of information. She said, 'I think I ought to warn you that the Turkish police think that your wife may be involved with this kidnapping.'

Curtis stood still and gaped at Judy. 'Debra?'

Judy nodded. 'You know that party I told you about, before Lili's gala in London. It turns out the anonymous

•

benefactor was Debra. We were only told this morning.'

Curtis's neat-featured face seldom registered emotion, but now he looked horrified. Somehow he knew that this time Judy was telling the truth. She said, 'The Turkish police got Scotland Yard on to the London hotel; they opened up their books and found that the money for the party had been anonymously paid, but it was traced through the paying bank. It came from Debra's account in Philadelphia.'

'My God!' Not for the first time in his life, Curtis wished that he had stayed in Switzerland with Judy, instead of bowing to the family ambition and marrying that bundle of trouble. He said, 'But Debra doesn't need ten million dollars! She's worth far more.'

'The Turkish police think that Debra might have arranged to have Lili killed, and that all these mad ransom notes are just a cover-up for the murder.' Judy's voice cracked. 'I've already been told that if Lili's body is found, Debra will be a murder suspect. I'm sorry to distress you, Curtis. It's obviously untrue and I don't believe it. Only a crazy person would do a thing like that.'

Curtis said, 'I'll have to get back home immediately.' He thought, I'll telephone Harry and Dr Joseph from the Hilton before I catch the plane. He dared not think further than that.

'Kidnapping insurance?' Hopeful ecstasy was on Judy's face. 'You mean, Omnium took out kidnapping insur-

•

ance? The insurance company can pay the ransom? Wonderful!' She beamed at the three men who had been waiting for her when she returned from her meeting with Curtis.

Oscar Sholto was head of the legal department at Omnium Pictures. He was accompanied by a chubby man called Steve Wood, who was from Special Risk, Inc., Omnium's Paris-based insurance consultants. A weary, pale Colonel Aziz had joined the group and now they sat around the table in a private dining room, which Colonel Aziz had commandeered for his investigations. Around the room spindly gilt chairs were stacked in fours. The bedraggled decorations from a party were fading and curling.

Oscar Sholto had been darkly handsome, but it had all dropped a little. He cleared his throat. 'As you know, Miss Jordan, it's not unusual for the star of a major picture to be insured by the backers. Omnium has millions tied up in *Helen of Troy*.'

Smiling, Judy sat back in her chair. 'I'm thrilled to hear this! I know it's tough for the insurers but if I get my daughter back . . .'

'I must warn you, Miss Jordan,' said Oscar, 'that Omnium cannot act in any way against Turkish police policy. And the police don't want the ransom paid, because it's against their national policy. No payment for kidnapping, because it only encourages other kidnappers. The main aim of the police is to *find* the kidnappers, and that will probably take time.' He folded his plump hands on the dust sheet which covered the round table and said, 'But the Turkish police have to decide between two

•

alternatives. They don't want an international kidnapping to take place in their country, but neither do they want to transgress their own laws by turning a blind eye to ransom payment.'

'Of course they've got to allow payment!' Judy's smile had disappeared.

Oscar said, 'What we're telling you is that the Turkish government may not allow us to pay the ransom *here*.'

Judy broke in, 'What are you going to do, as it's illegal to pay ransom in Turkey?'

'We have to work out how to get around the law. Maybe pay it over at sea, outside territorial waters,' said Oscar.

'All we can do for the moment,' said Steve, the insurer, 'is to wait for contact. The kidnappers will probably ask us to set up a safe, untapped telephone, so we can talk to them. Just give us time.'

'Time!' exclaimed Judy. 'How much time? Months? Years?'

'Two weeks,' said Oscar. 'Special Risk also covers Omnium for any other delay in shooting *Helen of Troy*. We're due to start shooting in a couple of weeks.'

'That should be ample time,' Steve confirmed. 'But, as you know, we first have to establish contact with the kidnappers, then establish that they really are holding Lili, then establish how we're going to get her back, then establish the price, then . . .'

'But we know the price!' Judy interrupted. 'They've already asked for ten million dollars.'

•

•

'At Special Risk we always try to bargain down,' Steve said evenly. 'If we draw out negotiations, it gives the police more time to discover where the kidnappers are holding their victim.'

'And your company saves its cash, of course. So what happens after that?' Judy had heard enough tactfully understated explanation; she wanted the bottom line on getting her daughter back. She had worked out the insurance company's old, familiar angle, which was always the same whether you'd had your bicycle or your Lear Jet stolen. Steve was only offering advance justifications for not paying the insurance in full. Judy was unimpressed; she'd used more ingenuity to string along the landlord of her East Eleventh Street studio, in the bad old days when she was starting out in business.

Smoothly Steve said, 'As soon as we are in communication with the kidnappers, we start stalling. We'll say that the payment has to be okayed by a lot of people in America, and then paid over discreetly, so we'll ask for five days' extension. Then we'll go back to them and say that we can only raise five million in cash, so we ask for more time. When they see five big ones within their greedy grasp, they'll give us more time. And then, in the end, we settle for six million.' Steve looked around the table, then added, 'And we take as long as we can over the whole business, so that the police and our special contacts can try to find Lili and perhaps obviate the necessity . . .'

'Of paying over your money,' Judy angrily interrupted.

•

•

She turned to Oscar Sholto. 'Lili's made a fortune for Omnium. She won't be able to make any more money for you if she's dead, will she?'

'Miss Jordan, both you and Omnium want the ransom paid fast,' said Oscar. 'That's why Omnium paid enormous insurance premiums to Special Risk.'

Steve said, 'I'm here to pay the ransom to the right people, provided we get the right results. Of course, we'll do everything we can to get Lili released as fast as possible.' He saw the panic on Judy's face. He had encountered parent hostility before, so he emphasized, 'Remember, Miss Jordan, as soon as we start to bargain with the kidnappers, Lili's life is much safer.'

Judy threw him a flinty stare. 'I'm Lili's mother and the way I see it is that the longer we wait, the more dangerous it is for Lili. I can't bear to think of her in the hands of those thugs.'

'They won't be thugs if this is a terrorist operation.' Steve tried to smooth out the hostile atmosphere. 'If we're dealing with terrorists, they're not likely to be disadvantaged peasants striking back at society, they're far more likely to be clever, well-educated, middle-class idealists, and they won't treat your daughter badly, Miss Jordan. They'll be in the whole business as much for the sake of their public image as for the money.'

Colonel Aziz said, 'Whoever they are, I don't understand why the kidnappers haven't been in touch, to instruct us where to pay the money.'

'The delay makes me think it's likely that the kidnap-

•

pers *are* terrorists,' offered Steve, 'because terrorists don't always want the money, they want the maximum publicity over the maximum time. Terrorists fight dirty because there aren't many of them, and they haven't got the money to run the sort of war they want. A kidnap is sometimes a really cheap publicity stunt. You don't need many people, or much equipment, and you get a nice financial bonus at the end. Their weapon is intimidation – kill one and frighten a million.'

'This is terrifying.' Judy looked at Oscar and Steve who had started to put their files back in their briefcases.

Oscar got up and extended a hand to Judy. 'Try not to worry, Miss Jordan. Lili will be in less danger as soon as we are communicating with the terrorists, and they see they're getting newspaper space for their message. It just takes time to set up the communication.'

Steve added, 'We're also concerned about your safety, Miss Jordan. We'd like to fly you out of here. There'll shortly be dozens coming forward with reports and information. All of it will be false, and every time another witness comes forward with another story, your hopes will be raised and then dashed to the ground.' For several reasons, Steve always tried to remove close relations of the victim. First, if any real communication was conveyed, then a distraught relative had only to tell *one* friend (and they always did), and the secret was general news within twenty-four hours. Second, you never knew what distraught relatives might do. They might refuse to cooperate with the police, or agree to cooperate with the

•

•

police and then change their mind without informing anyone, thus screwing up a carefully prepared police ambush.

'I'm not going anywhere!' Judy almost shouted at Steve. 'I've a right to be here! I'm not leaving my daughter and you've no right to make me leave. I also have the right to know everything that's going on – and I insist that you tell me everything!'

As he and Oscar climbed back in their car Steve muttered, 'Tough lady.'

'Are we going to keep her informed?' Oscar asked.

Steve looked at the rabble of photographers who still kept a disorderly vigil at the hotel. 'Of course not. We'd be crazy to pass on any information. She's emotional, and she might become hysterical, so she's a bad security risk. We're going to tell Miss Jordan as little as possible.'

Half an hour later Judy and Pagan sat together in Judy's hotel sitting room. In silence they sipped iced water. Judy had just finished telling Pagan of the conference with the Omnium lawyer and his security consultants.

Judy said, 'I can't stand this inaction. Just sitting around and talking is driving me crazy.'

Hoping to distract her thoughts, Pagan said, 'By the way, I got a letter from Kate today, sent on from London. She's bought a typewriter, a 1952 Remington which cost seven hundred dollars. The secondhand ribbon was fifty dollars extra. She says that the major powers – China, as well as Russia and America – are getting involved in

•

Chittagong and it isn't just the little jungle war that it appears to be. It could be as expensive and senseless and unwinnable as Vietnam, she reckons.'

'Any more good news?'

Pagan turned over the crumpled blue paper. 'They interrogated Kate for two hours, and she's afraid that the Bengalis are going to throw her out. Apart from that, she's well and happy. Isn't it odd that Kate's never happy unless she's uncomfortable?'

Judy didn't answer.

The only sounds in the room were the faint roar of the city and the insistent lapping of the water below.

A knock at the door brought Judy to her feet. Pagan watched expectantly as she opened the double doors; beyond them, a page boy held a cellophane-wrapped bouquet of roses, identical to the one that had concealed the original kidnap note. Judy snatched the flowers and ripped open the plastic to get at the envelope that accompanied them. 'Thank God, they've made contact at last!'

Pagan peered over Judy's shoulder as she ripped open the miniature envelope and pulled out a garish florist's card.

Judy gave a moan and dropped the card as if it had burned her, then fell into a brocade armchair and began sobbing. Pagan picked up the florist's pink and yellow card. Below the good-luck messages printed in Turkish were a few typewritten lines.

•

Put one million ten-dollar bills into a briefcase. At six o'clock tomorrow evening, let a man with a red armband take it on the Guzelhisar ferry that crosses the Bosporus. Further instructions will follow. Tell no one. Lili will be strangled with silken cords unless I am obeyed.

It was almost midnight and Abdullah was working at his desk in a soft green study scattered with rich rugs and hung with cream gauze curtains.

As the breathless Pagan burst in he looked up, and his frown of concentration changed to a smile as he grabbed a newspaper and said, 'Look what's in the *Tribune*.' He gestured to a two-inch front-page story which announced the death of Senator Ruskington in the Washington apartment of a French call girl. 'So now, Pagan, Lili is vindicated, and it looks as if Judy's money problems can be resolved.'

Pagan paused for breath after running along three corridors and up a flight of stairs. 'That's wonderful news, darling. I mean, I'm sorry he died, but the old bugger was asking for trouble.'

'Why are you out of breath, Pagan? What's happened?'

Pagan held out a bit of paper. 'I wanted you to see this as fast as possible. Judy's received a second note from the kidnappers. Here's a copy.'

Abdullah skimmed it. 'I still can't decide whether these people are cunning or crazy. This sounds like an eighteenth-century king's threat. If they wanted to get rid of one of the royal concubines at Topkapi Palace, the

•

woman was strangled with a silken cord.' He paused, then added, 'Common concubines were sewn up in sacks, weighted with rocks and thrown into the Bosporus. One king got rid of two hundred and eighty concubines like that. A few years later a diver found all those ghastly sacks, still upright on the sea bed, swaying in the invisible current, as if they were dancing to music.'

'I know, darling, you've told me before. A long time ago. But what do you make of the rest of the note?'

'Obviously, the police will lay an ambush on the ferry and at both landings, but often, with bandits, the first rendezvous is never kept, it's merely a test to check police reaction. However, this last sentence is strange. Why not just say that Lili will be killed?'

Pagan burst into tears. 'I can't bear to think of it.'

'My darling, it's late and we're both tired. Let's go to bed and I'll see what my people can deduce from this note tomorrow morning.'

SEVENTEEN

But Pagan could not sleep and turned restlessly on her bed in the hot night. Eventually, at three o'clock in the morning, she decided to take a soothing walk in the moonlit garden. It would be perfectly safe, because the grounds were guarded by sentries and also an electrical alarm system.

Pagan knew that someone would be watching her as she walked between the low clipped hedges of rosemary to the circular pool, where a family of terrapins were kept. It was impossible to be truly alone, wherever Abdullah slept. His bodyguards kept an endless watch outside his room, and in the corridors there were always silent servants waiting for commands or simply sleeping in corners.

As Pagan sat on the stone coping around the pool she disturbed a skinny, grey cat, which spat at her as it ran away in the half-darkness. Something in her head was prompting her; she felt that something important was

•

laying half-hidden at the back of her mind, like an un-answered letter on her desk.

Suddenly Pagan jumped up, and nearly fell into the terrace pool. As the moonlight painted the beautiful garden in strange shades of grey she abruptly remembered the exercise class in the *Verve!* office, when that exercise instructor had started to make strange jokes about his harem; that is, his grave remarks had been interpreted by the class as jokes, but Tony had obviously been nettled when the girls had laughed at him. And Pagan had told Tony that royal concubines were strangled with silken cords. It could not be a coincidence. Tony must be the person whom Lili knew and trusted, the person who had been able to lure her away from the hotel. Tony must be one of the kidnappers!

Pagan hurried back to the palace, losing a slipper as she ran along the tiled pathway, still slippery with dew. The palm trees stood out as dark silhouettes against the pre-dawn sky as Pagan ordered a limousine from the sleepy-eyed attendant at the main door, after failing to get Judy on the telephone. The switchboard staff of her hotel were obviously still asleep.

Speeding through the pale-grey streets, Pagan sniffed the spray of jasmine that she'd pulled from the garden's ancient, high walls, and thought how cruel this twice-over loss of her daughter was for Judy. Pagan remembered the *Verve!* cover photograph of Judy and Lili, and the way it highlighted their similarities: the tiny, doll-like build and the little, paw-like hands – as well as the differences

•

between mother and daughter. Judy looked so blonde, blue-eyed and Nordic whereas Lili was so dark and exotic. The cover photograph had also emphasized their odd apartness. However hard they tried, and however much they longed for intimacy, Pagan didn't reckon they'd achieve it; their relationship seemed almost a casual juxta-position of two completely un-alike people. There was so much they had shared, but so much they couldn't seem to share. However much a mother might want closeness, however much a daughter might want closeness, often it isn't truthfully possible because they have so little in common; hence those dutiful birthday cards, Pinteresque monosyllabic Christmas dinners and uneasy outings to the theatre or the movies: anywhere where they could avoid conversation.

Pagan thought of the intimacy that Judy and Lili had struggled to achieve, the intimacy of love. I wonder if it will be like that with Abdi and me, Pagan mused. Sometimes, when they made love, Pagan looked at her pale English skin next to his tawny flesh and felt curiously apart from Abdullah, no matter how sensitive his caresses, or how strongly her body responded.

In some ways, I suppose Lili's like Abdullah, thought Pagan, as she crushed the sprig of jasmine and sniffed the cloying perfume of the dying sprig. Lili and Abdullah are both aggressively defensive; they both have that quick temper; they both have that greedy, sweet tooth. And sometimes, when Lili throws back her head and glares, she has that same angry-falcon look as Abdullah.

•

Abruptly the kaleidoscopic jumble of Pagan's random thoughts fell into a sinister shape. Then, reluctantly, the corroborating evidence flooded into Pagan's mind. At first the conclusion that she reached was so unpleasant that she tried to push the whole idea out of her head and look out of the window at the leaden waters of the Bosporus, but the unwelcome notion pushed back into her mind with a force of its own. Could Judy have slept with Abdullah? Could he be Lili's father? Pagan remembered Judy's expedient lies, from the desperate deceptions of her early, poverty-stricken years to that odd white lie she had told Lili about her father. Why, she'd even repeated on television that Lili's father was poor Nick, who'd been shot in a jungle war, when Judy's friends knew that, although Nick had had a crush on Judy, she would have nothing to do with him. So certainly Nick could not have fathered Judy's child. Then Pagan remembered her dead husband Christopher's last joke. He had said that two clearly blue-eyed parents could not produce a brown-eyed baby; he had been definite about it. Curtis and Angelface both had blue eyes. Spyros Stiarkoz wasn't around when they were all in Gstaad, so it couldn't have been him. Maybe I won't win the Nobel Prize for genetics, Pagan told herself bleakly as the car drew up in front of Judy's hotel, but I can't ignore the facts.

'I'll bet Tony wrote that ransom note,' Pagan insisted to a puffy-eyed Judy, who was sitting up in bed. 'Don't

•

•

you remember that silly argument about harems we had in the exercise class in New York?'

'I vaguely remember.'

'But you were present when I told Tony about strangling disobedient concubines with silken cords,' Pagan insisted. 'The second ransom note is too much of a coincidence.'

'I should imagine that half Istanbul knows that tourist-guide story, Pagan, are you telling me that some guy who's only capable of pumping iron on Fifth Avenue could fix a kidnapping in Turkey?' Judy was still only half-awake.

'No, I don't believe that dumb ox could work this out by himself,' said Pagan. 'He must be working with somebody else.'

'That's certainly a possibility!' Judy jumped out of bed and pulled on an ivory-cream négligé. 'But that still doesn't tell us where Lili's being held.'

'I'm not so sure.' Pagan walked to the window and looked out. In spite of her tenseness, she appreciated the glittering sweep of water on which the Sancta Sophia Mosque and the Blue Mosque seemed to float. She said, 'The link between Tony and the second ransom note is the royal concubines. Where were they kept?'

Pagan looked at the rounded domes and soaring minarets of the Topkapi Palace and, suddenly, she had an idea where Tony might hide out. A place that would never be searched, because it was guarded: a place that nobody was allowed to enter.

•

Together Pagan and Judy tumbled into their limousine. As it drew away from the kerb another battered Mercedes pulled out from the side street and followed them.

In the limousine a reluctant Judy finally admitted to Pagan that Abdullah was Lili's father. So then she had to explain to Pagan how the conception occurred. In the nasty silence that followed, a grim Pagan finally asked, 'But why didn't you tell me at the time?'

'How could I?' pleaded Judy. 'You were my friend and you were in love with him. How could I tell you that your beau had raped me? And what good would it have done? I know that it probably didn't seem a rape to Abdullah. To him, it was merely a prince having his way with a servant. I'm sure he doesn't remember it, and I'm sure he wouldn't do it now. All our values have changed so much in the years since we were sixteen.'

Pagan was silent. Judy put her hands on her shoulders and turned Pagan to face her. Earnestly Judy said, 'Please don't wreck *your* future because of something horrible that happened years ago in *my* past.'

Pagan looked mutinous. Judy said, 'And you mustn't say anything to Abdullah about it, for the same reason I can't tell Lili who her real father is. Because the whole world knew that they had a passionate affair. Because, unknowingly, they committed incest. Why lay that burden of guilt on two human beings we care about, when it's unnecessary and will achieve nothing?'

Eventually Pagan asked, 'Does anyone else know about it?'

•

•

'Only one person. Maxine guessed, as soon as she saw Lili at the Pierre. She didn't say anything at the time, but she asked about it later, one Sunday when Tony was driving us up to Westchester to have lunch with Griffin. Maxine said that the resemblance isn't so strong today, but that as soon as she saw Lili she was reminded of Abdullah as a youth. Lili had his colouring, his features, his mannerisms . . . and his abrupt temper.'

Judy remembered that she didn't even have to admit it. Maxine had seen from her face that she'd guessed correctly. What's more, Maxine had immediately understood why Judy had found it difficult to establish a warm, loving relationship with Lili. Because Lili's beauty had come from a man who had raped Judy. She had always tried to push the thought to the back of her mind, but Judy couldn't help feeling forlorn because Lili was not a child of love. Lili didn't know it, but she was a child born from violence and hatred.

'We'd like to go into the other part of the Harem quarters, the part that isn't normally shown to tourists.' Pagan folded a 500-lira note and tried to tuck it into the shirt pocket of one of the palace guides. Accustomed to curious tourists with more money than sense, the guide said, 'I'm sorry, it is forbidden. There is nothing I can do.' He swept Pagan and Judy out of the entrance.

'Damn.' In the bright morning sun Pagan stamped on the ancient stone courtyard. 'I suppose I should have offered him more.'

•

Judy wasn't listening because she was peering across the courtyard. She jammed her tortoiseshell glasses on her nose, and again stared at the colonnade across the courtyard. 'Pagan, I know this sounds crazy,' she said, 'but I think I just saw Mark.'

Slowly they walked down the path to the entrance gate, then Judy spun around, almost tripping up two German tourists behind them. 'It is him! I'm sure I saw him. Mark! Mark!'

She ran towards the colonnade, still calling Mark's name, and the familiar khaki-clad figure appeared between two columns. Judy, breathless, stopped in front of him. 'What are you doing here, Mark? We thought you were in jail, number one suspect.'

'They let me out when my editor pulled rank, long distance, on Colonel Aziz. I've been following you, on the fire engine principle – follow the fire engine and you'll find a story at the end of it. So where's the fire engine, Judy? Why are you rushing off on this mad sightseeing tour with Pagan?'

Slowly Judy smiled. 'We think we've found out where the kidnappers have hidden Lili.' Judy wasn't ready to confess to Mark, but she needed help to get into the Harem. 'We think they're in the old part of the Palace Harem, but we can't get in because it's closed. D'you think you can help us to get in?'

Mark said, 'Should be easy. Come on, let's fall in with the next guided tour. It starts at ten o'clock.' He thought, first chance I get I'm going to grab her. I'm no good at explaining how I feel with words.

•

Again Judy and Pagan, now joined by Mark, were conducted through the labyrinthine palace. They inspected the Armoury, the Treasury, and the King's Robes. Some of the rooms were carved, some were gilded, some were tiled, and some were elaborately painted. They peered through pierced screens at the Valide King's apartments, and shuffled with the other tourists along the pillared façade of the Black Eunuchs' barracks.

The self-important guide reformed his group near the Harem entrance and, as he launched into another singsong speech, Pagan nipped to the far side of the group.

Suddenly Pagan clutched at the shoulder of a Japanese tourist, who buckled under her weight. Groaning, Pagan slid to the floor. The tourist party crowded around her lanky, prostrate body. The guide said, 'Get back, get back, everybody!'

As soon as Pagan's prearranged diversion had attracted the attention of the group, Mark and Judy slid unnoticed into the wide, dark doorway to the Harem. Above one of the doorways they had noticed a decorated grille. Between the top of the grille and the bottom of the stone arch of the gateway was a very small gap. Judy pulled off her shoes and climbed on Mark's shoulders. She could just reach the grille.

Quickly she scrambled up to the gap and wriggled through, then dropped into the open alley on the other side.

Mark followed her. They landed on a pile of builder's rubble and trash, and lay quiet, listening, as Pagan was

•

carried to the first-aid room. In the hot sun Mark and Judy lay on the stinking heap of rubble until the noisy band of tourists had moved on, behind the guide.

Then Mark took Judy in his arms and held her tightly against him as slowly he kissed her mouth with his sun-blistered lips. And, lying on the rubble, Judy felt that, for the time being, nothing else mattered.

Eventually Mark said, 'Do I make myself clear? It's you I love, not Lili. It's you I want and nobody else. On a scale of one to a hundred, I shall probably feel something for every beautiful woman I see. So would any other man. But you're the woman I want to spend my life with.'

A bit later he said, 'Why didn't you ever write back?'

'I never opened your letters. It would have hurt too much.'

'That's what I guessed. That's why I wrote to Lili. I asked her to explain things to you, I asked her to tell you how I felt about you. But she never once replied.'

'I expect your letters met with the same fate as the rest of her fan mail, darling. We can find out later. But right now, we should be looking for Lili.'

Judy opened her purse and pulled out her expensive guidebook, which included a map of the palace. Mark took it from her and pulled out a pen. 'This place is on a hill. We won't get lost, so long as we remember which way is up.'

'Famous last words. There are supposed to be over three hundred rooms in this place.' Cautiously Judy set off down a dirty, stone-flagged corridor, dimly lit by an

•

overhead skylight. Rusting iron bars braced apart the crumbling walls of the passage.

Gloomy corridors twisted through a maze of small rooms, linked by staircases and dark passages and tiny courtyards, where the sun scarcely fell. Sometimes a wall shone with blue or sea-green tiles, patterned with flowers. Through barred windows Judy noticed dusty, unlit lanterns hanging over the tiny rooms of long-dead concubines. She peered into the ornate, gilt, crumbling mirrors that still hung on the walls, dimly visible streaks of silver against the grey gloom. In some of the rooms they explored, the shutters of the windows were falling off, in others there were cobwebs, rotting sheets of rose velvet and tattered canopies.

As they peered into each debris-strewn room Mark methodically crossed it off their plan, but after half an hour he slowly realized that the tourist plan wasn't accurate. He checked his bearings, the corridor they were in, the rooms leading off it. Then he rechecked, and after that he was certain the map was inaccurate. But he didn't tell Judy that the map was wrong. He merely walked beside her in silence, noticing the frantic, mounting anxiety with which she searched each room

Some corridors led down half-broken flights of steps to yet more rooms on lower levels of the palace. Some rooms smelled damp, others of urine or rotting hangings. One room was alive with rats, which swarmed over the carcass of a dead cat.

As the sunlight turned golden in the late morning Judy

•

said, puzzled, 'I'm sure we've searched this room before. I remember those tiles with cypress trees on them.'

They were standing in the middle of a small, open courtyard. On all four sides the walls were pierced by small, screened windows. Below the windows were two iron-studded closed doors, and two doors that gaped open.

Mark said, 'I'm sorry, Judy, but the map's inaccurate. I hoped we might stumble on a way out, before I had to tell you. We're going to have a problem getting back, Judy. And we've nearly run out of matches.'

'Mark, this is hopeless, we'll never find her.'

'Yes, we will.' Mark took her in his arms and pressed her trembling body against his. She felt protected and consoled. Then, suddenly, she sniffed a scent that was familiar. There was nothing stale, mouldy, or rotten about it; it was a fresh, rich, delicious smell; it was Lili's carnation bath oil.

Judy pulled away from Mark, then raised her hand and put a finger to his lips. She sniffed, then so did he. He nodded, understanding. They looked around them. Nothing moved in the silence. Mark shook his head; they must have imagined it.

Then, suddenly, they smelled carnations again.

Outside, Pagan waited anxiously in the shade of the courtyard. Judy and Mark had been gone for ages. Pagan had just telephoned Colonel Aziz about her suspicions, but, as Judy had said, the colonel obviously

•

regarded them as a pair of interfering, 'hysterical' women. Judy had been right to try to get proof before speaking to Aziz.

Pagan decided that she'd try to get inside the Harem to look for Judy. She'd just look around for ten minutes and, if she found nothing, then she'd come outside again and telephone Abdullah. He would fix Colonel Aziz.

She'd had a brilliant idea for gaining entrance to the Harem. The official tour of the palace included a brief visit to the roof. She'd wait for the start of the next tour and then hide on the roof. Then, when the rest of the party had gone on, she'd find her way across the roof to the Harem quarters, and try to gain access from above.

Making sure that it was a different guide from the one she'd fainted in front of, Pagan carried out her plan and, when the party was shown that part of the upper palace which overlooked the Divan Council Chamber of the Imperial Ministers, Pagan hid in an adjoining room until the party had moved on, then she climbed out of the window and on to the wide parapet.

The roof of the Topkapi Palace, a forest of little gold-topped turrets and rounded domes, looks like a small, enchanted, deserted city. Pagan was easily able to get her bearings because she could see landmarks that she recognized in the city and the water around the palace.

Without much difficulty, Pagan picked her way around the domes and turrets until she judged that she was above the Harem quarters. This part of the building had been

•

uninhabited since 1909. Some of the windows that led on to the roof were rotting, some were only just hanging on their hinges.

Pagan picked the most decrepit window she could find, smashed the glass with the heel of her shoe, then carefully put her arm through the smashed pane, undid the latch and pushed the window open.

It led on to a small staircase. Pagan followed it down until it ended in a foul-smelling, dusty passage, littered with mouse droppings. Pagan picked her way along it, and turned the corner.

From behind, an iron grip grabbed her arms and pulled her to a panting male body.

Pagan screamed. Her arms were mercilessly twisted.

Half an hour later Mark and Judy had still seen no trace of Lili. 'Let's just look in that last passage, then we'll give up and grope our way to the entrance,' Judy suggested.

'It's no use, Judy,' Mark said reluctantly. 'We've run out of matches, and we may have a problem just getting back. Let's concentrate on that, huh?'

As they moved on, at the foot of the passage that Judy had wanted to explore, a heavy iron door opened a crack, and a dark eye looked out at the departing couple.

'Thank God he's taken our gags off,' Pagan hissed to Lili. Both women were lying on a dirty, green-striped mattress in the corner of a bare room. Light came from

•

two window apertures on the far wall; the window frames had long since rotted away.

'He knows no one could hear us, even if we yelled for help,' Lili whispered back. 'Any idea where we are?'

'In the Harem quarters of the Topkapi Palace.' Pagan wriggled into a new position. Her hands and feet were tightly bound with rope; Lili's wrists were handcuffed and her feet were also tied. The room was filled with rotting furniture that stank of cats' piss, rat-nibbled brocade bolsters, stained mattresses and semi-decayed hangings which had been arranged in a bizarre, conversational group around a brass table-tray.

Lili listened for sounds of Tony's return. In her four days of captivity she had grown acutely aware of his whereabouts, and since he had left the room five minutes ago she had tracked him mentally, listening to his fading footsteps. Now she could hear nothing.

'Lili, how did he get hold of you?' Pagan wriggled until she was sitting more or less comfortably against the cobweb-covered wall.

'It was ridiculously easy. I went to the Bazaar, bought a carpet, then took a cab back to the hotel. Tony was waiting in the vestibule. He carried my carpet up to my suite. He said that Judy had sent for him to look after the baggage. I wasn't surprised, because it had already been lost twice. Then Tony said Judy had asked him to tell me that she wanted me to meet her at the Saguchi Tea Room. He said she was seeing a diamond merchant there. He said she wanted to buy me a present. As we'd had

•

that row, I thought Judy was trying to say that she was sorry.' Lili gave an exasperated sigh. 'I'm so used to Tony acting as Judy's hired muscle I never suspected there was anything wrong until he laid me out in the taxi. With chloroform, I think. Anyway, some chemical on a pad that he shoved over my nose. And I woke up here.' She shivered. 'He's got guns, hand grenades and God knows what in the next room. So, act obedient, Pagan, don't give him anything to worry about. Who knows, maybe he'll untie us.'

Suddenly Lili jerked her head up and listened. She could hear Tony's footsteps in the corridor outside. 'I think something's gone wrong with his plan, because he seems to be panicking and he's reacting aggressively, like a cornered man.'

The rusting, iron-bound door crashed open and Tony glared at them. Gently Lili smiled at him, in a way that she hoped was friendly without being seductive. 'Won't you please free our feet, Tony. I can't feel my toes, the circulation has gone.'

'Maybe I'll untie you later.' Tony walked towards the window, turning golden rose in the late afternoon sun. As soon as it was dark, they'd have to leave this place.

Pagan tried her luck. 'Could we please have water, Tony?'

Tony grabbed a brass jug from the tray-table and walked over to Pagan. He drank from the jug himself, then held it roughly to her mouth and carelessly jerked her head back, as if she were a rag doll. Pagan spluttered

•

as the water ran down her face and stained her now grubby, black-and-white striped suit.

'Maybe you want something to eat, as well, Lady Know-It-All Swann?'

Tony moved to the low circular brass table, where a box of Turkish delight lay unopened. He ripped off the wrapper and took a piece of green, sugar-covered jelly out, walked back to Pagan and held it out.

Pagan said, 'But I hate Turkish delight, Tony.'

'Open your mouth!'

'No, Tony, it's OK, Pagan doesn't want any . . .'

'I said, open your mouth, Pagan.'

Reluctantly Pagan parted her lips and Tony jammed a piece of candy into her mouth. Before she had time to chew and swallow the sickly sweetmeat, Tony rammed another piece into her mouth, then another, then another. Pagan gagged but he roughly held her mouth shut until she swallowed the Turkish delight.

'And now, some pastry.' Tony picked up a honey-soaked baklava cake off the dirty brass tray-table and stuffed it whole into Pagan's mouth. She widened her eyes in helpless terror as he stuffed it down her throat, leaving her face smeared with honey and covered with flakes of pastry. Tears of anger began to dribble out of Pagan's blue eyes.

Suddenly Tony jumped up and listened. He grabbed the sub-machine-gun from the corner of the room and ran to the glassless window.

*

•

As Mark and Judy dejectedly left the Topkapi Palace they saw Gregg, Colonel Aziz and four minibuses packed with Turkish police, followed by armoured cars.

'Thank God Pagan has called the police,' said Mark as they moved forward to meet Colonel Aziz.

Colonel Aziz clearly believed himself to be on a wild goose chase but, as he had been summoned by the friend of the King of Sydon, he knew he would have to give a perfunctory search.

The small group marched briskly through the gardens surrounding the palace buildings, until Mark pointed to the corner of the building behind which, according to their map, the courtyard lay.

'I thought we'd never get out of there alive,' Judy muttered to Mark as she looked up at the ancient stone walls. Above, she could see the amazing roof of the palace: dozens of breast-shaped domes were crowned by gilt spires, while, between them, needle-like red-and-white turrets stabbed the sky. As she looked up, for one instant, Judy saw a face she recognized. 'There he is! Look! Tony's at that window!'

EIGHTEEN

5 September 1979

'I can't see anyone.' Using a pair of police binoculars, Mark scanned the windows, one by one. Judy followed his line of vision. 'Look to your left.'

'My God! Yes! That does look like Tony.'

With the binoculars, there could be no doubt. Colonel Aziz snatched up his own pair, then turned and issued a stream of commands into his hand-held radio.

Unaware that he had been seen, Tony spied on the small group in the tree-dotted park below. Aware that his attention had been distracted, Lili leaned over and, with her sharp little teeth, tugged at the ropes around Pagan's wrists. The thin nylon cord was harsh and slippery, but once Lili had succeeded in getting a grip on it, she pulled with all her strength, and the slippery knot unravelled with surprising ease. Pagan kept an anxious eye on the bulky back of her captor, who was trying to peer out of the window without being seen. With quiet, stealthy movements, Pagan freed her hands; then, with cramped and shaking fingers, she picked at the ropes around her feet, all the time aware that Tony might turn around at any moment.

Quickly Pagan wriggled down the bed and untied the knot that bound Lili's feet, but she could do nothing about Lili's handcuffs. Holding her breath, Pagan slid soundlessly off the bed. Barefoot, she tiptoed to the iron-studded door and gently touched the rusty bolt. Carefully she drew back the ancient catch, but a faint scrape of metal alerted her captor.

Tony whipped round, shouted, and bounded across the room, forgetting the central low brass tray-table, which tripped him. As he crashed to the floor Pagan slammed back the bolt, and fled from the room before he could reach her.

Outside the door was the square courtyard, overlooked by high barred windows, where, unknown to the captives, Mark and Judy had so recently searched for them. Wildly Pagan ran across the courtyard, hesitated, then bolted at top speed under the nearest arch. She found herself running along a dark corridor, with a massive green-tiled fireplace at the end of it. Ahead and to her left, a narrow spiral staircase of stone wound upwards.

She heard the sounds of Tony thumping across the courtyard in pursuit as she started to scramble up the spiral staircase.

Tony sprinted along the dim corridor, then he stopped, uncertain of the direction that Pagan had taken. He ran

•

to the fireplace that blocked the end of the corridor and looked up the chimney; he saw a magpie nest and the soot of centuries, but no Pagan. Then, from behind him to his left, he heard her scrambling up the spiral stone staircase.

Tony spun around, dashed back, then leaped in pursuit up the narrow stone steps. As he charged upwards he nearly tripped over his UZI machine-gun. Cursing, he propped it carefully in an alcove, then once more bounded upwards.

The staircase gave on to the leaded roof of the palace. As Pagan scrambled out of the opening at the top of the staircase she found herself in a shimmering hot landscape of ten-foot-diameter domes and small towers with catwalks between them. As she heard Tony's angry shout the panic-stricken Pagan tore along a catwalk between two rows of gold-spiked domes until, breathless and sobbing, she reached a parapet, beyond which was a sheer drop.

In desperation, Pagan jumped on to the parapet and ran along the narrow wall. At the corner she stopped and turned. Tony was nowhere to be seen. Pagan realized that she was an easy target and made a split-second decision to hide in the deep shadow behind one of the red towers. Quickly she fled to the nearest small tower and dashed behind it – straight into the arms of Tony.

Triumphantly Tony grabbed her, but Pagan ducked and managed to evade his grip. Terrified, she jumped back on to the parapet and ran from Tony along the narrow edge. Tony's long athletic strides quickly lessened

•

the distance between them, which grew shorter and shorter until Pagan could hear the rasping breath behind her. Sensing that he could almost touch her, Pagan panicked, screamed and almost lost her balance on the parapet.

Suddenly, down below, among the trees, Mark heard the scream, looked up, caught sight of the chase along the parapet, and started to run forwards.

Again Pagan screamed in terror, her arms flailing wildly as she tried to regain her balance. Somehow she succeeded and took a breathless step backwards to safety, but the enraged Tony was right behind her and, with one hand, he shoved her forwards, off the roof and into the sheer drop below the parapet.

Screaming, Pagan managed to spin round and clutch at Tony, her weight pulling him towards the vertical drop. For a moment they swayed together on the parapet, and it looked as if both the figures, silhouetted against the blazing late-afternoon sky, were going to plummet to the ground.

Then Tony managed to shake himself free of Pagan and violently shoved her forwards. Screaming, she fell over the parapet and plunged towards the earth below.

Transfixed with horror, Judy watched Tony recover his balance, scramble off the parapet and disappear from sight.

Down below, among the dusty foliage, police paramedics ran towards the copse of small trees where Pagan had fallen. A whistle blew and orders were barked. Colonel Aziz's men immediately scattered around the Harem area of the palace and, as Judy watched, police marksmen appeared on the domed roof and took up their positions behind the slender turrets.

Tony had again disappeared into the depths of the Harem.

Still handcuffed, her feet numb, Lili stumbled along yet another dark corridor. Her heart was pumping wildly and she was panting with fear but as she half ran over the uneven stones of the passage, her fright was nothing compared to the terror she had previously felt, lying handcuffed and helpless, as again and again Tony had loaded and unloaded his machine-gun, taken random aim at the wine jug, the window or the woman tied on the bed, then pretended to squeeze the trigger.

Suddenly Lili saw a faint glimmer of light and, hopefully, started to run towards it. Dimly she could make out a wide stone doorway.

Thankfully she reached it, then stopped in surprise. Beyond the doorway brilliant sunlight shone down like spotlights from the high arched windows of a big room; the far half was covered by a low platform surrounded by a golden balustrade. The ceiling was fretted and latticed in gold and the walls were edged with elaborate scrolls of gilt leaves and ribbons. The entire, sumptuous golden room was spotted with mould, and hung with cobwebs. Tiny, even rows of claw-marks on the floor showed where birds had hopped in the thick carpet of dust.

·

Opposite Lili, at the far end of the gorgeous room, was another elaborate doorway. Joyfully Lili dashed towards it, to find herself in another equally sumptuous, sunlit room with high, unreachable windows, and another elaborate doorway facing her. Each room led into another room and, as if in an eerie nightmare, Lili ran through salon after over-decorated salon, each one smothered with dusty, golden swags of fruit, and *trompe-l'oeil* paintings of formal gardens that seemed to offer fresh air and freedom, but then cruelly denied it.

Finally Lili reached the end room. It was a square, tiled chamber with no windows and no further door. The walls were covered in an ogee medallion pattern of neat blue flowers, and eight feet above the floor was a gilt frieze of inlaid Arabic script.

Frantic, Lili looked about her for a way out of this lavish, silent, cul-de-sac. But there was no way out, she realized. Despondently she started to stumble back along the way she had come, through all the golden rooms, following her own bare footsteps in the dust.

When she reached the last golden room, the dark corridor lay in front of her. Regretfully she turned her back on the treacherous sunlight. In the distance, echoing and distorted through the many passages, Lili could hear Tony's faraway voice, although at first she couldn't hear what he was yelling. Then, faintly, she heard him cry, 'I know you're there, Lili! I'm not going to let you get away!'

Lili firmly told herself that there was no need to be

•

frightened. All she had to do was to hide in a dark place until she heard the sound of a search party. Lili's heart thumped with fear as she plunged again into the gloomy labyrinth before her, looking for somewhere to hide. As she half stumbled, half ran along she noticed, in an alcove, a horseshoe-shaped trap door, raised and lying at a drunken angle against the wall. Below it gaped an opening, down which led stone steps, hollowed by the passage of many feet. Lili hesitated, then she heard a door crash open near at hand, and Tony's voice again threatened. Quickly Lili lowered herself into the darkness, taking care to make no sound.

Once below the level of the floor, Lili's eyes quickly adjusted to the darkness. At the bottom of the stone steps an underground passage beckoned and, in the faint light, Lili could see a low, half-open door to her left. She would hide behind that door, she decided, and pushed it.

The door was stuck. Lili leaned against it and shoved as hard as she could. As the door flew open Lili felt a rush of unearthly, fast, frightening terror. She seemed to be surrounded by flying demons as, with a flapping of leathery wings, she felt sharp little claws, furry talons, skinny limbs and blinding little creatures beat against her head and body.

In the darkness Lili screamed and screamed and screamed.

She heard Tony cursing as he crashed down the steps behind her and grabbed her by the hair.

★

•

·

'Is Pagan dead?' Judy anxiously asked Mark, as he crouched down beside her in the juniper brush.

'No, but she's badly hurt. It looks like two broken ribs, and a broken leg, shock and concussion. Luckily, the trees broke her fall. They've taken her to the French hospital behind the Divan Hotel. I saw her into the ambulance, then came back here to look after you. Colonel Aziz is informing the King.'

'Nothing's happened here for the last thirty minutes,' said Judy. They were both silent for a moment, listening to the interminable police megaphone as it ordered Tony to come out with his hands up.

'The police always string out a siege as long as they can,' Mark comforted Judy. 'The longer it goes on, the jumpier the kidnapper gets, and the more likely he is to make a mistake, or lose his nerve and surrender.'

A burst of machine-gun fire came from the window overhead as Tony opened fire on the policemen below. Everyone scattered to take cover.

Mark pulled Judy behind some juniper bushes, out of the line of fire, then he snaked forward towards the shooting.

Judy jumped as she felt a hand on her shoulder. It was Gregg, who had crawled up behind her, through the juniper bushes.

'How did you get here, Gregg?'

'Came up with the *Tribune* reporter. The hotel bar emptied as soon as they heard about this siege. Is Lili still in there?'

·

•

'Yes, Pagan said he'd got her handcuffed in one of those rooms. Then Pagan passed out, so that's all we know.' Judy nodded upwards. 'He's up there, where the shots are coming from.'

There was a burst of fire from Tony's Kalashnikov. Again Colonel Aziz turned on his megaphone and ordered Tony to surrender. Crouching low, a junior police officer ran up to the juniper thicket and ordered the three Europeans to vacate their inadequate cover and get behind one of the armoured cars, positioned below the palace walls.

As they cowered behind the hot metal vehicle Judy, her face sunken and pale, leaned against Mark's chest for comfort. 'Mark, what's going to happen?'

'I don't know.' He stroked her fine blonde hair. 'I've seen gunmen behave this way before. They get carried away by the excitement of it all, and by what appears to be their power. Then, as soon as they've fired the first shot, it's too late for them to get out, so, whether they know it or not, they're in it to the death.'

'And Lili's up there with that lunatic?' Gregg anxiously watched the window where Tony had appeared. 'Are the police inside as well?'

'Crawling all over the Harem by now, but there's not much they can do while he has Lili as a hostage!'

On either side of them young, eager Turkish policemen crouched with their weapons. Judy remembered Spyros Stiarkoz's warning about trigger-happy police. She said, 'Colonel Aziz won't let us go into the building. But I'm

•

terrified that if the police storm that room from the outside, someone will accidentally shoot Lili.'

'Judy's right. These boy cops are longing for a shoot-out; look at their faces!' said Gregg, picking up Mark's binoculars and scanning the palace walls. 'There are a lot of handholds on that building; it shouldn't be difficult to climb down it, from the roof, by rope.'

'What would be the point of that?' Mark asked.

'If somebody distracted Tony at one window, I could toss a smoke bomb in the second window and then jump in after it.'

'Smoke bomb?' queried Judy. 'Where do we get a smoke bomb?'

Gregg said, 'The police are sure to have some. If not, they'll have tear gas, which will be nastier, but even more effective.'

Mark said, 'I suppose you want me to steal a smoke bomb.'

'I'll offer the guard a cigarette while you sneak into the minibus.'

Ten minutes later Mark had a rope, two smoke flares, an axe and a distress rocket. Twenty minutes later he and Gregg were among the breast-shaped cupolas of the Harem roof.

Leaning over the parapet, Gregg pointed with one finger as he sketched his idea to Mark. 'This wall is at right angles to the wall with the windows in it. If you let me down on the rope to the little ledge, I can shuffle

•

along it, swing round the corner, get my foot on the ledge again, edge along until I reach the window, toss the smoke bomb through, swing in after it, and grab Tony from the rear.'

'Why not drop down from the parapet, straight above the window?' Mark asked.

'Because my legs would appear in the window; there'd be no element of surprise. And I wouldn't be able to manoeuvre into the window with the correct momentum. I'm going to have to dive into that window.'

Mark thought, the guy's got guts. 'OK, let's go. Tell me what you want me to do.'

Gregg showed Mark how to slip the rope around the nearest turret and take the strain, as Gregg tied the other end of the rope around his waist, then threw a leg over the parapet.

Hanging on to the rope, Gregg planted his sneakers on the ancient stone wall, leaned out and started to walk down. As he descended, Mark played out the rope. Gregg could not be seen by Tony because the corner of the building lay between them.

Gregg passed two ornamental ledges, then stopped at the third one. Inch by inch, with arms outstretched Gregg slowly shuffled sideways along the ornamental ledge towards the corner on his right. Trying to feel as if the wall were sucking him into it, he clutched at handholds in the rough stonework until his right fingertips eventually touched the corner.

Gregg silently looked up at Mark and nodded, then

•

swiftly he pushed the upper part of his body out from the wall and swung himself around the corner, feeling with his right foot for the continuation of the ledge he was standing on. He had checked from below, before he started, that the ornamental ledge continued round the building.

Gregg was sweating as he put his right foot round the corner. This was partly because of the blazing heat and partly because he knew that, as soon as he turned the corner, he would be within gunshot range of Tony. Dangling from the rope, Gregg felt naked and vulnerable. Firmly he told himself that Tony couldn't see him, and wouldn't see him, because Tony wouldn't risk putting his head out of the window, or the Turkish police would shoot it off.

Then, to his horror, Gregg realized that the continuation of the ledge on the far side of the corner was not the same depth as the ledge upon which he had been standing. It had not been possible to see this, either from below the palace or from the roof.

Gregg kept feeling for the ledge with his right toe, but the ledge was only about an inch wide – too narrow to stand on – and, as soon as Gregg put any weight on it, his foot slipped off.

He tried again, but the ledge crumbled, and again his foot slipped as soon as he put his weight on it.

Gregg turned his sweaty face up to Mark and shook his head. Slowly he began to inch back along the ledge. He was almost directly below Mark when his left handhold, a piece of decorative leadwork, came away from the wall. Gregg stumbled, swayed, then fell off the ledge, dangling on the end of the rope like a spider on the end of a string.

Mark braced his feet against the parapet and took the strain.

Very slowly Gregg swung his legs, searching with his sneakered toes for a foothold on the pitted wall. Eventually one groping toe found the ledge. Gregg leaned out, pulled on the rope, and began to slowly climb to the top of the parapet.

'Shit!' he grunted as he swung himself over and on to the roof.

Mark nodded.

Once again inside that gruesome room, her feet tied more tightly than before, Lili lay on the green-striped mattress, quivering with terror. 'Tony, for God's sake, let's give ourselves up!' she begged. 'Otherwise the police are going to kill us both.'

Sheltering behind the window embrasure, Tony said nothing, but fired a burst of machine-gun fire into the dusk.

Lili closed her eyes and linked her handcuffed fingers in an unconscious gesture of supplication. As she did so she felt – on her centre finger – the coral rosebud of the ring that her mother had given her. It comforted Lili.

'I'm pretty certain that if he lets me in, I can talk him out.' Judy stood in front of Colonel Aziz, a resolute

•

expression on her face. 'He knows me, he trusts me and, when he's in his right mind, he's devoted to me. If anyone can get through to Tony, I can.'

Covered with grey dust, Gregg added, 'There's only one guy in there; I don't see what we have to lose.'

Eventually Colonel Aziz said, 'As you say, it is worth a try. Very well. You will go in with six of my men. You will try to persuade him to open the door. You will stand aside as six of my men throw themselves into the room. If two men take the gunman, two throw themselves to the left, and two to the right, and shoot, we will have the best chance of getting Mademoiselle Lili out alive.'

'No!' Judy spoke quietly and firmly. 'I want to go in and persuade Tony to come out. I know exactly how to do it. If I fail, you can storm the room with smoke bombs, tear gas and bullets. But I won't have such unnecessary risks taken with my daughter's life until I've tried to get Tony to come out peacefully.'

Outside the studded wooden door Judy shouted 'Tony! Thank God I've found you. I'm alone. Please let me in.'

'What do you want?'

'To get you out of this alive. Please let me in.'

There was a long, nerve-racking pause.

'No.'

'Tony, I don't want you to come out, *I* want to come *in*.' Judy pleaded, 'I'm your friend, Tony. This is *Judy* out here.'

'Things ain't goin' as I hoped, Judy.'

•

•

'That's why I'm here, Tony, so that together we can work out what to do next.'

Nothing happened.

'You're sure you're alone, Judy?'

'I'm alone.'

Another long pause.

'OK, I'll undo the bolt and cover the door,' shouted Tony. 'Come in, then bolt the door behind you. If there's anyone behind you, I'll shoot.'

They heard the sound of the bolt slowly being pulled back.

Judy gestured frantically, and the men behind her took cover in the doorways.

Judy stepped forwards and pushed the massive door open.

'Bolt the door,' said Tony. 'Gee, I'm glad to see you, Judy.'

'Judy!' gasped Lili, struggling on the green-striped mattress. Judy looked at her with dismay, but fought back her natural inclination to run to her daughter. She ignored Lili and beamed at Tony.

'I've missed you, Tony.' Judy tried to behave as if they were still in the *Verve!* office. 'And I sure could do with a workout. I'm out of shape.'

'Yeah, well . . .'

'May I sit down, Tony?' Judy knew that she should move slowly and deliberately and, at any cost, avoid startling the gunman.

'Sure, go ahead.'

•

·

Judy sat on a stained, rose brocade mattress. 'May I eat a peach, Tony?'

'Sure, go ahead.'

From the central, low brass circular table Judy picked up a half-rotten peach, around which a few flies had been hopefully buzzing. She knew that the table was really a brass tray on a plinth, and she considered flinging it at Tony, then leaping to unbolt the door. But not yet. She was supposed to try to get him out peacefully.

Outside there was total silence.

Inside, Tony stood, sub-machine-gun in his hand, with his back to the wall by the window. Lili lay on the green-striped mattress, not moving.

'What was the plan, Tony?' Judy asked.

'I never meant it to get outta hand like this, Judy. I only wanted to help you.'

'You've always been wonderful to me, Tony. But why did you think I needed help?'

'I knew that the magazine was gonna fold. I heard Tom talking to the Lady Mirabelle people. Then, late one night, when I was waiting to take you home, I heard you tell Tom that you wanted someone to kidnap Lili.'

'*What?*'

'It was after Tom had said something about kids giving you more trouble when they was grown up than when they was small.' Tony shifted his weight from one foot to the other. 'Judy, you said you wanted a miracle to happen. You asked Tom to kidnap Lili for a ten-million dollar ransom, then give the money to you. But the putz said

·

he didn't know how to handle a kidnap. You called him a weakling, Judy. You said you couldn't rely on him.'

'But I *can* rely on you, Tony,' beamed Judy as, with horror, she vaguely recalled her joking conversation with Tom. She took another bite of the disgusting peach and leaned back against the pink brocade.

'Yeah, so I thought, I'll do Judy a favour and make a bit for myself as well, then hide out in Europe, change my appearance a bit, that stuff. I never had such a great life in the States until you appeared, Judy, and I knew that if the magazine closed, I'd lose my glamour job. But, like it says in the *Verve!* self-help articles, nobody has to put up with what they think they're stuck with.'

'The clever thing,' said Judy, hoping that she wouldn't retch, 'was those ransom telegrams. They got *front page coverage* Tony! How did you think of that?'

Tony looked pleased. 'The Greek guy was easy. He wanted to be Lili's sugar daddy. That's what gave me the idea. Originally, that is. I sorta kept this idea hangin' in my mind, then bits got added.'

'Like?'

'Like I hear the pop star yellin' at you on the phone. I think the guy's got no manners, the guy's rich, and the guy seems to think he's Lili's father.'

'Then?'

'Then I'm waitin' for you outside Mr Halifax's office and the door's open a crack . . . I can hear you cryin' . . . well, I guess I opened the door. His secretary's got

•

her own office, so she doesn't sit outside the boss's door.
I reckon that's a big mistake. So, anyway, I hear that Mr
Halifax has got the same idea as the pop star and I think,
little Miss Jordan, she sure kept them guessin', even when
she was a kid.'

'But how did you get here, Tony?'

'Simple. I flew to Britain, caught a ferry across the
Channel, then got here by train and bus. Don't worry,
Judy, I didn't leave a clear trail.'

'Then what did you do?'

'I had a copy of your travel itinerary, the one you left
for the office. So I knew where you'd be staying, and I
knew you'd have one of the fancy suites, facing the water,
so I rented a room on the Asian side of the Bosporus and
bought some hardware in the Bazaar. I followed you
pretty well as soon as you arrived. I know Lili likes to go
around by herself sometimes, so I just waited for a chance.
It came sooner than I expected.'

'And what did you plan to do after you'd got the
money?'

'My contact at the Bazaar, the guy I'd bought the guns
from, put me in touch with a seaman who was going to
hire a speedboat. After the man with the red armband
got on to the Guzelhisar ferry, I was goin' to wait until
the boat was in the middle of the water, then grab the
suitcase from him and jump over the side. Then the
speedboat was going to pick me up.'

'But wouldn't that have been very risky, Tony?'

'Judy, you know I'm a first-rate swimmer and the whole

•

thing took less than thirty seconds in our trial. You see, the ferry can't stop suddenly. I knew there would be police on board, but they probably wouldn't be able to shoot straight, not from a moving boat on choppy water, at a speedboat on an erratic course.'

Judy thought with horror, I wonder if he realizes that kidnapping is a crime punishable by death in some American states. Gently she asked, 'And then what were you going to do?'

'I was going to send another bunch of roses to tell you where to find Lili.'

'Such a *clever idea*, Tony.'

'Yeah, then I was going to fly to Egypt, meet you there, and give you half the cash.' He frowned. 'Maybe *lend* you half the cash. Until your business was straightened out.' Suddenly he raised his machine-gun as something outside the window distracted his attention.

But it was only a bird.

Neither Judy nor Lili moved. They were both terrified. Suddenly Tony relaxed and grinned. 'I also reckoned you musta bin quite a goer, when you was a girl, Miss Jordan.'

Judy gave a tight smile as Tony continued. 'Then the fourth telegram I sent to your friend, the King, after I heard you and Maxine talkin' on your way up to Westchester last fall. She said she guessed . . .'

Judy looked astonished when Tony mentioned the fourth telegram, then she quickly interrupted him, 'Maxine was right, Tony, and so were you, to send those telegrams to men with plenty of money. But what we

•

•

have to do now is figure out how to get out of here.'

'Yeah. I could do with a few ideas on that subject. Like I said, it ain't worked out as I intended.'

'How to get out of here *fast*, Tony. I've got a limo outside with smoked-glass windows. If we can make it into that, we've got a chance.'

'What about *her*?' Tony jerked his head to Lili, who was lying gagged and handcuffed on the green-striped mattress.

'What matters is *you* and *me*, Tony. All they want is her, so they can have her,' said Judy in a firm, reasonable voice. 'But you and I have to get to the limo.'

'How about we distract their attention by droppin' Lili outta the window?'

Judy's stomach turned over. She'd hoped to get Tony out and leave Lili in the room. 'Better if we use her as a hostage. Take her with us.'

Tony looked at her with an unnerving, cunning expression. 'How do I know there ain't an ambush out there?'

Judy swallowed hard. Dammit, she'd gone too far too fast, as usual. In a quiet, soothing voice, she reassured him. 'I'll walk in front and you follow, with the gun.' In a reasonable voice, she added, 'I'll hardly be likely to put myself right in the line of fire, would I? Anyway, the police don't know I'm in here.'

'You were in here before. With that guy.'

'Well, then you know I wasn't with the police. And I've shaken off Mark. You know, I haven't wanted anything to

•

do with him for months, after I caught him in bed with *her!*' She threw a contemptuous glance at Lili.

Tony thought about this for a few moments, then grunted in agreement.

'So how do you want this played, Tony?'

Tony thought again. 'Untie her legs.'

Judy slowly got up, walked over to the green-striped mattress and, without looking at Lili, she untied the nylon rope around her ankles, then helped Lili stand up.

Lili felt painful pins and needles in her legs, because the rope had been tight around her ankles. She looked at the floor, avoiding eye contact with Tony.

'Now what, Tony?' Judy asked, then realized that she had made another mistake, as Tony looked harassed. He had no idea what to do.

Judy said, 'Would you like me to unbolt the door? Then you can follow me, with the gun, and that trouble-making little bitch can walk behind you until we're safe. Then we can dump her.'

Tony moved away from the window to the wall behind the door. 'OK, Judy, open it.'

Slowly Judy opened the door and walked out. As she appeared Colonel Aziz's marksmen drew back into the shadowed doorways of the courtyard, out of sight. They couldn't jump Tony because he had his gun in Judy's back. If anyone shot Tony, Tony would probably shoot Judy as he died.

Judy stumbled along the corridor. Although fully dressed, she felt so naked and exposed, totally vulnerable

•

•

as they moved into the courtyard. Tony walked behind her. His right hand held his SMG trained on her back and, with his left hand, he dragged Lili by her handcuffs.

They reached the courtyard beyond the room. Judy thought fast. She screamed, 'My God, Tony, the police are on the roof!'

Tony looked up.

Judy threw herself to the ground, covering her face with her arms. Lili twisted herself from Tony's grasp and flung herself to the ground. Tony was momentarily thrown off balance, and staggered.

There was a burst of gunfire, bullets ricocheted around the small stone-enclosed space and then there was silence.

Judy uncovered her head and slowly looked up. First, she saw a pair of large, cheap black boots that belonged to a police gunman. Beyond them she saw a rivulet of blood trickling into the centre of the courtyard.

Tony lay dead on the stained stone flags in front of her. Suddenly the courtyard was full of activity.

Judy picked herself up and ran to Lili. 'Are you all right? Are you hurt?'

Lili shook her head. Crying, Judy beckoned to a policeman, who produced a knife and cut off Lili's gag.

'Where are the keys to your handcuffs?'

'In Tony's shirt pocket.'

Judy ran to the slumped figure of Tony and, with shaking hands, felt in his shirt pocket. She returned to Lili with the key, but her hands were shaking too severely

•

to unlock the handcuffs. Colonel Aziz stepped forward, took the key from Judy and unlocked the handcuffs.

As soon as Lili's hands were free, she flung her arms around Judy. 'You did come for me,' Lili said as she fought back tears of relief and happiness. 'My real mother did come for me, in the end.'

PENGUIN BESTSELLERS

These books should be available at all good bookshops or news agents, but if you live in the UK or the Republic of Ireland and have difficulty in getting to a bookshop, they can be ordered by post. Please indicate the titles required and fill in the form below.

NAME _____ BLOCK CAPITALS

ADDRESS _____

_____

_____

Enclose a cheque or postal order payable to The Penguin Bookshop to cover the total price of books ordered, plus 50p for postage. Readers in the Republic of Ireland should send £1R equivalent to the sterling prices, plus 67p for postage. Send to: The Penguin Bookshop, 54/56 Bridlesmith Gate, Nottingham, NG1 2GP.

You can also order by phoning (0602) 599295, and quoting your Barclaycard or Access number.

Every effort is made to ensure the accuracy of the price and availability of books at the time of going to press, but it is sometimes necessary to increase prices and in these circumstances retail prices may be shown on the covers of books which may differ from the prices shown in this list or elsewhere. This list is not an offer to supply any book.

This order service is only available to residents in the UK and the Republic of Ireland.